STEALING TRINITY

Also by Ward Larsen
The Perfect Assassin

STEALING TRINITY

A NOVEL

WARD LARSEN

Oceanview Publishing
IPSWICH, MASSACHUSETTS

ISBN 978-1-933515-17-5

Published in the United States of America by Oceanview Publishing,
Ipswich, Massachusetts
Visit our Web site at oceanviewpub.com

10 9 8 7 6 5 4 3 2 1

PRINTED IN THE UNITED STATES OF AMERICA

For
Lt. R. P. Larsen USNR
Pacific Theater
1941–1945

STEALING TRINITY

FOREWORD

For most, it was another day in a long war. Yet as a precursor to human tragedy, July 16, 1945, was a day without parallel.

The leading event came shortly before dawn, in the sparse desert of central New Mexico. In an instant that would irretrievably change the course of the world, a brilliant, searing explosion tore through the sky, turning night into day, sand into glass, and skeptics into believers. It was the world's first atomic blast, code named Trinity.

On that very same morning, two ships slipped from port and headed into the vast Pacific Ocean. To the east, the heavy cruiser USS *Indianapolis* steamed under San Francisco's Golden Gate Bridge, her task to deliver vital components of another atomic weapon — code named Little Boy — to the tiny island of Tinian in the South Pacific. To the west, a Japanese Imperial Navy submarine, designated I-58, also set sail. Her mission, ostensibly, was that of routine patrol, if there could be such a thing in time of war.

In a fashion, both ships would find success. Crossing the Pacific in record time, *Indianapolis* made her critical delivery, then steamed off to rejoin the fleet. And at the stroke of midnight on July 29, I-58 surfaced to find *Indianapolis* dead in her sights.

I-58's captain later claimed to have been astonished at his good fortune. Fortune or not, the results of the encounter have been well documented. *Indianapolis* took two torpedoes, and went down in twelve minutes. Of the ship's complement of 1,196, only 316 delirious seamen were eventually rescued.

At the end of the war, a court of inquiry investigated the disaster. Questions outnumbered answers, but a few were notably confounding. With the U.S. Navy swarming around the Japanese mainland, why had I-58 traveled over a thousand miles south in search of targets? Was it merely a cruel stroke of fate that *Indianapolis* was lost in the vicinity of Challenger Deep, the deepest abyss in all the world's oceans?

But perhaps the most vexing question arose from the testimony of one group of survivors. They asserted, to a man, that a short time after *Indianapolis's* demise, the silhouette of a ship appeared on the near horizon. One sailor went so far as to fire his sidearm in an effort to attract attention. On studying all evidence, the court strongly doubted that they had seen I-58 — she had remained submerged for nearly an hour after the attack. In the end, the court was entirely unable to account for the presence of a third vessel, and the matter was summarily dumped into the "unexplainable" category.

This much is known.

PART I

CHAPTER 1

Colonel Hans Gruber stood facing the stone wall at the back of his office, drawing heavily on a cigarette, a thick French wrap that filled the air around him with fetid gray smoke. On another day, in another place, he might have wondered if the acrid swill would bother the officers about to join him. But deep in an unventilated Berlin bunker, in April 1945, it was pointless. The bombing was mostly at fault, the Americans by day and the British by night, stirring the dust, bouncing the rubble, and creating more of each. Always more. Then there were the constant fires. Ash swirled in the air, at times indistinguishable from the snow, and subject to the whims of a bitter wind that somehow redistributed the mess without ever driving it away.

Gruber remained motionless, his tall, cadaverous frame hunched in thought, as fixed as the stony gargoyles that had once held watch over the building above. He stared blankly at the wall, glad there was no window. The Berlin outside was no longer worth looking at, a place unrelated to that of his youth. Even two years ago there had been hope. From his old office, he had looked down Berkaerstrasse on sunny mornings to see vestiges of the old city. Mothers pushing prams, stores still stocked with vegetables and thick sausage. Now he sat in a hole in the ground, praying for rain to dampen the ash, quell the fires and, most importantly, to hide the city from the next squadron of bombardiers.

A knock on the door interrupted Gruber's miserable thoughts. He turned and stabbed the butt of his smoke into a worn ashtray on his desk.

"*Kommen!*"

A corporal ushered in two guests. In front, Gruber noted without surprise, was SS Major Rudolf Becker. He strode with purpose and was in full regalia — black overcoat, shining jack-boots, skull insignia, and a wheel hat tucked tightly under one arm. Behind him came General Freiderich Rode, the acting number two of the Abwehr, the intelligence network that answered to Germany's Armed Forces High Command. Rode's appearance and carriage were very different, a thick-necked jackal to Becker's strutting peacock. He was a working soldier, boots scuffed and trousers wrinkled, a square face carved from granite. His bulldog neck was shaved close, disappearing into the thick collar of his jacket, and the eyes were wide-set and squinting — eyes that might be looking anywhere.

"Gentlemen," Gruber said formally, "please have a seat. Corporal Klein, that will be all."

Both men sat, and the corporal struggled to shut the solid door — something had shifted in the bunker's earthen support structure and it hadn't closed normally in weeks. With privacy established, Gruber sat at his desk facing two men who looked very tired. The room fell silent as he reached into the bottom drawer and pulled out a half-empty bottle of vodka, then three tumblers.

"It's Polish. They cook it in spent radiators, I'm told."

Gruber's guests showed no amusement. They were no doubt wondering why he had called them here. If they hadn't been good friends, they probably wouldn't have come. Rank was becoming less relevant with each passing day, and an unexpected summons to the headquarters of the Sicherheitsdienst, or SD, was enough to make anyone nervous. It was the Nazi party's own intelligence service, run by some of the most desperate men in an increasingly desperate regime.

Gruber poured stout bracers and issued them around. No

one bothered to toast anything — for three German officers a certain sign of lost hope — and three heads snapped back. Gruber set his glass gingerly on the desk and studied it before beginning.

"Have either of you made plans?" There was no need to be more specific.

Behind closed doors, Major Becker of the SS softened, his tone weary. "I have access to a boat, up north. But it will have to be soon. Ivan has crossed the Oder."

Rode said, "There is talk among the general staff of a convoy to the south. But I do not think big groups are good. Those who make it out will be alone, or in very small parties."

"I agree," said Gruber. He had his own escape, but wasn't going to share it, even with his most trusted peers. "How is our Führer holding together?" he asked, addressing Rode, who still attended the occasional staff meeting in the Führerbunker.

Rode shrugged. "The same."

Gruber knew, as did all who had seen Hitler in the last weeks, that their leader's mental health was deteriorating rapidly. He was despondent one minute, then bubbling with optimism the next as he ordered nonexistent divisions into battle against the advancing pincer. His field commanders were no help, making empty promises to avoid the Führer's wrath, each hoping to buy enough time to escape his own last-minute firing squad. Lies to feed the lunacy — and yet another multiplicand in the calculus of Germany's misery.

A rough, wet cough erupted as Gruber reached into his pocket. He extracted a silver cigarette case and plucked out another of the harsh French Gauloises. His doctor had advised him to stop, but Gruber decided it would be an improbable fate at this point to die at the hand of tobacco. The others sat in silence as he lit up, stagnant gray smoke curling up toward a ceiling stained black.

"Gentlemen, our immediate future is as clear as it is untenable. Within certain obvious constraints, it is up to us to plan for the future of the Reich." Gruber let that hang in the air for an appropriate amount of time. "Of course, the first priority is to establish ourselves in a safe place. This will require patience. The world will be in a state of confusion and recovery for many months, perhaps years, and this we must take advantage of."

"Our network in Italy remains strong," Rode suggested. "And Spain is possible."

"No, no. These might be good staging points for our departure, but Europe is out of the question for the near term. We will need a great deal of time to reorganize."

Becker added, "And a great deal of money."

"Yes, indeed. But here we are fortunate. Our Swiss friends are competent and extremely discreet in these matters. Considerable funds will be at our disposal. We will have the money, and we will take our time. But there is one particularly pressing matter."

Gruber stood and flicked his cigarette's spent ashes carelessly on the stone floor. "It concerns an agent of yours, General. Die Wespe."

Rode's eyes narrowed to mere slits. It was his signature stare, the mannerism that combined with his physical presence to wilt peers and underlings alike. Gruber, however, ignored it freely, in the same fashion that he ignored the flag-grade insignia on the man's collar. The structure of command was becoming increasingly fluid as a new order emerged.

"How do you know about Die Wespe?"

Gruber waved a languid hand in the air to dismiss the question as immaterial.

Becker asked, "Who is this Wespe?"

"He is a very special spy," Gruber said, "a fat little German scientist who works with the Americans." He shook his head derisively, still amazed that they could allow such a stupid breach. "He holds information that is vital to our future."

"Vital?" Rode scoffed. "I suspect it will be worthless." He turned to Becker. "The Americans have spent years and an incredible amount of money pursuing wild ideas. We explored the concept ourselves. Heisenberg, our top physicist, headed the effort. It came to nothing."

"We undertook a token project," Gruber agreed, "and it *was* a failure. However these academic types are a difficult breed. They consider themselves above the world, and some have a reputation for — conscience."

"Sabotage is what you mean," Rode countered.

"There were rumors. At any rate, our own work in the area has been feeble."

Becker asked, "What does it involve?"

Rode took a minute to explain the incredible details. He then added, "But it is only a whim on the chalkboards of certain scientists, a paper theory. Nothing has been proven."

The SS man, who knew his weapons, agreed, "I cannot imagine such a thing."

Gruber hedged, "Indeed, the concept has not yet been tested. But Wespe tells us this will come soon. Within months, if not weeks. Is this not true, Freiderich?"

Rode nodded.

"And if it should work?" Becker asked.

"There lies the significance. If it should work, my friend, those with the knowledge will control the future of our world."

Becker said, "And you think we should strive to acquire this knowledge?"

"We must have it!" Gruber paced with his hands behind his back, his angular frame leaning forward. "And it is still within our grasp."

"But are you not aware?" Rode warned, "Our agent in America, the only contact with Wespe, has been lost. He was uncovered, killed when the Americans tried to arrest him."

"Precisely," Gruber said, "which is why I have called you both here today. We must reestablish contact with Wespe, at any cost."

Rode blew a snort in exasperation, "Our networks are finished. Most of our agents have been captured or killed, and some have certainly talked under interrogation. Everything must be considered compromised."

"Agreed. Which is why we must start from the beginning." Gruber took a seat at his desk, coughing again, his lungs heaving to rid the spoiled subterranean air from his body. Recovering, he made every effort to sit erect and display strength, not the weariness that pulled straight from the marrow of his bones. Four thin file folders sat neatly stacked on the desk in front of him. Gruber split them, handing two to each of his compatriots. They were numbered for reference, simply one through four.

"We need someone fresh, someone unknown to your service, Freiderich. But, of course, there are requirements. This person must be absolutely fluent in English, and preferably has lived in America." Rode and Becker began to study the dossiers as Gruber continued. "These necessities limit our options, especially given that this person must be absolutely committed to our cause."

Gruber let that hang. He fell silent, allowing Rode and Becker a chance to take in the information. After a few minutes, they swapped files.

"There must be more information than this," Becker insisted. "Here there are only a few pages."

Gruber shrugged. "We are Germans, so of course volumes exist on each. I have taken the liberty of condensing the information."

Rode finished, and said, "You suggest that only one of these men be dispatched. If the matter is truly so urgent, why not enlist them all?"

"An intriguing thought, Freiderich. One which I entertained myself. But consider. Whoever we send must have enough information to contact Wespe." Gruber set his elbows on the desk and steepled his hands thoughtfully, as if in prayer. "Let me put forward a bit of wisdom from a friend of mine, a pilot in the Luftwaffe. One day, relating his flying experiences, he told me that he would prefer to fly an aircraft with one engine as opposed to two. He thought it safer. This seemed strange to me until he explained — an aircraft with two engines has twice the chance of a powerplant failure." He gestured toward the folders. "Sending them all would increase the probability of making contact with Wespe. But a single failure ruins everything."

The two men facing Gruber gave no argument to the logic.

"So the question becomes, which?"

Becker, the major, looked at Rode, perhaps deferring to rank, even though it held little substance here.

"Number two, without question," Rode said.

Becker nodded in agreement. "Number three is in the hospital, with injuries that might take time to heal. Four has been in Germany for a very long time. I suspect he might be too far removed from America. And number one, the Gestapo sergeant — he sounds like a killer, but perhaps more an animal."

"This one I know personally, and I would be inclined to agree," Gruber said. "But at least he would be true to our cause."

"Do you have reason to doubt number two?" Rode asked.

"No. His record is clear, although . . . something about it bothers me."

"I did not think anyone escaped the Cauldron on foot," Becker said, referring to the siege of Stalingrad, where Paulus's entire 6th Army was lost.

"Yes. I double-checked that. He is, as far as I know, the only one. He walked into a field hospital nearly a week after the surrender — von Manstein's relief Group. It was over fifty miles from the city. And in the middle of winter."

Rode said, "He is highly intelligent, and has fought for the Fatherland time and again. His performance reports are adequate. So what is it that you don't like about him?"

Gruber hedged, "I can't say, exactly. He grew up in America, but his father brought him to our cause at the outset of the war. Yes, he was brilliant academically, having studied architecture at the American's elite university called Harvard. But given that, his military ratings have been something less. Adequate, as you say, but nothing more. He has seen some of the fiercest fighting of the war, yet only recently found the rank of captain."

Becker said, "But any man who could walk out of the Cauldron — he is a survivor. This we need more than anything."

A distant rumble announced the arrival of another wave of American B-17s, and Gruber heard the plaintive wail of the air-raid siren.

"Where is he now?" Rode asked.

"He is assigned as a sniper, attached to the 56th Regiment."

"If this mission is as critical as you say, we must make the right choice. Let's send for him. Then we can decide."

"Yes," Gruber nodded thoughtfully. "But perhaps I will go find him myself." He gave a shout of summons, and Corporal Klein shouldered his way in against the warped door.

"When the raid has ended I will require a staff car."

The corporal shrugged. "We have none of our own, Herr Oberst. The last was taken this morning by a group of Gestapo officers. I can get on the phone —"

"Find something, you idiot!" Gruber shoved the files across his desk. "And secure these back in the safe."

Corporal Klein took the folders and headed out.

CHAPTER 2

The 56th Regimental Headquarters was easy enough to find, crammed into the rooms of a crumbling old school. From there, Gruber's difficulty began. No one seemed to know the man he sought. Captain Alexander Braun was recently attached to the unit, and here, organization was clearly beginning to deteriorate. The adjutant had lost all the regiment's paperwork in a fallback two weeks ago. The commander, an old-school Prussian with a shell-shocked gaze, was limited to muttered frustrations about his unit's lack of fuel and ammunition. The soldiers themselves were mostly silent, a few bantering halfheartedly about drink, cigarettes, and women — the pursuits of those who expect life to be brief, Gruber mused.

He searched for twenty minutes before being directed to a grizzled sergeant who sat cleaning his weapon at a schoolboy's desk in a corner. As Gruber approached, the man eyed the unfamiliar, well-fed headquarters officer. Gruber let his rank insignia suffice for introduction.

"I am searching for Captain Alexander Braun."

The sergeant shrugged, then spit on a rag and polished the shoulder stock of his disassembled weapon. Gruber was in no mood for interservice trifling. He moved closer and hovered, his holstered Lugar obvious in its message. There were Russians to the east and Americans to the west, but here, in the last crumbling corners of the Reich, lay some of the most dangerous men.

The sergeant, who had himself likely not seen a cleaning in weeks, put down the rag and set the butt of his weapon on the ground. "Braun. Yes. He is out on sniper duty."

"When will he be back?"

"I cannot say, Herr Oberst. He has been out for three days."

"Three days! How can a sniper team operate for such a length of time?"

"Captain Braun has set his own rules in his short time with us. He comes and goes as he pleases. And he always sends his spotter back. A lone wolf, you might say."

Gruber's eyes narrowed, considering this. "But is he effective?"

"As a sniper?" The sergeant cocked his head indifferently. "He claims many kills, but without a spotter to confirm them — who can say?"

"I must talk to his spotter. Is he here now?"

The sergeant smiled.

The journey to the front was amazingly circuitous. The sergeant led Gruber through a never ending maze of broken stone and twisted metal. At times they paused for no apparent reason, ducking into a bomb crater or behind a wall. Gruber had not been this close to the enemy since his days in France during the Great War. He recoiled as his basal senses registered long-forgotten details — the staccato echoes of gunfire, the pungent smell of cordite interlaced with death.

The sergeant moved in quick bursts, running, crawling, jumping past exposed openings. Gruber's heart raced as he mirrored each movement, knowing that the second in line had to be quicker than the first. The Russians also had snipers.

They passed a perfectly good truck that looked like it had just rolled out from the factory, probably stilled for lack of fuel. The sergeant stopped behind the burned hulk of a Tiger tank, and he pointed to a collapsed structure. Even in ruin it maintained a height of three stories. Fallen sections lay at odd angles, and the surviving walls were carved stone, ancient and ornate before the bombs had done their work. By the architecture, and the heavy granite cross lying in the street, Gruber could see it had once been a church.

"This is the place," the sergeant said. He peered once around the corpse of the tank and darted into the ruins. Gruber followed, half expecting a shot to ring out as he covered the last few meters through no-man's-land. Once safely in the remains of the building, the sergeant eased his pace. He led over piles of stone, and weaved among rows of shattered wooden pews, finally stopping in a corner where the perpendicular wall joint seemed to have held. A thick rope led somewhere above, and the sergeant yanked it three times before rappelling upward. He reached a landing of sorts, twenty feet up, and motioned for Gruber to follow.

Gruber hesitated, then grabbed the rope and clambered his way up, slipping now and again as his feet scrambled for purchase in the pockmarked wall. Out of breath, he reached the landing, a darkened slab that gave way to what looked like a small cavern. There, a single room lay solid and intact against the church's collapse, a cloistered retreat in better times. The place would be indistinguishable from the outside, as if God had spared a small refuge in the house of worship, an invisible sanctuary where His work might still be done. But as Gruber's eyes adapted to the shadows of the place, he realized he would find no men of God here.

There was little more than a silhouette at first, just back from the lone window. A man sat casually in a chair, his legs stretched out to rest on a box, the boots crossed indifferently. At his side was a table with thin, delicate legs, and on that a bottle and a glass, both shaped to hold wine.

"I see you have brought a friend, my sergeant." The voice was deep, strangely relaxed.

"Yes, Captain. This is Colonel Gruber, of the SD. He insisted on seeing you."

The man rose and sauntered toward the newcomers. As he came closer, Gruber was not disappointed in what he saw. Braun was tall, approaching Gruber's own height, and thin, like most everyone these days, but wide at the shoulders. The hair was blond, well trimmed, and the uniform strangely clean and pressed, out of place in such a dusty warren at the front. He moved languidly, and as he stopped in front of Gruber, the junior officer did not bother to come to attention.

"You are a hard man to find, Hauptmann Braun."

Braun shrugged. "Here, this is a good thing."

Close in, Gruber saw the scar — perhaps two inches, straight back along the right temple and disappearing into the hairline. It had been in the medical records, a noted wound, but no explanation. Braun held out an arm, inviting him ahead.

"Can I offer you a glass of wine, Colonel? It is a true Bordeaux, I can tell you. The priests here were doing God's work in style." He poured a glass and offered it, seeming more a landed baron socializing after a fox hunt than a sniper laying in wait.

"No, thank you," Gruber said.

Braun shrugged and put the glass to his own lips, allowing it to linger as he savored the contents. He then began to drift across the room, his free arm arcing out to their surroundings. "This church was once one of the few balanced edifices in Berlin." He directed Gruber's attention above. "The pointed arch is firmly Gothic, yet the carvings are high quality and detailed, reflecting Italy and the Renaissance. Here it was done well, probably thanks to timing — perhaps the late sixteenth century, before the Thirty Years' War." He took another sample across his lips. "You'd be amazed at the degree to which architecture is influenced by history, Colonel, the unpredictable path of events. Do you know why our entire city now smells like a sewer?"

"Not exactly."

"Decades ago our engineers thought it efficient to integrate water and sewer lines directly into the structures of our bridges. This was before the era of mechanized warfare, before anyone could imagine that aerial bombardment would target lines of transport. Now you see the result." The sniper's eyes drifted to the ceiling in contemplation. "War and uprisings. Famine and plague.

The source of commission for a building might be private, church, or state. Everything has its effect. Here, time was taken. You can see it in the end result."

"I see no more than a decorative pile of rubble, Captain."

"Indeed. The treasures of a thousand years have been trampled in this war — which only further proves my point. Yet for a brief interval in our militant history, this place was a masterpiece. There was one man with insight, with the character to bring it to realization. This kind of talent has not often prevailed in our design of things."

"The Führer has a talented architect."

Gruber watched closely and saw the reaction, a veiled smile.

"Albert Speer? He certainly has talent, but I would place it more in the category of propaganda than design. Grand monuments to feed grand egos."

"And you, Captain? You have this trait, this gift of vision? Perhaps when the war has ended you will help oversee the rebuilding of our cities."

The sniper-architect seemed to ponder this. "No, Colonel, I think not. We Germans are very exact in our measures and drawings, but beauty requires a very different kind of effort. When our country is rebuilt, there will be a lack of money and patience to do it properly, with style. The Berlin to come will be square and efficient. Nothing more."

Gruber weighed this silently, then noted the rifle leaning against the wall near the window. "Have you had any luck today?" he asked, pointing loosely to the gun.

"If I had, I would not still be here. One shot, then —" Braun snapped his fingers in the air, "one must not linger."

"Of course," Gruber said.

"There was a small unit, perhaps a dozen men. They settled their equipment behind a wall," Braun gestured out the window, "about four hundred meters away. They went off on patrol, but soon will return for their things."

"And then?"

Braun took the last of his wine before setting down the glass.

The ease that had enveloped him seemed to fade. His eyes narrowed and Gruber met his gaze, wondering what he must be thinking.

"What is it that you want, Colonel?"

There was the answer, Gruber thought. Full colonels of the SD didn't make house calls to captains on the front. Not without a damned good reason. Gruber started to speak, but then paused and looked at the sergeant, who was still back by the landing. Braun jerked his head to one side, and the sergeant turned and disappeared down the rope. Gruber spotted a chipped teacup on the floor. He picked it up, blew off some dust, and charged it generously from Braun's bottle.

"The war is nearly done, Captain. Given this, there are plans to be made for the future of the Reich." He was glad to see Braun remain impassive, nothing in his face to suggest what most Germans would now say: *Hasn't the Reich done enough?* "There will be an effort to regroup — in time. But we have one critical need." Gruber took a slug from the cup, no time taken to evaluate merits, but rather gulping as one would a beer. "There is a spy, a man with vital information that we must have. Unfortunately, contact has been lost. Our networks are finished —"

"In America!" Braun broke in. He beamed a satisfied smile. "That is it! You need someone who can pass as an American. Someone to retrieve your spy."

"Or at least his information."

Braun seemed to consider this before asking, "You can get me out of Berlin? Even now?"

"I think so."

"And where in America would I have to go?"

"This I will not tell you. Not yet." Gruber took another hard swallow from the cup. "First I must be convinced that you are the right man."

They eyed one another, two poker players searching for truth in their adversary's façade. A short, shrill whistle from below broke the standoff.

Braun raised his hand to command silence and eased to the

window. Only a small opening remained at the fallen frame of splintered wood and brick. He picked up a tiny spotting periscope and eased it into the opening.

"Our Russian friends have returned," he announced. "Would you like to see, Colonel?"

Gruber crossed to the window and was nearly there when Braun threw an arm to his chest like a lion striking a gazelle, pushing him to the side.

"The *light*, Colonel. It comes in here." He waved toward a shaft of dank illumination. "Not much, but one mustn't get caught."

Gruber nodded. He approached the window at an angle and took the periscope. After some searching, he found a group of ten Russians milling about behind a wall. Some were eating from tin cups, while others paced and rubbed their hands against the cold. The wall was tall enough to protect them from ground-level fire, but Braun had found enough elevation to see a bust of all who were standing. They seemed quite far away.

"How many can you take from here?" he asked.

Braun prepared his rifle. "One, Colonel. Never more than one. That way I can survive to shoot another day." He paused. "But then — will I have another day?"

Gruber looked again through the periscope, offering no reply.

The captain smiled. "This will be my last, I think. And for that, I will give you the honor. Which should I take?"

Gruber looked back at Braun. He had moved to the other side of the opening, their faces only inches apart. His blue eyes bored into Gruber, striking at his soul.

In a voice barely above a whisper, Braun said, "You are now God, Colonel. Who do I kill? The one with the fur hat? The one who limps?"

The eyes still penetrated and Gruber turned away to reference the scope. "There is an officer, near the back. That would be best."

"Best for what? For the Reich? I think not."

"What do you mean?"

"If I shoot the officer, someone will take his place. And if he was a good officer, they'll all want to kill more Germans. If he was a bad officer, they would thank me. But neither case helps our cause."

Gruber threw down the periscope. "Then who the hell do you shoot?"

Braun was now standing just back from the window, in a shadow, steadying the rifle on a shattered armoire. "For the Reich, Colonel, I will assist you. I should shoot whoever moves in front of the officer."

"What?"

"Whoever moves in front will have a hole in his head. Just another dead soldier to join the millions of others. But your officer," the rifle fell steady, "he will find the man's blood on his face. And tomorrow, the brains in his canteen cup. These things, my Colonel . . . these things make for a very cautious leader. A man who has many . . . second . . . thoughts."

Braun's stillness was absolute. The eye Gruber could see was closed, but he imagined the other, pale blue behind the sight, piercing an eagle's stare at a helpless prey. The calm was shattered by the crack of the shot. Gruber flinched involuntarily, and before the echo could reverberate back off the rubble outside, Braun was bolting toward the rope.

"Come," Braun called jauntily, "we must not loiter!"

Gruber hustled to follow, reaching the rope as the sniper, gun slung onto his shoulder, was about to rappel down. "But shouldn't we take one look, to see if you scored a hit?"

Braun paused for an instant, a bemused look on his handsome, scarred face. "What do *you* think, my Colonel?" Then he disappeared down the rope.

That evening, Corporal Fritz Klein watched as four men entered Gruber's office. The three who had been there this morning were joined by an army captain, a tall blond man who seemed strangely at ease. They met for three hours, summoning Klein only once to bring them coffee. When the gathering ended, he came to attention at his desk.

General Rode and Major Becker strode past to the hallway, ignoring him. Next came the captain. He had an unlit cigarette in his hand, and after a brief pat of his pockets, he raised an engaging eyebrow. Klein found a book of matches on his desk and offered them up. The captain lit his smoke, nodded appreciatively, then flipped the matchbook back on the desk before disappearing.

Colonel Gruber was the last to emerge.

"Corporal!"

Klein stiffened.

"These will be destroyed. Immediately!" Gruber dumped a short stack of files on his desk.

"Yes, Herr Oberst."

"Then destroy the rest. Burn them all."

Klein looked over his shoulder into the walk-in safe. The steel door was ajar, and six sturdy cabinets sat filled with what must have been a ton of classified documents.

"But sir, to incinerate them all will take—"

"Stay all night if you must!" Gruber shouted. "But do these now!"

The colonel rushed back to his office and Klein stood frozen, realizing what this meant. The end was getting very near. He locked up the vault, which could not be left open in his absence, collected the stack of files on his desk, and headed down the hallway.

The incinerator was in a separate room, three doors down. It was always stoked these days, if for no other reason than to counter the bunker's cool dampness. The heavy iron receptacle was built into the wall and glowed at the edges. Klein used the hooked heel of a poker to swing the heavy door open. Inside, the embers glowed white hot, and he tossed in the top two folders, which were clearly standard personnel files, titled with names and rank. He used the poker to adjust their burn before tossing in another, not bothering to note the name. He stirred again as manila and paper turned to cinder, and Klein reflected on the prospect of staying up all night doing the same. Not great duty, he reckoned, but a lot of grunts stuck in freezing foxholes right now would be glad to trade.

Klein looked at the last two folders in his lap. One was yet another personnel folder, but the final one was different. Not a person, but a mission or code name of some sort. Again, Gruber's words came to him. Troubling, desperate words. *Burn them all!* Corporal Klein looked back at the room's open door. Someone could come at any minute. Someone from another office, perhaps executing a similar command from their own colonel. *Burn them all!* But certainly he would hear anyone approach, heavy boots stomping across the cold, stone floor.

Klein opened the top file and scanned it. He saw a photograph of the army captain whose cigarette he had just lit. A few facts about the man's background were underlined. He shifted to the other folder, a mission dossier of some sort. Code names, contacts. He began at the top, but then footsteps stole his attention away. They were getting closer, but still down the hall. Looking again at the papers, one code name seemed to recur, in bold type again and again. The steps came near, and with a flick of his wrist Klein sent both files spinning into the fire.

"Hey!" said a familiar voice from behind. Rudi, the overweight sergeant from across the hall, tossed his own stack past Klein and into the inferno. "Something else to keep you warm, dumbass." He cackled and left.

Corporal Klein knelt at the open incinerator door and gave things one more jostle with the poker. Strangely, he saw the name a last time, the bold type slowly giving way as flames licked it into oblivion.

He wondered what the hell it meant. *Manhattan Project.*

CHAPTER 3

The Third Reich, designed to last a thousand years, in fact collapsed after twelve. On April 30, 1945, Adolf Hitler committed suicide in his Führerbunker. Admiral Karl Donitz was named as successor, but there was little to inherit. Sporadic pockets of resistance continued across Berlin, yet the Nazi chain of command had been shattered, and it soon became clear that the only remaining task of consequence was the formal surrender.

With few exceptions, the populace of Germany shifted its mind-set — from that of fighting a war, to mere survival in the face of a new order. Guns and ammunition were discarded, replaced in the hierarchy of needs by bread and potable water. Military uniforms and identification papers were burned or buried, and civilian replacements bought, stolen, and forged. Indeed, across Europe, millions of people, both victors and vanquished, began the awkward transition to a new life.

It was under camouflage of these distractions, two days later, that Major Rudolf Becker's boat departed at midnight, right on schedule. It was a tiny craft, eighteen feet of oak that looked like it might have been bent into shape a millennia ago. Black tar was slathered along the creases and joints, and there seemed precious little freeboard above the cold Baltic that was, at least for the moment, calm. The small German motor ran smoothly, though, as the boat pushed away from a rocky strand of coastline north of Rostock.

Becker was joined by three other SS officers and the boat's captain, a weathered old Bavarian who had spent the war smuggling for whoever had the most money. The plan took them to Sweden, for a join-up with an emerging association of former SS men who had already coined their name — ODESSA.

The hopeful plans were good for thirty miles. Near the midpoint of their crossing, a thick fog set in. The group didn't see the larger boat approaching, but rather heard it first. When the huge silhouette appeared it was ominously close and headed right for them. The junior SS man, a lieutenant, reacted badly. He pulled his service pistol and fired five shots into the air. As a warning, the act was as impotent as it was rash. The little boat's captain gunned his tiny motor and screamed for the lieutenant to stop, but the damage had already been done.

Aboard the larger vessel, a 110-foot passenger ferry running mostly legitimate business, the Danish captain was high and alone in the wheelhouse when he saw the muzzle flashes, slightly ahead off the starboard bow. He leaned forward to the salt-rimed windshield and barely made out the silhouette of a tiny craft sitting low on the water, headed north.

Having run this route through most of the war, he knew the waters well. And he suspected he knew who might be firing at his ship from such a tiny craft. The captain considered that his few passengers were below, insulating themselves from the cold. He considered that his boat was high at the bow — a slight turn to starboard would shield the wheelhouse from anything more. And he considered his brother, who had been strung up with piano wire by Nazi thugs, unjustly labeled as a partisan. The ferry captain gave a half-turn to the wheel and bumped the throttles forward ever so slightly.

The collision was little more than a shudder to the ferry. Underneath, the tiny runner splintered into a hundred pieces. After the collision came the propellers. Major Rudolf Becker was the only one to survive both, but the miracle was short-lived, as he was also the only one who could not swim.

General Freiderich Rode was the next to try. From a safe house near Stralsund, he kept a midnight rendezvous with an Fi-156 Stork. The utility aircraft was every bit as ungainly as its name implied. Long wings and landing gear sprouted from a boxy fuselage, and the craft flew so slowly that it could be landed backward in a stiff headwind. Despite this lack of elegance, the Stork was very good at what it was designed to do — take off from unimproved strips in 150 feet, and land in half that. It was the perfect vehicle for covert insertion and extraction.

Rode had also chosen the northern route — across the Baltic, then into an isolated sector of neutral Sweden. It had already proven successful on two previous occasions. Unfortunately, this time there were delays. Engine difficulties, according to the pilot, who by default had become his own mechanic. The craft's airworthiness in question, Rode brooded through the predawn hours as the man turned wrenches and hammered against the contraption.

Nearing sunrise, and with gunfire in the distance, the pilot gave up his tinkering. He announced to Rode that he was ready to try, although with the discomforting logic that ditching along the Swedish coast would be safer than staying in Germany to surrender to Ivan.

In fact, the Stork flew, but unusual headwinds slowed the trip. For a craft that cruised at only ninety miles an hour, forty in the face was a daunting handicap. The pilot kept the manifold pressure as close as possible to the red line, and the lights of Malmö came shortly before sunrise. The pilot pointed out the vague Swedish coastline to his passenger, who sat in the rear. Rode's outlook brightened considerably.

It was a pair of early risers from the Royal Air Force's 609 Squadron who spotted the Stork just at dawn. The two-ship of Spitfires eased up to the transport from behind, and the flight leader edged forward to be in the pilot's lateral field of view. He saw the Stork pilot clearly, and tapped his headset to suggest that a bit of radio contact would be in order. Instead, the Stork pulled down and headed for the dirt.

The flight leader shook his head with disbelief. Heaving a sigh, he sent his wingman to a covering position and armed his guns. He also double-checked that his gun camera was turned on. With three Messerschmitts and a Heinkel to his credit, he had nearly finished the war one victory short of becoming an "ace." Now, fortune had interceded. An unarmed enemy utility aircraft presented little challenge, yet, by trying to evade, the craft had fallen well within the Rules of Engagement. And as they said around the squadron, "A kill's a kill."

Little maneuvering was necessary. Two hundred rounds later, the boxy gray Stork pancaked hard into a foggy valley below. A brilliant incendiary flash stabbed through the mist for an instant before being swallowed by the low clouds. The Spitfires circled for a minute to confirm that there were no parachutes, then the flight leader arced his two-ship toward home. There he would make his claim.

Colonel Hans Gruber came the closest. Traveling with a young woman and a bodyguard, he departed a monastery just outside Vienna in the early morning, heading south. Hoping to blend in, his little group wore worker's clothing, old and in need of a wash. Neither of the men's faces had seen a razor in two days.

Unfortunately, the car, a dusty but still magnificent Hispano-Suiza, was altogether too conspicuous, and they ran afoul at the first roadblock. The Russian troops had no complaints with the fine counterfeit documents, nor did they notice that the occupants' polite answers were accented not in Austrian, but something farther north. The soldiers did, however, take exception when the nervous, heavyset driver pulled out a Lugar and plugged the nearest man in the chest before trying to race away.

The rest, a contingent of battle-hardened veterans, were quick to their Kalashnikovs and sure of aim. The Hispano-Suiza made no more than ten meters before its two left tires were shot out. The car skidded abruptly into a ditch, but the soldiers took no chances — they'd all made it this far, and with one of their brethren already lying in a pool of blood, they kept at it. Their weapons blazed until nearly spent of ammunition.

The soldiers approached the smoldering mess carefully, and one of the men pulled out his last grenade, icing for a ghastly cake. He was about to lob it through what had been a window when the authoritative voice of his lieutenant called clearly.

"*Wait!*"

It was a word that Colonel Hans Gruber, wounded and writhing in the wreckage, would later wish he had never heard.

CHAPTER 4

U-801 cut a rough line through the North Atlantic, choppy ten-foot seas washing across her dull black deck. Alexander Braun stood atop the sail — the boat's hardened oval watchtower — straining to see through the blackness that was amplified by a thin overcast above. The wind was out of the west, perhaps ten knots, but added to the fifteen-knot headway of the boat, and a temperature in the forties, it made for a brisk experience.

Two other men were also stationed atop the sail, the assigned lookouts, one to port and one to starboard. They'd started their shift thirty minutes ago, but neither had yet found a word for Braun. He wasn't surprised. It was part of the reason he was up here to begin with — to escape the crew, who were not enamored with the stranger who wore civilian clothes. Nine days ago they had plucked Braun out of a raft just off the Baltic coast, an orphan rescued from a war that was going badly in every quarter. From there, *U-801* had followed the balance of her orders and churned west.

She was a Type IX, a long-range variant, and each day her course remained steady, the longitude increasing. Aside from the boat's captain, no one knew the precise destination, but it mattered little. Everyone understood that they were getting dangerously close to the well-guarded shores of America — carrying no torpedoes, little food, and perhaps not enough fuel to make the return leg. The risks were enormous, and with the war nearing its end, the hardened crew of *U-801* wanted only to go home.

Footsteps clanged up the metal ladder from the control room below, and Braun turned to see the captain appear. He was a young man, only thirty Braun had discovered, though the war and weather had given him ten years more. He sported a scraggly beard, as did most of the crew, and his teeth were a sailor's, yellow and rotted from years of rough coffee and neglect. He sauntered ahead against the breeze and took up a post next to Braun at the forward rail.

"So, Wermacht, we are nearly there."

Braun had never volunteered a name, and the captain had never asked — probably guessing he'd not get the truth. He simply addressed Braun as "Wehrmacht," an unclassifiable specimen of the German war machine. And it always came in a pointedly derisive cadence.

"One more day beneath the surface," the captain continued, "and we will be rid of you."

Braun responded, "And I will be rid of you."

The captain grinned. "The seas, they have improved. Better than the first night."

The man was goading him. During daylight hours, the boat was forced to run submerged, to avoid being spotted by ships or patrol planes. But at night she surfaced to vent and charge the batteries, and also because, there, her speed was eight knots better. On the first night of the voyage a weather front had moved in, rocking the boat mercilessly. Braun, having not been to sea in years, had retired to his tiny room, and the crew clearly found amusement in his mal de mer. The next day Braun had recovered, and it had not been an issue since, but the captain still prodded.

"Have you taken any messages tonight?" Braun asked.

The captain's humor faded. "No. Our request for refueling on the return leg — it has not been answered. This is very unusual."

A rogue wave slapped audibly against the boat, and both men ducked their heads as salt spray flew over the rail.

"I expected them to deny it. But not even a reply."

"Are you sure the radios are working properly?" Braun asked. He knew the boat was tired. Her hull was pockmarked with dents, as if the ship's provisions were regularly dropped aboard from a great height. And the crew seemed to spend most of their time on repairs, often makeshift jerry-rigs to skirt around the shortage of spare parts. Every time they surfaced, a bucket-line detail emptied out the bilge. The engine fuel was being filtered through old underwear.

"Our radios are fine. We are just beginning to capture the broken signal of a Canadian radio station. No, it is not our gear."

"The end — it can only be a matter of days now," Braun said pensively.

"Yes. Which leads me to the question — should we continue?"

Braun himself had given the question much thought. He was to be dropped in a raft three miles off the coast of Long Island, with clothes, identity documents, and ten thousand American dollars that would allow him to immediately blend in. If the war should end before they arrived — or if it had already ended — what were his options? *U-801* would return to Germany for surrender. The crew would be vetted, and some would undoubtedly point their fingers at the man who claimed to be a military officer, but was certainly a spy. The Allies would be most interested, and jail time was possible. Of course, if it was the Russians doing the questioning, there would be nothing beyond a single bullet in Braun's future. Returning to surrender was not in his best interest.

"My mission is of vital importance," Braun insisted. "Your commander made this quite clear, did he not?"

The captain laughed. "Of course. But then, my commander is an idiot who has not been to sea since the last war."

Braun cursed inwardly at his error. Here was a man who had survived by thinking independently, making it through four years in a combat theater where 70 percent casualties was the grim fact.

He would not be cowed by threats from superiors when there
were far more immediate dangers in the skies and waters all
around.

Braun smiled. "You have not seen an idiot until you've met
my own commander. Now there is a bastard. But all the same, I
must get to America."

"For our Führer?"

"No, Herr Kapitänleutnant. For our country."

CHAPTER 5

Major Michael Thatcher pedaled his bicycle briskly at the shoulder of the Surrey road, the morning chill offering its usual incentive. His small, wiry frame gave minimal aerodynamic resistance, and he kept his head down to maximize the effect. The trip from his cottage to Handley Down was a matter of eighteen or nineteen minutes depending on the wind and, to a lesser extent, the condition of the road, which had a nasty tendency to deteriorate under heavy rain. Thatcher himself was not a variable.

His legs churned in steady time, notwithstanding the uneven gait — his left leg, artificial from the knee down, had never mastered the upstroke. Thatcher spotted Handley Down right on time as he rounded the last bend. Typical of the English country manors of its era, it was shameless and unrestrained, an overbearing statement of class and station. Huge fortress walls stood guard on all sides, protecting the forty-odd rooms that lay within. The place had been requisitioned for the cause in 1940 and, approaching the gated entrance, Thatcher tried to imagine what it might look like in another year's time. Minus the drab olive jeeps and sodden sandbags, it would revert to its proper owner, Lord somebody-or-other, and the offices and holding cells would be smartly reshaped back into dens, libraries, and servant's quarters. The crater near the stables had a number of possible uses, but would likely be filled in and smoothed over out of respect for the crew of the B-17 that had smacked straight in last August. Only then could the gentry return and the parties begin.

Thatcher slowed as he approached the perimeter gate. Six months ago he would have endured a stern challenge from the guards, but now, with things winding down in Europe, the mood had lightened considerably.

"Mornin', Major," a corporal called out as Thatcher approached, his lazy salute an apparent afterthought.

Thatcher braked to a full stop and balanced the bike by his good leg. His return salute was crisp. "Good Morning, Thompson." He looked into the tiny shack that served as shelter for the guards. It was empty. "Where is your second?"

"Ah . . . well that would be Simpson, sir. He's gone for our morning tea."

"Corporal, this post is assigned in pairs. It is a dereliction of your responsibilities to —"

Thompson interrupted, "Here he comes now, Major."

A chunky enlisted man waddled up the path from the main house, a battered teapot in his hand and a stupid grin on his face. Thatcher frowned and issued a firm warning, "We're not done yet lads, do you hear?" He pushed off and covered the last hundred yards to the house, knowing the two guards were probably enjoying a laugh at his expense.

He leaned his bicycle against a young beech tree and secured it with a chain and lock — the law was clear on securing all forms of transportation, and no caveat was made to exempt military installations. Thatcher entered Handley Down through its grand main entrance. Two massive oak doors, no less than twelve feet high, stood guard at the columned portico. On the wall next to these stalwarts was a poorly stenciled sign that read: COMBINED SERVICES DETAILED INTERROGATION CENTRE.

Thatcher heaved his way through the doors and into a voluminous lobby that swallowed all comers. Large enough for a small-sided football match, it was another study in contrasts. The

Italian marble floors were scuffed and encrusted with streaks of mud. A fine table held a lovely bouquet of roses, the vase a dented metal canteen. The walls were adorned with decorative columns and fine paintings that depicted past lords and ladies of the house, yet accenting this was a drab collection of army posters encouraging everyone to keep their lips sealed and buy bonds to support the war effort.

Thatcher strode to the familiar hallway, no attempt made to mask his limp. There had always been an unevenness about him, even before the air crash. His brown hair was typically askew, his nose had been broken more than once in a series of childhood skirmishes, and one leg had always been somewhat longer. The injuries he'd picked up from the ditching of a Lancaster bomber had actually leveled things on that count, though standing straight he was now often told that one shoulder drooped. None of it bothered him.

Thatcher paused to study a large cork bulletin board at the hallway entrance. Only months ago it had been strictly business — security directives, status reports, and detail assignments. Now the thing was dominated by situations wanted, job postings, and get-rich schemes. Everyone was moving on, it seemed, ready to put the war behind.

He navigated to his own wing and turned into the office labeled: COLONEL ROGER AINSLEY. Inside was a neat, orderly place. In better times it had served as the library. The walls were lined from floorboard to ceiling with books, rich and scholarly volumes that held no relevance whatsoever to the business at hand. The place held a harsh odor, a hundred years of cigars, brandy, and varnish mixing defiantly.

"Roger, we must do something about the security situation!"

Roger Ainsley looked up from his desk. He was a large man of indeterminate shape, a few extra pounds softening all his edges. His hair was prematurely white and thin, and a set of metal-framed reading glasses completed the grandfatherly appearance. In spite of a two-grade advantage in rank, he allowed Thatcher the familiarity of first names.

"Good morning, Michael. And yes, I know. We had this discussion last week."

"Lax, I tell you! I saw the breach in the fence as I was riding in. It's been over two weeks since that car skidded through and nothing's been done."

"I'll see to it, Michael. Coffee?" The colonel pointed to a pot on his desk. "You should have come last night. The rugby squad were spot-on in their debut. Quartermaster Harewood had a memorable try, although it was at the expense of three teeth and a fractured mandible."

Thatcher ignored the match report. He was in full mood. "This impending victory in Europe is having a positively corrosive influence on standards here. Our battle is not over! We're holding nine high-ranking Nazis, and it's imperative we get every useful scrap out of them. If any should manage to escape —"

"Eleven," Ainsley interrupted.

"What?"

"Eleven. Two more came in last night."

"Who are they?"

Ainsley shrugged. "That's always the question, isn't it? They were captured two days ago trying to leave Berlin. One had information regarding a freighter that was scheduled to sail from Rome to Cartagena, Colombia. Rather ambitious, if you ask me."

"Have we talked to them yet?"

"Phelps took one — he got name, rank, and a sworn statement that the other man worked for Gruber in SD headquarters."

"You're joking!" Everyone here knew that Colonel Hans Gruber was a senior officer in the Operations Directorate of the SD.

"This fellow is apparently only a corporal, mind you, but if it's true —"

"Can I have a crack?"

"I thought I'd give him to you."

"Capital," Thatcher said. "It's been two weeks since we've had any fresh blood. I'll see him straightaway. And I'd better take that coffee. You know how the new ones are — if they're of a mind to talk we could be at it all day. And he might have something I can follow up on." Thatcher was an interrogator, but he had also become the unit's bloodhound — when questioning divulged the whereabouts of important war criminals, Thatcher was sent to track them down. It had happened four times so far this year, and he'd found them all, although one was already in a pine box. "Have him brought to room three. And get Baker to stand watch, the big lad. That always intimidates —"

"Michael —" Ainsley interrupted, his voice thick in exasperation.

Thatcher lost his thought, seeing concern on his commander's face. Ainsley got up, went to the heavy oak doors, and eased them shut. Thatcher wondered what this was all about.

Ainsley spoke in a quiet voice, "Michael, I know you'll do a bang-up job on this, but there's something that's been bothering me."

"What? Have I cocked up? If it's about that Lieutenant I rousted yesterday over the condition of his sidearm —"

"No, no. Tell me — what day of the week is it?"

"Day of the week?"

"Yes, tell me what day it is."

"Well, I suppose it's Thursday." He watched Ainsley frown as he sat back at his desk. "Or perhaps Friday. What the devil does it matter, Roger?"

"What time did you leave here last night?"

"Around midnight, I suppose."

"And the night before?"

"Perhaps a bit later. I've been keeping the same hours for a year."

The colonel steepled his hands thoughtfully under his chin. "This war has hit you harder than most of us, Michael."

"Nonsense. I've recovered fully. My leg —"

"I'm not talking about your leg." Ainsley had turned things around, and now he was the one steeped in stony seriousness. "Have you given any thought as to what you're going to do?"

"I'm not sure what you mean."

"Afterward, Michael. After the war."

In fact, he had not. Not really. Before the war Thatcher had been a happily married man, well on his way to becoming a solicitor. Two years remaining at King's College, Cambridge, and a lifetime to spend with Madeline. Then the damned war had taken it all away. It was strange to even imagine going back to school, yet he could think of nothing else to say. "I suppose I'll go back and finish my law studies."

"Have you contacted them?"

"No. How can I without a schedule? Roger, we'll be chasing down these scoundrels for years. There's so much to be brought to light. You saw those photos last week, the classified ones of this Dachau camp. It was barbaric! They *must* be brought to justice, and it's our job to shoulder."

"It's our job to chase down and interrogate suspected high-ranking Nazis. Right now we're having a field day. But, Michael, I went to a meeting yesterday. For the moment this is between the two of us — but Handley Down is to be closed in early September."

"What? That's only three months! How can we do our job in that amount of time?"

"You know we're not the only ones. There's Kensington Palace Gardens and, of course, the Americans and the French."

"So we'll be transferred?"

The pause was deafening. "It's not out of the question, but even then — six months, or a year. You and I will soon be demobilized. I'll retire, but you're barely thirty years old, with the balance of your life ahead. Michael, you were a man on the rise before the bloody war. You must go back."

Thatcher's crooked shoulder sagged and he stared at the floor in thought. Go back? Go back to what? The university seemed like a lifetime ago, and if he did return it would be without Madeline. Would the memories be insurmountable?

"I know how much this work means to you, Michael, but you must move on. You *must*."

Thatcher stood slowly and spoke in a quiet voice, "Of course you're right, Roger. Someday I'll return to finish my studies. But until that time there's work to be done."

Prisoner 68, as he was internally known, was already in the interrogation room. It was a spartan place, one of the few rooms in Handley Down that could be made so. Formerly occupied by one of the lesser servants, the color scheme was institutional gray. A single table divided three chairs — one versus two, subliminal reiteration to the prisoner that he was outmanned at every turn. Baker's hulking figure loomed near the only door, and dim light came by way of a lone bulb hanging naked from a wire.

Number 68 had been sitting in place for thirty minutes, long enough for him to understand that prisoners and guards might have their time wasted, but interrogators were far too busy to bother with punctuality. So far, under the watchful eye of Baker, Number 68 had been calm as he sat with his manacled wrists crossed on the table.

Thatcher crashed through the door and bustled in, Baker springing to rigid attention. It was a mockery of the military bearing normally shown around Handley Down, but served as a clear message for their guest — this was an officer not to be trifled with. Thatcher carried a thick file under his arm and he took a seat without making eye contact with the prisoner. He opened the file like a book and began sorting and sifting through the pages, as if an encyclopedic dossier already existed on the man facing him.

In fact, most of the pages were blank, and what they really had would fit on a single page with room to spare. Number 68 was supposedly Corporal Fritz Klein, secretary to a top Nazi spymaster. If it was true, more documentation would confirm these facts in time — the Nazis were sticklers about records — but it might take months or even years to sort through all the captured information. Thatcher paused at a paper here and there, narrowing his eyes critically like a doctor regarding the chart of a terminally ill patient. He finally slapped the file down on the table and addressed the prisoner.

"*Guten Morgen.*"

The prisoner nodded. He stared at Thatcher with dark eyes that held firm. He was rather heavy, of medium height, and his skin had a vibrant, healthy hue, absent the pallor and perspiration usually seen on the first session. Number 68 seemed to have a purpose. Thatcher wondered if the man might have been involved in interrogations himself. He poised a pen over paper.

"*Was ist dein name?*"

No answer, but an easy shake of the head. Thatcher continued in fluent German.

"Your unit and service number?"

Nothing.

"Do you wish to say anything?"

The man sat in silence. Nearly half did on the first session.

Thatcher put down the pen and leaned back in his chair. Pinching the bridge of his nose, he sighed, then refocused on the German with a piercing glare. It was no act. "Why don't we get things straight right now. You are here to answer our questions, and you will do so until we are satisfied. Whether it takes ten days or ten years is of no consequence to me. We will eventually find out everything. If you have committed crimes, your degree of cooperation will be considered when punishment is assessed. I will ask once more. Do you have anything to say?"

The German nodded once. With two index fingers that were chained in close proximity, he pointed toward the pen and paper on the table. A thankful Thatcher poised again to write.

"Manhattan Project."

The German's accent fell hard on the English words, but there was no mistaking them. Thatcher looked up quizzically and Number 68 again gestured for him to write. Reluctantly, Thatcher did, only to be rewarded with more silence. The prisoner was done for the day. Thatcher took the paper and crumpled it into a ball as he rose. He strode from the room, Baker again steeling to attention as he passed, and slammed the door shut.

Alone in the hall, Thatcher paused. At first he had thought Klein, if that's who he really was, was going to be the defiant, silent type. But a bloody gamesman. Unusual, but good. They had agendas, deals to make. In a matter of days this one would be offering everything for a price. And then the words came to Thatcher's mind. *Manhattan Project.*

He wondered what the devil it meant.

CHAPTER 6

The day's run had been without incident. *U-801* ran quietly at ninety feet, her black hull easing closer to the coast of Long Island. Braun had divided his time between the navigation table, monitoring a plot of the boat's course, and below in his quarters preparing his gear. He was eager to get the drop over with before anything changed, any message or scrap of information that could take away the legitimacy of the ship's standing orders. If Germany surrendered, the Kriegsmarine would recall the fleet. And Braun would lose control of his destiny.

Shortly after dark, *U-801* began her final approach. She rose to periscope depth where the captain confirmed that conditions were adequate. Scanning the surface, he addressed Braun, "The seas are light, Wehrmacht, but a low moon in the east will give some illumination."

He moved to the chart table to join Braun, who was dressed for his mission — khaki pants, heavy shirt, wool sweater, and workman's boots. The ensemble was worn, but clean and serviceable, the labels all authentically American.

"We will soon be in place," the captain said, pointing to a drop zone circled on the chart, just off the eastern end of Long Island. "You are ready?"

"Yes. How long will it take for your men to deploy the raft?"

"We will be on the surface no more than three minutes."

Not much of an answer, Braun thought, but it conveyed the idea. He would climb up the sail, then back down onto deck while a raft and oars were stuffed up through the forward hatch. With any luck the thing would land upright in the water. From there, Braun was on his own. *U-801* would seal her hatches and submerge, leaving him to negotiate the final, most dangerous miles.

With the drop imminent, the control room of *U-801* took on a surreal air. Red lights basked gauges, instruments, and faces in a bloody hue. The crew fell silent, and the scents of the submarine seemed to magnify. Oil from machinery, brine from the bilge, and the sweat of fifty sailors. All mixed regularly in the damp, stale atmosphere, but now it was traced with something else, something Braun recognized from the rat holes of Stalingrad — fear. The tang of the unexpected.

The crew stood at their stations, grasping wheels and levers, but all eyes were locked on the captain. On his command, *U-801* started to rise. Just short of the surface, the boat leveled and the skipper turned once more to the periscope, scouting for any last sign of trouble. Apparently satisfied, he gave the final order.

"Bring her up!"

Compressed air hissed into the ballast tanks, voiding water and providing enough buoyancy to bring 900 tons of warship back to the crew's natural surroundings.

"Captain!" The shout came from the aft passageway. An ordinary seaman from the radio room stood waving a paper.

"Not now!" the captain ordered.

"Captain, please!"

The crewmen stared down the sailor, but the skipper eyed the man with interest. Braun knew what he was thinking. No one would interrupt at such a moment without good reason. The captain nodded and the sailor scurried to hand over the message. The boat's deck pitched forward slightly, and a gentle rocking motion told everyone that *U-801* had surfaced.

Braun watched intently as the captain's face cracked into a

weak smile. He looked up, his eyes darting between crewmen before making the announcement. "Gentlemen, our war has ended."

There was no cheer, no refrain of joy as would certainly have been the case on an American or British boat, but the relief was palpable. Some bowed their heads, perhaps in thanks to whatever god had delivered them this far, while others grinned at their buddies, open hope that a better life might soon lay ahead.

"Germany has conceded unconditionally," the captain continued, "and we are to return immediately to Kiel — to surrender our boat." Unease stirred as the crew swallowed the bitter order. The captain said, "I think, perhaps, it would be appropriate to take a moment to remember our fallen brothers-in-arms."

He dropped his chin to his chest, and the crew followed suit. Braun went along with the motion. After a very short minute, the skipper ended the exercise. "And may God have mercy on their immortal souls."

"Captain," the helmsman broke in, "shall we rig to dive?"

The captain looked disdainfully at Braun. "Ah, I almost forgot. My friend, any previous orders are now certainly overridden by this bittersweet news. Do you not agree?"

Braun met the skipper's gaze coolly. "I do not. We have come this far. I must still undertake my mission."

The captain seemed amused. He strolled toward Braun, who held his ground, and the two exchanged a hard stare. The tenuous authority of Braun's orders, his only control, was now lost.

"Captain," the executive officer insisted, "we are exposed! Request permission to dive."

"Yes! Yes! The war is over, but there might be a destroyer captain about who has not gotten the news." He smirked and gestured to the ladder. "Still, we must not take lightly the sacrifices of our other services. Standby to man the deck!" he ordered. "*U-801* will complete her last mission. Prepare the raft at the forward deck hatch." The captain turned to Braun. "The coastline is three miles off," he grinned and pointed to starboard, "that way."

The pressure door above opened and residual seawater splashed down the ladder. Braun moved for his gear, but the captain stepped in the way.

"No, my friend. We have brought you here at great risk. Your things will stay with us — a reward, of sorts, for our efforts."

The two men glared at one another. A half dozen crew members took their skipper's lead and eyed Braun menacingly. The duffel, wrapped in oilskin, contained everything he needed — documents and uniforms to run his cover as a soldier, a Lugar 9mm, and 10,000 U.S. dollars. For a brief moment he wondered how they knew. But then Braun understood. He should have anticipated it. At the beginning of the voyage, when he had tried to hide the money in the nooks and crannies of his stateroom, he'd found three bottles of liquor and an indecent book. Nothing could be hidden here without the crew's knowledge. It was their territory, every inch, and they would have been intensely curious about anything Braun had brought aboard. It was the money they wanted, a rare chance at spoils for the vanquished.

"All right, keep the money. But I must have the rest." Braun reached for his bundle, but the captain kicked it away. He knew about the gun as well.

"Go now, Wehrmacht! Before I lose my benevolence!"

A stocky sailor, built like a squat stone pillar, brandished a heavy wrench. Braun considered his options. He could easily take the captain, and perhaps a few others, but the odds were extreme. There was no way to get his gear topside without unacceptable risk. Even then it would be pointless without the raft, to be delivered on deck through a separate, forward hatch. Braun put a hand to the ladder. His pale blue eyes focused on the captain, yet fell obscure, a fog covering what lay behind.

"Until we meet again, Captain." With that, he climbed to the sail.

Above, the salt air hit with its customary raggedness, an altogether different realm from the smooth darkness of twenty fathoms. Braun searched across the black sea. He could just make out lights along the coast. It looked farther than three miles, but judging at night was difficult. Forward, the deck of *U-801* stretched out before him. He could just see the outline of the forward cargo hatch. It would open at any moment to disgorge his salvation, the raft and oars that would carry him the last miles to America.

Then Braun heard it. At his feet, the solid clang of the hatch closing. A churning astern as *U-801*'s screws were engaged. *Bastards!* The boat eased forward, and her bow planes extended with a downward tilt.

Braun scampered down from the sail and ran forward to the cargo hatch. He stomped on it with his boot, the rubber sole thudding against a steel fortress. The boat picked up speed, and soon foamy water began to churn over the top of her black hull. When the water reached his knees, he succumbed to the futility. Braun jumped as far as he could, hoping to clear the twisting screws. The water was cold and hit like a shot of electricity, but for the moment only one thing mattered — *kick, swim, get clear!*

With his head down, Braun pulled for all he was worth. The water transmitted a throbbing pulse to his ears, closer and closer. His body twisted against waves and whirlpools that seemed to pull him toward the spinning propellers. He went under, tumbling, not sure which way was up, which way was clear. Then, finally, he surfaced. He shook his head to clear the water from his face and saw *U-801* slip down and disappear into a maelstrom of foam. The sound of her engines faded and the seas quickly reverted to their standard, uniform chaos, no traces left to betray the steel black monster lurking just below.

Treading water, Braun scanned the horizon for the shoreline he had seen only moments ago. It was hopeless. The gentle waves that had caressed *U-801* now seemed huge. Braun rose and fell on the swells, yet even at the crests he was too low to make out the horizon. He had to act fast. With water so cold his time was limited. There was only one reference, the moon, still low to the east. As long as he kept it at his back, he would be moving in the right direction.

Braun began swimming at a brisk pace, but quickly realized

his problem. The clothes were impossible, dragging like a sea
anchor. He curled down and took off his boots, then tore away
the heavy jacket. He tried again, but progress was still impeded,
and when he stopped a breaking wave caught him flush in the
face. Braun coughed and spit out the briny mess. He cursed
inwardly. He had survived far too much. *It will not end here*, he
thought. *Not like this!*

He reached down and frantically stripped off everything —
shirt, pants, briefs, and socks — until he was naked, save for the
Swiss-made timepiece strapped to his wrist. Now the water
seemed colder still, and for a moment Braun despaired. But he
knew the one thing that would save him. He could just make out
the second hand on his watch. One minute.

He took a deep breath and fell back, floating fluidly on the
churning sea. Above, he saw the stars in their familiar patterns, an
unmoving reference against the roiling ocean. It was the same
constant he had found in the skies over Stalingrad. There, on clear
nights, the black stillness above was the only thing to hold against
the chaos of bullets, knives, and explosions all around. Time and
again over the last years he had watched men panic in the face of
such trials. He'd seen them throw their guns down and run
screaming from foxholes, seen them rush suicidal into enemy
onslaughts, perhaps hastening what they saw as inevitable. He
had watched men who were not on regular terms with God fall to
their knees and pray for His intervention.

Braun, however, had always been the provider of his own
salvation. This was where he differed from other men. Purging
the cold, purging everything, he closed his eyes and set his mind
to a blank. He soon acquired a tranquility that mirrored the heavens above. It was his advantage, a mental structure that always
held form and foundation. He would waste no thoughts on cursing Colonel Gruber or the captain of *U-801* for bringing him
here. He would not brag inwardly that he would win, or that he
had never been beaten. He simply fell calm. Braun allowed his
limbs to float freely in the ocean's cold, aqueous womb. His mind

acquired order and a singular, absolute constant fell into place — the task of swimming a few miles in the correct direction through a freezing ocean.

He noted the time, referenced the moon, and again started off. His arms and shoulders did the work, stroking at a firm, rhythmic pace as his mind considered the variables. How far was it to shore? He was a strong swimmer, but the cold would take his strength. Would he have an hour? Two? The winds were light, but what about the current? Sourced from the south, he decided, the Gulf Stream flowing up along the coast. Perpendicular. He hoped it was so. A knot or two against him would double the task. Braun concentrated on his form, and his muscles filled with blood from the exertion. It felt good, but he realized that the warmth his body manufactured was ultimately no match for the ocean's cold. There were limits. Even he had limits.

The breaking waves were merciless. He sucked in seawater, coughed up brine and bile. Every few minutes he paused to reference the moon, rising steadily behind him. He went for nearly an hour when, at the crest of a wave, he thought he saw a light on the horizon. His spirits rose. But on the next rise he saw nothing. Braun returned to pulling through the water, his limbs straining with less authority now. Had it been a light on shore? A low star? Or perhaps a boat? He felt the first cramps in his back. Yes, a boat would do nicely. A fisherman. He could make it work. Somehow. He looked west again, but still saw nothing. It was very cold.

He ignored his watch now, and Braun's mind began to drift — odd, directionless thoughts. Minnesota, Cambridge, the steppes of Central Russia. Useless thoughts. Had it been another hour? Two? What did it matter — he had the rest of his life. The cramps forced him to adjust his stroke. From an overhand crawl he shifted to the breaststroke, but with the seas in his face it was impossible. He went to a sidestroke, alternating, and made far less headway. Soon his legs began to cramp, and Braun began to shiver. His teeth chattered uncontrollably against the temperature drop. He knew what it meant — his body was nearing the end of its ability to function. This, too, he had seen in Russia, but always in others. Braun had never been this far himself.

Still no lights. His mind began blanking. The waves seemed bigger. Or was he simply moving lower in the water? His right leg seized, the muscles rigid. Headway was nothing. *Just stay up!*

Waves slapped mercilessly, and then suddenly all was calm. His surroundings fell still and dark, shrouded like an overcast Russian sky. And with the last vestige of consciousness, Alexander Braun realized he had gone under.

CHAPTER 7

Michael Thatcher strove desperately to find the virtue of routine. When he woke at five thirty, his customary hour, the first stop was always the washbasin. He stirred shaving cream in a cup and was about to apply it to his face when he paused to regard the image in the mirror. Five o'clock shadow notwithstanding, the face staring back at him was a sad sight. His thin, narrow features seemed to strain along the vertical axis, as if some great weight was pulling everything down by the chin. Dark circles lay under murky, tired eyes. And his brown hair was too long, tousled, and untidy. *I've let myself go,* he thought. *Or perhaps Roger is right. I've been working too hard.*

After shaving, the tide continued against him. Laundry had been piling up and there was no clean underwear in his top drawer. Thatcher eventually found a pair wedged in the gap between his dresser and the wall, and he thought they looked clean enough after he'd shaken off the dust. Once dressed, he placed a pot of water on the stove.

He had spent the previous night with Mr. Churchill on the radio, finally hearing the words the country had been waiting years for — *"The German war is over. God save the King!"* He had been tempted to go down to the Cock and Thistle for a pint — the place must have been riotous. But he'd been tired. Very tired.

That's what war does to you, Thatcher had reasoned before falling asleep in his best chair.

This morning things seemed strangely unchanged. There was no brilliant sunrise — an early morning drizzle tapped against the windows — and the same stack of cases would still be scattered over his desk, oblivious to the formal surrender. Thatcher was pouring his morning tea when the telephone rang. Roger Ainsley sounded weary.

"Michael, I need you here right away."

Thatcher was taken aback. Roger worked hard, but never found his way to the office before daybreak. "Can I ask what this is about?"

"It has to do with Number 68. I can't say anything more."

"I see. I'll be right in."

Thatcher turned off the stove and donned his uniform, wondering what had happened. Roger sounded in a state. Had Klein done himself in? It had happened once before, an SS major who'd certainly been up against the gallows. But Klein was a nobody, a corporal. He might have useful information, but the man hardly seemed a war criminal. Thatcher remembered the results of his questioning — Manhattan Project. More than ever, he wondered what the devil it meant.

Thatcher stepped into Ainsley's office twenty-five minutes later, his boots muddied and his uniform peppered with moisture from the early morning drizzle. He saw Ainsley flanked by a pair of serious men. One was tall with angular features, and wore the uniform of a U.S. Army colonel. He stood rigidly for the introduction. The other looked a civilian, a slight man with close-cut reddish hair that receded on top to reveal a freckled scalp. He swam in a tweed jacket, and held a casual stance. A cigarette dangled loosely from two fingers.

"Major Thatcher," Ainsley said in an uncharacteristically formal tone. "These gentlemen would like a word with you. This is Colonel Rasmussen of the U.S. Army Intelligence Corps."

Thatcher exchanged pleasantries with the officer.

"And Mr. Jones is a representative of the United States War Department."

The civilian offered a soft handshake, then retreated to the side and leaned against a bookcase. Thatcher decided that the man was trying to imply, by his aloofness, that he effectively out-ranked the colonel.

"Gentlemen," Ainsley began, "Major Thatcher here is an interrogator. He's also our tracker — when we find reliable evidence of important Nazis on the run, we send Thatcher to hunt them down. He's quite good at it."

"I see," Rasmussen said. "Yesterday, Major, you interviewed Number Sixty-eight?"

"I did."

"And what were the results?"

"Well, the only thing I got was this phrase — Manhattan Project. The prisoner clearly thought it would mean something to me. It didn't, so I asked around a bit."

"Who did you discuss this with?" Rasmussen asked.

"A couple of the officers here. I also made a call to a friend in intelligence at SHAEF," Thatcher said, referring to the Supreme Allied Headquarters.

"A Major Quinn?" Rasmussen suggested.

"Yes, that's right. He's an old acquaintance, and always knowledgeable."

"Why did you feel the need to ask someone in *our* intelligence services about this?"

Thatcher thought it was obvious enough. "The name of course. *Manhattan* Project."

The American officer clasped his hands behind his back. "I see. And was anyone able to shed light on this name?"

"No. Not yet. Is it something important?"

"Nothing vital. A shipbuilding project in New York. But it is classified. We'd like to find out what else Number Sixty-eight knows."

Thatcher's voice was edged in skepticism, "This project is nothing vital, but you've rushed over straightaway in the middle of the night — just in case there's something more?"

Rasmussen frowned and Ainsley stepped in. "We'd like you to interview Sixty-eight again. Really press in and see if he has anything else. We've confirmed his identity." Ainsley tapped a folder on his desk. "Just as we thought — Corporal Fritz Klein."

Thatcher recognized the German Army personnel folder. "Where did you get that?"

"Berlin. We pulled it out of the Wehrmacht's records."

"Berlin? That usually takes three weeks. We got it overnight?"

The man called Jones finally entered the match, his tone impatient. "Major Thatcher, we're asking for a little help here. I know you're an investigator by nature, but let's remember who pulled Europe's ass out of this fire."

Thatcher bristled and was ready to lash back when Ainsley again turned referee. "Michael, this comes straight from White-hall. Let's see that it's done. I've already arranged for Sixty-eight to be brought to The Stage."

Thatcher knew what that meant. The Stage was a unique interrogation room, the only one with a mirrored viewing area. Ainsley and the Americans would be watching. He was being steamrolled, but there wasn't much he could do about it. Thatcher locked eyes with Jones like a prizefighter staring down an opponent.

"All right then. Let's get on with it."

The brightness was incredible. Braun opened his eyes and squinted severely against the brilliance. The sound of the ocean remained, echoing in his ears, yet when his hands clawed there was no longer water. Something firmer, yet still liquid through his fingers. Sand.

He shielded his eyes for relief and slowly began to see, slowly began to remember. *U-801*. Swimming, gasping, breathing. Just barely breathing. And then sinking, falling slowly, helplessly until his feet finally hit something. *Push! Push back up!* At last another breath. Then fighting the waves until he could stand, crawling the last few meters. The cold had been next. Not like Stalingrad, but the same vital thoughts. *Keep moving. Find protection, warmth.*

Braun's vision focused more clearly. He registered dunes and outcroppings of long grass. He was in a recess dug into the side of an embankment — a bed of coarse sand and a blanket of straw-like grass to break the wind and absorb the rays of the sun. He tried to move, only then remembering that he was still naked. Rising, the sand and grass gave way, exposing his body to a steady breeze.

Braun stood tall. He stretched as he looked out across the ocean. He had prevailed. Just as he had over the steppes of central Russia. And the bastard captain of *U-801*. And Colonel Hans Gruber. He had survived them all, and here he stood, thrown onto the shore of America as if reborn. To hell with Russia, he thought. To hell with Gruber and his derelict Nazi partners. After five years, Braun's war was done. Finally done.

He walked slowly to the shoreline and stood at water's edge, his feet sinking into soft sand. He checked his watch only to find the hands stilled, beads of salt water rolling aimlessly under the crystal. Braun unlatched the useless thing from his wrist and dropped it into the surf at his feet. The rebirth was now complete.

Braun would never believe in God — not after what he'd seen — but he did believe in Providence. He had been delivered to this shore on a quest commissioned by three wretched Nazis. Men who would today be running for their own lives, assuming they'd even managed to escape Germany. Braun had been sent on a mission for the salvation of a Reich he cared nothing about, washed ashore without even a shirt on his back. They had given him a few scant pieces of information — the time and place for a rendezvous, and the code names of an agent and a project. It was a mission he had never intended to complete, and now, with the principals of the fiasco certainly routed, Braun was free. But free to do what?

This was the thought that had stirred ever since he'd learned he was headed to America. Could he return to finish his work at Harvard, the study of European architecture? What was left but a continent in ruins? Yet something of his old life must remain. It had been good, nibbling at the edges of a social station he'd never before imagined. Evenings with his friends at their private clubs in Boston, summers at the ocean. Braun had hung to the coattails of a pleasured existence until his damned father had yanked him away.

And then the nightmare, five years of doing what was necessary to stay alive. Looking out across the ocean, he smiled. What did the Americans call it? The silver lining in the cloud. Five years ago Braun had seen the life he wanted, yet had no idea how to acquire it. Now, for all the suffering, the war had taught him much. He would take what he pleased, by any means necessary. And he knew precisely where to start.

At the water's edge he paused to look left and right. There was nothing but empty beach in either direction, two barren, opposing pathways that might lead anywhere. The immediate choice seemed natural. Just as in the Cauldron, Braun turned west and began to walk.

Forty minutes later he had taken up an observation position. Hidden in a dense outcropping of bushes, Braun watched sporadic traffic along a two-lane road. Across the street lay a diner, host to only two cars at the early afternoon lull. He found himself critiquing the structure — it was probably no more than twenty years old, yet the wood frame had already begun to sag, and the shingled roof needed repair. The Americans built things quickly, but rarely to last.

Minutes earlier, a vagrant had trudged by, an old tramp with grey stubble across his face. The clothes were tattered, the gait unsteady. Easy prey, but hardly satisfactory. Braun needed three things — clothing, money, and, if possible, transportation. The tramp would provide only one, and that marginal. As he waited, scents from the diner drifted across the road. Hunger pulled at Braun's stomach, but it was a well-ingrained task to force the urge aside. How many men had he seen die from such simple impatience?

The answer to his problems presented itself in a cloud of dust and black diesel smoke. A large delivery truck creaked to a stop on the near shoulder of the road in front of him. The driver, a chunky, middle-aged sort dressed in workman's clothes and a flat cap, climbed down from the cab and trundled across the street to the diner.

Braun studied him as he had come to study all men. Size, strength, carriage. The driver did not wear glasses. There was muscle in the man's shoulders, but also thickness around his belly. His hands were small and thick, the fingers like fat sausages. His gait was compact but even, nothing to indicate infirmity. He would be strong, but stiff and immobile. His hair was long enough — it could be grabbed and held if necessary. And he wore suspenders. No man with experience would ever go into a fight wearing straps so close to the throat. But then it dawned on Braun — for the first time in years, his adversary would not be expecting a fight.

The truck's engine was left to run, suggesting a short stop. A call of nature? Braun wondered. Or perhaps a cup of coffee? Either way, the opportunity was clear. Taking the truck directly was not an option. The driver would report it missing within minutes. Braun checked left and right along the road, making sure no other traffic was approaching to see a naked German spy crawl from the woods. He edged out of the weeds and climbed to the running board of the truck's passenger door. He saw two seats in the cab, but nowhere behind them to hide. The passenger door was unlocked, and he noted a tire iron on the floor between the two seats. His tactics evolved.

The driver emerged from the diner five minutes later. He carried a thermos in his hand and Braun adjusted his mental blueprint. He would have to deal with that first. It was heavy, and no doubt filled with some type of scalding liquid. He stayed low behind the passenger door as the driver's side opened, then slammed shut.

He counted to three before throwing the door open. Braun lunged into the passenger seat and spotted the thermos on the floor. He swatted it aside and scanned for any new threats. The pause was designed to give the driver a good look at the hostile, naked man who had just violated his coffee break. His reaction was as rash as it was predictable. He lunged for the tire iron, head low, right arm extended. At the bottom of this motion, Braun brought his right bicep up under the man's neck, pinning him helplessly and keeping the hand with the iron bar locked uselessly beneath. He then completed the constriction from behind with his left, and one vicious twist ended the affair in a crunching noise. The driver slumped toward Braun, his ear lying unnaturally against his shoulder, the eyes bulging in terminal surprise.

Braun shoved the man to the floor on the passenger side and removed his shirt, sliding it over his own shoulders. He would tidy up later, but for the moment he had to drive, before a waitress came trotting out with change, or some other complication. He assumed the driver's seat, donned the dead man's cap, and put the truck into gear.

CHAPTER 8

When Thatcher entered the room, Number 68 was again sitting quietly, his manacled hands resting on the table. Today the guard was outside the door, yet another irregularity to fuel Thatcher's curiosity. He took a seat opposite the prisoner and eyed him directly. Today's offer had already been set, Ainsley the architect, but with the approval of the Americans. Thatcher's job was to make it convincing. As he began in German, he wondered if Rasmussen and Jones understood the language. He suspected they did.

"Corporal Klein, this will be your last meeting with me. We are very busy, as you can imagine, and we can't waste time with someone such as yourself." He paused before his strike. "You were an aide to Colonel Hans Gruber in Abwehr Headquarters. Given this, you may have come across valuable information during the course of your work. Today you will dictate to me anything of possible value regarding matters of intelligence and war crimes. In exchange, I am authorized to make the following offer. You will stay in our custody for a period of two months. During this time we will verify the evidence you give. If it proves accurate and true, we will deliver you to your hometown of Wittenberge with the sum of one hundred British pounds in your pocket. From there you will be free to make your way in whatever existence you can find. This is a singular and immediate offer." Thatcher added a glare to make sure he was clear on the next point. "It will *not* be made again."

The lack of alternatives to the offer was quite intentional, and Thatcher watched the young man fidget, his fingers prying together. Yesterday's calmness and confidence were gone.

He continued, "If you wish, I will leave the room for five minutes while you decide."

More fidgeting, then Klein spoke. "What guarantees do I have that —"

"*None*," Thatcher interrupted, not allowing any east-west into the conversation. "You can agree to our terms — or not."

The corporal's eyes glazed as he no doubt considered a million things. Home. Prison. The unknown. Predictably, he relented. "Yes. All right."

"Good. We will begin with what we have. You are Corporal Fritz Klein?"

"Yes."

"You were assigned to work for Colonel Hans Gruber?"

"Yes."

"Yesterday you mentioned something called the Manhattan Project. You obviously think it is important. Why?" Thatcher poised a pen over his notepad.

The prisoner arranged his thoughts. "Colonel Gruber held a meeting on his last morning in the office —"

"When?"

"April twentieth, or maybe the twenty-first."

"Who was present at this meeting?"

"Yes. This I remember. General Freiderich Rode and a Major Becker of the SS. They discussed a mission, I think, but I did not hear the details. The meeting was short, yet re-formed later that day, with the addition of a captain from the army. Immediately after this second gathering, I was ordered to destroy all the files in the office. But my first priority was to eliminate five folders — the Colonel was very specific on this point. I think they related to the meeting."

"And this was when you came across the words — Manhattan Project?"

"Yes. The first three files were personnel folders. I did not see the names. Of the last two, one involved this secret project. There is an agent — in Mexico, I think. Code name Die Wespe."

Die Wespe, Thatcher thought. The Wasp. "This agent, is he American?"

Klein shrugged. "I remember nothing else. There were only moments to look."

"What about the final file? You looked at this one as well?"

"Yes, briefly. It was a personnel dossier on the army captain. He lived in America before the war — this was circled — and he attended university there."

"Which one?"

The prisoner frowned in concentration and Thatcher scribbled away, increasingly sure that the man was giving all he could. "Harburg . . . Harbor. Something like this."

"Harvard?"

"Harvard! Yes, that was it," Klein said.

"You're sure?"

"Yes."

Thatcher wrote down the name and circled it idly. Not that he would forget. Klein probably had no idea that Harvard was among America's most elite institutions of higher education. It was also, like Oxford and Cambridge, academic territory reserved for the children of the very wealthy and privileged. He thought it curious that a man from such a background might end up as an officer in the Wehrmacht.

"Give me a physical description of this man."

"Tall, strong build, blond hair. He wore a sniper's badge. And there was a scar — here." Klein pointed to his temple. "I also remember his name."

He motioned for the pen and paper with his cuffed hands, and Thatcher slid them over. Klein wrote the name, then proudly turned it toward his interrogator. ALEXANDER BRAUN.

"There is one other thing," the prisoner added. "I saw a strange classification, a note handwritten on the cover of the folder. We file by a single letter, then a number. This one said 'U-801.' "

"Why do you find this strange?"

"Because the U file doesn't go that high. Maybe fifty is the highest. And Braun starts with a B."

"So perhaps Braun was not his true name?"

"It is possible."

Possible, Thatcher thought. *So much was possible.*

The interview lasted another twenty minutes. Convinced that Corporal Klein had given his all, he released the man to the custody of the guard. Thatcher quickly made his way out of The Stage, wondering if the Americans were still watching.

As he walked down the hall, the word Roger Ainsley had spoken yesterday suddenly came back. *Demobilized.* Thatcher wondered how long he had. Might this be his last case before heading back to university? Civil Law and Procedure. The Rules of Evidence. How trite it all seemed in the face of a world turned upside-down.

Of course, someday the world would right itself. Thatcher only hoped he could do the same.

CHAPTER 9

The meeting reconvened in Ainsley's office an hour later, a round-table discussion of the slim facts. As earlier, Jones sequestered himself from the conversation, staring out the window with a brooding expression that mirrored the slate gray sky outside.

"Not much to go on, but he was very consistent," Ainsley said.

"Yes," Rasmussen agreed. He seemed to look to Jones for guidance. "It all sounds pretty sketchy. I'm not sure if it's worth pursuing."

"I found it compelling," Thatcher disagreed. "We should have another go tomorrow. I'd like to try to jog his memory on this Braun fellow. We know where he went to school before the war. If I called there and—"

"No!" Jones broke in. "No. We're done here." He moved to the coat rack. "Colonel Ainsley, there is no need to pursue this matter any further. Keep Klein in solitary until we approve his release."

"We told him he'd be released in two months," Thatcher countered. "And surely solitary can't be necessary."

"Keep him isolated until we tell you otherwise. It might be two months or two years."

"But we agreed—"

"Major," Jones cut in again, "that man is a Nazi!"

"He's a soldier."

"Soldier or not, he's locked down. And I will also require the two of you to maintain absolute silence about this."

Thatcher limped over to Jones and stood in his face. "You'll *require* us? What the bloody hell does that mean?"

Jones shrugged his baggy coat over his shoulders and said, "It means that by the end of the day you will have very specific, written orders relating to this matter. Drop it and zip your lips. That's it!"

The civilian strode out the door, Colonel Rasmussen tagging along behind.

Thatcher bristled. "Who the devil does he think he is?"

In a practical sense, Thatcher and Ainsley found out three hours later. The orders came straight from the War Office. Isolate Klein indefinitely, and don't breathe a word about any of it.

Ainsley broke the news to his friend over an ale at the Cock and Thistle.

"This has come from the very top, Michael. We must honor it."

Thatcher studied his Guinness. "Bloody eejits! It doesn't make sense, Roger."

"What do you mean?"

"If this Manhattan Project is such a minor issue, why all the huff?"

"So there's more to it. The Yanks want to investigate the matter themselves."

"But they're not! That's what doesn't follow. If it was a breach of some critical program, they'd be grilling poor Klein six ways. Instead, they order him locked down, tell us to shut up, and disappear."

Ainsley shrugged and took a long pull on his mug.

Thatcher continued, "It's something terrifically important, I tell you. Braun, Wespe, and this Manhattan Project—it all goes beyond the war."

"Our hands are tied, Michael." Thatcher didn't respond and Ainsley gave him a stern look. "*Tied,* I tell you!"

"Of course, Roger."

A hard silence fell. Thatcher looked to the wall at the back of the bar. There were two dozen photographs of young men and women. They were nailed into every space, a makeshift memorial to the locals who had given their lives for the cause. Each would have had families, friends, comrades-in-arms. So many, Thatcher thought. So much suffering. He paid for the round and told Ainsley he was going home.

They both knew it was a lie.

It wasn't so strange, Braun thought, being a spy. In a way he felt like he'd been one his entire life. He had taken a gunfighter's seat in the posh restaurant — his back to the wall and with a commanding view of the entrance. It seemed a natural precaution.

He'd only been in America for thirty hours and, though exhausted, everything was falling well into place. The truck he'd stolen yesterday in Westhampton was now parked amid a half dozen similar rigs at a roadside restaurant, this one far busier than the place where he'd first found it. The choice of the truck had been fortuitous. It was a mover's truck, delivering the worldly possessions of some well-to-do family. Braun had stuffed a suitcase with clothes, which were far better in fit and quality than the squat driver's, along with a considerable collection of jewelry. The driver himself, minus eighteen dollars that had been in his pocket, was now folded neatly into a large trunk at the front of the trailer, and the rear doors secured by a padlock.

Next had come a bus ride into the city, and a night in an anonymous hotel in the borough of Queens. This morning, an inexpensive breakfast prepared him for the riskiest maneuver — quietly exchanging the jewelry for cash. Claiming it to be an inheritance, Braun split the collection and pawned it at three different shops. He allowed the merchants a steep premium for cash, knowing the magnitude of the bargain would suppress any unease about the source of the goods. In the end, he pocketed three hundred eighty dollars—more than he'd ever had in his life.

Only now did he allow himself the luxury of a good meal. In spite of being famished, he lingered for twenty minutes over the menu, studying the offerings like a fallen priest in a whorehouse. It was the waiter's description of the chef's *selection du jour* that sealed things. Preceded by a generous *salade assaisonnee* and a glass of Chablis, the rack of lamb proved sumptuous, the meat literally falling from the bone. Braun lingered with each bite, pausing, appreciating.

As he did, he watched those around him. Amid dark wood trim and velvet seats, middle-aged businessmen sat at their regular tables. They mingled in clusters or, in a few cases, were paired cozily with much younger women. Martinis came and disappeared in a constant flow. Braun found it all entertaining, and he imagined that in both groups the lies flowed as freely as the alcohol. It occurred to him that the men seemed quite confident, sure of themselves in these gilded surroundings. He doubted a single one had ever killed a man. It made him feel like a wolf among sheep.

The fine meal was a pleasure he had not experienced for nearly five years, and he left nothing but a scattering of bones picked clean. Braun winced when the bill came. He paid, allowing a nice tip, and headed outside into the warm sun. There, he practiced his new trade.

Braun walked to a corner, turned, and ducked into a shop. He studied the scene out the front window. The lessons had been rushed. On leaving Berlin, he'd spent three days in a safe house before boarding *U-801*. There, his instructor was Frau Schumann, a graying woman of about fifty who had probably been attractive in her time. She'd given Braun a crash course in the arts of deception. How to build a radio from commonly available parts. How to work with invisible inks and simple codes. Her particular quarter of expertise was an adult version of the child's game of hide-and-seek, the nuanced mechanics how to see but not be seen, how to follow but not be followed. He found her information useful, steeped in an unsavory brand of practicality. Braun took to it naturally. Frau Schumann was pleased.

She had kept him busy for sixteen hours the first day, and at the end she shared a little about herself. She had worked for the Abwehr in Spain, Italy, and France. She spoke seven languages. Her husband had died in the Great War, a victim of the gas. Braun listened politely.

The second day had lasted twelve hours. She then tried to seduce him, which he allowed. The final day's lesson lasted ten hours and, after a pleasant dinner, Braun had put a bullet in the back of her head as she stood washing dishes. Those had been his instructions — Gruber wanted no possible trace of the spy sent for Die Wespe. Braun suspected it was also another part of his education. A final exam, as it were.

Now, as he walked out of the shop, Frau Schumann's words echoed. *Crowded places are best. Know every exit. Listen freely, look sparingly.* It all made perfect sense.

CHAPTER 10

Penn Station was busy in the early evening rush. Office workers swarmed in every direction like ants across a pile. Braun suspected the bustling atmosphere was amplified today, victory in Europe adding a spring to everyone's step. He sat quietly on a bench, waiting for the six fifteen train to Boston. In fact, he would not go quite that far, exiting two stops before the ticket's final destination. The extra cost had been minimal, and while he was quite sure that no one was presently seeking him out, there was comfort in the small lie.

A whistle blew and steam billowed around the frame of a departing engine. As he waited, Braun tried to use the time constructively. In the conversations around him he picked up slang. He noted the New York accent that held a stronger edge than his natural midwestern tone. Braun would have to be careful — five years of speaking only German and a smattering of Russian would creep in if he wasn't careful. He would have to be deliberate and precise. Bit by bit, information came. The Yankees were winning, but struggling in the pennant race. La Guardia was still mayor.

A young boy scurried toward him barking a pitch to sell the *New York Times*. More to learn. Braun waved him over.

"Hey, boy. I'll take one."

"Five cents, mister."

Braun paid and took a copy. The headline, of course, was

GERMANY DEFEATED. The city had climaxed in a spontaneous explosion — liquor and confetti, strangers kissing strangers. The celebration would last a day or two, probably until the next horrible casualty count from the Pacific.

He turned to the paper's latter sections and flicked his eyes across the pages. He wondered what was happening in Germany. Amid the chaos and muted relief, had Gruber and the others escaped? An image came to mind — it had been in the Ukraine. His unit had set a barn on fire during a rushed retreat, not wanting to leave anything for Ivan. Amid the blaze, a few chickens had run out, screeching and flapping their smoldering wings. Yes, he thought with a smile, that's how it must be. Braun was sure he'd never see any of them again.

He tucked the newspaper under the arm of a fine charcoal gray suit he had purchased only hours ago. It was used, but in excellent condition, an expensive Italian cut that fit perfectly and retained the signature label. The shoes were also Italian, and together the ensemble reeked of wealth. Even second hand, it had cost thirty dollars. Fortunately, the rest of Braun's needs were modest. He would eat another meal, take a room, and tomorrow find a quality haircut and a shave. When the time came, he had to be eminently presentable. The Coles of Newport would expect nothing less. Or would they?

It had been five years. He knew that Americans, in spite of their patent wealth, had been making sacrifices for the war. Rationing of gas and sugar, copper and tires. But Newport, where the robber barons of capitalism sunned their egos so openly? Would Newport sacrifice? Braun smiled inwardly. Of course not. Discretion. That would be the order of the times. Let the hedgerows grow higher. There would be no shortage of beef on the dinner table or tea to accent one's afternoon. The industrialists would make a mint out of this war, the only concern being not to flaunt the local ease.

Not that there wouldn't be hardship. There must certainly be a shortage of able bodies to keep the gardens lush and the stables clean. The sons of proper society, those who couldn't manage

4-F, would have to take their commissions and go away, even if it was only to plum headquarters assignments in D.C. or Rome. And there would be no end to the tedious fund-raisers and War Bond drives. In her own inimitable way, Newport would do her part. As would the Coles.

A vision of Lydia came to mind, her long dark hair and curving figure. He wondered how much she had changed in five years. She'd sent a picture back in '41 or '42, tucked into one of the last letters that had found him. Still attractive, in an ordinary sort of way, and with the same hopeful pout. Braun had returned a few letters in the beginning, but his enlistment in the Wehrmacht predictably intervened. From there, a friend in Paris had forwarded a few of her buoyant missives, but the arrangement was unsustainable. Lydia would never hold him at fault for not writing — she knew he'd gotten lost in the fight. Braun had simply neglected to tell her for which side. When he finally walked in the door after so many years, she would forgive. Of this, he was sure.

The rest of the family might have questions, of course. He would concoct a few vague stories, but nothing heroic. Everyone knew the true warriors were the ones who said the least. With the war winding down, men would be coming home by the boatload. Braun would claim to be a soldier on leave, a slim departure from the truth. Two weeks to begin. Or maybe three. Long enough to reestablish himself in good stead with the Coles of Newport.

He'd met her at a Harvard-Wellesley mixer, and they'd done exactly that, wantonly, during the summer of 1940. At first, Braun had been amused by the prim, reserved Lydia, seeing her as simple fare, a light challenge for conquest. The results came immediately, and if she demonstrated a distinct lack of expertise, it was more than compensated for by rampant enthusiasm. The entire, exhausting affair would have fizzled quickly had it not been for Lydia's prescient invitation — two weeks with the family at Harrold House. This was where Braun had become truly enraptured.

He remembered his first impressions driving down Bellevue Avenue. Expansive lawns gave separation from the road, allowing the commoners a glimpse from a suitable distance. And farther back, along the shoreline, was madness. Forty thousand square foot "cottages," occupied only a few months each summer. It was an impossible mix of styles and themes, an architect's playground and nightmare at the same time. A Louis XIV chateau next to a Georgian Revival. French Normandy sandwiched between Gothic and Tudor. The resulting hodgepodge was an assault to Braun's trained eye. He preferred symmetry, consistency. Yet there was something more behind it.

In the days that followed, Braun realized the error of his first appraisal. He saw a greater force at work, an influence that overrode any architectural misdemeanors. These were not structures, they were statements, each a reflection of the individual owner's imagination and ego. Crass and unenlightened as they might be, the buildings and gardens were only props, a setting for the true occupation of Newport. Evenings in full dress, elbow to elbow with senators and ambassadors. Old money magnates and respectable crooks mingling to proper music served up by forty-piece orchestras. It was pure theater on a scale Braun could never have imagined. By day, the men competed, the more ruinously expensive the sport, the better. Polo ponies and racing yachts. Ruthless golf and tennis. By night, the parties rotated among the estates, and here the women competed — better caviar than the tripe served by the Smythes last week, or three bands to top the Wynn's two. There was backstabbing and manipulation. Deal making and lust. But more than anything, there was money. It was the constant, the standard by which foolish excess was measured.

For Braun, the leisures of Newport had been fleeting, interrupted when the telegram had come from his bullheaded father. *Come to Paris right away.* No explanation, no suggestion of reason. He had little alternative. Unlike most of his brothers at Harvard, Braun held no trust fund, no reserves from which to draw his final year's tuition, room, and board. He had explained to Lydia that the trip was academic, a scholarly study of the facades of a Paris that might soon be at risk from the impending storm of war. She'd been a model of understanding.

Newport had lasted only two weeks, but it had burned into

Braun's mind. Memories that would later hold against the starvation of Stalingrad, the desperation of Berlin, and the killing grounds in between. Yet if he remembered vividly the mansions and galas, Lydia herself fell almost forgotten. He tried to recall her eyes. Were they blue? Or perhaps green? No matter, he decided. He would learn soon enough. Lydia, eager young Lydia, would be his ticket back.

A train pulled to the platform and he rose from the hard wooden bench. The cars were full, and he took a seat to the rear, next to a plump young woman who was firmly engaged in a dime novel. He coughed and snorted roughly as he sat. *Feign sickness . . . people always avoid it.* He sensed the woman pull away.

Braun settled back and closed his eyes, reflecting on the last days. Yesterday he had killed a man for nothing more than the clothes on his back and the few dollars that might be in his pocket. He mused on the progress this posed. Five years ago, as a third-year man at Harvard, the mere thought of killing a person would have been intolerable. Now it seemed perfectly natural.

He remembered Stalingrad and Berlin. There, Braun had met men who killed for pleasure. He was proud, at least, to have never gone down that road. *I am not a cruel man,* he reasoned, *I only take life when there is a purpose.*

The train rocked gently, picking up speed, and Braun closed his eyes. Minutes later he drifted off, his thoughts already having moved on.

Thatcher arrived at work well before dawn. His night had been sleepless as questions swirled in his head, a result of yesterday's frustrating afternoon. He had always been wired with a peculiar internal circuitry. It stipulated that everything must fit, falling into the universal order of logic and reason. A leads to B, and, in turn, C follows up. The war had short-circuited his world in the most terrible of ways, and Thatcher found relief only in work. It was his outlet, the channel for his energies. That being the case, he would not be put off by a troublesome Yank, or even victory in Europe. The issue of Alexander Braun was his to tackle.

He'd so far drawn a blank on the Manhattan Project, and asking the Americans again would only bring the hot water he was in to a boil. He wondered what a German spy could possibly be doing in Mexico, but the thoughts never advanced beyond pure supposition. To the positive, he had at least been able to ascertain that Major Rudolph Becker's body had been found washed up on the Northern Baltic shoreline, the cause of death indeterminate, but immaterial. And there was a sketchy report that General Freiderich Rode had been killed, a passenger in an aircraft shot down over Norway. It was plausible. Two years ago the place had been a German possession teeming with Nordic spies. Now the reciprocal had emerged. Thatcher assigned Sergeant Winters, his most capable assistant, the task of finding proof. If the information could be authenticated it would be one less Nazi for Thatcher to hunt.

The fate of Colonel Hans Gruber had proven more elusive. Thatcher doubted Corporal Klein would possess knowledge of his boss's escape plan. Gruber was an intelligence man who would understand the game — each extra person who knew his plans only increased the chance of failure. But Gruber was well known to the Allies, an easily recognizable target. Thatcher doubted he could evade for long.

Yet as the field narrowed, the last target became even more elusive. Only one other person remained from the meeting Klein had described, and that person was the most important, the key to uncovering a spy called Die Wespe. Unfortunately, without another witness, someone who knew where the man was headed, Thatcher was flailing in the wind. It had to be America. But how could Alexander Braun get there? And what use could he be now with Germany defeated?

It all weighed on Thatcher, each fact a piece on his mental game board, each unknown a pending roll of the dice. He reached across his desk and picked up a medallion. It commemorated the Arsenal Football Club's 1938 League Championship. Madeline was a supporter, and the medallion had been his first gift to her, one of those lighthearted gestures that had risen to become a landmark in their lives. Thatcher rubbed it slowly between his thumb and forefinger, feeling the sappy words he'd had inscribed on the backside — MY DEAREST MADS, ALWAYS.

Always — except for the blasted war. England was singing, dancing, drowning in the pubs. And Thatcher sat mired, his investigation stuck in a ditch. The Nazi regime was a plague, a disease that had to be eradicated completely. And who was going to do the work? A bunch of drunk louts who, out of sheer relief, were ready to let bygones be bygones?

He put the medallion back on his desk. Thatcher knew what Roger Ainsley would say. *Drop it.* But something about this Manhattan Project, about Gruber's meeting during the last days of the Reich. There was desperation in it, a menace that wouldn't necessarily die with the formal surrender.

He wondered if Braun had already made it to America. Or perhaps he was sitting in a British internment camp right now, spinning the tale of a hard-fighting soldier who'd done his duty and was now ready to start life anew. There were millions of them. Thatcher could go through the camp rosters and search for the name Alexander Braun. It was common enough. There might be dozens. And would Braun even give his real name?

With a sigh, Thatcher pulled a stack of papers closer and began to read.

CHAPTER 11

"Forty, love," Sargent Cole called.

Lydia stood at the net and watched her father serve to her partner. He used the overhead style, a method she herself had never bothered to learn. It looked terribly difficult, and aside from that, there was something decidedly unladylike in the motion. The ball went whizzing over the net, landed four feet beyond the service box, and would have struck Edward in the privates had he not twisted his plump frame and protected himself with his racquet.

"Out," Edward mumbled. Recovering from his defensive scramble, he established a proper ready stance.

Lydia heard her mother giggle from across the net. The next serve fell into play, and the two men exchanged a short rally before Edward was outdone, his last effort a weak, fluttering lob that Mother was allowed to finish.

"That's it then!" Sargent Cole boomed, rushing to the net. "Six-one, six-love."

Glad to be done, Lydia complimented her father on his form, while Edward, still not accustomed to the thrashings, endured a brisk handshake.

"Don't worry, my boy," her father said. "In time. All in time."

The four retired to the patio where a large round table sat in wait, stocked with fresh juice, pastries, and coffee. Mother busied herself serving.

Sargent said, "Lydia, we must work on your backhand. I'll set up some lessons next week with Serge."

"Father, it's no use. I've already got a thousand-dollar backhand."

"But you were better when you were a girl."

Lydia couldn't argue that. She'd been decent a few years back, but lately had been gaining weight. She was slower now, more cumbersome, and her enthusiasm for the game had disappeared. It seemed such a trivial pastime, given what the rest of the world was enduring.

"Monday," her father decided.

"All right, Father."

"And Edward, what about you? Shall I set something up?"

Edward said, "No, sir. I'll be in the city Monday. In fact, I'll be going in this afternoon as well. I should get cleaned up now." He trundled toward the main house, his round shape straining the white tennis togs.

"All work, that boy," Sargent said. "He needs to break more of a sweat out here."

Lydia was about to select a pastry when she saw the signal from inside the house. It was Evans, the butler, standing in a window and beckoning her with a rapid hand motion. She excused herself and went discreetly into the house.

"What is it, Evans?"

"A gentleman to see you, miss."

She looked out the window, toward her parents, and wondered why it had not been a general announcement.

Evans, who had been with the family for thirty-two years, clearly understood her confusion. "Come with me, miss. I think you'll understand."

A perplexed Lydia followed to the library. When Evans opened the door, she froze at a vision that had died in her dreams a thousand nights ago.

"Oh, God!"

Her knees buckled and she felt dizzy. Through a semiconscious state she felt Evans at her side, supporting an elbow. And then another, stronger presence anchored the opposite side. They guided her to a chair and she sat, grasping the soft fabric arms so that the world might stop spinning. When Lydia finally focused, the apparition was still there, now balanced on one knee at her side. Then came the voice.

"Hello, Lydia."

That strong, undeniable voice.

"Alex?" she managed. "Dear God — is it really you?"

His watery blue eyes seemed to embrace her. And then the cavalier, one-sided smile. He reached out and took her hand.

"It's been a very long time."

"Oh, Alex. I thought . . . I thought you were dead." Tears flowed over her cheeks. "I stopped hearing from you, the letters. And I knew you were fighting —"

"Yes, yes. It's a long story. But all that's over now. Done."

She saw a ragged scar on his temple. It was prominent, but somehow almost an improvement on Alex, a touch of visceral splendor to accent his strong features. She reached out to touch it softly with her hand. What had he been through? Lydia wondered. What other scars might there be?

"Can I get you some water, miss?" Evans asked.

The question brought her back, and Lydia stood gingerly, collecting herself. "What kind of hostess am I? Evans, we have a guest. Bring coffee, would you? Alex enjoys coffee."

Evans acknowledged the order and disappeared. Alex stood back and she realized he was looking at her. His eyes wandered carelessly across her body, the half smile still intact. What was he thinking? No, she knew exactly what he was thinking. Is he disappointed? *God, what stupid thoughts.*

"You look well," she blurted.

"A few scratches, but mostly I came through unscathed."

"You're not in uniform. Are you on leave?"

"Yes. I just got back from Europe. My uniforms are at the cleaners. God knows they needed it. I have three weeks before I'm scheduled to report for duty on the West Coast."

"Of course. We're not done yet, are we? Those pesky—" Lydia froze when she saw Edward stroll in the doorway.

"Darling, have you seen my red tie?" Edward asked before noticing the guest. He paused to study the man for a moment. "Sorry, I don't think we've met."

Lydia said, "Oh, forgive me. Edward, this is Alex, an old friend. Alex, this is Edward Murray . . . my husband."

She saw it for an instant. A crack in Alex's easy smile. He shook Edward's hand and exchanged niceties.

"Alex was at Harvard, before the war."

"Harvard, was it? Bad luck. I was Princeton myself. Law. What did you study, Alex?"

"Architecture, although I wasn't able to finish."

"Oh yes, of course, the war. You know, I tried to enlist myself but there was some rubbish about an eardrum. What I do now is the next best thing. All those tanks and guns don't get built without contracts. My firm does almost half their work with the defense industries. Boring, of course, but it has to be done."

"Soldiering is mostly boring, to tell you the truth. But at least the food is first class."

Edward looked baffled before recognizing the joke. He laughed. "Yes, I'm sure." He turned to Lydia, "Now, dear, I really have to be on my way."

"On the hook in your closet," she said.

"What?"

"The red tie."

"Oh, right." He closed in and gave Lydia a peck on the cheek, then added, "Good to meet you, Alex."

"And you, Edward."

Edward disappeared and the room fell silent. Having seen him off, Lydia's back was to Alex. She couldn't bring herself to turn. What must he think, she wondered, fighting the war for so long, only to come home to this? But if only he'd written. If only she'd known he was alive. Lydia folded her arms tightly, still not able to face him.

"Alex, I—"

His hands took her by the shoulders and guided her around until she faced him. What Lydia saw in his eyes was not anger or disappointment. It was strength. Understanding. She stayed locked to his gaze until her father's voice interrupted, bellowing her name from out on the lawn.

Alex smiled again. "I should go say hello to Sargent."

"He always liked you, Alex."

"Except when I beat him at his games."

"Can you stay? At least for a few days?"

He paused. "I don't see why not. Actually, I'd rather been planning on it."

She sighed and closed her eyes, his hands still on her shoulders.

"He seems like a nice fellow," Alex said.

"Who?"

"Edward."

"Oh . . . yes, he's very nice."

He gave her a look of assurance. Lydia knew they were stirring the same thoughts, yet he seemed so calm. Perhaps the war had something to do with it. He must have seen unimaginable terrors. A tragedy like this must barely register. Yet the guilt rested like an anchor on Lydia's very soul. While he'd been out fighting, she'd been—

"It's all right," he said, as if reading her anguished thoughts. "This war has turned a lot of lives upside down. At least we made it through."

With that, he drew her closer. She felt his breath on her neck as he whispered into her ear. "It's all right, Lydia. It's all right." Alex put his lips gently to the side of her forehead, lingering much longer than he should have. Lydia knew she should pull away. She didn't. Not until she heard footsteps on the marble outside the library. She pulled back just as her father appeared. Lydia tried to compose herself as he paused at the door jamb.

"Father, do you remember Alex?"

Sargent Cole studied them a moment before breaking into a smile.

"Well, I'll be damned! How could I not? He beat the pants off me on the tennis court for a week straight."

Lydia's father strode over and shook Alex's hand.

"He's just back from the war," she said.

Alex clarified, "It's a temporary reprieve. I'm off to the Pacific in a few weeks."

"Good! Good! Give 'em hell, eh?"

"Father, I've asked Alex to stay for a few days. Is that all right?"

He eyed her before answering. "Sure. Let's show him a good time. But I will insist on a rematch, Alex. Have you been practicing?"

Alex replied breezily, "The last time I played was here."

"Christ, that was years ago. You have been busy. But it might give me a chance."

"Perhaps — although one likes to believe in the constancy of things."

Lydia remembered that Alex was the only person she'd ever known who could goad her father and get away with it. Evans materialized with a tray of Scotch and tumblers — her father's presence had superseded the request for coffee — and he poured without asking.

"So," Sargent asked, "kill any Germans?"

"Father!"

As the guest, Alex was offered the first Scotch. He took it and ran a sample over his palate. "Three," he said indifferently.

Even Sargent fell quiet.

Lydia, not wanting to think about such things, changed the subject. "Father, let's put Alex up in the East Room." It was the biggest guest room, with stunning views of the ocean.

"All right," her father agreed. "Evans, something special for dinner tonight. A warrior's feast!"

Evans acknowledged the order.

"I've already played today, but it was an easy two sets of mixed doubles. What do say, Alex — two o'clock?"

"I don't think I brought the proper clothes, sir."

Sargent waved it off. "No excuses, now. We'll dig something up for you."

"All right," Alex said. "Done."

CHAPTER 12

Braun stood trancelike, staring out the third-floor window of the East Room. Outside, four men, two very young and two very old, groomed the shrubbery with hand shears. The landscaping was impeccable, a well-designed layout of gardens and walking paths, with lovely arcing lines and nice proportions. The entire arrangement flowed pleasingly away, ending abruptly two hundred yards off, where a rocky cliff gave way to the roiling Atlantic. It was a study in contrast, a masterpiece of the controlled against the uncontrolled.

In Braun's hand was yet another tumbler of Scotch, this one on the rocks. He rolled it slowly, ice tinkling gently against the glass. The thoughts in his head tumbled far more energetically. Lydia married. It had never crossed his mind. She was so malleable and timid — her father must have arranged it. If Sargent had wanted her married, he would have found an Edward, a pathetic little man who would be as easy to control as she.

But now what? Braun wondered. With Lydia unavailable, what options did he have? A week or two here would be pleasant, but each day would bring more raised eyebrows — the long-lost suitor returning to find the object of his affections taken. And the longer he stayed, the more agony Braun would find in leaving. The exquisite meals, the games, the servants. The leisure of it all.

He'd been so close. It was like taking a sumptuous appetizer, only to find that you would never be served the remaining courses.

Perhaps there was a God after all, he thought, some supreme being who kept him alive for mere sport, to see what tortures one man could withstand before breaking. When Braun had gone to Europe, his father had made him join the German Army. And not just any unit, but Paulus's 6th, doomed to extinction at Ivan's hands. Starvation, escape. Back to the fight in Berlin, then again, salvation. And finally a deliverance to America, the home to which he'd never imagined returning. Braun had endured the Russians and the Nazis. But now the royalty of Newport were inflicting the most wicked wound of all.

He whipped around and threw his glass crashing into the fireplace, crystal shards scattering back onto a rich marble floor. *What now?* His pockets were nearly empty. His old connections from school were of no use. The war had affected everyone. Marriages and love, death and loss. No one could pick up where they'd left off in the halcyon days of the Ivy League in 1940. Everyone had different tangents now, different lives. And what did he have? Memories of a hell no one here could imagine. And a few useless scraps of information. Die Wespe. Santa Fe. A place called Los Cuates in a few week's time. A vital mission for a cause that was now lost.

A knock on the door interrupted.

"Come in."

A young maid, prim and slender, stepped into the room.

"Dinner in ten minutes, sir."

Dinner, Braun mused. Conventional measurements of time meant nothing here. Instead, the sequences of the day revolved around games and meals. Newport War Time.

"Thank you," he replied.

The maid said, "Is there anything I can — oh, dear! You've had an accident!" She scurried to the fireplace.

Braun turned away, his gaze fixed again on the ocean. "Yes. Silly of me."

"Not at all, sir."

He heard her dropping pieces of broken glass into her hand. "Shall I send for another drink?" she offered.

Braun closed his eyes and rubbed his temples using a thumb and trigger finger. Gradually, the ill thoughts dispersed. Calm reemerged, and he cocked his head around to see the slim girl bent at the fireplace.

"Yes. Yes, another Scotch would be most enticing."

Clad only in a form-fitting slip, Lydia studied herself at the full-length dressing mirror in her room. Her hips were bigger than five years ago, rounder. Some men liked that, she reasoned. Her breasts were bigger too, but gravity was taking its toll. She sucked in her gut, stood on her tiptoes, and turned to the profile. Not bad. More mature. But what would happen if she ever had children? She lumbered to her dressing table and sank into the chair, twisting a strand of dark hair around a finger. How had she worn it back in college? Good God — two months ago she'd found her first gray. At twenty-five!

Lydia closed her eyes and sighed. Such thoughts. *Stupid, stupid girl.* What did it matter? Edward was the man in her life. Her husband. Alex would stay and chat for a few days, just to be decent, then he'd be gone.

She pulled a brush through her hair as memories swept in. Alex had been so different from the other boys she'd met — a young man at odds with himself. Calm yet exciting, cultured but primitive. And he had come back to her. He had finally come. She tugged harder with her brush, raking until it hurt. Now he'd go back to Wisconsin or Minnesota, or wherever it was he was from, find some slim Scandinavian beauty and together they'd raise a perfect little flock of blond children. Lydia would never see him again.

She dropped the brush to the floor and broke down in despair. Her chest heaved and her face crumbled as tears began streaming out. *Why?* she thought. *Why hadn't Alex written?* If only she'd known he was alive —

"Hello, darling. I'm home!"

It was Edward, calling from the adjoining room. Lydia sat up straight and tried to collect herself. She took a handkerchief and wiped her eyes, blinking to work away the creases of misery. She sensed him closing in from behind.

"See, I told you I'd be home for dinner." He bent down and pecked her head, simultaneously reaching around to present a mixed bouquet of flowers.

"Oh, darling, how kind!" She reached out and buried her face in the arrangement, using it to hide the dampness around her eyes. "What a lovely scent." Edward squeezed her shoulders.

"Glad you like them. Let's get ready for dinner. We mustn't miss cocktails."

"Of course not. I'll find a nice vase for these."

Edward disappeared.

The last time he'd brought flowers had been on Valentines Day, the obligatory dozen red roses. The same ones she'd be getting for the next fifty years. Lydia set the flowers on her table. She felt heavy, ponderous as she rose and walked to her closet. At the rack of formals she slid out Edward's favorite, a blue evening gown. He had picked it out himself as a Christmas present. It was incredibly expensive and fit like a satin potato sack. Behind it on the rack was a spicy red number she'd bought on a whim, but never worn. Frightfully deep at the front, she'd never been able to screw up the courage after bringing it home.

Lydia held the two side by side and bit her bottom lip.

The main course was an exquisitely tender roast pheasant selection. By the time it made its way to the table, Sargent Cole had already commandeered the topics of conversation through one war, two presidents, and four post-conflict industrial opportunities.

Sitting quietly, and certainly enjoying the meal more than anyone at the table, Braun remembered the act from his previous visit. Sargent lorded over these gatherings like a king holding court. As a host, he was the social equivalent of a blunderbuss — blunt, archaic, and never distracted by matters of accuracy. He eventually got around to pressing his guest of honor.

"Tell us about the three Germans you killed, Alex. Was it in one battle?"

Braun tipped a tolerable glass of Cabernet to his lips. The number, in fact, was accurate. Thankfully no one had asked him how many Russians he'd killed — Braun had no idea. Of course, he could never divulge the true circumstances. Nearing starvation in Stalingrad, he'd quietly killed a fellow German officer in order to steal a stashed loaf of bread. Another, a civilian in East Prussia, had fought for his bicycle against the much younger and stronger soldier who'd been caught alone in a frantic regimental pullback. And then there was the incident involving the first sniper's spotter he'd been assigned in Berlin, a pudgy teenager who'd proven hopelessly inept. He would have gotten them both killed in time, and Braun had simply taken the matter under his own sight, saving the Russians a bullet. Three Germans, three good reasons.

"It was nothing heroic, if that's what you mean. I was just doing my job." He'd heard the soldiers on the train say it time and again. *Just doing my job.* It was all he had to say.

"Oh, Father! Please!" Lydia intervened. "It must have been horrid. Let Alex find his peace."

Even Sargent Cole had his limits, and he went back to tearing limbs from his pheasant. Braun knew the family patriarch had avoided the First World War, no doubt by way of family ties. He saw no need to antagonize the man by mentioning it. Alex locked eyes with Lydia, who was directly across the table, and smiled appreciatively.

Edward piped in, "So tell me Alex, when the war is over will you go back to Harvard and finish up?"

"I haven't given it much thought, really. Of course, I was studying the architecture of Europe — so much has been lost."

"Well," Edward reasoned, "someone will have to build it all again."

Braun cocked his head. "Yes . . . but that's rather not the point. When a building falls, the history it represents is lost as well."

"History?" Sargent barked. "Who needs it? I say look forward. This is a tremendous opportunity to build a continent for tomorrow." Sargent held up his wine glass. "Here's to tomorrow!"

The crowd echoed the words with feigned enthusiasm. Braun doubted any of them cared a whit about Europe or her future, aside from the odd chance that they might vacation there after things had been swept up. He found the conversation tiresome. It was time to redirect. He turned to Sargent. "A rematch tomorrow, sir?" he suggested airily. The afternoon's match had been close, Sargent dominating the first set while Braun shook off the rust. The second had been Braun's in a tight affair, and by the third he'd found his form, a resounding 6-1 win to decide things.

Sargent jumped at the challenge. "Yes, by all means. Let's say ten o'clock. I'll be fresh in the morning."

"Ten it is."

With the next day's recreation firmed up, dinner drifted to its natural conclusion. Edward was the first to leave, ambling off to the library to catch up on work. Lydia excused herself, and Braun watched as she stood. He allowed his gaze to settle obviously on the deep cleavage that fell between the folds of her crimson dress. He then looked up at her eyes, which told him everything he needed to know.

The knock came just after midnight, a quiet rap against the hardwood door of his room. Braun had known it would come. He opened the door to find her in a sheer nightdress, her shape silhouetted against the dim light beyond. He took her by the hand and pulled her inside. Neither spoke. Lydia pulled the nightdress over her head and walked to the window, her figure clear now as moonlight filtered in. Braun went to her and she fell back onto the window seat, pulling him down.

A cool breeze swept in, but did nothing to cleanse the aerosol of confusion in Braun's mind. His senses were overwhelmed and he closed his eyes, perhaps hoping one less input would help him find control. It did nothing. His head ached from too much

Cabernet. Lydia writhed beneath him. Pulling, tugging, moaning. His body responded. Pleasure teasing an insurmountable pain. There were bright flashes, explosions that echoed in his head like thunder. It was not a dream, nor a nightmare. Only the vicious circumstance of his existence.

He felt her rhythm. He felt the heavy, ice-cold marble under his feet. Braun heard her panting against the sound of waves breaking outside. Finally, he opened his eyes and found them drawn not to her, but up toward the open window. The moonlight seemed exceptionally bright, as if Sargent Cole had been able to purchase something more. The grounds were immaculate, torches lining the paths for no particular occasion. A servant had placed chairs around a table on the lawn, carefully setting the stage for yet another day's calculated idleness. Everything would again be perfect.

His thoughts turned frantic, parallel but somehow separate from the bucking underneath. When relief came it was overwhelming, and with little regard for the woman below him. He was sure it could have been any woman.

In the period of reconstitution that followed, everything fell to silence and stillness. Eventually Lydia spoke, a sweaty murmur buried deep in his chest. Braun did not hear the words. He could do nothing but stare out the window and wonder.

CHAPTER 13

While attendance at dinners was mandatory, breakfast at Harrold House was a more leisurely affair. All were expected to make an eventual appearance, but no schedule was drawn, and the members of the household crossed paths randomly. Braun entered the dining room to find Edward at the end of his coffee and financial section, while Lydia was parked behind a huge plate of eggs and meat.

"Good morning, Alex," Edward chimed in.

"Morning, Edward, Lydia." Braun watched her smile through a mouthful of food. "You look famished," he prodded.

With Edward lost behind his newspaper, Lydia smiled brazenly and winked.

Braun went to the buffet. He found a half dozen selections in such huge quantities that he knew most would go to waste, even after the servants had had their chance. He paused at a massive stand of bacon. No one here could imagine the conflict he felt as he reflected on the last time he'd seen such a pile of pork. Desperate for any warmth on a subzero Russian night, he had slept huddled against a sow. The next morning, his fellow troops had slaughtered the animal and gorged themselves. Braun moved to the eggs.

"Are you working today, Edward?" Lydia asked.

Edward peered around the *Journal*. "Of course, dear. A few

hours, anyway. I'll never make partner if I don't at least show my face each day."

Partner, Braun thought. The summit of his ambition.

Edward said, "But my doctor *has* prescribed fresh air, so I'll be taking the boat out this afternoon. What do you say, Alex? Are you up for some sailing?" He turned to Lydia. "I'd invite you as well dear, but the forecast is for strong southeasterlies — it might be rough."

Lydia said, "You know I don't enjoy the nasty weather, darling."

"Alex, what do you say? I suppose you haven't been on a boat in some time."

Having just spent nearly two weeks crashing across the Atlantic on a U-boat, Braun smiled. He had always regarded sailing as an aimless discipline. Drifting slowly, the wind blowing you where it wanted. It was far too serendipitous. He preferred to live by design. On the other hand, he had nothing more pressing.

Braun looked at Edward and beamed. "Why not?"

PART II

CHAPTER 14

Two weeks. Two frustrating weeks. Thatcher again made his way down the hall to the Records Section. He'd averaged six hours a day there, pouring over rosters from the British and American POW camps. There were millions of names, thousands of lists. Some were organized alphabetically, some by rank, and others not at all. So far he'd found no Alexander Braun. It weighed on Thatcher that the man might have used a false name. It weighed on him that Braun could have been taken in a Red sector — if so, he'd likely never be heard from again. Even with a lack of new arrivals, other work was accumulating on Thatcher's desk. Perhaps it was a wild-goose chase, as Roger had insisted. As the American Jones would have him believe.

He decided to give it one more day. If he didn't find anything, he'd move on. Passing through the office entrance, a lethargic young sergeant greeted him.

"Mornin', Major. Back for more?"

Thatcher was about to answer when he stopped abruptly. He turned and glanced at the open door. *Something, but what?* He stared at the words stenciled onto the wood: RECORDS SECTION. He then shifted to what was beneath. C-18. Room C-18. Something about it stirred his gray matter. U-801. Letters and numbers. They could be used for many things. U-801. Klein had assumed it was a filing note. Thatcher scurried into the room.

"I must know if the Germans had a submarine designated *U-801*. If so, I need to find out where it is now."

The clerk at the desk yawned, his breath laced with coffee. "I thought you was lookin' for a bloke, sir."

Thatcher gave a hard stare.

"Right," the sergeant said. He meandered into a back room, reappearing five long minutes later. He plopped a file on the counter. "If it's the German Navy you're after, these'd be all the messages we have. They're not separated — some are confirmed sinkings, some ships were captured, and the rest surrendered. Goes back for years."

"What if I need to find the crew of a particular boat?"

The man shrugged. "Best of luck, sir. One or two might have crew manifests attached."

"If I want to find a specific captain?"

"I suppose most mention the commanding officers, aside from the ones that went down."

"And if I find a name, can we locate that person?"

The sergeant smiled wryly. "If we got to him before the Russians? Piece of cake, just like that other one you're lookin' for. Only about two million names on the prisoner of war rosters."

"All right. First we'll concentrate on the boat."

The sergeant's smile evaporated as Thatcher cut the thick stack and shoved half his way.

"We? You want *me* to get on with this?"

"We're looking for *U-801*. With any luck, she's surrendered or been captured in the last few weeks."

Thatcher pulled up a chair and dove into his stack. When the enlisted man didn't follow suit he shot the man a pointed look. Soon both were scouring a thousand messages in search of a single boat.

The break came after four hours.

"Bollocks!" The sergeant waved a message. "*U-801*. She surrendered to an American destroyer off the coast of Cape Cod, in the States. Two weeks ago. They escorted her to the Naval Air Station Quonset Point. The boat was given up and the crew interned."

"So she *did* go to America!" Thatcher said excitedly. He thought it through. "And she turned herself over in America for one of two reasons. They were either low on fuel, or they didn't know which adversary had occupied their home port in Germany — if surrender was inevitable, the Americans or British would have been much preferred to the Russians."

He took the message and saw that it had no reference to *U-801*'s captain or where he and the crew were being held. Thatcher felt a stirring in his blood. He had to find out, and there was only one sure way.

"Absolutely not!" Roger Ainsley slammed a palm down on the bar. "I need you here Michael, not traipsing around America looking for ghosts."

It was mid-afternoon, but the usual crowd at the Cock and Thistle had come early. The celebration had been nonstop since victory over the Jerries had been declared, and Ainsley's raised voice was lost amid a room buzzing with raucous chatter. Thatcher sat calmly in the face of it all.

"It's the only way, Roger. This mission was something big. We have to be sure it's ended."

"It *has* ended. This U-boat surrendered."

"The boat was lurking off the coast of America. And it was there to deliver Braun."

"We know no such thing!"

"He's probably in a prisoner of war camp," Thatcher reasoned. "If not, the crew can tell us what became of him. Either way, I can't miss this chance to close the book on Alexander Braun."

"It's too thin," Ainsley argued. He then changed tack. "Anyway, I need you here, Michael."

"No you don't. You told me they're closing the place down. It's only natural that the pipeline will slow. And besides, I haven't been off station in two months, since I tracked down that cut-throat Smoltz."

The bartender slid a pair of replacement pints in front of the two officers without asking, and removed the first-round empties. It was the final installment of their customary order.

"Roger, it's my job to hunt down the ones that have slipped through — the high-profile cases. Let me get on top of this one while it's still fresh."

Ainsley shook his head and took a long draw on his mug.

"My mind is made up," Thatcher said. "You know what a nuisance I can be when my mind is made up."

"You've really slipped your moorings, Michael. I should deny it just for the sport. And make you take a week's leave."

"If you give me a week's leave, you know where I'll go straightaway." Thatcher waited patiently.

"Bloody hell! Two weeks. Not a minute more."

Thatcher grinned. "I'm sure it won't take any longer."

CHAPTER 15

The next morning Thatcher took his tea with honey, hoping to soothe the unmistakable rawness that was building in his throat. His body ached — more than usual — and the pressure in his sinuses sealed it. He was coming down with a cold. The timing was miserable, but there was nothing to be done.

He stood with his hands on his hips wondering what he might have forgotten to pack. Thatcher had done his best, but it still looked like an eggbeater had been turned loose in his suitcase. For so long it had been Madeline's chore. She would have had the spare set of briefs on top, followed by the extra uniform trousers, undershirt, and shirt. Done that way, he could dress more quickly, donning each item straight out of the case. She'd always had a wonderful economy with things like that, the simple practicalities that so often escaped Thatcher.

He went to his nightstand and lifted the small framed picture of Madeline. It had been taken in late '43 at a Christmas bash, only three days before the Heinkel, still laden with its bombs, had crashed into their Chelsea flat. It was the last picture taken of her, but that wasn't why he liked it. It was her demeanor, the effervescent spirit that had enveloped her during those last days, captured in a moment of irreverence near an overdone Christmas tree. Madeline had turned positively buoyant during some of the darkest days of the war. Only later did Thatcher find out why. Doctor Davies had come to the funeral to pay his respects.

"*I'm so sorry for your loss, Michael. It must have been doubly cruel given her condition.*"

"*Condition, doctor?*"

"*Oh God — hadn't she told you?*"

Thatcher had changed the subject, not wanting to hear any more. Yet the truth would not be put down. Days later he found it in the unopened Christmas card she had prepared for him — a horrible dagger preserved in a dressing table drawer in the rubble of 27 Kingston Street. *Dearest Michael. Let's enjoy our last Christmas alone. Congratulations!*

She had been waiting, holding her most precious gift for the perfect moment. A moment she would never live to see. The loss of one life so dear had seemed unbearable. Yet the second, never even to be realized, had put Thatcher over the edge. He made every effort to ignore the thirst for revenge, but it was quite impossible. It was, he supposed, the essence of most wars.

As the Ordnance Officer for 9 Squadron, he was in charge of twenty-eight men who loaded bombs and bullets on the unit's Lancaster Mk II heavy bombers. It was not outside the purview of his job to tag along on flights, the intent being to verify the accuracy and performance of weapon systems. Prior to Madeline's death he had been aloft a number of times on maintenance test and training sorties. But never across the channel and into action.

His opportunity arose from a series of malfunctions — the new five hundred pounders were developing a nasty tendency to hang up, not releasing properly from their bomb racks. This created an inherently dangerous condition, and Thatcher suggested to the squadron commander that he should go along on a few combat missions to diagnose the problem. The commander was less than enthusiastic, but Thatcher had done his homework. He made a strong engineering case for solving the issue, and the commander had little choice but to approve his request for limited combat flight status.

The first five missions passed easily. He had watched the

bombs on every release, finding one hang-up due to a broken lug. But Thatcher had still not gotten what he really wanted. He'd spent hours behind the guns, regularly volunteering to relieve the gunners from their tedious watches, and quietly hoping they'd get jumped while he was on the trigger. His chance finally came on the sixth mission. Over the target area, Bremen, they came under heavy attack from the air. The tail gunner took a round from an ME-109, killing the lad instantly. With the fighters still swarming, Thatcher took up the position and returned fire at the swooping machines. Unfortunately, while he knew the mechanics of the .303 Browning intimately, he'd never been trained to fire it at a moving target. He only knew from bar talk that you had to lead the target.

One after another, the Messerschmitts dove in with guns blazing. Thatcher responded in kind, forcing himself to fire in front of the fighters, hoping they'd crash into his own deadly stream. Pass after pass, bullets raked into the thin skin of the Lancaster. Smoke burned into his lungs and he heard crewmen screaming, but the huge beast kept lumbering ahead.

Finally, one of the Germans got impatient. Instead of a slashing attack from a high angle, the fighter pulled directly behind the Lancaster and closed in. Thatcher and the fighter pilot eyed one another straight on, no angular movement to complicate the firing solution — it was simply a battle of nerves as the much faster fighter closed in. At one hundred yards both began firing. Thatcher's bubble canopy shattered, and he fell back as bullets ripped viciously into his leg. There was blood everywhere, his own now mixed with that of the original gunner. His fate seemed sealed, but he clawed his way back to the station, praying the gun would still work in the next seconds. The Messerschmitt filled the sky as Thatcher squeezed the trigger, not even trying to reference the sight. An orange fireball erupted, enveloping everything, and shrapnel from the screaming fighter peppered the Lancaster's tail. It was the last thing he remembered.

The copilot later filled in the rest. The bomber had managed to lumber back and ditch in the English Channel. Thatcher, a tourniquet around his mangled leg, had been picked up with the three surviving crewmembers. Two months in hospital followed.

There, Thatcher was able to reflect on his actions. Madeline had been killed by the crash of a German bomber, shot down by a British fighter over London. He'd then found his own way to the fight, shooting down a German fighter over Bremen. Time and again he had wondered — had the remnants of that aircraft crashed into a building below? Perhaps, in the great circularity of war, killing a German soldier's pregnant wife? There were moments, disturbingly, when he hoped it was so.

These were the thoughts Madeline would have hated, but he couldn't shake them away. While on the mend, he'd been surrounded by others who had lost limbs or their sight. But Thatcher was sure he had lost his mind. He wanted nothing but to go back and shoot down another Messerschmitt. And another and another. He wanted nothing less than full settlement for the death of his wife and their unborn daughter — somehow he knew it had been a daughter. Thatcher couldn't sleep, and while his body mended, his soul festered.

His chance for salvation came by way of Roger Ainsley, one of his old professors from King's College. Roger had visited him at the rehabilitation center and offered a transfer to a new section — MI-19. It was part of the Directorate of Military Intelligence, responsible for interrogating prisoners of war. Thatcher, the nearly solicitor–at-law, saw it as an ideal means to his end. Uncover the worst offenders and hold them responsible. No bullets or explosions, but a guaranteed gallows for the deserving. And as the war in Europe ground to a messy stop, the time had come for accountability.

Thatcher slid the photograph carefully back onto the nightstand. He washed his teacup and put in on the drying rack. He then eyed a struggling, withered plant by the window. It was the only survivor, the rest of Madeline's crop having already fallen to rot under his care. Along with the once productive garden out back. She had turned it over to vegetables for the war effort. Now it was a horticultural disaster, a muddy tangle of weeds and vine.

Thatcher sighed. Perhaps he could salvage something when he got back.

His flight, the first available, would leave from RAE Farnborough in two hours. It was an American B-24 being repositioned to the Pacific theater. The third landing would deposit him at a place called Westover Field, a U.S. air base in Massachusetts. From there he would track down the crew of *U-801*. Alexander Braun might still be among them. Or perhaps not.

Thatcher would simply have to find out.

CHAPTER 16

The three flights took two days, slowed by a broken oil cooler that had grounded them for twelve hours in Halifax. The B-24, designated *Big Red* by her nose art, touched down in America at six in the morning and deposited Thatcher on the tarmac of Westover Field in Massachusetts. To his surprise, he was informed that a message was waiting for him at Base Operations. He took his bag, thanked the crew, and trudged wearily across the ramp.

The American bomber had proven no more comfortable than the Lancasters Thatcher was familiar with. Deafeningly loud, it had a heavy vibration when the propellers weren't perfectly synchronized. This, complemented by a temperature well below the freezing point, had resulted in no sleep whatsoever during the journey. To top it off, Thatcher's head cold was ratcheting up. His throat was raw and his joints ached.

Base Operations was a small, hastily erected clapboard building that hardly owned up to its lofty title. Inside, he found an enlisted man at the reception desk. The soldier stiffened slightly, and Thatcher suspected he probably had no comprehension of British rank insignia. He put the man at ease.

"I'm Major Thatcher. I was told you have a message for me."

"Oh, yeah," the man smiled and began fishing into a drawer. "Here you are, sir."

Thatcher unfolded the paper to find what he'd been hoping

for: CREW OF U-801 HELD AT FORT DEVENS MASSACHUSETTES.

Sergeant Winters had done well, Thatcher thought. But nothing about Braun. In a perfect world they might have already found him. He turned back to the enlisted man. "How can I get to Fort Devens?"

"Devens? It's about eighty miles northeast, almost to Boston. If it's on your orders, they'll set you up with a car at the motor pool. Otherwise, the bus station is a few blocks outside the main gate."

Thatcher's initial reaction was to go with the bus, but as he walked out of Base Operations he decided that a car might speed things considerably. He'd always heard America was a big place and getting around might be a problem.

The sergeant in charge of the motor pool was of British descent, bored, and took right away to the amiable major who needed a car for a day or two of the king's business.

"I have a sedan, sir. The only thing is, I've got to have her back by midnight on the third day."

"Of course," Thatcher agreed, having no idea if he could keep the bargain.

Ten minutes later, map in hand, he drove out the main gate and concentrated on his driving. He owned a car, a dilapidated Austin 7, but since the start of the war he'd rarely driven it for lack of petrol. Now came the added complication of staying on the right side of the road.

Once comfortable, he allowed his eyes to drift to the surroundings. The traffic was heavy, like he'd only seen before in London, but absent were the bombed-out buildings, blackout curtains, and sand-bagged batteries of antiaircraft artillery. The stores along the street were all open and seemed well stocked with goods. There were signs of the war, of course. Soldiers strolled the sidewalks with girls on their arms, and patriotic posters were plastered in the shop windows. Still, he had the impression that the war's influence here was less direct, a distant threat that touched all but harmed few.

The drive to Fort Devens took over two hours. On arriving,

his first order of business was to establish approval for an interview. Thatcher lacked any official, written authorization to con-
duct his investigation, so he tread lightly with the request. Fortunately, the camp commander was a disinterested sort who saw
nothing wrong in an Allied officer pursuing a distant inquiry. "If
you've come all this way," the man decided, "you must have a good
reason."

Thatcher next talked to the captain who had already investigated the case. He confirmed that *U-801*'s entire crew was incar-
cerated at Fort Devens, except for her executive officer, who'd
been taken elsewhere for medical attention. He also learned there
was no Alexander Braun on the crew roster. The American officer
had questioned *U-801*'s captain once, but the results were limited, giving Thatcher none of what he was after. Not wanting to
waste time, he requested that Kapitänleutnant Jürgen Scholl be
brought right up.

If the interrogation rooms at Handley Down were utilitarian, those at Fort Devens were minimalist. Inside a tent, three
chairs sat on wet dirt. They were the folding metal type, sure to
inflict equal discomfort to the backsides of all participants. The
table separating the chairs was nothing more than a thin sheet of
laminated wood resting crookedly on two uneven stacks of bricks.
Thatcher took a seat and did not rise when Jürgen Scholl was
guided into the room. The guard looked inquiringly at Thatcher,
who shooed him off with a wave of his hand. "No need, Sergeant.
You may wait outside."

The man did as instructed. Thatcher switched to German.

"Have a seat, Kapitänleutnant."

The Kriegsmarine man moved guardedly to a chair. He was
small, slightly built, though not in the sense of being malnour-
ished as were so many of the prisoners Thatcher had seen. He
wore an unkempt beard, but behind the mask a pair of piercing
blue eyes held strong. Thatcher reached into his pocket and
offered up a cigarette and a light.

The German accepted with a nod of appreciation. "Thank
you."

"I am Major Thatcher of the British Army. I am not assigned to this facility. Are they treating you and your crew well?"

Scholl's eyes sparkled. "Each of my men has his own bunk, we shower every day, and the food is excellent. We might not wish to leave."

Thatcher smiled thinly. Civility established, he set his course. "I have come here seeking information about a man, and I think you may be able to help. After today, Captain, you will not see me again. That is, assuming what you offer is found to be — accurate."

The U-boat commander showed no reaction, and Thatcher realized that any attempt to instill fear would fall flat on this one. Years under the Atlantic had certainly deadened whatever nerves he still possessed. Other means would be necessary.

"You are from Kiel?" It was one of the few facts established from the previous session. That was where Jürgen Scholl would want to go.

"Yes."

"And you have a wife and son there?"

"Who knows." The German shrugged and took a long draw on his cigarette. "Major, tell me what it is you wish to know. The sooner we settle these things, the sooner we can all go home."

"Indeed." Thatcher leaned forward and interlaced his fingers on the wobbly table. "I wish to know about your last mission, the one that brought you here to America." Thatcher saw little reaction. "Did you deliver a spy?"

"Yes. A Wehrmacht captain. I do not know his name — not his real one. Our instructions were to make best speed and deposit him ashore at the place they call Long Island."

"And you did?"

"Yes. We received a message regarding the war's end only moments before the drop-off. The spy insisted on going ashore anyway. We sent him topside with his things and a raft, three miles out. It was the last we saw of him."

"I see. The conditions were good? The weather?"

"Nothing out of the ordinary."

"So in all likelihood this man is now in America."

"I suppose. And don't bother asking me what his mission was, Major. As I said, I did not even know his true name."

"All right." Thatcher raised his voice, "Sergeant!"

The guard peered in the door.

"I need the best map you can find of the United States. The northeast coast in particular."

"Yes, sir."

Thatcher turned back to the prisoner. "What did he look like?"

"Rather tall. Blond hair, blue eyes. And a scar, here." He drew a slash across his temple.

"Tell me, what time of day was this drop-off?"

"Shortly after dark. Once the drop was complete, we went back out to sea. However, I could not make contact with head-quarters. We were very short on fuel and would never have made it back to Kiel. I thought it best for my men to surrender here."

The questions ran until, ten minutes later, the guard returned with a schoolboy's geography book in his hand.

"This was all I could find, Major. Sorry."

"We'll make do." Thatcher took it and leafed through to a page that showed the northeastern United States. He turned it on the desk to face Scholl, and *U-801*'s captain tapped a finger straight on the spot.

"Here. Just off the eastern end of Long Island."

Thatcher saw a town called Hampton. "All right. I'll double-check the position with your executive officer."

The German suddenly seemed hesitant. "Fritz? He is not here with the rest of the crew."

"No. He's in a hospital, over in Rhode Island. Recovering nicely from his infection, I'm told."

Thatcher watched carefully as the man who had battled the sea for so many years shifted slightly in his seat. It was a classic interrogator's tactic. He knew that with the crew interred together, any story line could have been concocted among them.

The executive officer was conveniently outside, an unassailable cross-check to the captain's story. The two men locked eyes and a new atmosphere fell into place. The captain had either lied or not told the entire truth. Was he doing it for the good of the fallen Reich? Thatcher doubted that. More likely he had done something improper, perhaps even criminal.

Thatcher lowered his voice and spoke slowly, suggesting a departure from the previous track. "Kapitänleutnant — I suspect there is something more. I'll offer two options. First, I can go to every man on your crew, including the executive officer, and compare their stories. This will waste a great deal of my time, which will make me angry. If anything should be brought to light that is questionable under the rules of this war, I will push very hard to have you and any culpable members of your crew prosecuted. On the other hand, if you tell me everything here and now, and I believe it to be true, you will not hear from me again. On this, you have my word as an officer. I will tell the Americans you have cooperated fully." Thatcher paused. "We have just finished a long and very nasty war. I am dedicated to cleaning up the loose ends, and this man you delivered to America may be a very significant one."

The U-boat commander found his balance. Far from being cowed by the ultimatum, he grinned, the blue eyes piercing into his interrogator. "I am glad, Major, that you spent the war in places like this and not in command of a destroyer. You might have given me trouble."

"We all have our uses. Now, what have you not told me?"

The German studied his adversary, a luxury he must rarely have had when he'd guided a ship under the ocean, Thatcher thought.

"The Wehrmacht captain is dead, Major. Put your mind at ease."

"What happened?"

"He was a bastard, but I only did him a favor. If he had been captured with the rest of us, he would have been identified as a spy and hanged." The German dropped his spent cigarette to the floor and twisted the toe of his boot over the remains. "We surfaced three miles from the shoreline, right where I showed you, and sent him above. Then we shut our hatches and dove. He had nothing. None of his equipment — and no raft."

"You don't think he could have swum ashore?"

"I can't imagine it. The water was cold. The currents. He is gone, Major."

Thatcher now understood Scholl's omission. It was certainly a crime, and as captain he was responsible, notwithstanding the logic that the spy would have been executed in any event. Yet by its very criminal nature, the confession was dressed in truth. They had thrown Braun overboard with almost no chance of survival. *Almost* no chance.

"But how can I be sure?" Thatcher wondered aloud.

The Kriegsmarine skipper grinned and shook his head. "Major, there were many times when I heard my torpedoes hit their mark, yet with destroyers buzzing around like angry wasps above, I could not venture a look to verify the kill. You must do what I did. Give yourself the benefit of the doubt. And move on to the next target."

The two weeks had passed like two years. Braun drifted through the currents of leisure — golf and tennis, lunch at the Newport Country Club, and even a formal dinner at the Van DeMeer's. Each affair was little more than a tease, like studying the design of a magnificent castle, knowing all along that a wrecking ball was imminent.

He was enjoying breakfast for once, so far alone in the huge dining room. As Braun gorged himself, he studied the abomination on the wall behind Sargent Cole's place at the head of the table. An exquisite Renoir was on display, one of the master's latter works emphasizing volume and contour. Hanging next to it was the most god-awful piece of modernist trash Braun had ever seen. That was what money allowed, he decided. Take something extravagant and, if the whim strikes, spit in its face.

He was tired, having been up nearly all night contemplating his course. He would have to leave soon, if for no other reason than to carry his false existence to a natural conclusion — the Japs were on the back foot, but not done yet, and Alex Braun, the soldier of obscure rank and service, had work to do. With Harrold House soon to be a distant memory, he needed something new, a plan to take him forward. Unfortunately, his only other connection with this country involved a rendezvous in New Mexico — for a mission he had no intention of completing.

He was taking his coffee when Edward bustled in.

"Good morning, Alex."

"Good morning, Edward."

Edward scooped sausage and a hard-boiled egg onto his plate. "What are your plans today?"

"Oh, the usual. A bit of tennis, then maybe lunch on the terrace." On his last day, Braun thought, he might add, *And screwing your wife as a nightcap.* Lydia had come to his room each night. After the first liaison, Braun had been unsure of what to do. He found Lydia's passion frustrating, distracting given the current circumstances. Continuing the affair carried risk, yet he had always answered her knock, satisfied her impulses. To what end he had no idea.

Edward said, "I'm taking *Mystic* out this afternoon. Care to come along?"

Braun would have preferred pistols at dawn. He'd already been out on the boat twice. It was a tedious affair as Edward blathered about his work and nautical exploits in inverse share to the demands of the boat — the greater the wind, the less he talked.

"How's the weather?" Alex inquired.

"Should be a strong breeze today. A storm's working its way up from the Carolinas."

"Might be fun." Braun weighed the thin positives of wasting another day at sea with Edward. But then his thoughts ricocheted down a very different path. He found himself saying, "Perhaps Lydia would come along."

"*Lydia*? Good heavens, she hates heavy seas. It's all I can do to get her out on the bay."

"Well, we'd be good sports to ask."

"Ask if you like, but I know what the answer will be."

Braun got up to leave, taking a cup of coffee with him. "What time?"

"Oh, let's say three."

"Right."

CHAPTER 17

With Edward at the office and her father tied up with business, Lydia decided it would be an ideal day to invite Alex to lunch at the Newport Country Club. And while she desperately wished she could spend the time alone with him, there was no choice — she had to bring mother. Lydia was an awful liar. If it were just she and Alex, the old hens roosting at their regular tables would see it in her eyes, and their tongues would wag mercilessly.

She found Alex in the library, standing in front of a large wall map of the United States, one finger planted on a spot to the lower left.

"Hello," she said.

Alex turned sharply, but then his eyes softened. His gaze drifted over her body in that open appraisal she so enjoyed. "You look fetching," he said.

Lydia brushed by him as if not hearing the comment, and hoping he'd get a whiff of her new perfume. She went to the map, which displayed two dozen red and green dots, all in the northeastern states. "Father keeps track of his holdings, all the factories and projects."

Alex looked at the display. "These circles?"

"Yes. I can't tell you exactly what they represent, but Father likes visual things. I suppose in another ten years the whole map will be covered with his dots." She went next to him, closer than was necessary. "What were you doing?"

"Oh, just checking the route I'll be taking when I head out West."

Lydia's mood sank. Another reminder — soon he'd be gone.

"But let's not talk about that." His hand fell and brazenly cupped her bottom.

Lydia heard footsteps outside the library door. She pulled away, and moments later a uniformed maid appeared at the entrance.

"Sir, your whites are ready now. Mr. Cole is waiting on the tennis court."

"Thank you," he replied.

The woman disappeared. Lydia leaned back against the sofa and heaved a sigh. "Oh, Alex —"

"I know, darling. I know." He started toward the door. "Your father doesn't like to be kept waiting."

She'd nearly forgotten why she'd come. "Alex, wait."

He paused.

"Can you come to the club for lunch?" Lydia felt the need to add, "We'll bring Mother along."

His smile was an answer. "Of course. Oh, and what about you — are you doing anything this afternoon?"

"No, why?"

He hesitated. "Well . . . just keep it free. I may come up with something."

Lydia watched him leave. She crossed her arms tightly. It was all so insufferable. She knew the status quo was doomed to ruin. In particular, if her father ever found out all hell would break loose. Edward had not yet become suspicious — the two of them kept separate rooms at Harrold House, and she'd been feigning headaches in the evenings to ensure her privacy — but sooner or later she'd slip up. On one hand, she hoped Alex would never leave. On the other, Lydia wished she could abandon the affair. She felt wretched about having been unfaithful to Edward. He'd done nothing to deserve it. If only Alex would do it for her, she thought. Perhaps one morning she'd wake to find a sincere, agony-swept good-bye-my-love note slipped under her door.

Lydia looked again at the map on the wall. In one corner was Newport, her home, surrounded by dots. The rest was a tremendous open expanse — and it would soon swallow the man who had turned her heart inside out. A thin sheet of glass covered the map, and her attention was drawn to where she'd seen him pointing. There was a smudge where his finger had been. Lydia read the name of the town underneath and, while she was not a worldly traveler, it made instant sense.

Of course, she thought. *He's traveling by train.*

Thatcher kept his word. He dismissed Scholl without relaying the confession about Braun's fate. He knew from vast experience that war crimes of the type were viciously hard to prove. Scholl could easily excuse his actions by saying that he felt his ship was exposed or threatened. The crew would back him up. In any event, the war was at an end, and prosecutors would be inundated with cases that were both far more deserving, and far easier to establish in a court of law.

The morning spent, his next step was obvious. Thatcher would drive to Long Island and search for anything about a German spy who might have come ashore three weeks ago. A look at the map told him it would be a considerable drive, stretching well into the evening, and so he stopped at the first roadside restaurant he came across. It would be his first true meal since leaving England. Thatcher needed it — he felt listless, weak, and his head throbbed from the congestion. After parking, he again studied the map and decided he would also order a sandwich to take away, thus avoiding another stop later.

He went into the diner and was immediately told by a middle-aged woman in a tired dress and splattered blue apron to, "Sit anywhere." Thatcher was halfway down the row of worn booths along the front window when he sneezed.

"Gesundheit!"

The voice came from the booth he had just passed — and it

was vaguely familiar. He turned to see Jones, the irritating American he'd met in Ainsley's office. Jones pointed across the booth to an empty seat and a suspicious Thatcher eased himself down.

"Welcome to America," Jones said. A thin smirk edged across his lips as he reveled in his little ambush. The man had the subtlety of a rock crusher.

"So you've taken to following me."

"Let's say I found you, Major. And you're awfully far from the office. On vacation?"

Thatcher would not play games. "You know damned well why I'm here."

"Pursuing the case you were ordered to drop?"

He eyed the American defiantly. "Precisely."

"Really? So you think your ghost is here somewhere, sabotaging our factories, stealing information for — no, wait. Who would he be working for now?" Jones chuckled as a waitress skidded to a stop at their table.

"What'll it be, boys?"

Jones ordered coffee. Thatcher forced his attention to the menu and saw that breakfast could always be had. "Eggs, sausage, toast, and tea, please. And a ham sandwich to take away." The waitress scribbled on a pad before scurrying off.

Jones lit up a cigarette. "Fueling up for a long day?"

"How long have you been watching me?"

"How about I'll ask the questions — what were you doing at that POW camp?"

Thatcher bristled, but strove for patience. Jones had some measure of authority, and antagonizing him would not help matters. He pulled the sharpness from his voice. "I discovered that our German agent, Braun, might have been sent to America on a U-boat. In particular, one that surrendered here in the states recently. I went to Fort Devens to talk to the captain of that ship."

"And?"

"I was right. They dropped Braun off along the coast of Long Island three weeks ago."

Jones' humor faded. His high, freckled forehead gained new creases. "He actually got here?"

"He got to within three miles of your coastline." Thatcher added deftly, "From there we can only guess." The American fell quiet and Thatcher pressed his advantage. "Worried about your Manhattan Project?"

Jones cut a swift glance over his shoulder before locking eyes with Thatcher. His voice was low and harsh, "Do not mention that name again!"

"All right. Under one condition — you tell me what it is."

"*Tell you what it is?*" Jones stuttered incredulously. "Just like that?"

"Mr. Jones, or whatever your name is, our interests are mutual. We don't want this man anywhere near your precious secrets. But to find him I must know what he's after."

The waitress arrived with cups of tea and coffee. When she left, Jones raised his mug in a mock toast. "God save the King. Now listen, Thatcher —"

"FBI."

"What?"

"You're FBI," Thatcher repeated. "All that nonsense about the War Department."

The American rubbed his temples. Thatcher hoped he was giving the man a headache.

Jones aimed a finger at him. "I can have you sent back to England under armed guard within the hour."

"And I'll be back on the next B-24."

The two locked glares.

Thatcher continued, "In England you didn't even talk to Corporal Klein. It was me you were after. This project is something big, and the mere mention of the code name threw up a red flag. You only wanted everything swept clean and shuttered."

"Can you guess why?"

Thatcher considered it. "Because the whole thing is nearing fruition. It won't be a secret much longer."

Jones sat back and took a long draw from his cup. "You're a smart man, Major. As we say here in America, maybe too smart for your own good."

"I can help you find Braun," Thatcher implored. "He could still be a threat, couldn't he?"

Jones set down his cup and looked across the room again. When he spoke, it was in a voice only Thatcher could hear. "This is the biggest secret of the war. And it's also the biggest single industrial program ever undertaken. Billions of dollars."

It was Thatcher's turn to fall nonplussed. "Surely you didn't say—"

"Yes, *billions*. Without the approval of Congress, I might add."

"What does it involve?"

"That I'm not telling you. I like my job. Let's just say it's a weapon, and it's taking an incredible amount of resources to build. My job is to make sure nothing gets in the way. And there are a hundred guys like me out there, not to mention the Army."

Thatcher filed away this information. "It's almost complete?"

"Almost."

"Will it be used against Japan?"

"How would I know? The point is, this project is expansive, and so far along that one lone saboteur could never make a difference. He'd have to destroy huge facilities all over the country. With the security that's already in place — it would be absolutely impossible."

Thatcher chose not to argue the point. "But then why?"

"Why what?"

"Why this whole mission? The Nazi's knew the war was over. What would be the point of sending Braun here? It's not the kind of thing they could steal?"

"No way," Jones said. "But they say it's something that will change the way wars are fought."

Thatcher chewed on that — *change the way wars are fought*. How many times in the history of armed conflict had that happened? The bow. Gunpowder. Mustard gas. In this war it had been the airplane. The goddamned airplane. And now some new terror to trump them all. He wondered what it could be. Did Jones even know?

The waitress rushed up with Thatcher's food, a heavy plate clanking onto the table. When she left, he said, "What about Die Wespe? Klein said there was an agent."

Jones shook his head definitively. "Nobody could threaten a program of this scale." He slurped crudely from his cup. "You really think this Braun guy is here?"

"I'm sure he was dropped off. But . . . I do have doubts as to whether he made it ashore."

"Why?"

"Leaky raft, nasty weather. The captain of this U-boat seemed skeptical, but no one can really say." Thatcher began cutting his sausage into neat, half-inch cylinders. "You just need to get out to the end of Long Island and start looking."

"*I* need to start looking?"

"Yes. You represent a large law enforcement agency — you could find out a great deal, probably with no more than a few phone calls. And while you work on Long Island, I'll take a different tack."

Jones' amusement was evident. "I'll bite. What's that?"

"If he made it here, Braun might be difficult to track down, especially since he's gotten a big head start. I want to find out more about him."

"How?"

Thatcher's answer made the FBI man laugh. "So you want me to do your leg work while you prance off to an Ivy League school to look at yearbooks? I'll give you this, Thatcher, you got big brass ones." He shook his head and crunched his cigarette into an ashtray. "Give me one good reason why I shouldn't have you sent back to England right now."

Thatcher took a knife and meticulously trimmed the edges from his toast. "I'll give you two. First, because I'm right. And second, because, if he's here, I'll find him."

• • •

Thatcher was back in his car thirty minute later. His map held a new fold, now showing the road east to Boston. Jones had succumbed, agreeing to search for any evidence of the last German spy coming ashore on Long Island. He had also given a telephone number where he could be reached. It would be an uneasy partnership, he and the crass American — the man was like a barnacle, a scraping irritant. But Thatcher was on foreign ground. He needed help, and he hoped that Jones, for all his arrogance, was at least proficient at his job.

As Thatcher drove, the rolling countryside and small towns he passed through would have been an easy comparison to home. He never noticed. Instead, he stared blankly at the road ahead, his head aching. A doctor, if he had one, would have prescribed rest. Madeline would have prescribed hot soup. He should have ordered the soup.

Never one for self-pity, his thoughts moved on. Miles passed quickly as bits and pieces of information turned in his mind. The Manhattan Project. Three high-ranking Nazi intelligence men plotting a mission in the Reich's dying days. But what was it all about?

The only way to know for sure was to find Alexander Braun.

CHAPTER 18

A waiter produced a tray of scones as the feast wound down. Mother demurred, while Alex took two. Lydia had hoped lunch would be a distraction, but so far the time with Alex had only served to muddle her nervous thoughts further. She couldn't speak without examining every word, lest anything incriminating slip out. A cinnamon scone fell to her plate.

"You act like you're eating for two, dear," her mother remarked.

She had indeed taken a full lunch, but the words sent Lydia reeling. *God, I never even considered it — what if I should become pregnant by Alex?*

"They're quite good," Alex remarked.

"Take another," Mother said. "You still have to deal with those dreadful Japs. I know the Army takes care of its troops and all, but you may not see a proper scone for some time."

"Indeed," Alex agreed.

"And when *will* you be heading out, dear? How much leave have they given you?"

Lydia thought the question seemed casual enough, nothing pointed to suggest that Alex's welcome had thinned. Still, it got her thinking. Had her parents been talking? Of course they had. She reached for her mimosa.

"I have to be out west in ten more days. Of course, I might take some time in Minnesota."

Her mother said, "And how is your father?"

"Actually he's away, in Europe," Alex said breezily. "There's a lot of reconstruction to be done — he's a businessman at heart, you know."

Lydia watched her mother smile at this perfect logic. Mother knew little about business. It was simply what rich men did. It came to Lydia's mind that she should try to learn more about Edward's dealings. A good wife would understand such things. *A good wife.*

Alex said, "I'll stay just a bit longer, assuming I haven't challenged your gracious hospitality." He smiled rakishly. Lydia knew he was always at his most engaging with her mother.

Mother giggled, having had three mimosas herself. "Oh, dear boy. It's a pleasure to have someone around who can beat Sargent at his games. You do vex him." She giggled again before adding, "Now if you'll excuse me, I have to go powder my nose."

When Mother was gone, Lydia turned to Alex. His gregarious mood had already descended — he was feeling the stress just as she was. Both his hands were wrapped around a water glass on the table, and he studied it intently, as if deciding something.

"So you really will go soon?" Lydia asked.

He spoke without looking up. "Yes."

The ensuing silence was harsh, and Alex finally spoke in a low voice, "Darling what we're doing — you know it can never last."

She nodded, then more silence before he announced the news she'd been both hoping for and dreading.

"I'm going to leave tomorrow."

"Oh, Alex! Then tonight will be —"

"No! Not tonight." He looked at her and his expression softened. "There's too much at stake. I can't allow you to ruin your life for my own selfish —" he stopped and once more studied his glass. Then his tone was lighter, almost glib. "Listen. I'm going sailing this afternoon with Edward. Come with us. There's nothing untoward as long as Edward is there. That way we can at least be together."

"Sailing? Well, it's not my favorite. But if it's our only chance — then all right."

"Good."

Lydia saw that Alex was pleased. It might be her last chance ever to spend time with him. She couldn't possibly have said no.

After lunch, Braun borrowed a car, telling Lydia he had to run errands to the bank and the cleaners. On returning to Harrold House, he separated himself for a stroll to the water's edge. A winding path worked through gardens and toward the shore. At the edge of the property an offshoot continued to one side, meandering to the northern boundary where a rocky point jutted defiantly into the ocean. From there, the shoreline curled back inward and receded into a small, natural cove where Edward's boat *Mystic* lay protected at a dock.

Braun eased slowly down the stone steps that led to the dock. He surveyed the boat, familiar now after two outings, and studied her layout. She was solidly built and attractive, if a bit square, and her upkeep was top-notch, thanks to a gardener who doubled very competently as a dockhand. Her teak rails were glossy and the winches polished to a high shine. He studied the lines and stanchions, the pulleys and cleats. And he wondered which components would help him kill Edward Murray.

He wasn't sure when the idea had begun circulating in his mind, but with each day it gained clarity, came more to the forefront. Strangest of all, the more Braun tried to push it away, the more insistent the urge became. The mechanics varied. A vision of Edward tumbling hard down the stairs, interrupting high tea. Edward's body crushed on the rocks at ocean's edge. The risk was enormous, of course, but if done properly, neatly, the rewards could be commensurate.

Braun was sure that Lydia herself was within his grasp. But if Edward should die under suspicious circumstances, eyes would fall hard upon him. Not only those of the police, but Sargent Cole as well. The man was a consummate opportunist who would easily spot the same. Braun's very existence was less than a house of cards — it was nothing. He had no identity papers, no accounts. Only words and stories.

But those stories were presently held as fact by the Coles of Newport, and from that foundation he worked in reverse. The police would allow Sargent Cole to vouch for the soldier who was their guest. Sargent, in turn, could be convinced by Lydia. He would be blinded, not by her cunning and guile, but rather her lack of it. If she could truly be convinced that Edward had fallen victim to a terrible accident, the die would be cast. Braun would answer a few questions, then leave to finish his tour of duty. From a distance he would watch and listen. If no questions were raised, he could return at the war's conclusion. Return to console the grieving widow — and eventually take his place at Harrold House.

It would only work if done well. There was an art to killing well. Braun had seen all varieties — messy bayonets, random artillery, clumsy strangling. It was in sniping, however, that he found a strange, arcane beauty. He possessed a natural flair for it — the intricacy of stalking, the quiet patience, the geometry of the shot. It all came together in one precise, deadly instant, a moment that could be countered at any time by an opposing shot. Braun put two fingers to the ragged scar on his temple. Once he'd gotten greedy, gone for the second shot, and it had nearly cost him his life. The other sniper had missed by a fraction, the bullet skimming off Braun's sight to leave its harmless mark. Was he pressing his luck now?

He studied *Mystic* and wondered if it could be done perfectly. Purely. His eyes narrowed as a blueprint began to form in his mind. Next to the dock was a small boathouse. Once a place to lodge the occasional guest, it had fallen in status over the years to become nothing more than a storage shed for *Mystic's* gear. Braun went to the door. The brass handle was green, corroded from sea spray, but the door swung open smoothly.

He turned his head, recoiling momentarily at the musty odor, then scanned across a room full of lines, tackle, and canvas. He found a large, sturdy sailbag and set it aside. A mushroom anchor, sized more for a skiff than *Mystic*, also drew his attention. The plan began to form. Braun visualized *Mystic*, the layout of her cabin and deck. Details fell naturally into place. As in any blue-print, the key was simplicity. Start with a strong foundation, ensure balance, and function would follow. The principles were universal.

Into the sailbag went the anchor and an old fishing reel that, judging by the degree of corrosion, had long been separated from its pole. He also came across a blunt, sturdy knife, of the type used to pry open shellfish, and this too went into the bag. He then shouldered the lot and went out to *Mystic*.

Fortunately, the padlock on her companionway door was unlocked — Wescott, the gardener-cum-dockhand, had already begun his preparations. Braun looked around to make sure the coast was clear, then went below. Thirty seconds later he emerged empty-handed and jumped back to the dock. He paused for a final look at *Mystic*'s deck before walking briskly to the house.

Thatcher had parked and slept in his car for a short stretch — his body rhythm was not yet adjusted to the local clock — and was bleary-eyed when he arrived in Boston in the mid-afternoon. A short walk, however, reinvigorated his senses before arriving at the Administration Office of Harvard University.

The woman behind a large wooden counter smiled. Any man in uniform, Thatcher suspected, even an unfamiliar one, would have taken the same smile.

"Good morning, I'm Major Michael Thatcher of the British Army. I'm investigating a possible Nazi spy."

The woman's smile evaporated. "You won't find any of those around here, Major."

"Hopefully not now, but I'm interested in a young man who might have attended your school before the war."

"Before the war?"

"Yes, 1940, and perhaps a few years before that. Might I trouble you to check your records?"

"Well, I suppose there's no harm in it. What's the name?"

"Alexander Braun. B-R-A-U-N."

She turned to a filing cabinet, opened a drawer, and mumbled aloud so that Thatcher could follow, "Let's see — we had a Bratton and a Braswell — Braverman. But no, no Braun."

Thatcher was dumbstruck. There had to be a mistake. Corporal Klein had been certain about the name. "Are you sure?"

The clerk closed her filing cabinet. "Major, I run this department — have for fifteen years. There was no Braun at Harvard in '39 or '40."

He grasped weakly for an explanation. "There isn't another university by the same name, is there?"

"Mister, there's only one Harvard."

Thatcher sat on a barstool an hour later turning an empty mug by its handle. He'd already drained it twice, enduring the piss-yellow liquid that passed for beer in America. Time and again he tried to make sense of it. Such a simple equation. He knew the school and the name, yet the records, which he suspected were painfully accurate, showed nothing. Had Braun lied about his name? Or his education? The Germans were sticklers for records, thank heavens, but had Alexander Braun put one over on them? And if so, why?

Frustrated, he decided to check in with the FBI. He went to a phone booth at the back of the bar and pulled the piece of paper from his pocket. *Tomas Jones,* it read, followed by a number. An operator picked up on the first ring, and moments later he was talking to Jones.

"Any luck on Long Island?"

"No. At least no straight evidence of someone coming ashore. The only thing out of the ordinary was a murder. Some truck driver was robbed and stuffed into his trailer — happened the morning after you think this guy came ashore."

"It might have been him," Thatcher said.

"I would have expected something more dramatic from the last Nazi superspy. Any luck at the university?"

"No. Nothing." Thatcher wished he had a more positive

reply. He rubbed the small paper with the telephone number between two fingers, eyeing it distractedly. *Tomas Jones. Tomas*—

"Look, Thatcher, we've hit a dead end here. This guy probably never made it to shore from the submarine."

Thatcher suddenly wasn't listening. He stared at the paper. *Of course!*

"I've got bigger fish to fry," Jones continued, "but if you do come across anything, call me at this number. All right, Thatcher?" The FBI man's tin voice kept coming from a handset that swung freely by its cord. "*Thatcher, are you there?*"

Twenty feet away Thatcher threw a dollar bill onto the bar as he raced for the door.

"Brown! B-R-O-W-N."

The woman behind Harvard's administration desk had been preparing to go home. She sighed at the Englishman, her patience wearing thin. "All right."

She went back to the same filing cabinet and in a matter of seconds pulled out a manila file. "Alexander Brown?"

"Yes! That's it!"

She gave it to Thatcher who began rifling through loose pages — transcripts, application for admission, personal data sheet. There were also tuition payment records.

"Is there not a photograph?"

"Photograph? No." She looked over the transcript. "The seniors have one taken for the yearbook, but this boy never made it past his junior year. Good grades, though. Do you really think he's a Nazi?"

Thatcher ignored the question. "Can I have this?"

"The records? Not a chance, mister. I'd lose my job." She looked around the room. "Of course, most everybody has gone home for the day. If you really think he's a Nazi — I could stick around and let you copy some of it."

Thatcher smiled.

CHAPTER 19

An hour into the trip Lydia wished she hadn't come. She was laid out miserably on a couch in the main cabin, an arm draped across her sweaty forehead and a bucket waiting on the floor. The bucket was empty, so far, but with *Mystic* rolling heavily it was only a matter of time. The skies outside were dark and wind whistled through the rigging. She wondered what had possessed her to come. One last afternoon together with Alex? And this is what he'd remember. Still, he'd been very understanding — checking up on her, the occasional comforting touch. Edward, on the other hand, was lost on deck tending to the boat. Her husband was not a mean-spirited man, but there would be no compassion for her suffering, nor any thought of cutting the trip short — he had told her not to come.

A fresh wave of nausea swirled through her innards and Lydia moaned. She heard the two men talking above, their voices loud enough to overcome the thumping of waves into *Mystic*'s hull, and the rattle of sea spray raining across her deck. With another muffled thud, *Mystic* gyrated yet again. Lydia rolled to the bucket just in time, her stomach heaving lunch into the pail. She remained curled in a fetal position, retching violently, again and again until there was nothing left.

Spent, she rolled into a ball, shaking, the putrid taste in her mouth, the sour smell in the air. How embarrassing. How utterly embarrassing. If only she had the strength to get up and empty the bucket. But she just couldn't do it. *Yes,* she thought, *this is how Alex will remember me.*

Footsteps pounded to the top of the companionway. She hoped it was Edward. Even in his I-told-you-so mood he'd have to have the compassion to remove the humiliating evidence. Alex appeared. She could only see his legs as he stood strongly against the wind. He was yelling toward the front of the boat, something about the foresail. She heard a muffled reply, and then Alex clearly, "Watch your step up there, man!"

He descended to the top step, one arm extended back out of sight to hold the tiller, which was just aft in the cockpit. He paused on seeing her. *What a revolting sight I must be,* she thought. Lydia heard something drop to the deck up front, and Alex shouted again to Edward before refocusing on her.

"Are you all right?" he called down.

She nodded, trying to force a smile. Alex left the steering long enough to trot down and remove the bucket, sliding it above and out of sight. He then scurried back up and divided his attention between her and the compass.

He said, "I should never have asked you to come, Lydia. This is my fault. I'll tell Edward we're going to turn back."

"No, it's not important. I feel better now."

"This weather is miserable. I'm not enjoying it."

Another ill wave rose in her stomach and Lydia rolled away, moaning. When it passed, she felt his gentle hand on her cheek. "Oh, Alex," her lips quivered, "it's all right, really. I'll be fine. Edward won't want to turn back."

"Then I'll make him."

"No. Please don't."

He seemed not to hear her as he moved to the stairs, but in the next moment *Mystic* lurched hard. Lydia heard the rigging creak and she was nearly thrown to the floor as the boat heeled severely to port.

"Dammit!" Alex raced above to the tiller and the boat soon righted. Lydia heard him yelling again. "Sorry Edward —

Edward!" Alex's head twisted back and forth. "Where the devil are
you?"

There was an edge to his voice Lydia had never heard. "What
is it, Alex?"

"I don't see Edward!"

"What do you mean? Where is he?"

She saw Alex scurry forward on deck, then reappear
moments later. "I don't see him! I think he's gone over!"

It took a moment for Lydia to register the significance of
those words. "What? You mean he's in the ocean?"

"Quick, come here! I need your help!"

Adrenaline overrode her suffering, and Lydia scrambled topside. Alex was at the helm, his hands feeding lines, his eyes scanning *Mystic*'s wake.

"When I left the steering the boat heeled over hard. He's gone
overboard. We have to come about and find him."

"Dear God! Edward!" She stood next to Alex and began scanning the waves. White patches of foam where waves had broken
dotted the surface everywhere. She squinted as the wind whipped
salt spray into her eyes.

"Look over there," Alex pointed. "I'm reversing course."

He worked the sails and soon they were looking ahead.
Lydia's stomach churned again, but the source was different now
— sudden dread, a panic that swept over her. Time and again she
thought she saw something, but it was only the tossing seas,
splashes of foam bristling to life and then receding into the cold
black water. After what seemed an eternity, Alex turned the boat
again.

"We'll go back over it once more!"

Lydia looked to Alex for hope, but his face had turned grim.
She instinctively took his arm. "We have to find him, Alex. We
have to!"

He put an arm around her shoulder and said with certainty,
"We will."

The second pass was no more use than the first. Alex turned
the boat toward shore.

"What are you doing?"

"We have to go for help."

"No! No, Alex, we can't leave him out here!" Her body trembled and Lydia felt herself losing control. "We have to find him!" she screamed, reaching for the tiller.

He took her by the shoulders and forced her eyes to his. "Lydia, we must get help! We can't do this on our own. Within an hour there will be twenty boats out here. *That's* how we'll find him."

Lydia felt his strength, his will, but her heart sank at the idea of leaving Edward out here alone.

"It's his best chance," Alex insisted.

Lydia nodded, tears welling up as she looked helplessly across the reeling ocean. "All right, Alex. You know best. But please hurry!"

Indeed, within the hour, twenty-three boats were scouring Rhode Island Sound for Edward Murray. They swarmed across the water like a colony of bees in search of a lost queen. Captains considered wind and current. Sailors, police, friends, and family scanned relentlessly until the light was lost. Even then a handful kept at it, waving flashlights and lanterns, shouting into the inky darkness in hope of a weak reply. The last boat docked shortly after midnight, Alex Braun and Sargent Cole aboard.

Sargent, looking more tired than Braun had ever seen him, mumbled to Wescott, the dockhand, "Keep her ready. We'll head back out at first light."

The words were belied by a hollow expression.

"Sir—" Braun began.

"I know, Alex. He won't be alive in the morning. A man in his marginal physical condition—he wouldn't have lasted more than an hour." Sargent looked up the hill. "I'm going to tell her now."

"Would you like me to come?" Braun offered.

Sargent shook his head. "No. It's for me to do." He turned silently and began a slow climb up the steps to the main house, a man with an impossible weight on his shoulders.

Braun watched him disappear into the back entrance of Harrold House. Minutes later, from a hundred yards, he heard her plaintive wail. He turned to the water, now bathed in a soft moon, and lit a cigarette. Braun took a long draw, held it, then purged the smoke in a smooth, controlled exhalation. How quick, he thought. How easy. Tomorrow the authorities would launch the fleet again, this time looking for a corpse—in the sea, or perhaps washed up on the beaches or jetties of Newport. The boats would crisscross Rhode Island Sound in a determined quest for whatever remained of Edward Murray. Braun took another draw from his cigarette and smiled. He worried little, for he knew that they would all be looking three hundred feet too high.

Thatcher sat on the bed in his hotel room, papers stacked in three piles. Night had fallen in the four hours since his arrival, and the only illumination came from a single lamp, a cone of amber that rose above a fabric shade to scatter weakly across the place. There were other lights in the room, but Thatcher was far too engrossed to notice—he had stopped at the first hotel, taken the first room offered, and turned on the first light switch. His suitcase sat unopened at the foot of the bed, and the drapes were still pulled across the room's lone window, the potential of a nighttime overlook of Cambridge Common never having crossed his mind.

He'd spent two hours at the Administration Building scribbling notes from Braun's university records, only stopping when the clerk had threatened to shut him in for the night. Not having time to record everything, Thatcher had prioritized the most important information while mentally reserving the option of returning tomorrow for the rest. He had also taken from the receptionist a list of professors in the School of Architecture.

The guiding principles of his investigation were shaky, and knowing so little about the Manhattan Project—Braun's assumed target—Thatcher had to fall back on assumption. Wherever Braun was headed there was a chance he'd need help—since *U-801* had dumped him ashore without his gear, he might require money or a means of communication. Thatcher knew that Germany's spy networks in America had been shattered by J. Edgar Hoover's FBI, so it was reasonable to assume that Braun would specifically avoid any existing Abwehr contacts. This left two options — he might return either to his old school or to Minnesota, where he'd grown up.

Minnesota had been first. During Braun's time at Harvard, from September 1937 to May 1940, his tuition had been paid through his father's bank in Minneapolis. This funding stopped abruptly in the winter of '40, when Braun apparently paid his spring tuition, in part, from his own standing Boston account. The balance was never paid, and after summer break that year he had not returned.

Hours earlier, Thatcher had put through a call to First Savings and Trust in Minneapolis, connecting just before the place closed for the day. A Mr. Snell, in Accounts, was leery of the long-distance investigation, as any good bank man would be, but on hearing the name Brown he minced no words. Mr. Dieter Brown, Alexander's father and only known relative, had been an outspoken Nazi supporter. In the years before the war the local timber magnate had forged an uncomfortable name for himself in local circles, and in '39 the widower sold his stakes and emigrated to Germany. The banker's tone made it clear that the elder Brown had burned his bridges upon leaving, casting America as doomed in the face of the German Reich.

It made sense, Thatcher reasoned. The elder Brown had gone back to Germany — no doubt dropping the Anglicized spelling of his name — and then called for his son to join him. Perhaps the son declined, comfortable in his situation at the time. Might the father not cut off funding? Logical, but pure supposition. The banker's information did make one very useful point, however. Alexander Braun would find neither friends nor support in Minnesota. With his family name tied firmly to the Nazi cause, it would be the last place he'd go.

Thatcher had then turned to the other records. Alexander

Braun had been a strong student, with excellent grades and superior written evaluations from his professors. He had played football, run on the track team, and made extra money as a German language tutor. Thatcher decided there had to be a fair number of professors, friends, and acquaintances who could offer insight to the man. It had only been five years, he reasoned, so some of them must still be around. He turned to the faculty list for the School of Architecture and reached for the phone book, but a look at his watch gave pause. It was five minutes after midnight. *Where had the time gone?* Thatcher wondered. And how much farther away had Alexander Braun slipped?

He put down his papers. The pain in his head was mounting, and he went to the wash basin for hot water and towels. His stomach also stirred, and he realized that he had forgotten about his sandwich. Was it still in the car? He sighed. *How ever do I survive?*

Thatcher draped a hot, damp towel across the back of his neck. It felt wonderful, and he decided that a good night's sleep and a hearty breakfast would bring everything to rights. Then he could get back to work. Someone in Boston would remember a man like Alexander Braun. They'd know his friends and his haunts. If the spy needed help, this was where he'd come.

CHAPTER 20

Braun spent the morning on the water, but official enthusiasm for the search faded by midday. The initial inquiry came next. Questioning that normally would have taken place at police headquarters was deferred to the library of Harrold House — the Cole family had suffered a loss, and a sympathetic detective gathered his information over tea.

Lydia, lightly sedated, sat quietly in a leather chair. Sargent hovered over her, a bear minding its cub. Braun was across the room, a visual ploy to reinforce the concept of distance between him and Lydia. He had not been any closer since taking her hand yesterday as she stepped from *Mystic* onto the dock, to collapse into her father's waiting arms.

The detective was a burly local who had a quirk of scratching the back of his neck. The man tread lightly, and wasted his first twenty minutes with condolences and offers of support. He then moved on to establish the basic facts concerning who, what, when, and where. The *why* was nicely forgotten.

In time, the detective had quiet words with Braun. The most critical issues were dealt a glancing blow. Where was Edward when Braun had last seen him? Did he seem in good spirits? Had anyone been drinking? Braun naturally tried to assume some blame, cursing himself for leaving the tiller free and losing control of the boat. It was a novice's error, committed by an unseasoned sailor. A mistake for which he would never be held accountable. Edward had been the skipper, and he'd been working on deck in heavy weather without a safety line. Still, Braun brooded openly in a punishment of conscience.

When the detective finished his questions, Braun receded to a remote corner of the room to sulk further against the tragic events. While the investigation ran its tender course, Braun mentally reviewed the death of Edward Murray for probably the twentieth time. The thoughts had nothing to do with regret, nor even a sense of victory, but were rather an accountant's appraisal of the efficiency of his work. It was a mirror of the well-practiced analysis that had evolved during his time as a sniper. With each kill he gathered new elements of use, and tossed out the ineffective. It was an application of learning that his old professors at Harvard would never have imagined, though something, he was sure, many would have appreciated from a purely academic standpoint.

Lydia had been firmly entrenched in the bunk below, Edward above, working at the bow. Braun had simply carried his sailbag up front, extracted the mushroom anchor when Edward was turned away, and struck him on the head. The blow had not been fatal, only enough to knock him senseless — a bloody mess to clean up would have cost valuable time. Braun caught Edward as he fell, avoiding any loud thumps on the deck to alert Lydia, then quickly removed the remaining items from the large canvas bag before stuffing his victim in. Braun was intimately familiar with the nature of decomposing bodies — he knew they exuded a tremendous amount of gas, so he used the oyster knife to puncture a few holes through both the bag and Edward. As anticipated, any blood that came from the wounds was neatly contained inside the canvas. He then dropped the knife and the anchor into the bag, drew the opening shut, and tied it securely. When he eased the lot over the side it was dead weight, disappearing in no time into the churning black waters.

This part of the sequence had taken just over a minute — but he was not done yet. A single item from the bag remained, the old fishing reel. He pulled out twenty feet of line and tied a knot at the base of the reel. Holding it aloft, he kept the tension constant and threaded the line through rigging as he moved aft. Braun kept up a disjointed conversation as he approached the companionway, adding muffled replies in something resembling Edward's voice. The indistinct words were further masked by the sound of *Mystic* crashing through the seas. On reaching the cabin, Lydia had spotted him right away. She looked awful, an arm draped across her forehead. Braun released the fishing line and the reel thumped to the deck.

Do you need help with that foresail, Edward? Two more quick thumps for good measure, and after a pause, *All right, I'll tie it down. Watch your step up there, man!*

With the right thoughts fixed in Lydia's head, the rest had been easy. Disconnect the tiller at the right time, allowing the boat to heel. After the lurch, find Edward missing and kick the reel overboard. Quick, clean.

Now Lydia was reciting Braun's story chapter and verse to the investigating authorities. A perfect mix of grief, naïveté, and innocence. He could not have imagined a more perfect spokesperson. All that was left was to sit back, wait, and watch.

The morning at Harvard had been difficult. With summer recess in full swing, many of the professors and nearly all the students were away. The only advantage was that, lacking classes to attend, those who remained were highly accessible. Thatcher was able to track down two of Braun's professors, but only one remembered him, and that a vague recollection. The man did, however, direct Thatcher to a graduate student who would have been in the same class.

Thatcher navigated the basement of Grays Hall, a narrow passage sided with slabs of stone that gave the place a tomb-like ambiance. He found Nicholas Gross in the Structures Laboratory. The young man was slouched casually on a stool, examining some kind of experimental framework. Tall and thin, he was smartly dressed and well manicured — more dapper than a student ought to be, Thatcher thought. Gross looked up curiously, no doubt put off by the uniform.

"Can I help you?" he asked.

"Yes — or at least I hope so. I'm Major Michael Thatcher, an investigator for the Royal Army."

"Which one?"

"I beg your pardon?"

"Which Royal Army? There's a lot of royalty in the world."

Thatcher's thoughts stumbled until he saw a grin emerge on the young man's face.

"I'm just kidding, old man. With an accent like yours —"

"Oh, yes," Thatcher recovered, "I see."

"Whatever could a servant of his majesty be investigating in a dungeon like this?"

The flippant attitude kept Thatcher off balance. On closer inspection, Gross was probably nearing thirty — rather old, even for a graduate student. And he fenced with the sharp words of a man striving to appear more clever than he was. Thatcher knew the type from his own days at Cambridge, career students who had the financial means to prolong their aimless academic careers to no end. Gross had probably spent the entire war in this basement, or somewhere better, notwithstanding holidays and school breaks when he would have returned to the soft bosom of his family.

"I'm trying to track down information on a former student. I was told you might have known him."

"Who?"

"Alexander Brown."

"Dear God, Alex! We all wondered what became of him."

"We?"

"Yes, yes. Alex was a stray when we found him — absorbed him into our little pack of liars. Roy Kiefer, Anna Litsch, Eddie. With a little guidance and a lot of booze Alex became quite a hit."

"Do you know where he was from?"

Gross thought about it. "Can't remember. He wasn't proper East Coast, but he wasn't one of those loony Californians either. Something in between."

Thatcher yanked a handkerchief from his breast pocket and stifled a sneeze. The internal pressure of the act brought on a spectrum of minor pains. "I see."

"So did he make it through? The war, I mean. We all knew Alex didn't finish school so he could enlist."

"That's what I'm trying to find out. When he left, did he keep in touch with anyone?"

Gross laughed and spun a full circle on his stool. "Lydia! Dear, rich Lydia." Dismounting, he sauntered over to an icebox and pulled out a Coca-Cola. "Can I offer you a drink, Major?"

"No, thank you. Who is Lydia?"

"Lydia Cole, of the Newport and Palm Beach Coles. Filthy rich, but not snobby in the usual old money way. We all had our eye on her, but Alex won the prize."

"They were involved — romantically?"

Gross hooked the lip of the bottle cap on a sharp corner of the bench and whacked down on the bottle. The cap went spinning to the floor. He made no effort to retrieve it.

"Romantically?" He chuckled. "Scandalously, Major. At least as far as Alex was concerned. Though I suppose Lydia was smitten enough. They spent some time together with Lydia's family in Newport — it was the summer before Alex left school."

"That would have been 1940?"

"Yes, I think that's right. Then Alex left for Europe. I always thought that was odd."

"What do you mean?"

"Well, the war was brewing, but we Yanks weren't involved yet. And I was never clear about which service he'd joined or why he went straight to the battle. Doesn't one normally go to boot camp or something? Anyway, Lydia got a few letters and she wrote back in spades, but after a year or so I didn't hear much."

"And *you* haven't heard from him since he left?"

"Good Lord, no. He and I got along, but only in the liquid sense. There was something different about Alex. He was witty — engaging when he wanted to be. Everyone knew him, and everyone liked him. But I doubt anyone would say that they were really close to him. Except Lydia." Gross swilled his drink, got back on the stool and brought his heels to rest on the lab bench. "So tell me, Major, why are you looking for him? Old Alex hasn't gotten into trouble, has he?"

"I'm not sure. Right now I just want to find him. Do you know where this woman, Lydia Cole, might be?"

"I haven't seen her in years. But it *is* summer, Major — the rich are frightfully predictable. I think there's a good chance you'll find her at the family house in Newport. If not, they'll point you in the right direction."

"Yes, I see. Well, thank you for your time. I won't take you from your work any longer."

"Work? Oh, right. Someday I'll finish this thesis. And then whatever will I do?"

Thatcher moved toward the door, but then paused. He looked squarely at Gross. The man could not be shallower if the tide went out. He said in a somber voice, "You'll marry a very wealthy woman who will grow to dislike you. Eventually, one of you will begin to drink to excess."

The young man looked dumbfounded, but soon his face cracked into a smile and he began to laugh uncontrollably. As Thatcher retreated down the hall, the laughter quickly dissipated until only his footsteps echoed through the place.

The rest of the afternoon at Harvard gave Thatcher little else. He tracked down another professor, this one an aging Renaissance historian who remembered nothing about Alexander Brown. The only other student acquaintance Thatcher could identify was away in Canada for the summer. This left him with one more chance — Lydia Cole.

He considered simply tracking down her telephone number and calling directly, but something warned him against it. According to Gross, Lydia would be the best lead. An experienced interrogator, Thatcher always preferred direct contact.

He returned to his hotel and took a late supper in the dining room. Veal was the chef's special. It turned out to be anything but, the meat overcooked and the boiled potatoes mushy. Thatcher was quickly coming to the conclusion that the Americans cooked like they fought — quantity and brute force over quality and nuance. He would have walked anywhere in town for a nice steak and kidney pie.

Thatcher studied a map while he ate, checking the route he would take in the morning. Newport wasn't far, slightly more than an hour down Route 1. Thatcher wondered if Jones had done anything useful yet. It aggravated him to no end that the boorish FBI man had the assets to find Braun but not the interest. He wondered what he could do to change the man's outlook. With Germany trounced, all eyes in America were shifting west. And when Japan succumbed, as she inevitably would, then what? Would there be an emphasis on tying up loose ends like Alexander Braun? Thatcher suspected not. Russia would be the new threat. Everyone had trusted Stalin to beat down Hitler's eastern flank, but who would trust him now that he occupied most of Germany and eastern Europe? The thoughts made Thatcher's head hurt that much more.

He pushed away a clean plate, tidied up under a napkin, and rubbed his forehead. The cold had gone to his sinuses, sharp pain stabbing behind his eyes. He ordered a pot of tea to take to his room. American tea, he thought miserably.

"*Hot* water, please," he told the waiter, "a rolling boil." His last cup had tasted like a bag of dust swept up from the kitchen floor, steeped briefly in bath water.

When it came, he carried the tray to his room and set it aside to steep. He called the front desk and asked if he'd had any messages. While they checked, Thatcher mused that there were only two people in the world who might try to contact him here. Roger Ainsley and that blasted Jones fellow. Chances were, they'd both want the same thing — Thatcher heading back to England on the next available flight. That being the case, he was happy when the clerk told him there was nothing.

Thatcher removed his prostheses and laid out his clothes for the next day. Easing onto the bed, his entire body ached, and he suspected he had a fever. The last time he'd been this sick was just before the war, in the London flat. Madeline had taken care of everything then — hot soup and biscuits, warm towels, tea with honey. And that infernally pungent menthol-and-eucalyptus rubbing cream. Madeline had always kept their flat spotless; she could balance the household accounts to the penny. Yet for all her practicality, when it came to illness she'd always had a peculiar bent toward mystical herbal remedies. Thatcher remembered telling her how silly it was, that none of it would help against a viral disease. To which Madeline would reply, "Of course not, dear," as she massaged deep circles into his aching muscles.

Thatcher turned to the papers on his bed and began shuffling. He sorted the important from the less so, and the extraneous went crumbled onto the floor, joining a scattering of used Kleenex tissues that now littered the place like wood shavings across a mouse's cage. Twenty minutes later Thatcher was sound asleep. On his rhythmically rising chest was one of the papers, the name *Lydia Cole* scribbled in the margin.

His slumbering thoughts, however, were with another woman, and in a better place and time.

CHAPTER 21

Thatcher had drawn certain expectations about the place called Newport. From the insinuations of Gross, and the hotel clerk with whom he'd settled his bill, the place would be astounding, littered with synthetic castles for a capitalist royalty. It was home to a nouveau aristocracy of wealth, where the titles involved were not lord and baron, but rather chairman and founder.

It was a disappointment, then, that the outskirts of Newport looked little different from the other half dozen towns he'd passed through this morning. The homes were modest, the businesses small. Along the waterfront fishing boats were moored haphazardly, and a few daysailers lay up to the shore. Thatcher was beginning to wonder if there was perhaps another city by the same name when he turned onto Bellevue Avenue.

Here things changed, though not on an unfamiliar scale. Thatcher's own office was in a castle, albeit a temporary arrangement, and if any people on earth were practiced at enduring the excesses of the upper crust, it was the English. Yet he found the mansions now before him curious, both individually and collectively. Each held a different style, though none that seemed "native." The odd mix of expensive imitations left Thatcher with the same general impression as the huge country estates back in Hampshire and Surrey — utterly wasteful.

The one called Harrold House was easy enough to find, its

name artfully carved onto each of two stone pillars guarding the main entrance. There was no gate, so he drove directly to a large circular parking area that fronted the entrance of the main house. His government-issued sedan was the only car in sight, and he wondered for a moment if the Coles were not in residence. A look around one side of the house allayed his fears — the gravel driveway spurred an offshoot, and he could see the corner of a large garage. In residence or not, he suspected a fleet of fine cars were nestled inside.

Getting out of the car, Thatcher smoothed the wrinkles from his uniform coat and climbed marble steps to the front door. The huge portico was awash in useless architectural trimmings — lions, cherubs, and carved coils of rope. He rang the bell, and moments later a uniformed butler appeared.

"May I help you, sir?"

"Good morning. I'm Major Michael Thatcher. I'm an investigator with the British Army. I'd like to speak to Lydia Cole. I thought she might be able to help me locate a man by the name of Alexander Brown."

"Mr. Brown? Mr. Brown is here, though I'm not sure if he's yet awake. Please step inside, sir, and I'll inquire."

Thatcher's heart surged. *Good Lord!* he thought. *He's here! Right at this moment!* He stepped inside to an atrium as the butler ascended a wide, arcing staircase.

He suddenly realized how rash it had been to come straight here. Thatcher had no authority to arrest the man. There were no established crimes, no warrants. The fact that Braun was here, delivered by a U-boat, made him a spy. But proof of even that was thin at the moment. Thatcher had immersed himself so deeply in the search he had not even considered what to do when he found the man. It was foreign soil. Should he contact the local police? Or perhaps Roger, or that idiot Jones? These were the thoughts spinning in his head when another man entered from a side room.

It was definitely not Alexander Braun. He was in his fifties, a big man with thick gray hair and a vibrant gait. He strode over and thrust out a hand, a severe upward chop that reminded Thatcher of an Oriental martial arts maneuver.

"I'm Sargent Cole. Is Evans assisting you?" The voice was strong, the handshake crushing.

"Yes. I'm Major Michael Thatcher. I've come looking for a man by the name of Alexander Brown."

"Alex?" The American eyed Thatcher's uniform. "Yes, I think he's around here somewhere. What's this in regard to?"

Thatcher stumbled for a good answer, but the effort was cut short by a scream. He turned to see a young woman plummet from the top of the staircase. She tumbled hard, smacking over the stone steps, and came to rest halfway down, crumpled against the balustrade.

"*Lydia!*" Sargent Cole screamed as he bolted for the stairs.

Thatcher followed, his crippled stride slower up the steps.

"My darling! Are you all right?" Sargent Cole said, cradling her.

Thatcher paused long enough to hear Lydia Cole moan. She was battered and bruised, but alive. He kept moving to the second-floor landing, and there he found the butler lying in a heap on the floor.

"*Where is he?*" Thatcher demanded.

The servant pointed down the hallway.

Thatcher moved as fast as he could. He heard a crash from a room just ahead. Thatcher tried the door, but it was locked. Taking two steps back, he lunged at the door with a lowered shoulder. His body bounced back into the hallway. He rushed straight back with even more determination. This time the wood frame gave a distinct crack. Thatcher heaved himself a third time, and the door gave way.

He tumbled into the room, sprawling face down on the floor. Rolling onto his back, Thatcher saw a flash of steel. He twisted to one side as a fireplace poker smacked the marble floor where his head had just been, chips of stone stinging his cheek. Instinctively, he grabbed the shaft and looked up. Alexander Braun was standing over him, rage written across his Teutonic features. They grappled fiercely and Braun fell to the floor, straddling Thatcher's chest. It seemed a tactical victory, getting Braun down to his own level, but then Thatcher felt the man twist and pull the iron bar until it was straight across his throat.

He heaved and rolled, got both hands on the weapon, but Braun was stronger. The killer used his weight to press down on the rod. Thatcher heaved and squirmed but he knew he was no match. The cold rod pushed harder. His breaths were no more than stifled gasps.

I need a weapon, he thought. But even if there had been something, he couldn't free either hand for an instant. Thatcher tried to lock his arms, keep the bar from pushing any further, but it was no use — it was only a matter of time before his guttural rasps would be cut off.

The veins in Braun's thick neck bulged, the muscles strained like taut rope. As Thatcher weakened he found himself staring at the man's eyes. They were pale blue. Yet unlike the rest of the killer's tense features, the eyes held an unnerving ease, a calm as he finalized his murderous task. Thatcher felt his strength slipping. The blue eyes turned gray. Everything turned gray. Then, suddenly, a breath.

His vision returned and Thatcher looked up just in time to see Braun heave the poker toward the door. An instant later a shot rang out. Braun scrambled to his feet and ran. Thatcher watched the man put a foot to the window sill in perfect stride and jump.

Thatcher struggled to his feet, holding his nearly crushed throat, gasping for air. Sargent Cole ran past him to the window. He carried a cracked shotgun, his free hand feeding a fresh shell into the smoking chamber. Thatcher reached his side just as Cole fired again from the second-floor window. He saw Braun swerve severely as a cloud of dust and gravel sprayed to his right.

"Shit!" Sargent Cole bellowed. "He's headed for the garage."

Thatcher staggered to the hallway, passing an oval buckshot hole in the plaster wall. He stumbled downstairs, past Lydia Cole, who was now being tended to by the butler. Outside, he paused at the front steps. Thatcher heard an engine being gunned from around the side of the house. He ran for his car.

Thatcher was halfway across the gravel parking area when he froze. A big black sedan flew into view, fishtailing to one side around the bend — when it straightened out, the car was headed right for him. With only an instant to decide, Thatcher dove left, pushing up and away with his good leg. He was airborne when the car hit his prosthesis, sending him spinning across the gravel. Stones tore at the exposed flesh on his hands and face. Thatcher scrambled up in a cloud of dust and kept moving toward his car. His limp was more pronounced than usual, the blow from the fender having dislodged his artificial leg. There was also pain in his good leg, but he could still move.

He got in the Army sedan and launched it up the driveway. Braun's car was no longer in sight, but a trail of dust led to the main road. There, Thatcher turned right — as far as he knew, it was the only way out of town. A mile later came the first intersection. Thatcher stopped. He looked left, right, and straight ahead. It was no use.

He slapped his bloody palm on the steering wheel. "Damn it all!"

CHAPTER 22

Braun drove wildly down the dirt road he'd scouted the day before. The back of the car slipped around corners and loose stones went flying through clouds of dust. On another day it might have been exhilarating.

All along Braun had known he was taking a tremendous risk by killing Edward. It was one thing to do it and not fall under suspicion by either the police or Sargent Cole. It was quite another to do it as a spy, a man with no identity.

And he thought he might have pulled it off. The police had questioned him thoroughly about Edward's "accident," but never asked for any kind of identification or military orders. As hoped, they'd simply relied on a powerful family's familiarity. Who would suspect Sargent Cole of harboring the last Nazi spy? Sargent himself had clearly been rattled by the tragedy, but so far his attention had fallen to comforting his daughter — not to accusing Braun.

All the same, Braun had stayed alert. He had been at the library window when the military sedan pulled up. He watched a lone officer in an unfamiliar uniform walk to the front portico. Alarm bells sounded in his head. He noticed that the man limped slightly, and when Evans answered the door, Braun heard the soldier introduce himself in a clipped British accent. *Good morning.*

I'm Major Michael Thatcher. I'm an investigator with the British Army... help me locate a man by the name of Alexander Brown.

The alarm screamed. Braun had rushed upstairs to collect his cash — and run straight into Lydia. She paused on seeing him, perched at the top of the stairs. Then Lydia had smiled. As always, so completely trusting and unaware. Silly girl. Braun had acted on instinct — a gentle shove was all it took. Then all hell had broken loose.

Now, as he drove, Braun wondered what had gone wrong. Had he been careless, perhaps slipping up on his accent? Had someone at Harrold House become suspicious? Or maybe the police had become curious about Edward's disappearance. Yet none of that fit a lone, gimpy British officer tracking to his door like a hound on a scent. For an instant Braun had considered staying, to talk to the man. But now he was sure he'd done the right thing by running. Major Michael Thatcher had to be something else. A new threat. Maybe the Allies had uncovered his mission. Maybe the bastard captain of *U-801* had talked. But how had the man tracked him here?

The car burst into a clearing and Braun's objective came into sight. The questions would have to wait. He slowed as he approached the place, eyeing everything carefully, measuring it against what he had seen yesterday. Two small aircraft hangars were separated by a modest office that displayed a sign advertising Mitchell's Flying Service. Behind the buildings was the long, freshly cut strip of grass that served as the runway. Braun pulled the car next to one of the hangars, cursing under his breath. All the doors were shut and the office was locked down tight. Old man Mitchell had not yet arrived for work.

He brought the Buick Special to a stop and smacked his fist on the dashboard. This had been his insurance if things ran foul. He'd come here yesterday after lunch to make an idle inquiry about flying lessons. Years ago, during his summer with Lydia, he had tagged along on some flights with her cousin Frank, who was a licensed pilot. Braun had met old Mitchell back then, and the little airfield, a remote strip of level ground cut from the surrounding forest, was now his first choice for escape. The authorities might think of it, but it would be far down their list after scouring roads, buses, and train stations.

Yesterday the old man had been at work, tinkering with an airplane in one of the hangars. There were no formal business hours posted on the office door, and Braun suspected that Mitchell kept his own schedule. It was nine fifteen — still early. Would he be here by ten? Noon? Or might this be his self-appointed day off? Braun couldn't wait to find out.

He left the car and walked quickly to the office. An after-hours telephone number was posted on the sign. He committed it to memory and circled the small building. Braun knew there was a telephone inside, and it would be far less risky than heading five miles back to town to use a telephone booth. The only door to the place was locked and looked solid. He circled around and found a window on each side. The second, in the back, gave way with a solid tug. Braun climbed in, quickly found the phone, and dialed the number. Mitchell picked up on the second ring.

"Hello, Mr. Mitchell, this is Alex Brown. We spoke yesterday out at the airfield."

"Yes, yes. What can I do for you? Have you decided to go ahead with the lessons?"

"Well, in a way. I actually have a crisis on my hands. I've got some important business back in Minneapolis, and I was hoping to hire you out on a charter."

"*Minnesota?* That's a long way from here, boy."

"Yes, I know, but I thought we could combine things — do some instruction along the way."

"I see. And when did you want to go?"

"That's the catch. It would have to be right away. I'm near the field now. I could be there in fifteen minutes." There was a pause, and Braun imagined the old man cupping his stubbled chin as he had a penchant to do.

"I have a lesson scheduled for this afternoon," Mitchell said.

"And Minnesota would take two days — maybe more, depending on the weather."

Braun forced a slight British whim into his voice, a tendency he had adopted from the local upper crust, a quiet registry of social standing. "I know it must be a terrible bother, but I'll gladly make it worth your while. Would two hundred do it?"

"*Two hundred dollars?*"

"Plus expenses — fuel and that sort of thing."

"Young man, you got yourself a deal."

Mitchell showed up thirty minutes later. Braun was leaning on the fender of the Buick, toying with a lit cigarette. He'd already closed up the office and made sure nothing inside had been disturbed. It would set an uncomfortable precedent if the old man discovered that he had broken into the building just to use the telephone.

Mitchell parked his old truck next to the office. "I'll have to get a few things," he said, pulling a handful of loose keys from his pocket. He tossed one to Braun and pointed to the nearest hangar. "We'll take the Luscombe. She's the gentler of the two, plus she's the one with the fuel ration." The old man winked. "I carry mail a few times a week — it gets me all the gas I need."

Mitchell unlocked the office and went inside. Braun took his cue and unlocked the hangar. Two corrugated metal doors, sagging on rusty hinges, had to be lifted and dragged aside. Fortunately, the white Luscombe nestled inside had seen far better care. She looked clean and tidy. There was one engine, a single high wing, and, as Braun had heard around the airport, she was a tail-dragger — high at the front on two main wheels, and a small pivoting wheel underneath the tail. Mitchell came out of the office with an armful of charts and books. He locked the office door and strode to the hangar.

"I checked the weather. Might be a few rain showers this afternoon in Ohio, but just the usual summertime puffies. Let's get her out into the daylight."

Braun moved a toolbox and an old bicycle clear so that the aircraft could be brought outside. He remembered the first time he had moved an airplane, surprised that such a big machine could be so light.

"Now, if you're gonna fly there's bookwork to be done. But since we're in a hurry, I'll bring the manual with us. It'll be three long flights to Minnesota. On the first, you watch and I'll fly. You'll get your stick time after that." He walked around to the far side of the aircraft and threw his gear into the cockpit. "Grab a strut, son. On three —"

Braun put both hands to the support brace that ran from the fuselage to the bottom of the wing.

"One, two —"

Both men pushed, and in seconds the Luscombe was clear of the hangar. Mitchell busied himself checking the oil and fuel, talking as he went. Braun wasn't listening as he stared at the empty building. He said, "Since we might be gone for awhile, can I leave my car inside?"

"Sure. Don't have much trouble out here, but lock her in if you want."

Five minutes later Braun had the Buick secured neatly in the hangar.

"I'll start in the left seat," Mitchell said, "then we'll switch out at the first fuel stop."

"All right."

"Now, watch close." Mitchell put a hand to the propeller. "She won't start now 'cause the ignition's not on. When I say 'contact,' you turn it like this." He pulled down on the propeller. "Then get the hell clear. Got it?"

"Sure."

Mitchell climbed into the small craft and took the left seat. He flipped a few switches before shouting, "Contact!"

Braun turned the propeller and the engine coughed once, then stopped.

"Again!"

On the second try the engine caught. It spit a cloud of blue smoke, as if trying to rid itself of some respiratory malady, before latching to an idle. Braun kept clear as he scurried around and climbed in on the right-hand side. With the old man running through his checks, Braun struggled to pull the door shut. One shoulder was jammed against the side window, the other against Mitchell. The last time he'd flown, it had been in a different type of aircraft — he didn't remember it being so cramped.

Braun studied his new surroundings. There was a control stick between his legs. The dash in front displayed a half-dozen gauges, along with some levers and switches. A few of the gauges were obvious enough — airspeed, engine tachometer, altimeter. "Why is the compass up there?" he asked, referring to the lone instrument above the dash.

"It's magnetic. You have to keep it away from the rest. I set a metal thermos up on the dash one day — ended up over Lake Erie before I figured it out."

Mitchell pushed the throttle forward and the Luscombe began to move toward one end of the long clearing. He explained his choice as they went, "Not much wind today, and the trees are lower at the east end. She's a testy old kite when she's heavy."

Braun looked at each end of the clearing, noting little difference in the height of the trees. Perhaps a few feet. How could it matter? he wondered.

Mitchell went through a few checks, running the engine up to power, then back to idle. Finally he turned down the strip and added full throttle. The machine shook and rattled as the propeller pulled them ahead, the big wheels bouncing jauntily over ruts in the grass. Acceleration was slow, the airspeed indicator barely rising. Indeed, the trees at the far end of the clearing began to fill the windscreen. But then the bumps and noise dampened as the Luscombe levitated away from the ground. Braun looked down as they cleared the trees by at least a hundred feet.

Here was his first lesson about flying. If all went well, the trees were inconsequential. Yet by planning for the unexpected, old man Mitchell had given himself every edge. Today, a few feet meant nothing. On another day it might be the difference. Braun understood completely, drawing any number of parallels to his own exploits of the last years. Never leave food or ammunition behind when you have an empty pocket. If you lose a button, sew it back on securely because staying dry was paramount. The small things.

Mitchell banked a smooth arc to the west where a series of low ridgelines dominated, huge waves on an evergreen ocean. In the distant haze behind, Braun could just make out the coastline. The individual mansions were dots, and he couldn't begin to discern which was Harrold House, where a small army of lawmen were no doubt gathering. Along with Major Michael Thatcher, whoever the hell he was. And Lydia.

She was such a simple, transparent woman, Braun thought. In spite of the years, she had still been under his charm, throwing herself at him freely, no regard given to her husband or her family. He was sure this was not her habit—Lydia was not a tramp. She was naïve, a child in a woman's body. He briefly wondered if he had harmed her by sending her clattering down the stairs. It hardly mattered. His designs on Lydia were dashed, and Braun shrugged the thought away. She meant nothing. Lydia was little more than a conveyance, a channel to the existence he wanted. Braun would simply have to find another Lydia. Or perhaps something else. The other opportunity that had been quietly nagging. Die Wespe. Could there still be value in what the spy offered? Perhaps. But the immediate task was to get clear.

Braun watched Mitchell's boney hands as they caressed the controls. He watched his eyes alternate between the instruments and gauges, a firm pattern established. There was purpose in every movement and Braun decided that he liked the concept of flight —the control, the delicate accuracy. He kept studying the old man as Newport dissolved into the haze behind.

CHAPTER 23

The library at Harrold House became a center for recovery. Thatcher tended to his own wounds while the rest — including the family doctor, a bespectacled, white-haired man — saw to Lydia. The palms of Thatcher's hands were raw from his dive across the gravel, and his foot had swelled heavily at the arch — he wasn't sure where in the scrum that had happened. His throat was sore on the outside now, a complement to the internal rawness he'd started with. It was all a constant reminder of how close he'd come. *If Sargent Cole had shown up thirty seconds later—*

Thatcher had called Jones right away upon returning to the house. The FBI was on the way, to arrive within the hour. In the meantime, the local police established temporary jurisdiction. The detective in charge peppered Sargent Cole, his wife, and the servants about the man they knew as Alexander Brown. Thatcher wiped antiseptic gauze over his hands and listened closely.

"He arrived unexpectedly on our doorstep," Sargent said, "just over two weeks ago. He was an old friend of Lydia's. Said he'd been serving in the Army. He was on leave and had to report soon for duty in the Pacific."

Sargent Cole carried on until the detective finally said, "I wish I'd known more about this yesterday."

Thatcher stepped in. "Yesterday?"

The detective answered. "I was here to investigate a disappearance. Mrs. Cole's . . . er . . . Murray's husband, Edward. He was lost at sea."

"Lost at sea?" Thatcher pleaded.

The detective hesitated, sounding like the foreman of a hung jury. "Our suspect, Brown, and the Murrays were aboard the family sailboat when Edward disappeared. It seemed to be an accident—" his voice trailed off.

"It would hardly seem that way now," Sargent said.

Thatcher eyed the widow, Lydia Murray, who was presently laid out across a couch. Her head rested in her mother's lap as the family doctor tended to a knot over one eye. She also had a nasty gash across a shin, and bruises mottled her pale skin like spots on a jaguar. Thatcher knew he was to blame. He had barged in on a dangerous man—a mistake he would not make again.

The detective addressed Thatcher. "So tell me, Major, why are *you* after this fellow? Is he a deserter?"

"A deserter? Anything but. We think he's a Nazi spy."

"*Nazi?*" Sargent Cole boomed. "We've known him for years, he's an American!"

"He was born here," Thatcher allowed, "but he fought with Germany. And in the end, probably because he was so authentically American, he was recruited by the SD, German Intelligence."

Sargent Cole, standing by his daughter's side, grew visibly angry as the prism of this new information cast a shifting light. "So he really might have killed Edward."

Lydia moaned. The doctor eased a hypodermic needle into her arm.

"It's a distinct possibility," Thatcher said.

The policeman suggested, "If he's a spy, like you say, then the FBI will take over."

Thatcher said, "The man I called earlier has been lightly involved in the case. I expect he'll go deeper now." He addressed the Coles. "We have to find out where Braun might be headed. Did he say anything to suggest a destination?"

"Alex played himself off as a soldier — one of *ours*," Sargent said. "He told us he'd be heading out west soon to join his unit."

"Did he give any specifics?"

"No," Sargent admitted, "it was all very general. A pack of lies — I see that now. But I do know he's from Minnesota. His father was a timber man there."

"At one point, yes," Thatcher said. "But those interests were sold before the war. And his father was an outspoken supporter of Hitler. I can't see Alex Brown going back there now."

Sargent Cole said, "So where in the hell will he go?"

Thatcher eyed Lydia who was catatonic on the couch. "Where indeed."

The first fuel stop came in Pennsylvania, a little strip called Franklin. Mitchell guided the Luscombe to a gentle landing, talking through it as he went.

"First settle the mains, but keep flying. *Always* keep flying. Then you ease the tail down." The little craft settled, bumping to a crawl before Mitchell turned it toward a small building. "The next one'll be yours," he said.

They were on the ground only long enough to take on fuel and drink a soda. The old man then walked Braun through a pre-flight inspection, checking the propeller, oil, fuel, and flight controls. When they got back in, Braun took the left seat while Mitchell stood at the door and walked him through the starting procedure. He pulled a worn card from under the seat, greasy fingerprints smudged across the thick paper. Braun had not seen it before. "This is a checklist. It'll help you not miss anything until you get the hang of it."

Braun took the card and went through the steps systematically. When all the switches and levers were set he shouted, "Contact!"

Mitchell turned the propeller and the warm engine caught right away. The instructor scurried around to the passenger seat and belted himself in. "Flying's the easy part," he said. "If you can

drive her on the ground you've got it licked." He pointed down to
the pedals at Braun's feet. "It's got heel brakes. If you want to go
left, give her some power and tap the left brake."

Braun executed a jerky turn to point them in the general
direction of the landing strip.

"Keep her to one side as you taxi to the end," Mitchell said.
"You never know when another airplane is gonna show up."

Braun looked skyward. The only other plane he could see
was sitting outside a hangar, and that particular craft was missing
an engine. Still, he took the lesson — some airfields would indeed
be busier.

At the end of the runway they paused to run up the power
and check the magnetos, the electrical wonders that sparked the
engine. With the checks complete, Mitchell talked Braun through
the takeoff. Directional control was maintained using the pedals
on the floor, which controlled the rudder on the tail, much like
the rudder on a boat. The ground roll was bumpy, but as soon as
the main wheels lifted everything smoothed out.

Climbout seemed simple, and Mitchell instructed a level off
when the altimeter reached 5,000 feet.

"Straight and level is the first lesson," he said. "Remember,
pull back on the stick, the houses get smaller. Push forward, the
houses get bigger." He cackled while Braun concentrated intently.
"The instruments are secondary for now. You want to fly as much
as possible by looking outside. Pick a bug spot on the windshield
and keep it on the horizon."

Braun did and the aircraft stayed remarkably level.

"If you change power to go faster or slower, you'll have to
change the aim point just a bit."

Braun experimented, first with the wings level, then adding
a few mild turns. The next lesson involved something called stalls,
a discomforting term that had nothing to do with the engine, but
rather aerodynamics. If you got too slow, in the Luscombe's case
below forty-five miles an hour, the aircraft no longer flew. Fortunately, the recovery was tame — the nose dropped, power was
added, and the airspeed quickly recovered.

For the next two hours they went through maneuvers and procedures. All the time the Luscombe kept roughly on a westerly heading, making distance as the learning took place. With the fuel gauge getting low, Mitchell turned to navigation. He pointed out the window. "See the road down there? That's Route Six. I've been watching it this whole flight. It's the easiest way to navigate — follow the roads."

He handed over a map that showed the highway in red. Braun studied it, but thought the picture outside was less clear. Intersecting side roads and small cities swallowed the highway at unpredictable intervals.

"I see the road, but how far along it have we traveled?" Braun asked.

"Well, there's a few ways to tell. Dead reckoning with time and speed, checking the layout of the towns and roads against the map. But I have my own personal favorite."

"What's that?"

The old man grinned. He took control of the aircraft and rolled it until they were nearly upside down. Braun gripped the door as the nose dropped. When the wings righted again the Luscombe was diving toward the ground. Mitchell leveled out no more than a hundred feet off the deck, straight above Route 6. The airspeed approached the red line on the gauge — 145 miles an hour — and the Luscombe shot past a truck and two cars like they were standing still.

Mitchell pointed ahead and shouted over the rushing noise of the wind stream, "There you go!"

Ahead, a billboard stood at the side of the road. It read:

WELCOME TO SOUTH BEND INDIANA

HOME OF THE FIGHTING IRISH

CHAPTER 24

The name was Spanish for "The Poplars," referring to the cotton-wood trees that grew in thick clusters at the bottoms of the canyons. Los Alamos, New Mexico, sat high on the eastern slope of the Jemez Mountains, a desert mesa that provided breathtaking scenery and isolation in equal measure. In 1917 it had become home to the Los Alamos Ranch School, a curiously popular and expensive boarding school that provided a "hardening experience" for those privileged young men of good society whose parents saw the need.

Twenty-five years later, in December 1942, the school was presented with its notice of eviction. The directive came from none other than Secretary of War, Henry Stimson, who announced that the school was to be "acquired for military purposes." The owners and staff were asked, in grave tones, to maintain a patriotic silence on the reasons for the school's closure.

The Army's logic was straightforward. The closest city of note was Santa Fe, and that reachable only by an hour's car ride on an unpaved road that suffered seasonally — syrupy plots of mud in the summer and slick sheets of ice in the winter. Unfortunately, it also lacked both straightness and guardrails, leaving little to keep one from launching into the picturesque canyons below. Few of Los Alamos' new inhabitants — all either government employees or dependents — made the harrowing voyage regularly.

The reciprocal result, by strong design, was that virtually no one from the outside world found reason to make the trip up to the isolated canyon community, known by its residents as "The Hill." Those who tried were asked to leave by surly Army sentries at checkpoints along the road. Anyone attempting to circumvent this would have to deal with barbed wire fences, and the soldiers on horseback who patrolled them continuously.

Because of this isolation, the new residents of Los Alamos were allocated a miniature city to themselves. There was a school for children and a store for groceries. The church doubled as a movie theater, and so each Sunday morning the prefects were forced to arrive early at the house of holy worship to sweep popcorn off the floor. This was Los Alamos, a city with a singular purpose — to be the olive drab birthing room for the most deadly weapon ever conceived by man.

If there was a heart to the organism that was Los Alamos, it was the community center. At two o'clock in the morning, music blared to a scratchy crescendo from a worn phonograph, the sound from the highest notes and most egregious vinyl imperfections stabbing out across an otherwise quiet compound. The crowd, twenty-odd scientists and a handful of support staff, all cheered drunkenly. Dr. Karl Heinrich was a silly sight.

At five foot two, two hundred and five pounds, he had never been one to cut a dashing figure on the dance floor. Now, however, with a Navajo blanket draped around his shoulders and a huge sombrero atop his nearly bald head, he resembled a child's top — thick, brightly colored, and spinning to a wobble before inevitably falling to the floor. It was a controlled collapse though, the physicist dissipating his kinetic energy without losing a drop of tequila from the bottle in his hand. Sitting in a heap, Heinrich snorted, took a swig, and yelled in a thick German accent.

"To the conservation of momentum!"

"To gravity!" someone countered.

There was a modest cheer, something less than what would have come an hour ago. Half the crowd had already left, and the remaining hardcores were rightly toasted.

Heinrich pushed himself to his feet as another song began. It had a catchy beat. "Now there is something to dance to!" he sang out. Heinrich scurried over and latched onto Marge, the sixty-year-old widow who ran the cafeteria by day, and dragged her to the center of the floor. She allowed herself to be taken and tried to keep up, but after five minutes she was out of breath. Marge edged aside to watch as Karl Heinrich twirled and shuffled his feet.

"I must have a partner!" Heinrich yelled. He grabbed Arne Pederson, an engineer, and the only man fatter than Heinrich himself. The crowd applauded as the two big men tried to keep time with the beat. Pederson only lasted a minute. Heinrich kept going. Sweat covered his face and neck, and his jowls jiggled. Once again the tireless little Bavarian, whose good-natured smile seemed permanently etched into place, was the center of attention. The crowd began clapping in rhythm to the music, and Heinrich again raised his bottle. "To Ernst Schrödinger!"

The name of the legendary physicist brought a mix of cheers and catcalls. Aside from a smattering of chemists, mathematicians, and the odd metallurgist, the scientists of Los Alamos fell into two overriding groups — engineers and physicists. Each faction was naturally convinced of the superiority of its own discipline. The physicists, aided by Albert Einstein himself, had given birth to the project. In their minds everything relied on the basic theories and mathematical models they contributed. The engineers, on the other hand, insisted that theories were meaningless until applied. Anyone could imagine a bridge over a river, but to build one that wouldn't collapse — that was something else.

As in most circles of academia, competitive banter was rampant. But high in the canyons of northern New Mexico, a new paradigm had been created. The Manhattan Project was a collection of mental talent perhaps unrealized in the history of mankind. Universities and industries across the world had been raided for the most gifted minds in existence. As the local jest went, "Here, university department chairs are a dime a dozen. Nobel Laureates a quarter."

Yet along with that intellect came a commensurate display of egos — men and women who believed that they were the best in their fields. For the most part they were right, but it made for an insufferable social scene. The Saturday night "Potluck and Dance" get-togethers had emerged as the most casual affair. After a long week in the labs everyone was ready to blow off steam, though anyone who ruined a night by making an ugly scene was not invited to the next.

The music came to an end, and the room was lost to the familiar *tic tic tic* as the needle on the phonograph hit the end of the rotating album.

"More, Karl! More!" someone yelled.

Heinrich smiled and leaned against a wall. His plump chest heaved for air and his shirt was sodden with sweat. "Yes, yes," he agreed, "in a moment."

A young woman, a secretary from the director's office, moved unsteadily to the turntable. Many of the men watched — while she wasn't particularly pretty, she was shaped along the lines of Rita Hayworth, and for a gaggle of love-starved scientists, many of whom had been forced to leave their wives and girlfriends behind, she was an eyeful. She also drank to excess.

"Any requests?" she slurred in a raspy voice.

"Something we can dance to!" came a shout.

"You drunk bastards can't dance when you're sober," the woman said. An instant later she stumbled, crashing into the table that supported both the phonograph and a ceramic toilet that served as a punchbowl. The whole lot clattered to the floor, alcohol-laden punch dousing everything. The woman was splayed out awkwardly, her white dress now wet and red. "Christ!" she sputtered.

A dozen men moved at the opportunity, but Heinrich was

closest. He put down his bottle, scurried over and helped her up by the elbow. "Are you all right, dear?"

"Yeah, yeah," she said in a coarse East Coast accent. The woman rose unsteadily and looked at Heinrich with bland appreciation. Then a physicist from the explosives lab grabbed the other elbow. Heinrich knew he was a new man, from Vanderbilt, an expert in blast wave propagation. He was also six foot three and very handsome. The secretary immediately leaned away from Heinrich and swooned toward the Vanderbilt man.

"Maybe you should call it a night," the fellow suggested.

"Yeah, that's just what I was thinking," she agreed.

He leaned to her ear and spoke quietly, but Heinrich heard the words as he backed away. *Can I give you a lift to your place?*

Her reply was a smile and a nod.

The lack of music soon had a dampening effect. When the last two women left — in protective company of one another — the mood among the remaining men soured.

Forlani, an Italian mathematician, pointed to the toilet bowl that was cracked and surrounded by a sea of red. "You see? No woman can be around such untidiness. It goes against their nature." He went to the coatrack and made his grand proclamation. "*I* am going home."

Major James, U.S. Army Regular, and the only uniform in the place, picked up the tequila bottle Heinrich had put down in the ruckus. Heinrich rushed over and took it from the major's hand. "Oh, thank you, sir. I might need this later."

James laughed — in the good-natured way that fellow drunks did — and started for the door. Others followed. Heinrich and Peter Bostich, a Serbian colleague from the theoretical branch, were the last to leave.

The high altitude night air was cool and dry, even on the cusp of summer. The two engineers strolled a path that led to the housing community, gravel crunching crisply under their feet. Heinrich still carried his bottle, and Bostich cradled an armful of albums from his private collection, minus the one that had been lost in the disaster.

"It is amusing, is it not," Heinrich said, "that the creation of America's greatest weapon has been fueled so heavily by whiskey?"

Bostich laughed. "Yes, but it will not be so amusing if we fail." The Serb paused. "Will you be coming into the lab tomorrow, Karl?"

Heinrich's smile remained. "No, Peter. I will sleep rather late, I think." He had taken Sundays off this last month, a departure from the previous year when seven-day work weeks had been the custom. "Our share of the task is largely complete." He sighed. "Perhaps tomorrow I will go to church."

Bostich laughed. "I have never once seen you in church, Karl."

Heinrich put a hand to Bostich's shoulder. "We are close to our goal. Perhaps a little prayer to go along with so many calculations?"

The Serb nodded. "It is exciting, is it not, to be this near."

"Ja, ja. Only two more weeks."

"Will you go to the test?"

"Of course, Peter, I must see the result after so much effort."

"Oppenheimer seems nervous," Bostich said, referring to the director of the project. "Do you think the gadget will work?"

"Ah, the billion dollar question. Teller still insists it could ignite the earth's atmosphere," Heinrich prodded, a jibe at the famous Hungarian physicist.

"Teller still pursues his fusion miracle. Let us hope he is wrong on both counts."

The path gave way to a clearing where the housing compound lay. Heinrich gave Bostich a friendly embrace, noting the sour smell of old beer. "I will see you Monday, Peter. But call me tomorrow if anything arises."

The two parted ways, and Heinrich took a meandering path toward the back where his own room was situated. He often walked the woods at night, finding the evening air far less oppressive than that of the day. It sometimes seemed like the only time he could breathe.

Halfway to his room, Heinrich detoured momentarily into the low forest of squat piñon pines and emptied the water from his tequila bottle. When he had first arrived in Los Alamos he would never have considered such a ruse. In his initial weeks here he had cultivated a careful image — outgoing, free-spirited, sociable. And not afraid to tie on a few drinks. His first dinner party at the club had not ended until the following morning, when he had awakened stark naked under the billiards table. The banging in his head had not been an element of the hangover, but rather the cleaning lady's vacuum striking him repeatedly on the crown.

He was amazed at how easily the Americans had taken to him. Karl Heinrich had made no attempt to hide his Germanness — the accent would have been impossible to lose, and besides, many of the scientists here knew him from his teaching days at Oxford and Hamburg. There were other Germans here, and they all had two things in common. They were experts in their fields, and they professed a uniform hatred of the Nazi regime. Heinrich had never confided in any of the others, but he sometimes wondered if he was the only liar.

He had come late to the National Socialist movement. In the early 1930s he had been too consumed by his work to worry about politics. As a visiting professor at the University of Hamburg, he was a well-respected theoretical physicist, and Heinrich's lectures on alpha particle scattering were in high demand. His frustrations began in 1935 when an Austrian Jew, Simons, had beaten him to the punch by publishing the authoritative paper *Mass Determination of Component Nuclei* as Heinrich was nearing completion of his own parallel work. The field was one over which he had been considered lord and master, so the letdown was heavy. It was as if a renegade cardinal had usurped the pope's podium in Saint Peter's Square to issue Mass on Easter Sunday.

The next misstep involved one of his previous works, relating to the projection of mixed nuclei in a radiant beam. Errors were discovered in Heinrich's methods by another Jew (a graduate student no less), and while the basic principals were solid, a year's work previously thought to be groundbreaking had fallen suspect. Full tenure never came at Hamburg, and Heinrich began a nomadic series of "Guest Lecturer" appointments. It was in Bremen that he attended his first National Socialist rally. The message fed his suspicions about Jews. They were evil, inbred thieves. Destroyers.

On Hitler's usurping of the Sudetenland, Heinrich had found himself at Oxford, a German patriot watching from the other side of the fence. Two years on he was invited to Columbia University in America, and it was in early 1943, with the eastern war going badly for Germany, that Heinrich was invited by a colleague to join a group of scientists working on a "war project."

At the outset there were standard questions from the Army about Heinrich's sympathies, his political leanings—but here he was rescued by his friends. The scientists of Los Alamos, dozens of nationalities among them, were a network of intellectuals who considered themselves above borders and politics. They righteously vouched for one another with blind confidence. In the end, it was this support, along with Heinrich's command of theoretical physics, that carried him past the Army and into the heart of the Manhattan Project.

He opened the door to his quarters and stepped inside, pausing to catch his breath. First the dancing, then the climbing—if he didn't slow down, he thought, he was going to have a heart attack. The walk to his room had been uphill, and even after a year he was not used to the thin air at 7,300 feet above sea level. He would not miss it. Indeed, the entirety of this desert he would not miss. It was clearly America's dustbin, good as nothing more than a place to hide her defeated indigenous people. Round them up and put them on "reservations." Such a nice word, he'd always thought, as if a maître d' was holding a table at a fine restaurant. The Germans used a different word, and of course it involved Jews, gypsies, and homosexuals. Still, Heinrich reasoned, the concept was the same. And in all practicality, he did understand why the Manhattan Project had found its home here. Heat, dirt, wind —who would bother looking for the world's greatest secret in such a place?

The room was a single, modest in size, situated at the end of a row of four identical dwellings. The adjacent apartment was occupied infrequently by Enrico Fermi, the Italian physicist from the University of Chicago. Fermi had spent most of the last year at his university lab, and traveling to the other facilities in Tennessee and Washington. Lately, however, he'd been more of a regular at Los Alamos, probably because the project was reaching fruition. It made Heinrich's work that much more difficult.

He set a pot of coffee to brew on his electric hot plate before starting to work on the curtain. There was only one window in the place, and Heinrich was meticulous about sealing it off whenever he worked. Having lived for a year in England during the blitz, he was an expert at the task.

When he finished, the coffee was ready. Heinrich poured a cup and added a hearty serving of sugar. The mix gave him energy, acting as a catalyst to shift his mental transmission into a different gear. It was time to put the evening's frivolity behind.

Tonight would be strictly photography. At the start, a year ago, he had copied the critical elements of each document by hand before resorting to the camera. If the film should go bad or become damaged, he had reasoned, there would be a backup. Now there was simply no time. With the war nearing its end, Heinrich's days at Los Alamos were numbered. Over the last two weeks he had taken many risks, scouring records and files, secreting bundles to his room. The scientists here regularly brought work to their rooms — though it was officially forbidden — but none on the scale Karl Heinrich managed.

He pulled a suitcase from under the bed and unlocked it. Inside was everything, a year's worth of work — documents, drawings, film, and the camera. He had considered something more secure, perhaps devising a secret compartment somewhere in the room, but Heinrich eventually decided it would be of little use. If he fell under suspicion, the Americans would tear the place apart. His only regular concern was the cleaning lady who came twice a week, a Zuni Indian woman who, if she could get by the lock, probably couldn't even read. Heinrich simply had to be careful.

He set today's stack on his working table and spent the first thirty minutes deciding which documents were worthy. Quietly, so as not to wake the Nobel Laureate next door, Heinrich dragged a shepherd's hook floor lamp across the room until it was over the table, then mounted the Leica camera. At the beginning he'd managed the Leica and documents by hand, an awkward series of repetitive movements that begged for better efficiency. He had fashioned a mount for the camera that attached to the frame of the lamp — the engineers would have been proud — and this simple advance had nearly doubled his progress. In a good hour he could take a hundred pictures, and by his most recent estimate there were at least nine thousand photographs, documents, drawings, and prints in his bulging little suitcase, covering every aspect of the Manhattan Project. Plutonium production, canning of uranium slugs, measurement of detonation waves. In all, three years of work fueled by the world's greatest minds.

Tonight Heinrich would concentrate on the arrangements for the actual test — design of the tower, capture of data for yield estimation, and the layout of radiation monitors. He discarded the sections on range safety and security, which were handled by the Army and seemed obvious enough.

The shutter began to click, and as Heinrich shuffled documents through his fingers his thoughts drifted ahead. After tonight, only one vital vein would remain to be mined — the results of the test, the world's first atomic explosion. It would take place in two weeks, and the data was of critical importance. He wondered if he would still be here, still have access. But soon the larger question flooded his thoughts — the one that had bothered him increasingly over the last months. What would he do with it all?

Heinrich read the newspapers each day and the latest headlines could not be more grim. The Reich had been dealt a terrible blow. He had no doubts that it would reemerge — but how, and where? Such uncertainty. Still, Heinrich held faith. The cause was right, and pure — particularly ridding the world of the filthy Jews.

As he focused the Leica on a diagram — a layout of seismographs, spectrographs, and ionization chambers — his thoughts drifted to Santa Fe. The day was fast approaching when he would reach for the last thread that connected him to the old country. Would his new contact be there? Karl Heinrich sighed as the camera clicked. It had to be so.

It had to be.

CHAPTER 25

The outline of downtown Chicago was just visible in the haze behind them. Braun concentrated on correlating details on the map in his hand to the features below. Once again, the instructor had taken the right seat, the student the left.

This flight had gone deeper into the subject of navigation, with a few stall recoveries at the outset. They had practiced landings yesterday evening in South Bend, just before dusk. After seven touch-and-go's Braun had become comfortable, if not completely proficient, and at the end he noticed Mitchell's hands did not hover over the controls as they neared each touchdown. The student was making progress.

After the last landing, they'd taken a room at a boarding house near the airport. Braun had drifted to sleep wondering if the authorities in Newport had found the Buick Special stashed in the hangar.

This morning he and Mitchell had risen early. After stuffing down a sugary Danish and a tar-like cup of coffee, the journey had resumed.

"Route Sixty-one," Mitchell said, tapping on the map. "That'll take us northwest through Wisconsin."

Braun nodded as he held the controls. Until now, the terrain below had been the same for hundreds of miles — an endless layout of farms, pancake flat, and arranged in orderly squares by roads that were true to the cardinal directions of the compass. Mitchell called them section lines. Here, though, the contours began to change. Carpets of forest, deep green in mid-summer foliage, swallowed the landscape, and soft hills provided basins for white pockets of early morning mist.

"The future's right down there," the old man remarked.

"What future would that be?"

"Trees. Lumber. This war's gonna be over soon, and all the boys will be coming home. When they get back they'll start families. A family needs a house. And for a house you need wood. Lots of it."

Braun shrugged. "I suppose so." There *would* be an epidemic of cheap housing, he thought. Row after row of uninspired boxes stamped out in a frenzy of construction, as if from one of Mr. Ford's assembly lines. But the deeper irony of Mitchell's observation was notable. They were getting close to Braun's home, the land he remembered, flush with the rich timber that had so distracted his father. Of course, if it hadn't been the timber, it would have been something else.

Braun's father had always been the chief designer of his misery. The man had come across the ocean a classic immigrant, arriving penniless from Germany in 1912. He'd seen land, opportunity. And he stopped at nothing to take his share. The first tract had been small, the trees taken down by hand, hauled by horses. But the old man was relentless. By the time the Depression hit, there were hundreds of acres, mechanized transportation, and a mill. The early thirties were hard — parcels had to be sold and the mill closed — yet his father survived, recovering all his losses before the war came around. As was always the case, however, success came at a price.

The elder Braun rarely found time for his family. He was a virtual stranger in his home, and when he wasn't at the office he was at Schmitt's, the corner bar that pulled authentic German beer for the neighborhood. While Alex's father was gone to pursue either the riches he demanded or a good pint, his mother was left to bear the load at home.

So it was, when a new sister came into the world two months early, it was Alex who was forced to run six miles to town in a violent snowstorm to fetch the doctor. When the two eventually made it back, hours later, the newborn and mother were both still, the bed drenched in blood. Ten-year-old Alex had been inconsolable, and when his father finally showed up that night, obviously drunk, Alex had struck him the best blow he could muster. His father, through some mix of whiskey and guilt, had responded by beating his surviving child senseless. Only the doctor's intervention had saved Alex's life.

Any ties that had ever existed between the two were ended that night. Alex was committed to a series of boarding schools, rarely seeing his father, and the divide only cemented their estrangement. Holidays were spent in dormitories, and each year on his birthday Alex received a remittance of ten dollars, the handwriting on the envelope that of his father's secretary. As time passed, most of what he learned about his father was garnered from the newspapers and school gossip — his elder was becoming richer and more prominent. This, at least, was something appreciated around Alex's preparatory school, and the teachers, administrators, and other students allowed him a certain status of acceptance.

And then there was the matter of Alex's acceptance to Harvard. His grades had been decent, but somewhat erratic. He strongly suspected his father had arranged the admission, just before selling his holdings and fleeing back to Germany. The question was why. To offer his sole issue an elite education? Or was it simply a business move on his father's part, a card to be later played in some arcane game? Young Alex Braun chose not to dwell on the matter. Instead, he simply took what he could, a precept that would harden severely over the next five years.

A familiar voice drove away the memories.

"Yep," Mitchell continued, "lots of boys coming back. By the way, what did you do during the war, son?"

For those who had stayed behind it was the hard question, the one that could not be taken without a certain underlying sharpness. Braun's answer was pre-forged and sturdy. "I served in

Europe. I'm only back for a few weeks before I head out to the Pacific. That's why I need to get to Minnesota in such a hurry."

Mitchell seemed convinced, yet Braun was curious as to why he had suddenly turned conversational. The previous 8.4 hours of flight, so precisely measured on the aircraft's Hobbs meter, had been entirely business. The instructor taught, the student performed. Braun decided it was a display of confidence, an affirmation that he was indeed flying the aircraft well.

"That's the Mississippi over there," Mitchell announced, pointing off in the distance. "Follow that for an hour and it'll take us right to downtown Minneapolis."

Braun saw the meandering river ahead, a heavy vein on the earth's surface to move her life's blood.

"How long will you need in Minneapolis?" Mitchell asked.

"My business should only take an hour or two. We can start back East this afternoon." Braun's hands were steady on the controls. The altimeter read a perfect five thousand feet.

"Okay. Maybe we can get back home tonight. My wife promised to bake an apple pie — her way of getting me back home!" Mitchell cackled. "And by the time we get back, you'll be ready to solo."

Braun looked out at the forest below. It was punctuated by countless small lakes that mirrored the low eastern sun, like a thousand diamonds shining against an emerald blanket. He saw only one small town, distant to the west. Braun looked at his instructor and smiled.

Hiram Mitchell smiled back at his student, thinking he'd add a scoop of ice cream to the apple pie. He was happy with the boy's progress, happy that he'd taken the job. It was the easiest two hundred dollars he had ever earned. Mitchell decided to use part of the money to take his bride to the Poconos for a week — it had been nearly a year since they'd gotten away. The rest would go for an engine overhaul on the Avion, which was already overdue. *Yep,* he thought, *easy money.* He leaned forward for a chart.

It came out of nowhere. The pain was excruciating, like a

sledgehammer had smashed between his eyes. Mitchell tried to push himself up, but his limbs wouldn't respond. *What was happening?* His hands groped awkwardly, clawing for a grip, anything to right himself. His head spun and his vision was blurred. And then he felt the oddest sensation, something warm spreading across his face. "What—" There was no time to finish the question. The second blow, to the side of his head, brought only stars.

Mitchell's world faded. Time stopped. The next sensation was movement, his body being shoved and tugged, back and forth. He tried to get his bearings, to understand, but the pain was agonizing. Suddenly he felt wind, and then his stomach lurched in freefall. It was like being on the roller coaster at Coney Island. His arms and legs flailed, and the wind came stronger — a hurricane all around. He'd always had dreams about falling, spinning down through an endless void. But when Mitchell wrenched a hand to his face and wiped the blood from his eyes, he saw that there was indeed an end. The forest rushed up at him, larger and larger, filling his view until there was nothing else.

Hiram Mitchell screamed.

Thatcher led Tomas Jones across the back lawn of Harrold House. The FBI man had arrived early, but been buttonholed by the local police detective before Thatcher was able to usher him outside for privacy. Meandering the walking paths, the two found common ground for the first time.

"Looks like this Sargent Cole is some rich sunnava bitch," Jones noted crassly.

Thatcher eyed the manicured surroundings with equal distaste. "Perhaps it has something to do with why Braun ended up here."

Jones chewed on the remark. "So somebody at Harvard told you he'd be here?"

"A fellow student told me he was involved with the girl, Lydia. I came to talk to her, but I never suspected Braun might actually be here."

"That was pretty dumb, just going right up and banging on the door."

Thatcher's blood rose, but he let it go. He deserved that one. They paused on reaching the ocean, the waves breaking just below, the air laced in a salty tang.

"Have your people taken over the search?" Thatcher asked.

"The FBI? Hell no!"

"But Braun was just here — he's killed a man!"

"We don't know that for sure. He shoved that girl down the stairs, and roughed up you and the butler. Stole a car too, I guess, but that doesn't make it a federal case."

"He's a Nazi spy — you know how he got here! His mission involves your precious Manhattan Project!"

"*Does it?* Then why the hell is he diddling around here playing Jay Gatsby?"

Thatcher fell silent for a moment. "Maybe he needed money. He came ashore with nothing."

"So he kills this gal's husband to weasel his way into the family fortune? Today a funeral, tomorrow a wedding? That's a new way to fund sabotage. Come on, Thatcher, you're better than that."

He fumed, trying to see a way around the American's logic.

Jones said, "He may have been delivered here as a spy, Major, but the war is over. He knows that as well as we do." He turned toward the house. A rack at the edge of the lawn displayed a neat array of colored croquet mallets. Jones lifted out the red one and walked to where a wooden ball sat on the grass waiting to be sent through a wire hoop twenty feet away. He swung and scuffed his effort badly. "And the fact that he was laying around this goofy amusement park only proves it — he ain't a threat. At least not to our national security."

"So you won't pursue it?"

"Oh, we'll get involved. If there's been a murder, we'll find him. But it's not a high priority."

"*Not a priority?* Listen —"

Jones swung the mallet down to the turf like an axe splitting a log, then pointed it at Thatcher's head. "No, Major, you listen! You get out of my hair. We'll find this guy in time, but we'll do it our way. That's it!" Jones tossed the mallet onto the perfectly trimmed, sunlit lawn, and headed for the house.

Thatcher turned back to the water. Under a thick haze the Atlantic looked nearly black, fading to obscurity at the horizon. He was angry. Angry he'd been so close, yet bumbled away the chance to catch Braun. And angry that what Jones said made sense. Why *had* Braun come here? What was he after? And most importantly, where had he gone now?

CHAPTER 26

The cheese was foul and Braun spit out the first bite of his sandwich. Adjacent to the airport in Lamoni, Iowa, along Route 69, there had been only one motel and one restaurant. It was a traveler's lodge, a place to rest for as long as one could ignore the heavy trucks that rattled in and out from the grain elevators across the street. The room was dank, one small bed with stained sheets and the musty odor of mothballs. Wanting to keep as low a profile as possible, Braun had ordered a ham and cheese sandwich to take to his room, but now he wished he'd risked a hot meal.

There had been enough fuel and daylight to fly at least another hundred miles, but a huge thunderstorm had blackened the sky to the west. When Braun spotted the little airstrip he decided not to press his luck. The landing had been wobbly, but his confidence was growing. He had covered three hundred miles since disposing of Mitchell, stopping once for fuel. On only one occasion had he become unsure of his position, and he'd tried Mitchell's silly tactic of going low to check the road signs. Surprisingly, it worked. He had easily correlated city names to fix his position on the map. Unfortunately, Mitchell's aviation charts ended at the Kansas border. Braun would have to find something else tomorrow. If he couldn't get a proper flight chart, he reckoned he could do as well with a good road map.

He had already arranged to have the Luscombe fueled — the attendant seemed to accept his story about delivering the craft to a rural postal service in Colorado — and now Braun would try for a decent night's rest as he sorted through the next steps.

He heard a spray of light taps against the window. Braun pulled aside the tattered curtain to see a turbulent scene. The storm front had arrived. Swirling winds blew dust across the road as the first heavy raindrops smacked down, tiny explosions erupting in the dirt parking area. He let the curtain fall closed and reconsidered the once bitten sandwich and warm bottle of beer next to his bed. Perhaps something from the wine cellar, he mused. Braun sat on the bed, springs squeaking under his weight, and he forced down the rancid meal. How quickly he had been spoiled, he realized. A few months ago he would have celebrated this as a special feast.

He thought again of his decision to go to Santa Fe for a meeting with Die Wespe. It had not been an easy choice. The voice of the Englishman intruded constantly . . . *Major Michael Thatcher . . . help me locate a man by the name of Alexander Brown.* Had someone — Rode, Gruber, or Becker — been captured and talked? The crew of *U-801*? Perhaps, but none of them would have known about Newport. How had the Englishman tracked him there? His name — the authorities had discovered his name. From there how difficult would it have been to connect Alexander Brown to Lydia and Newport? Not very. It was likely the Americans had helped. And that led to one thing — this Manhattan Project, whatever it was, might indeed be important.

He wondered if the authorities had uncovered Die Wespe. There was no way to be sure. But if so, they'd be waiting for Braun in New Mexico. He remembered Colonel Gruber's last words to him . . . *You must bring the information Die Wespe holds. It is priceless, vital to our future.* Priceless. He found that one word inescapable.

A knock on the door startled him. Braun couldn't see outside. If he moved the curtain aside to look, the movement would be seen. With no other way out of the room, he decided the direct approach would be best. Swilling down the rest of his beer, Braun grabbed the bottle firmly by the neck, covered it with a pillow to muffle the sound, and smacked it hard across the edge of the nightstand. With the jagged remainder firmly in his hand, he went to the door. Braun squared his feet in a strong stance and pulled it partially open, keeping his weapon out of sight.

"Um, hello there, sir."

It was the service boy from the airport, a skinny teenager whose skeletal frame swam inside greasy coveralls that were spotted with raindrops. Braun's hand remained tense on the broken bottle, yet his eyes sparkled with ease.

"What is it?"

"She could use some oil. You want me to go ahead and add it?"

"Yes, please."

"Okay." The boy rubbed a chin that was just sprouting its first few, reddish whiskers. "Ah, it'll be two dollars."

Braun pulled out the wallet he'd taken from Hiram Mitchell's back pocket before dropping him five thousand feet to his death. Still holding the bottle, he fumbled behind the door to use both hands, and eventually shoved out three dollar bills.

"Thank you, sir."

Braun gestured to the storm outside. "Assuming this lets up, I plan on leaving at first light."

"Oh, it'll be cleared up by then, mister. And I'm always at the hangar by six. Let me know if you need anything else." The kid gave a two-fingered salute, and dashed through the rain to a weary old truck.

Braun closed the door and leaned into it with a shoulder. He tossed the jagged bottle into a trash can and took a deep breath. Three days until the meeting with Die Wespe. He wondered what this Manhattan Project could possibly be. A rocket-bomb like the V-2? An airplane? Braun simply had to find out. And he had to be very careful.

He went to the bed and stretched out on top of the sheets.

The room was hot and uncomfortable. New Mexico would be even worse. Yet for all the hardships Braun had seen, this he did not mind. He only wanted to never be cold again.

When Braun arrived at seven the boy had the airplane ready to go, tie-downs removed and fully serviced. Breakfast had been better — it was hard to mess up eggs — and by ten minutes after seven he was cruising westward, following the Rand McNally map he'd purchased at a gas station near the motel. It would take the entire morning to traverse Kansas, and the Luscombe would need one more refueling to reach New Mexico.

He considered what to do with the airplane when he arrived in Santa Fe. Should he try to keep it hidden as a potential means of escape? Sell it for cash? Unfortunately, the Luscombe was the one thing that tied him to Newport and a missing flight instructor.

The flight across Kansas was familiar — flat, incredibly uniform features. Endless dirt roads demarked square farm plots. Each was tended by a small house, with larger buildings to shelter equipment and harvests. Braun had taken to following a rail line, easily distinguishable from the roads, and punctuated with precision regularity by grain elevators. It was all very orderly and functional, a well-thought-out design, he decided.

The fuel stop came after four hours, a place called Liberal, Kansas. The midday heat was insufferable, its companion a stiff breeze that did nothing to cool but instead acted as a bellows to the fire. The facilities around the airfield looked in decent shape, but Braun was surprised to find that there was no fuel service here. He was forced to walk two miles to the nearest gas station, where he again tried to use Hiram Mitchell's postal credentials. The surly attendant groused that he'd been having trouble getting letters through to his son in the Pacific, but ten dollars eventually sufficed for eighteen gallons of high-test, the use of two ten gallon cans, and a ride back to Liberal Municipal. It was noon when he departed.

As he taxied to the end of the runway, Braun noted the different landing surface. It was a hardpan dirt strip as opposed to the grass he was used to. There was a stiff crosswind, and when he began the takeoff roll Braun wrestled awkwardly with the controls to keep the machine headed in the right direction. The Luscombe seemed to hesitate, building speed much more slowly than in the past. His first idea was to shove the throttle forward, but it was already against the stop.

He felt a sudden pang of discomfort. Was something wrong with the engine? Was a dirt strip different than grass, some coefficient dragging him back? He watched the airspeed build with glacial speed. The end of the runway came closer — not trees or a fence, but rather squat bushes, the boundary where clearing work had simply stopped. At fifty miles an hour it was clear that the Luscombe might not get airborne. A wall of tangled brown bushes rushed toward him. Braun considered trying to stop. But could he? Or would he only go careening into the scrub?

Finally, the tail began to respond, rising lazily to his command. Braun waited until the last moment, then pulled back firmly. The main wheels came up, lumbering, and the wings seemed to wobble. Somehow the plane rose just enough, skimming across flat terrain as the airspeed crept upward. He milked the thing up until he had a hundred feet, two hundred, and finally a thousand. Only then did Braun realize how his heart was racing.

Outside, the remains of what looked like a tumbleweed was tangled in his right wheel, fluttering crazily in the wind stream. He took a deep breath. *How had that happened?* Braun wondered. *Have I become reckless?* He measured it all, and soon the answer filtered down. No, he was not reckless. Braun was unaware of his specific mistake during the takeoff, yet he knew where it was rooted. Overconfidence. He had gotten too comfortable in an unfamiliar discipline. Braun remembered the grip of success he had felt as a new sniper — one good shot tempted another. And another. But the odds would find you.

He looked ahead and found his railway, the curvilinear guide that had brought him here. It still meandered west. The sky had filled with clouds, thick and puffy, and to the north he saw a thunderstorm, classic in its anvil shape. Braun figured it must be beating the hell out of a farm somewhere. He recalled that Mitchell had always checked the weather by phone before each flight. Braun should have learned how this was done. Of course, now it was too late. And in any event, his next landing would likely be his last.

It was Hiram Mitchell's wife who broke things open. The untouched apple pie on the sill above the kitchen sink loomed ominously, and when she didn't hear from her husband by midday on the third day, she got worried. If the Luscombe had broken down he would have called. Not knowing who to call to report a missing airplane, she decided on the local police. The operator there almost pushed her off on the Civil Aeronautics Board before an astute desk man made the connection.

A squad car was sent to the airfield, and it took another ten minutes for the officer to get permission to whack the padlock off the hangar door. He reported that he'd found the missing Buick, and a short time later the news reached the library at Harrold House.

CHAPTER 27

Lydia was in her room, arranging the flowers Edward had given her only a few days ago. They were beginning to wilt, black at the edges, and she turned the freshest side of each forward. She wondered, perhaps, if she could plant a row of the same variety on the east side of the house and tend to them herself. Lydia knew nothing about gardening, but Wescott could teach her.

Hearing the telephone ring in the distance, Lydia headed for the library. It was a considerable effort, the aches and bruises from being sent down the stairs still fresh. The pain pills made her woozy, keeping the world in a haze. She hated the drugs, but the doctor had insisted.

When she reached the library her father was already talking, scribbling down information. Major Thatcher was also there, and Lydia took a chair next to him. Father had put the Englishman up in a small room, and he'd become a fixture around the place. Lydia studied the little man with the limp who seemed so direct and focused. It was odd, she thought. She'd always imagined her father to be a strong man, and physically he was, but the Englishman carried a different sway, an intensity of purpose that she recognized, but didn't quite understand.

Her father hung up the phone.

"Have they found him?" Thatcher asked.

"They found the car," Sargent Cole said. "Mitchell's Flying

Service — it's a little operation off State Road Seventy-seven."

Thatcher winced. "We've been looking everywhere else — the bus and train stations, the airport in Providence."

Through her drug induced stupor, Lydia made a connection. "Frank! Of course, I should have remembered."

Thatcher said, "Remembered what?"

"Cousin Frank — he and Alex went up for a few flights the last time Alex stayed with us. He'd know about the airfield. How stupid of me not to remember."

"Did Brown know how to fly?" Thatcher asked.

"No, I don't think so. He and Frank just went joyriding, as I remember it."

Sargent Cole said, "That was five years ago. For all we know, he could be a Luftwaffe ace by now."

Thatcher moved to a large map of the United States that was situated centrally on the wall behind an ornate writing desk. He stood with his hands on his hips and wondered aloud, "So where have you gone now, my friend?"

Lydia looked at the map and instantly knew the answer. "Santa Fe!" The words came in a strong, clear voice that belied here foggy mind. She took Thatcher by the elbow and pulled him closer to the map. "He's going to Santa Fe! The other day I came into this room and he had his finger parked right on it. He gave me some story about tracing his route out west. I remember the name perfectly because I decided he was taking the train. The Santa Fe Line."

Sargent Cole said, "What do you think, Major? Could there be something to it?"

The Englishman seemed to hesitate as he stared at the map. "Possibly."

"We have to tell the FBI," Lydia said, her eyes boring into the map. "They'll catch him."

"All right," Thatcher agreed. "I'll call Jones."

Thatcher made the call from another room, needing privacy to sort through the ideas churning in his head. Santa Fe, New

Mexico. *New* Mexico. He remembered Corporal Klein's words. *There is an agent, in Mexico I think, code name Die Wespe . . . the Manhattan Project.* Did it really make sense? Thatcher wondered. Or was he grasping at the breeze?

When Tomas Jones came on line he was noncommittal about the news of the getaway car having been found. "So he's out flying around with some old geezer. Any idea where they're headed?"

"Mitchell's wife says her husband was hired out on a charter to Minnesota."

"Shouldn't be hard to find," the FBI man said. "We'll put out a bulletin to check all the airfields along the way."

Thatcher wondered how many there could be. Thanks to the war, England had become littered with them. Then he remembered Lydia's idea. "I think we should cast the net a bit wider," he insisted.

"Why?"

"Well, does this project of yours have a site in New Mexico?"

Jones exploded. *"God dammit! That's it!"*

Thatcher held the receiver away from his ear.

"You're done, Thatcher! Pack your bags and go home! If you're feet are still on American soil by nightfall, I'm sending the two biggest oafs I can find to escort you to a very slow boat. Go home now! That's an order!" The click was next, and when Thatcher hung up he smiled. He had his answer. He went back to the library.

"Well, is the bastard going to do anything?" Sargent asked.

"Yes. He's going to send me back to England because I'm interfering."

Sargent seethed openly.

"Will you go?" Lydia asked.

"Eventually. But I've always wanted to see the Grand Canyon. Is that in New Mexico?"

"Arizona," Lydia said.

"Close enough."

"What can we do to help?" Sargent said.

"My official capacity here is — well, let's say it's always been on unsteady ground. In all honesty, I'm a little short on funds right now. I wasn't planning on such a long stay."

"Whatever you need, Major. Somehow I think you have a better chance of tracking down Alex Brown than the FBI." He went to the writing desk and scribbled out a check. As he held it out he studied Thatcher. "What is it, Thatcher? Why do you want this guy so bad?"

It was a fair question, one Thatcher had been asking himself. "He's been sent here to contact a spy, and I think that's why he might head to New Mexico. It's simply my job to stop him."

"Bullshit. I'm a good judge of people, Thatcher — this is personal. Did you ever know Alex?"

"No. I never knew he existed until a few weeks ago."

Sargent Cole pressed. "Has he hurt someone you know? Committed a war crime?"

Thatcher shook his head. "Not that I'm aware of. I suppose he represents something to me. My war was more quiet than some. Chasing after the likes of Alex Braun — it keeps me in the fight." He paused. "Anyway, I'll leave first thing in the morning." He held up the check. "And thanks for this. I'll repay you when I get back to England."

Sargent Cole waved it off. "Just find him, Major."

"Yes," Lydia added, her eyes glassy and fogged, but her tone clear, "you *must* find him."

Thatcher looked at her squarely. The girl was shattered, yet trying to hold up. He ought to tell her that time would heal everything — that's what he'd been told. Of course, it was a lie. His own wounds had proven incurable. Blight lingered on his soul. There was, Thatcher knew, only one truth he could offer. "I'll do my best," he said.

The changes came subtly. The earth's hue was based in brown, but striations of red and orange swept in more frequently. The farm fields of Kansas and the Oklahoma panhandle gradually ceded, the land almost barren now for want of water. Riverbeds cut deep into the rocky ground but, as far as Braun could tell, all were dry.

The remoteness increased as each mile passed beneath him, and there were few signs of civilization. The colors deepened further as the Luscombe passed into New Mexico, darker shades of red that made it look as if the world had begun to oxidize. Braun was beginning to understand why the Americans had chosen this place. He hoped the remoteness was a sign that Die Wespe's information was indeed as important as Gruber had held it to be.

The lack of anything manmade did not aid his navigation. The last recognizable town had been a place called Tucumcari, a dusty group of buildings that had bulged along the rail line thirty minutes earlier. There, he'd left the track he was following to pick up another, one that would lead to Santa Fe. Since that time, he'd seen nothing he could use to cross-check his progress as the Luscombe bumped along through turbulent air. And there were other problems.

He'd first noticed it on landing back in Kansas. There, the field elevation had been 2,800 feet above sea level, far higher than the other places he'd landed. Now, with the airplane struggling to hold altitude at 7,000 feet, he thought the ground looked much closer. The roadmap disclosed that Albuquerque was situated at over 5,000 feet. Braun wondered if Santa Fe might be even higher. He saw mountains ahead, clear on the horizon. Could the Luscombe even manage it? Braun tossed the map to the passenger seat. If nothing else, he was close. He might have to find an airfield and land short. Even a road would do. There were still two days until the scheduled rendezvous with Die Wespe. If he couldn't fly into Santa Fe, he would find another way.

Cumulus clouds had begun to build in the mid-afternoon heat. Unable to fly over the cotton white obstacles, Braun turned left and right to skirt between them. As he tried to keep the railway in sight, turbulence shook the little plane with more authority. The airspeed needle bounced erratically, gaining ten miles an hour, then losing five. He remembered yesterday's storm in

Kansas, and old Mitchell's penchant for worrying about the weather. A look ahead, however, eased Braun's concern. The lower clouds were still scattered and soft, topped by darker versions above. He would simply slide beneath it all.

Approaching the mountains, he noted yet another change in the landscape — the sides of the hills were increasingly green, covered in thick vegetation. The mountain tops lay obscured, lost in a curtain of gray and black clouds. With the Luscombe at 8,000 feet now, the airspeed had deteriorated to only sixty miles an hour. Braun thought it a logical trade.

The railway meandered into a deep valley between two imposing mountains. Braun soon found himself guided less by his steady reference and more by the terrain. This had to be the gap where the tracks cut through the mountains, he decided. On the other side would be Santa Fe.

Craning to keep the railway in sight, Braun clipped the corner of a cloud, everything turning white for a few seconds. When he burst back in the clear, another was straight ahead. He turned hard to the left, but yet another patch of white swirled before him. This time it took longer to come out, and when the little plane broke clear there were darker shades in every direction. He continued to turn as he hit the next cloud deck, and after a few glimpses of white, the world turned a heavy gray. The Luscombe rattled and suddenly seemed to strike a wall of water. Rain smacked at the windscreen like rocks against a sheet of tin. The plane lurched and Braun's head struck the ceiling.

He saw nothing outside now, only a swirl of black. He was flying blind. The instruments had gone haywire, the altimeter now showing 10,000 feet, but dropping, the needle spinning backward like a clock gone crazy. His senses told him he was in a turn, and he fought against the stick. Eight thousand feet. Still fighting the turn, he yanked on the stick. The Luscombe gave a shudder — and began a freefall. The stick flopped uselessly in Braun's lap. He had lost control.

Seven thousand feet. He felt dizzy, disoriented. Braun tried to make sense of instruments that were spinning wildly, an incoherent jumble of information. Outside, the ocean of darkness kept swirling, swallowing. Sixty-five hundred feet.

He took a deep breath. Just as in Russia and the Atlantic, Braun let go. He took his hand from the control stick and it bounced aimlessly between his legs. He closed his eyes. *One minute,* he thought. But for the first time, Braun knew he didn't have that long.

An instant of confusion swept in. Then, suddenly, a sensation of light. Calm and bright. Braun opened his eyes. The Luscombe had broken clear of the clouds — but it might have been more merciful had it not. A mountain filled the windscreen, huge evergreen trees, slate gray rock in the gaps. The angle of dive was impossible, the earth and trees seconds away.

His hands instinctively went to the control stick. It felt firmer now, the craft somehow having found purchase on the thin air. The crash was imminent —— but there was one chance. Braun forced the stick to the right and pulled back for all he was worth.

Ben Geronima Walker stepped quietly through the woods. As a Mescalero Apache, the art of stalking game came quite naturally. He had learned from his father, a hunter of considerable skill. Of course, fifty years ago, before the opening of the Mescalero Grocery, the knowledge had been substantially more important. In fact, Ben Walker had not killed a deer in six years, his last a buck taken with a clean shot from fifty yards. On that occasion he'd done the fieldwork, dressing out over a hundred pounds of venison and hauling it to his truck.

Now, at seventy-two years old, he had no desire to take any more from the forest. He knew that kill had been his last. But he still went into the woods, the rifle his excuse. His quarry was different now — he enjoyed the solitude, the spirituality of the forest. Throwing a tent in his truck, he would come here for days at a stretch to escape his nagging wife and the idiot who lived next door, a self-taught auto mechanic who banged away at ridiculously late hours. Here, in the mountains east of Pecos, Ben Walker found peace. And he'd had it all morning.

As was often the case, however, the afternoon had brought storms. The sky darkened quickly, and gusty winds swept through the pines, bringing the sweet scent of ozone. As was his custom, Walker planned on sitting out the showers in the cab of his truck, three or four cigarettes before edging back out into the fresh, cool air.

He was headed in that direction when he saw a flash through the trees. At first glance he thought it was a bird, big and white, swooping over the hill. But then he recognized the glint of metal, and heard the sound of snapping tree limbs violate the forest's stillness. Birds flushed and animals scurried for cover. But then the interruption ended as suddenly as it had come, and the woods again retreated to a natural rhythm.

If he hadn't seen it, the metallic reflection, Walker probably would have kept going. But there *had* been something, just over the ridge to his right. It was a steep climb and he moved slowly, his knees and hips not what they were so many years ago. The Winchester rifle on his shoulder seemed heavier than usual. Cresting the rise, he saw the source of the commotion. At first he didn't recognize the mess for what it was. He saw dust and smoke, but gradually a white tube of sorts came into view. It was bent and twisted, looking vaguely like an airplane. But the thing had no wings.

He scampered as best he could, weaving between saplings and shrubs. Fifty feet away he stopped. He saw the tail now, clear with numbers and lettering. It was definitely an airplane — and there was someone in it. A man crawled out, bent and twisted, just like the metal frame. Covered in blood, he stumbled clear and came unsteadily to his feet.

Walker rushed to him. "Let me help you!" he called.

The man used a shirtsleeve to wipe blood from his face, revealing a dazed expression.

Walker glanced into the airplane as he got closer. He saw no one else. "I can help! Are you able to walk? My truck is at the bottom of the hill. You need a hospital, mister."

Ben Walker took the Winchester off his shoulder and leaned it against a nearby tree. He held out a helping hand. Oddly, the bloodied face looking at him wrenched into a smile.

CHAPTER 28

It was four in the morning when Lydia moved gingerly down the stairs. Each step was a new revelation in pain — her hip, her ankle, everything seemed to hurt. But it was her own doing. The nurse her father had brought in had dispensed a ration of pills last evening. Discretely, Lydia had dropped them all behind her bed. She'd had enough of the drugs. Unfortunately, without them she'd not been able to sleep a wink.

Lying awake, Lydia had decided on a trip to the kitchen. When she arrived, she was surprised to see a light burning. The Englishman was seated at the servant's table with a plate of left-overs and a pot of tea. He stood when he saw her.

"Good morning, ma'am."

"Oh, please, Major. That makes me feel so old. Call me Lydia."

"All right, but then 'Major' is far too formal. I think Michael will do."

She smiled and turned toward the refrigerator. The movement was a bad one, and Lydia grimaced.

"Are you all right?" he asked, standing. "Can I get you something?"

"No, please. I . . . I'm rather tired of people doing things for me." She poured herself a glass of milk and joined him at the table. "What are you doing up so early?"

"I have to catch the first bus down to New York. Then a flight. And you? Are you having trouble sleeping?"

She grinned. "That's all I've been doing, Michael. Sleeping." She wanted to add, *my entire life*. Lydia shifted to a less uncomfortable position. "Actually, I stopped taking my medication last night."

"I see."

"I've been walking around the house in a daze. Yesterday I found myself in the garage, but I wasn't sure how I'd even got there. And do you know what the last straw was?"

"What?"

"I woke up and saw a dim light outside my window, but I had no idea — none whatsoever — whether it was dawn or dusk."

He nodded. "That happened to me once, in the hospital after my accident." He gestured to his leg.

She saw his ill-fitting pant leg. Somehow Lydia knew he wouldn't mind if she asked. "What happened?"

"I was the ordnance officer for a squadron of Lancaster bombers. I tagged along on a mission to do some troubleshooting, and we tangled with a flock of ME-109s. Our ship eventually went down, but not before . . ." he hesitated, "not before I actually took up a gun position. The lad who'd been manning it was killed."

Lydia was riveted. "Did you actually shoot at any of them?"

He nodded. "It was the only chance I had through the entire war to look the enemy in the eye and pull a trigger." Thatcher looked blankly at the table. "I remember it like it was yesterday — the Messerschmitt exploding. The fireball filled the sky."

After a moment of reflection, Lydia found herself saying, "Tell me, Michael, how did it make you feel?"

His reply came right away, as if it had been a perfectly natural question. "It was exhilarating — the most fulfilling instant of my life." They locked eyes, and he added, "Even if my wife, Madeline, would have hated it."

Lydia nodded. "She must have been terribly worried about you."

He seemed put off, and Lydia eyed his wedding ring.

"Actually," he said in a quiet voice, "my wife was killed in the Blitz."

"Oh, God! Michael, I'm so sorry. I only assumed —"

"No, no. It's all right. I still wear the ring — can't get it off, actually."

Lydia looked at her own wedding band. Would the thought of taking it off ever come? She watched Thatcher as he buttered a piece of bread. His face was rather bony and narrow in the dim light, angular and at odds with itself. The eyes, however, seemed soft, more so now than she'd noticed before. But then every other time she'd seen him he'd been engrossed in his hunt for Alex.

"Do you miss her?" she asked.

"Yes. Terribly."

Lydia felt a new pain emerge, one that the drugs could never help. "I miss Edward too." She felt a tear fall freely down her cheek. "You know, it's funny. When Edward was alive I could only see the worst in him. Wrinkled shirts, working weekends, the spots where he'd missed shaving. Now I only think about the flowers he gave me, and the trip to Niagara Falls he wanted to take over the holidays."

"Yes, I know. Madeline and I had so many plans. But the last thing I ever said to her was something stupid about a wing — what you call a fender — that she'd bent on our car."

Lydia shook her head. "But for me it's worse, Michael. You see, it's my fault Edward died."

"You can't believe that."

"I brought Alex here."

"He was an old college flame who thought —"

"No! When he came back, I should have turned him away. But instead I embraced him. I led Alex on, without a thought for my husband!"

He offered up a handkerchief and she began to wipe.

"Lydia, *Alex* is the killer."

"No! He couldn't have done it without me! Michael —" she felt the confession rise, "I carried on with him!" The tears began to flow, but she couldn't stop. "Right in this house, with Edward only a few rooms away!" Lydia fell forward on the table, sobbing into her folded arms. She felt his hand on her shoulder.

"You must think I'm disgraceful."

"I think you're human."

Thatcher made no attempt to dissuade her from her guilty thoughts. He simply sat in silence until her convulsions eased.

"And useless. I'm so damned useless! I failed Edward, and I've been a failure through this entire war. I just heard today that our former cook's son, Mario, was killed in the Pacific — one of those dreadful kamikazes. I grew up with Mario, he and I played together when we were children. He goes off to the war and makes that sacrifice, while my biggest concern each morning is . . . is what shoes to wear!"

Thatcher said nothing.

Lydia straightened up in her chair. "Look at me. I'm a blathering mess."

"Yes, you are. But I suspect there are at least a thousand like you at kitchen tables across the country at this very moment."

She eyed him thoughtfully.

He said, "This war has caused incredible suffering, Lydia. No one has come through untouched."

"I suppose you're right. But my wounds are self-inflicted. I only have myself to blame."

She handed back his handkerchief, now a soggy ball of cotton. Thatcher then helped her up the stairs to her room where she collapsed on her bed. He gestured to the pill bottles on her nightstand. "Are you sure you don't need these?"

"I'm sure," she said. "Please take them away."

He did. "I've got to go and catch my bus now." Thatcher took her nearest hand, which had a nasty bruise, and rubbed lightly over the mottled patch of skin. "Time heals, you know."

"Does it?"

Lydia thought his smile looked strained.

"Take care of yourself, Lydia."

And with that, he was gone.

PART III

CHAPTER 29

It took two days for Thatcher to reach Santa Fe. After a short night in a hotel, he called Sargent Cole.

"Have you heard anything new?"

Cole had been getting regular updates from the Newport Police regarding the almost certain murder of his son-in-law. He was Thatcher's source for current information.

"Yes. They tracked the airplane through a series of fuel stops. Last night it turned up — he crashed in New Mexico, about fifty miles east of Santa Fe. Near some little place called Villanueva."

"And Braun?"

"The airplane hit hard, but it clipped a couple of trees perfectly — ripped both wings off. The police figure that absorbed the impact of the crash. The cockpit was pretty banged up, but it was in one piece. They found blood inside, but not Alex."

"Blast! Does this man have no end of luck?"

"Oh, it gets better. Right next to the wreck was the body of some poor old Indian — had a nice hole in his chest. Apparently he was out hunting. Must have seen the crash, gone to help and —"

"And Braun gets another!"

"Looks that way. The guy's rifle and an old beat-up truck are missing."

Thatcher asked for a description of the truck, but Sargent Cole couldn't help. "Have you talked to Jones?" he asked.

"God damned right I did! When I heard about this I called and ripped him good. He says he's working on it, but not very hard if you ask me. He seemed more interested in you, Thatcher."

"Me?"

"Yeah, they seem to have lost track of you. I told him you were back in England, as far as I knew."

"Good. How is Lydia holding up?"

"It's been rough. They haven't found Edward's body yet."

Thatcher was not surprised. "They may never."

"I'm worried about her."

Thatcher understood perfectly. And it wasn't only Lydia. He heard it in Sargent Cole's voice as well — grief combined with anger. Thatcher knew how frustrating it could be, how it burned constantly from the inside. At that moment, he considered telling Sargent Cole the truth — that finding Braun would not end his family's misery. Life as they'd known it would never return. The pause was a long one.

"Thatcher? Are you still there?"

"*Yes . . .*yes. Give her my best, would you?" He then gave Sargent Cole the telephone number of his hotel. "Call me if you find out anything else."

Karl Heinrich looked nervously toward the entrance of Los Cuates. He mixed the last of the food on his plate, stirring rice and chicken into the green chili sauce. He'd be leaving New Mexico soon, yet for all he disliked about the place, Hatch green chili was the one thing he would miss.

The place was dark, more resembling a cave than a restaurant. Heavy wood beams held up the roof, and the walls were adobe, the mud and grass medium that dominated nearly every building, fence, and wall in Santa Fe. Heinrich had always wondered why it all didn't wash away in the heavy rains of monsoon season. The floor was dull and unvarnished, smooth not from fine craftsmanship, but rather years of wear. It was caked in a layer of brown dirt, probably swept in by the incessant wind. The wind he would certainly not miss.

He'd arrived an hour earlier — fifteen minutes before the place had opened for lunch — to ensure he got the correct table. It had probably been overkill. Even now, approaching noon, only three other tables were occupied. Eleven thirty, the time for the rendezvous, had come and gone. And still he was alone.

Again the questions gnawed. What if no one came? How would he reconnect with the Reich? His information was of such value, certainly vital to the rebuilding effort. Heinrich knew that his last contact, Klaus, had been killed by the Americans. This surprised him — even if they were the enemy, the Americans seemed a civilized lot, the type to handle prisoners in a fair and honorable manner. He could only assume that such severe justice was reserved for spies. Spies like him.

It had been a massive relief to find the new message last month, coded in a newspaper classified advertisement. A new contact would be made, someone to escort him back to the folds of the Fatherland. Heinrich again looked desperately around the restaurant. *So where was he?*

"*Scheiss!*" he muttered under his breath.

He scraped his plate clean. Should he push it away? Order something else? He'd never been good at this game. In the labs of Los Alamos he was on familiar ground — there, stealing secrets had become second nature. But Santa Fe was different. It was the only place where The Hill's scientists and workers were able to mingle with the general populace. Given this, the Army Intelligence G-2 men were on every corner. They were agonizingly obvious in their pin-striped suits and wing-tip shoes, against the locals who were partial to blue jeans, Stetson hats, and bolo ties. Heinrich had decided that the disparity was intentional, a message of intimidation. He was also convinced that some of the bolos were watching as well. It all made him feel like a fish washed up on the beach — flopping around and trying to breathe in an unnatural element, praying for a wave to come and sweep him away.

The chime on the front door jingled, and Heinrich looked up hopefully. He was disappointed. A skinny Spanish-American boy scurried in. The lad walked quickly, pointing at each empty table he passed, as if counting. When he reached Heinrich's table he stopped.

"*Cinco!*" The boy dropped a piece of paper next to Heinrich's empty plate. "*Para usted, señor.*" He then held out his hand.

Heinrich was stunned to inaction. *No*, he thought, *this is not the plan. This is not the way it is supposed to happen.* He collected himself enough to fish a few coins from his pocket and drop them in the boy's hand. He smiled and scurried away.

Heinrich looked around the room expecting all eyes to be on him. In fact, none were. He took the note, undid one fold, and palmed it like a poker player with a tight hand. It read: *Petroglyphs, fifteen minutes. End of southern path.* There was no signature.

Karl Heinrich's spirits soared. His wave had come.

He tried to walk slowly so as not to draw attention. Heinrich ignored the Indians hawking trinkets from their blankets on the sidewalk, and tried to ignore two G-2 men who were chatting near a lamppost. His pace quickened as he passed La Fonda, the town's main boardinghouse, and continued east toward the foothills.

The petroglyphs were a local curiosity, situated near the terminus of the Santa Fe trail. The topography altered slightly just outside of town, the crusty hardpan soil giving way to clusters of boulders. Here the vegetation, scant to begin with, almost disappeared, a few desperate weeds fighting for survival amid the cracks between rocks. A thousand years ago the indigenous people, the Anasazi, had used the sides of the boulders as their canvases, engraving human and animal figures, along with more elaborate, artistic designs. A handful of these images remained with remarkable resolution, and the petroglyphs had become a mildly popular side trip for the scientists of Los Alamos. Today, however, at noon on the cusp of summer, Karl Heinrich was alone as he trudged across the informal walking path toward the southern end of the outcropping.

He'd been here once before, a year earlier with Bostich. Then, he had thought the petroglyphs indeed remarkable, but less so than the fact that the Anasazi had chosen to live in such a godforsaken place. Today these thoughts were completely lost to exhilaration — the possibility of reconnecting with the Fatherland.

The final segment of the path climbed a moderate rise. Combined with the altitude and excitement, it had Heinrich panting like a dog. A vulture turned lazy circles in the sky above. Heinrich spied it with defiance. *Not today, you bastard.* The path ended near an unusually large formation, a red-brown boulder the size of a truck. Heinrich stopped and bent over, his hands on his knees, his open mouth gasping for air.

"*Guten Morgen, Herr Wespe.*"

Stunned, he turned to see a man behind him. He was tall and blond, Aryan in appearance. He also looked like he'd taken a recent beating. There was a large bruise on his forehead, and he carried one arm close to his chest, bent at the elbow as if injured.

"We should use English, no?" Heinrich suggested.

His contact shrugged and smiled easily. "I've been watching closely. We are alone here, and the approaches are easily seen. But if you prefer —"

"No, no. I would like to use our native tongue. It has been a very long time for me."

The man came forward and extended his good hand. "My name is Rainer. It is good to finally meet you."

Relief swept across Heinrich. He lunged ahead and took the hand with both of his. "I am Karl. Dr. Karl Heinrich." He had to suppress tears as he held the man close. A hundred questions rushed to his excited head. "It has been very difficult to be isolated for so long — to hear only the American's view of the war. Surely it cannot be as dire as what I see in the newsreels and papers. What has come of our Reich?"

The man whose name was almost certainly not Rainer smiled confidently. "The Reich . . . it endures, Karl. It endures."

Heinrich was overwhelmed. He stood back and eased his bulk down on a rock, smiling as those words played in his mind. Even if Germany's situation had seemed bleak, Heinrich had never lost faith. And now here was the reward for his confidence. "What about our Führer? Is it true that he is dead? No one has produced a body, so I suspected it might be a ruse."

"No, Karl, it is true. Hitler is dead. But the Reich remains strong. If we have lost the battle for Germany, the greater struggle will go forward."

"This I have never doubted," Heinrich insisted. "The next time the world will fall not to our sword, but to our cause, our logic. The impure races are a scourge on humanity, weighing the world down."

"Yes, without doubt," Rainer replied. "But it will take time for us to rebuild that cause."

"Yes, yes. Where will we go? I have guessed South America — Brazil."

There was a pause. Rainer smiled. "A good guess, Karl. Very close. It will be Argentina."

"Yes! Argentina!" Heinrich had been to Buenos Aires many years ago for a conference. It was a comfortable place. No dust. No wind.

"The military there will work with us," Rainer said as he took a seat on a nearby rock.

Heinrich watched the man. Even with his injured arm he moved languidly, like a strong cat. His eyes regularly checked the path that led back toward town, searchlights scanning for any possible threat. The Reich had chosen well, Heinrich decided. A dangerous man for a dangerous mission. And he would know what to do. Rainer would get him out of here. He said, "Have you seen the level of security in town? Army Security — G-2 they call it — is very busy here."

"Yes, they are everywhere indeed. Which is why I brought you here using that note. But the G2's, as you call them, they are easily seen."

Heinrich looked at Rainer's shoulder. "You have been injured?"

The man shrugged dismissively. "A minor accident. It will heal soon."

Heinrich bent forward and put a hand on Rainer's good shoulder, wanting again to feel the strength of a compatriot. He could no longer hold back his most important question.

"*When*? When can we go? My work here is nearly complete. It is critical that we provide it to the Fatherland."

"Yes, our mission is most vital. The specific arrangements for the journey have been left to me." His eyes skimmed up to the horizon, yet this time it seemed more in contemplation than watchfulness. "But I must tell you, Karl, when I was given this assignment I was told little about your work. This was a protective measure for you, in the event that I might be — intercepted. From here we will work together until arriving in Argentina, and it would be helpful for me to know something about this Manhattan Project."

It made sense to Heinrich. "Yes, you must know the importance of our mission." He organized his thoughts, beginning with his own story. He explained how the Jews had infiltrated the world of academe to spoil many great careers, including his own. He proudly covered his conversion to the National Socialist Party, and how easily the Americans had taken him into the center of their great secret. Finally, he took an instructional tone, a vestige of his days at the university.

"What do you know of physics and chemistry, Rainer?"

"I am an architect by training, so I have studied each at a basic level."

"An architect, yes! This is good. You see, the atom itself has structure and dimension. Have you ever heard of atomic fission?"

"I believe it involves splitting the atom."

"Precisely. And when this happens under specific conditions, a chain reaction can be initiated. Most importantly, huge amounts of energy can be released."

The student did not look impressed.

"*Huge* amounts," Heinrich reiterated, "with distinct military applications."

"So this process can bring about an explosion—a bomb of sorts?"

"A single weapon of this type can cause destruction an order of magnitude beyond anything ever imagined by mankind."

Rainer did not seem to appreciate the scope of what he was saying. He was distracted, again monitoring the pathways. It did not matter, Heinrich decided. Who could imagine such a thing as this bomb? He paused and regarded the blackened stick figures on the rock before him. It was strange, he thought, to be explaining the most fearsome weapon ever conceived while in the presence of such trivial, ancient testaments.

Rainer said, "Tell me, Karl, the information you have—what form is it in? Do you simply keep it in your head?"

"Ha!" Heinrich laughed. "God, no. I am on the Oversight Group, with access to all divisions of the project. There are thousands of pages—drawings, documents, and photographs. I keep it all in a suitcase in my room."

"A suitcase? Is this safe?"

Heinrich shrugged. "What else can I do? Each scientist has a personal safe in the laboratory, but one of the American wunderkind has made a hobby out of breaking into them."

"This is tolerated?"

"You must understand, the Army oversees this project, but it is run—or perhaps I should say overrun—by scientists. In any event, the Manhattan Project is nearly complete. The test will come soon. After this, I am to leave for the Pacific."

"The Pacific?"

"Yes. The gadget—that's what we've taken to calling it—if it actually works, the Americans will waste no time in using it against Japan. I have been assigned to personally accompany certain components to the field for final assembly. This journey is the best chance for me to disappear—after the delivery, on my return."

"When will you leave?"

"Immediately after Trinity."

Rainer was no longer gazing down the path. His interest had come full.

"Trinity is the code name of the test," Heinrich explained. "It will take place next week, south of here in the desert. From there, I will fly to Hawaii and join a ship, the USS *Indianapolis*."

"So we must arrange for an escape during this journey."

"Yes." Heinrich looked at his watch and frowned. "I must return soon. The bus back to The Hill leaves in twenty minutes."

"All right," Rainer said. "Get the details of your travel plans— tell me exactly where this ship is going."

"I'll do what I can, but everything is kept most secret."

"Find out as much as possible. When can we meet again?"

"I do not think we should meet here, in Santa Fe. The risk is too high."

"Agreed. Do you have any ideas?"

Heinrich though for a moment, then smiled. "Yes." He explained the plan.

"It should work," Rainer said. He then paused. "There *is* something else, Karl."

"What?"

"We have hinted of this project to the Argentine military. It is possible they will lend some support. But we must have details to convince them, some kind of hard information to prove the value of what we possess."

"My information is priceless! No one, not even Oppen- heimer himself, the director of the project, could hold such a comprehensive body of information. And we must be careful. What if the Argentines try to take it for themselves?"

Rainer turned up the palm of his good hand. "My thoughts as well, Karl. But we need help at the moment. We must trust the new leaders of the Reich. They are good men, Karl, strong. They need only a sample—a few detailed documents to prove the worth of what you possess."

Heinrich hesitated.

WARD LARSEN

Rainer said, "By your own plan it will take a month or more for us to reach Argentina. In that time we can set much into motion."

"You can send it securely?"

"Yes. Of that I'm sure."

"All right. I will give you enough to raise everyone's appetite. I'll include it with the rest, as we discussed."

"Good."

Rainer went over the details of the plan once more for good measure, adding in a contingency should something go wrong. Heinrich tried to listen, but his thoughts were already drifting to the hero's welcome he would receive in Buenos Aires. He imagined addressing the leaders of the new order. *For what I give you now, I have one inviolate demand*—then a proper pause before the grand punch line—*a schnitzel and a proper beer!* He could hear the laughter now.

Rainer stopped talking. He sauntered toward Heinrich, seeming taller now, more imposing.

"Until we meet again, Karl." He offered his hand.

Heinrich backed away one step, stiffened, and snapped his palm up in a Nazi salute. "Long live the Reich!"

Rainer stood back, almost looking surprised. But then, with the most serious face Heinrich had seen, he responded in kind. "Long live the Reich."

Heinrich trundled away down the path, confident that the spy would disappear as magically as he had appeared. That's what men like Rainer did. Heinrich was giddy, and the swirl of dirt that came spinning across the path—the locals called them dust devils—did nothing to dampen his mood. Soon he would be free of this place, free of the life of deception that had grown so tiresome. And soon he would be recognized for his genius. Karl Heinrich—the father of Germany's atomic age.

From the shelter of the piñons, Braun watched the pudgy scientist waddle away down the path. *So this*, he thought, *is Die Wespe.* Hardly a figure to cast fear. Still, Braun would not underestimate the man. Whatever his shortcomings, he must be a top-notch physicist to gain involvement in this American project. Heinrich was no fool. But then neither were Hitler, Himmler, and the rest.

He traced one of the petroglyphs, a delicate deer-like figure, with his finger. He was glad he'd thought things through carefully before the meeting. With the war in Europe over, Braun had anticipated three possibilities. First, that Karl Heinrich might have wanted to get out, a reluctant spy or perhaps a conscientious scientist who only wanted to return home, perhaps to a family. But he now knew that there was no family. The man had asked about no one except Hitler, which led to option two—a hardened Nazi who would go to any length for the nonexistent Reich. Here Braun had been ready, his answers sure, confident, and swallowed whole. And he was thankful that the last contingency had not proven the case—that Wespe was of Braun's own mind.

He moved slowly through bristly vegetation to the place where he would wait for nightfall. The gully, or "wash" as they called them here, was a mile outside town. Again, Braun found himself living outside, exposed to the heat and cold, hunger pulling constantly. The recent weeks had been an exercise in extremes. He had slept on fine linens at Harrold House and on rocks in the open. He had taken an exquisite Chablis in Waterford crystal and brown water in a rusty cup. It all started five years ago, when the pleasurable sins of Paris had given way to the brutal sins of Stalingrad.

Braun wondered what would come of it all. Was the Manhattan Project really something valuable? The little scientist was sure, but Braun remembered from his time at Harvard how full the highbrow intellectuals could be of themselves. A new weapon? It sounded fantastic. How much power could be found in splitting a few atoms? Time, perhaps, would tell.

CHAPTER 30

Lydia sat in the dark surrounded by a mass of people. They were laughing at the antics of Abbot and Costello on the big screen. The smell of popcorn and candy sweetened the air, further sugar to coat the bitter reality that was the world outside.

Alice Van DeMeer sat next to her, dressed properly for the matinee in a conservative skirt and modest flats. Alice had called with the invitation at noon, but Lydia was sure it had been arranged by her mother, who'd been coming up with diversions all week. Shopping trips, excursions to the beach — anything to get Lydia's mind off the indelicate fact that she was now a widow at the age of twenty-five. Alice was two years younger, properly reared, and single. A perfect companion in Mother's eyes, Lydia supposed. And, of course, Alice was still full of that joie de vivre so common in young women not encumbered by the weight of dead husbands on the bottom of the ocean.

The movie had started thirty minutes earlier, but Lydia stared blankly. Any positive leanings in her mood had been ruined by the newsreels. The first had been about the battle in the Pacific, smiling young soldiers, boys jousting and ribbing one another lightheartedly before throwing themselves onto another death trap of a beach. But it was the second news clip that had imprinted so awfully in her mind. Footage of more American boys, these liberating a concentration camp — dead bodies stacked like cordwood, skeletal figures whose very shapes seemed to defy biology. It played over and over in her head, like a terrible song whose lyrics couldn't be pried away.

A roar of laughter erupted in the theater. Alice Van DeMeer doubled over in a very unrefined guffaw. Lydia could take no more. She jumped up and shoved rudely past ten sets of legs to reach the aisle. When she burst onto the street the brightness took her gaze down. It was just as well—she didn't want oncomers to see the tears streaming down her face.

Lydia walked quickly, though she doubted Alice would try to catch up. The whole affair had been awkward, Alice trying to be cheery and Lydia in a supremely dark mood. More importantly, she thought, the entire afternoon had been a waste. Another day of idleness, nothing done to help.

Lydia gathered herself as she walked. She passed a WAC, a smartly uniformed brunette of the Women's Army Corps. *Why couldn't I have done that?* Lydia thought. She could have been a nurse or a messenger. She could have gone to work in a factory building trucks or airplanes. Her mother would have been apoplectic. But Edward would have permitted it. Kind Edward would have seen how important it was to her. Instead, she had played tennis and gone to parties. She had learned how to drive, taking joyrides with no concern for the rations of fuel and rubber. While the world had suffered, she had gone to tea.

The afternoon heat bore down as Lydia walked home, fitting the ideas that were simmering in her head. Self-pity turned to self-loathing as she succumbed to the painful facts. She had let Alex seduce her, and the rest had followed directly.

As awful as it was, this realization brought great clarity. She had failed Edward. That was done. If there was any redemption to be had, it would be in helping to find Alex. And that would never happen until she finally took control of her life.

When Lydia arrived at Harrold House she was hot in sweat. Her mother was the first to see her.

"Where have you been, dear? Alice called to say that you'd left the matinee in a state."

"Where is Father?" she demanded.

"Lydia, I don't like that tone of voice. There's nothing respectable about being—"

"*Where is he?*" Lydia shouted.

Her mother stood back. She pointed toward the back lawn.

Lydia strode out to find her father seated in a chair at the bottom of the lawn, a cold drink in one hand, a newspaper in his lap. He seemed to be staring at the dock, where *Mystic* bobbed gently against her lines. Lydia stomped to a halt at his side. I must be a sight, she thought. She hoped her eyes were not puffy, evidence of her breakdown. She had to be strong.

Her father did not look up, but instead kept looking at the boat. His thumb and forefinger cupped his chin in contemplation. "I'm going to sell her," he murmured.

Lydia looked at *Mystic*. She was stunned. The boat had been Edward's joy. Something inside her snapped.

"No!" she shouted. "Absolutely not!"

Her father looked up patiently. Patronizingly.

"I won't allow it," she insisted. "Edward loved that boat. It was his, and now it's mine. I will never sell it. Never!"

Her father's response was to raise the newspaper. He began a study of the financials.

Lydia took a deep breath. "I'm going to New Mexico."

"New Mexico? Really, Lydia—"

"I want to help Major Thatcher find the man who killed my husband."

The paper still hid his face. "The major is very competent, dear. You mustn't worry—"

Lydia swatted the *Times* to the ground. Her father looked up in amazement.

"I do worry! I . . . I apologize for my impertinence, Father, but I'm going. I have sat around here far too long playing silly games and living a gilded life. The rest of the world is dealing with death and starvation. It's time I pitched in to help. And I'll do it with or without your approval."

Lydia braced for his rage. He would rise and tower over her

to deliver the verbal dressing-down that would end her little rebellion. And then what would she do? What would she do when he denied her?

Strangely, her father sat still for a moment, and his expression turned to something else. Something very unexpected. If Lydia was not mistaken, it was pride.

"All right then," he said, "go."

Braun had hidden the old Indian's truck in a derelict barn on the outskirts of Santa Fe, not sure if he'd even go back to it. But Heinrich had been right about one thing — Santa Fe was crawling with Army G-2 men, and probably the FBI. Braun knew he couldn't stay here.

He decided it was likely that the authorities had found the remains of the Luscombe and the body of the Indian. If so, they'd be looking for the truck. But they'd also be watching the train and bus stations. If he traveled at night, the truck remained his best bet.

He headed south at midnight. In three hours he passed only four cars, one a police black and white that fortunately showed no interest. During the drive Braun reflected on his meeting with Die Wespe. He would not see the scientist again until their rendezvous in the Pacific. And as soon as Braun was in possession of the trove of documents, he would dispose of the little Nazi. The question then became what to do with it all. If the information about this atomic weapon concept was indeed valuable, Braun had to find a way to sell it — to a country, most likely. Given the present dynamics of world affairs, there was one obvious choice.

Braun arrived in Albuquerque just before dawn, rattling along with a nearly empty gas tank. With daylight less than an hour away, he had to find a place to dump the truck for good. He found it on the southwest side of town, along the banks of the Rio Grande. A junkyard sprawled out behind a wooden fence, five acres of metal, rubber, and glass to blight the landscape.

He paused in front long enough to be sure no one was around. The "office" was little more than a shack, and a pair of guard dogs came running — German shepherds, perhaps, with something else mixed in that made them thicker in the chest and jaw. They barked and snarled behind the fence, and made Braun doubly sure that no one was inside the place.

He drove another hundred yards to find what he wanted — a telephone pole next to the road. He steered the truck carefully, accelerated a bit, and smashed into it, corrupting the left front quarter panel. He reversed, then charged again, this time giving treatment to the right headlight and bumper. The truck was a cosmetic disaster to begin with, but after ten minutes of battering it looked like a casualty from the Russian front.

As Braun guided it back to the junkyard, the radiator spewed steam and the steering wheel pulled hard to the right as rubber scraped metal. For a final resting place, he pulled the mess up to a swinging section of the fence that served as an access point to the junkyard. He was sure that by noon today his donation would be drug inside, no questions asked.

Five minutes later, the license plate and key went spinning into the Rio Grande. Once again, Braun began to walk.

CHAPTER 31

He spent three days in a flophouse south of Albuquerque. It was nestled in the Manzano Mountains, near Route 60, and run by a Spanish-American couple who spoke little English. Braun had learned long ago that it was the have-nots, the simple people, who would ask the fewest questions. The police would be less welcome at the Manzano Inn than the quiet patron who had paid cash in advance for a dirty room — simple breakfast and dinner included. The arranged term had been two weeks, though Braun only expected to stay half that long.

He'd hitched rides south to the area, and had immediately stumbled onto the place. It was ideal for his purposes — quiet, and only three miles from the strange dead-drop location Karl Heinrich had chosen. Braun had already made one dry run, borrowing a bicycle from the innkeeper for a late morning ride. On that occasion, he had picked out the correct cement road marker and climbed to the crest of the hill. There, he'd found nothing aside from the clearing Heinrich had described, and a magnificent view of the Rio Grande Valley. Tonight he hoped for more.

It was three o'clock in the morning, and the slim moon was little help. Braun found the road marker again, but only after passing it once. He walked the bike into the scrub and leaned it against a tree. From the handlebars he unhooked a kerosene lantern, also borrowed from the inn, and Braun stoked it to life.

The climb, which had been simple in daylight, would be a far greater challenge at night.

Braun started off carefully, keeping the lantern low and in front to illuminate trouble spots — loose rocks, fallen tree limbs, stray roots. The forest here was similar to Santa Fe, thick, stunted vegetation that clawed its way across dusty soil to probe every crevice for water and nutrients.

He reached the top at precisely three forty-five. Heinrich had been insistent on the time, thought Braun could not imagine why. By definition, a dead-drop meant that Die Wespe would be nowhere near the place. And Braun could hardly envision anyone else coming to this godforsaken wilderness at such an hour. He was breathing heavily and, as he stood straight, he imagined that the fat little Nazi must have been panting like a dog after such a climb. Again, he wondered what was so special about this time and place.

At the crest of the hill was the same clearing he'd seen last time, but in the lantern's light he saw something new. A tripod, the kind used by photographers, was centered on the best level ground. It was equal to his own height, and a small box was mounted on top. Braun went to it and put the lantern close. A metal plate read: SPECTROGRAPH. On the opposite side was an orifice of sorts, oriented toward the south.

Braun looked out and saw the wide valley, barely visible in moonlight that filtered down through broken clouds. A few tiny clusters of light punctuated the landscape, all many miles away. He remembered Heinrich's next instructions. *Go twenty paces toward the valley.* He lowered the lantern and counted steps. Reaching sixteen, a knee-high rock blocked his path. Immediately behind it was a canvas bag. Braun set the lantern carefully on the rock and opened the bag. A handwritten letter was on top.

Rainer,

> *Our plan is progressing well. Here are the documents you asked for. They are enough to convince anyone with a background in the field that my*

information about the Manhattan Project is invaluable. I have also detailed everything I know with regard to my travel plans. We must meet on the island of Guam. The ship we discussed will make port at 9:00 a.m. on July 27th. I will come ashore with everything at the first opportunity. From there we must rendezvous with the others as quickly as possible.

Look at the papers later, Rainer. At this moment it is more important for you to check your watch. At precisely 3:55 you must use the protection in the bag and look to the southern sky. The test is scheduled for 4:00, forty miles south of where you stand. You are about to witness history, my friend, assuming this incredible thing works.

Karl

The test, Braun thought. That's why Heinrich had chosen this place. *Rendezvous with the others* — he truly believed the Reich would carry on. Braun marveled at how an educated man could be so blind. But then the ranks of the Nazi Party had included many such learned men, and they had proven blind indeed — every vision, every idea obscured by the blackness of hatred.

He checked his watch — 3:51. Braun reached into the bag and pulled out a thick folder of documents, a welders mask, and a bottle of suntan lotion. Suntan lotion. He wondered if it was Heinrich's idea of a joke. He stood and again regarded the nighttime vista.

Braun shook his head. He could not bring himself to apply the lotion, and he tossed it back into the bag. He did, however, resign to pulling the welder's mask over his head. It was heavy and ill-fitting. The dark glass faceplate turned the world nearly black. Braun could no longer see his watch, and the resulting limbo of time made him tense. He had seen every kind of explosion known to man, some at an uncomfortably close range. What kind of thing, he wondered, could require such precautions? And forty miles, a ridiculous distance. At this range there would be nothing — perhaps a momentary flash on the horizon.

He waited for what he thought was fifteen minutes. Nothing happened. A coyote howled a plaintive wail. Braun heard a rumble in the distance, but it was only the familiar, gentle roll of a distant rain shower. He took off the mask and tossed it aside in disgust. So where was the awe-inspiring weapon, this revolutionary idea? Had it been a failure? Had the Americans spent billions of dollars pursuing worthless, chalkboard theories? He eyed the folder of documents. Did Wespe have *anything* of value?

Braun again sat on the rock and began to read. The first document was some kind of scientific synopsis, an introduction to a collection of diagrams and calculations that were attached. The handwriting on the cover page was clearly Heinrich's, matching the letter Braun had already read:

Uranium Enrichment: The Gaseous Diffusion Method

Several pounds of the fissionable isotope U-235 are necessary for a single bomb. This desirable isotope exists naturally at the ratio of only 1 part in 140, thus physical methods of separation are required. Three possible solutions were originally identified: electromagnetic separation, thermal diffusion, and gaseous diffusion. Of these, gaseous diffusion has proven the most effective, though it requires significant industrial capacity.

In principle, when uranium is converted to a gaseous compound (uranium hexafluoride), it can be forced through a porous screen. The heavier U-238 isotope moves more slowly and is effectively "filtered." This process must be repeated roughly 5,000 times to achieve the nominal weapons-grade purity of 93% U-235.

Attached are copies of blueprints of the American K-25 plant, a forty-four acre facility at Oak Ridge, Ten-

nessee. The magnitude of this production site cannot be underestimated. It was built at a cost of 500 million U.S. dollars. I believe it is feasible to construct a smaller scale version. By avoiding certain errors, efficiency can be improved. Particular attention must be given to the materials used in construction. Uranium hexafluoride is extremely corrosive, and will react violently with grease or oil. Also, maintenance is paramount, as contaminants have resulted in a continuous series of setbacks and shutdowns. The Union Carbide Corporation runs this facility, and a copy of their operating manual is included here . . .

Braun pored over the letter and attachments. Most of the papers were hand-drawn duplicates, but a few originals bore the header: **U.S. Army Corps of Engineers – Manhattan District.** These were stamped TOP SECRET. There was also a second file, regarding a place called Hanford, Washington. The cover letter, again in Heinrich's hand, was titled: PLUTONIUM — THE TRANS-MUTATION OF U-238. Braun read it, then found himself carrying on to the rest, a thick volume of blueprints, diagrams, and equipment specifications. The project was industrial in nature, different from the artful works of design Braun had studied at Harvard. Yet he recognized enough to see the legitimacy of the information. The scale of this place in Tennessee was unlike anything he had ever seen.

Braun was seized by excitement. He pored over page after page by light of the lantern, checking dimensions, awed by the immensity of it all. *500 million dollars,* he thought. For one industrial plant? Had the Americans gone insane? He looked at every page, his heart pulsing by the end. There was so much here — details, calculations. And this was only a sample of what Heinrich possessed. It *had* to be of value.

Braun stood. His back ached from sitting on the rock. He locked his hands above his head and stretched like a cat. The injured shoulder was better, almost no pain. A look at his watch told him it was nearly five thirty. He'd lost track of time and spent over an hour consuming Heinrich's file. But what good was any of it, he thought, if the whole project was a failure? Dejection stabbed in. Once more, Braun looked across the land. He saw only tranquility — a desert still, silent, and black. And then the sky exploded.

The universe fell ablaze in white light. The brightness was incredible, like nothing he'd ever seen. He instinctively stepped back and turned his head aside — yet Braun forced himself to look. The flash did not fade, but rather grew in intensity, as if the sun had crashed into the desert valley. His eyes adjusted to the light, and he saw a mountain of dust rising into the sky. He stood transfixed as smoke and light churned into a hellish orange fireball, rising up and up. Then Braun saw something else. A wave of destruction sweeping out, rolling across the desert at incredible speed. Rolling right at him. He braced himself.

It hit like a hurricane. Braun tried to stand firm against the pressure. He squinted and his hair was blown back. The sound came now, not an instantaneous crack, but a rumble that grew and grew like a thousand bass drums. It seemed to have no end, pulsing echoes that pounded off the surrounding hills.

Braun stood still. Watching, listening. Stunned.

After what seemed like an eternity, the sounds dampened and were lost. Silence gradually returned, and the tremendous ball of fire ebbed, taking with it the light. In the end there was only one thing — a gigantic column of smoke, a cylinder capped on top by an even wider ball of tumultuous, roiling dust. In the muted dawn it rose up as if trying to black out the heavens. He stared in raw astonishment, and a single number came to Braun's mind. Forty. He was forty miles away.

His lips parted, and the words came in a hoarse whisper.

"Mein Gott!"

CHAPTER 32

Lydia looked out the window as the train pulled into the station at Albuquerque. The place looked like something straight out of a western movie. The building was a skeleton of heavy wood beams supporting some kind of earthen material. Most of the men on the platform wore cowboy hats, and there was actually a horse tied to a rail in the dirt street.

The women, at least, were a mix. The Indians, with uniformly long, silky black hair, were wrapped in colorful robes, while the white women generally dressed in a more contemporary manner. A few wore skirts and blouses, but most seemed to prefer pants, a few even sporting denim blue jeans of the kind Lydia had only seen men wear. Stepping off the train through a mist of steam, she realized that there was a time in her life when these local fashion trends might have tipped her into the first clothing store. Now, however, she had far greater concerns.

She scanned the platform but saw no sign of Thatcher. She had kept in touch with him by telephone during her journey and he'd promised to meet her. He'd been scouring hotels and hospitals in both Santa Fe and Albuquerque, looking for any trace of a man who had survived a plane crash a week ago. So far he'd come up with nothing, but Lydia had brought her secret weapon — a photograph of Alex Braun. She'd nearly forgotten about it, a group picture of Alex and four other students acting silly on the beach. Her father had taken the negative and had it enlarged, and Lydia hoped it would jog someone's memory.

A look at the station clock told her why Thatcher wasn't here —the train had arrived early. Lydia flagged down a porter, a wide-shouldered Indian boy, and arranged for her trunk to be taken off the train.

She walked into the terminal. The place was busy, but nothing on the order of the big stations back east. Hers was the only train, resting on the only rail. People milled about, but none seemed in a hurry, perhaps slowed by the heavy heat that hung on the breeze. Lydia decided she should go out front, collect her trunk, and wait for Thatcher. As she steered through the light crowd, a hallway took her left, then right, and finally deposited her at the front of the station near the ticket booths. There, the first person she saw was Alex Braun.

He was in a fog. It had taken much of the morning to get back to Albuquerque, paying the innkeeper's brother twenty dollars for a ride to the station. Braun remembered none of it. His mind was completely absorbed by the enormity of what he had seen. It was an image of fire, a wave of destruction rolling across the landscape. A sight he would never forget.

He carried one bag. A change of clothes, a jacket, a razor — and the files Karl Heinrich had left on the hill. There were fewer than a hundred pages, yet the bag seemed heavy in his hand, a wonderful weight. He found himself gripping so hard that his fingers were numb. Of course, this was only a sample of what Die Wespe possessed. How heavy would the fat little scientist's suitcase seem? Braun wondered. How much could the world's greatest secret weigh?

He stood in the ticket line, one man in front of him. Braun had only discovered his destination five minutes ago, the third coin and third telephone operator having provided the answer.

The man in front of him disappeared and Braun edged forward, forcing his attention to the girl behind the window. She was very attractive, and met his eyes directly. Then she smiled. He tried to remember if she had smiled for the last man. He usually noticed such things.

"Where to, sir?"

"San Francisco. I'd like a sleeping compartment."

"We have roomettes in first class — it's not much extra."

"That will be fine."

"One way or round trip?"

"One way, please."

Her hands worked, but her eyes darted between the papers and her customer. "So . . . you won't be coming back?"

He smiled engagingly. She was young, flirtatious. For the first time since this morning Braun entertained a thought other than Trinity. But the notion was fleeting. Carnal lust was an impulse he could control, switched on and off like a light. His impatience, he knew, lay elsewhere. "I'm afraid not. Not anytime soon."

"Pity," she said, sliding a ticket through the window. "That's twenty-six dollars and twenty cents."

Braun didn't even flinch. He paid and walked to the platform. His train was waiting.

Lydia stood behind a column and watched him leave the ticket counter. Fortunately, he turned away and headed toward the train. She looked out to the street, hoping to spot Thatcher. He was nowhere in sight.

She didn't know what to do. There were no policemen around. And if she went to one of the rail officials, what could she say? *Would you please detain this customer — he killed my husband.* Alex would know how to handle that. He'd smile his disarming smile. Lydia had once been vulnerable to it. But now, much too late, she knew his act for what it was — a simple tool. If confronted, Alex would exercise his charm until he was either turned loose or forced to kill again. No, Lydia thought, he was too dangerous to simply plead for help from a stranger. And the only other person to appreciate that risk was Thatcher. She looked desperately toward the street again, willing him to appear.

Alex walked to one of the forward cars, presented his ticket to the attendant, and disappeared into the coach. The big schedule board said the train would be leaving in five minutes. Lydia had to do something. She rushed to the ticket counter. A man was talking to the girl behind the window. Lydia couldn't wait.

"I'm terribly sorry," she said, elbowing in. She tried to give the fellow an attractive smile. "Would you mind? I'm in a terrible predicament."

The man eased back, annoyed, but trying to be polite.

Lydia turned to the attendant, whose jaw was working furiously on a piece of chewing gum. "A tall blond man just bought a ticket from you. Where was he going?"

The girl looked suspicious. "Is he a friend of yours, miss?"

Lydia blurted out the first thing that came to her head. "He's my husband."

The girl frowned. She said, "He's going to San Francisco. One way."

"Oh. I see."

The girl's face turned sympathetic. "It leaves in five minutes," she said.

Lydia stared at the first car. Inside, the man who had killed Edward was now settling in comfortably. She opened her purse. "Give me a ticket to San Francisco."

"Are you sure, miss?"

Lydia answered by widening her eyes severely and cocking her head.

"All right. What class?"

"Well — where is he?"

"He has a roomette in first class."

It was the same car she had come in on. "I'll take the day coach."

Lydia paid and walked quickly to the train. She would be in the open for a few seconds, and she kept her face turned away from the front passenger car. Lydia wished she'd worn a hat, something modest to pull down over her eyes.

She passed three sleeper Pullmans and stepped up onto the last car, boarding the same train she'd gotten off twenty minutes earlier, though much farther back. For as long as Lydia could remember, she and her family had taken the train to their winter home in Florida each year. In all that time, she had never ventured farther back than the dining car. *After all,* her father would say as he admonished her to keep her station, *I hold a considerable interest in the Atlantic Coast Line. I know who rides back there, and I know that we make more money for each cow we carry.*

Inside the coach, a worn wooden aisle separated two rows of bench seats that stretched all the way to the rear door. The seats had no cushions, and the air was still and hot. The mix of faces here was far less homogenous than what she was accustomed to — brown and white, dirty and clean, happy and miserable. All seemed to ignore her.

She shuffled and stumbled down the center aisle, a strange setting for a former Newport debutante. Lydia had been deeply heeled in the importance of making entrances. Dress well, eyes forward. Keep the chin high but don't overdo — regal as opposed to overbearing. Now she fumbled her way to the back of the last grimy train car, ducking her head desperately to see out the station-side window. What if Alex had gotten back off? Lydia wondered. Was it possible he'd seen her?

There were no seats open at the windows along her left, but Lydia spotted a soldier, clean cut and very young, with a single aisle seat open next to him. She recognized the uniform as Army, but struggled for anything more. Judging by the lone stripe on his shoulder and a complete lack of decorations, she decided he must be a new recruit. Lydia tried to wipe away the worry that had to be chiseled into her face.

"Is this seat taken?"

The boy looked up and smiled like he'd won a trifecta at Pimlico.

"No, ma'am."

Her voice was sugar, "I hate to be a bother, but do you think I might take the window?"

The young man slid over like he'd been parked on a hot-plate.

"Thank you," she said, sliding demurely into the seat. She instantly surveyed the station for any sign of Alexander Braun. Or even better, Michael Thatcher. She saw neither.

A distant voice disrupted her thoughts. "— I said, where are you headed?"

She turned to find the young soldier eagerly awaiting her reply. Smoke billowed from the front of the train and she heard the conductor make his last call.

"Ah, San Francisco." Not wanting to be rude, she added, "And you?"

"Los Angeles. My unit is going to ship out soon. I can't tell you exactly where, you know."

Lydia kept searching outside. "Of course." The train began to move.

"My name's Tommy. Tommy Moore."

Lydia nodded and offered a light handshake. "Lydia Murray. Nice to meet you, Tommy."

Tommy began to talk nonstop, and Lydia gave back an occasional nod in return. Trying to analyze her muddled situation, she suddenly realized that she carried nothing more than her purse — her trunk was sitting out on the curb waiting to be claimed. I should have stayed, she thought. Thatcher will turn up soon. Together they might have convinced the police. Alex could have been arrested at the next station. Instead, she was alone. There were rail employees and a few soldiers, but Lydia had never been good at authority, at badgering people. And Alex? She knew better than anyone how convincing Alex could be — engaging, confident, persuasive. God, how she knew.

The station disappeared and the train built up speed as it headed into a vast desert. Lydia's heart raced. *What on earth have I done?*

*   *   *

Thatcher parked his new car along the street in front of the station. It wasn't actually new, but a decent ride. The owner hadn't bothered with any paperwork once Thatcher had forked over four hundred in cash. He only wished Sargent Cole's money could procure Alexander Braun so easily.

Santa Fe had been a dead end. Knowing Braun had certainly been injured in the airplane crash, Thatcher's first stop had been to the only hospital in town. No one there remembered a tall, blond man. They'd even checked the logs to confirm that there was no record of a patient with suspicious injuries on the days in question. Thatcher had next tracked down every private doctor and nurse he could find. Nothing. He'd then tried the hotels and boardinghouses, coming up empty. To top it all off, the investigation back in Newport had gone equally cold.

Thatcher also noticed that the FBI men in Santa Fe — they seemed to be on every corner — paid him no attention whatsoever. Tomas Jones knew that Braun's stolen airplane had gone down nearby, yet there didn't seem to be any official search. Not for the first time, Thatcher thought the Americans seemed terribly confident in their security arrangements.

He walked across the front platform of the station, searching for Lydia. When Sargent Cole had told him she was coming, there was a sense of conveyance in his announcement — as if to suggest it was Thatcher's turn to hold her hand for a while. He'd do nothing of the sort. In fact, he expected she'd be quite useful. Lydia knew Alexander Braun better than anyone, and had strong reasons for wanting to find him.

A cloud of dust washed into the station from the street, blurring everything in a haze of red. Thatcher sneezed. He had thankfully recovered from his head cold, but something in the desert air was playing havoc on his sinuses. He spotted a sturdy young porter who was standing at the curb next to a large steamer trunk.

"I beg your pardon, but I'm here to meet a friend. Has the three o'clock from Amarillo arrived yet?"

"Yes, sir. Came in thirty minutes ago and she's just gone back out."

The man pointed and Thatcher saw a trail of black smoke to the southwest. He thanked the porter and entered the station. The crowd was modest, and everyone moved slowly in the heat. It took less than a minute to cover the entire place — Lydia was definitely not here. There were few remaining possibilities. She could be in the ladies room, or she might have walked down the street for a bite to eat. Thatcher took a seat on a long, empty bench. There was nothing to do but wait.

Lydia watched the desert drift past her window. It seemed endless, particularly at the tops of the hills where she could see mountains that must have been a hundred miles away. The openness was a comfort, daylight against the dark shadow of Alexander Braun.

The more Lydia thought through the situation, the more she calmed. Even if Alex were to come back, she was safe here, surrounded by dozens of people, half of them strong young men. He was a killer, but not a stupid, reckless one. She had certainly erred by getting on the train, but now the way out seemed clear. She would simply sit here in coach until the next station, a place called Winslow, Arizona. They were scheduled to arrive in an hour, and at the station she'd get off and call her father. It would work perfectly as long as Alex didn't see her.

Then Lydia remembered something Thatcher had said. Alex was here to contact a Nazi spy. The question rushed to her mind — could that person also be on the train? Perhaps in this very car? Lydia looked all around. A man two rows back was leering at her obviously. His face was narrow and pinched, with a rodent's black eyes. A shiver went down her spine, and Lydia turned away in fright. Had it been the sneer of an old lecher? Or something else?

She tried to see him in the reflection of the side window, but it was no use — too many faces, too much commotion. Still, it felt as if the man's eyes were boring into her back. But he couldn't be the one, she reasoned. If there *was* a spy on the train, it would be a stranger, someone who couldn't possibly recognize her. Unless . . . unless Alex had pointed her out.

She imagined the black eyes, felt his stare still fixed on her. Lydia had to do something. She turned to Tommy. He was nearly asleep, having long ago given up his offensive in the face of her cool, distracted responses.

"I'm sorry to bother you —"

His eyes opened fully, but the earlier excitement was gone. "Yeah, what is it?"

"There's a man back there — he's staring at me."

He started to turn, but Lydia took his arm. "No, don't look," she whispered. "He's middle-aged, wearing a brown shirt and a flat cap."

His chest puffed out. "You want me to go set him straight?"

"No, no. Look, it's probably nothing." She hesitated. "Listen, I'm going to go up to the next car. Could you just make sure he doesn't follow me?" She squeezed his skinny bicep. "It would really mean a lot."

The soldier grinned, awash in confidence. "Sure, sweetheart."

Lydia got up, walked quickly to the front, and passed into the next car. It was a sleeper, and there were more soldiers here, lounging in bunks on their elbows with magazines and cigarettes. More smiles. When Lydia reached the front of the car she ventured a look back. The man had not followed her. Ahead was another Pullman sleeper, also loaded with soldiers, many more solid and steeled than the wisp who was already serving as her guardian.

The sea of uniforms gave her a sense of security. Lydia gained confidence. Alex was up there, she thought, only a hundred feet away. The man who had killed Edward was relaxing, perhaps taking a Scotch. Enjoying a casual afternoon. But what was he doing here? Lydia wondered. And why San Francisco? Or was he even going there? It dawned on her that Alex might also get off the train in Winslow. If he did, he could disappear forever. And how many more would he kill? How many more women would feel what she felt at this very moment? Anger. Even hate. It made her seethe. Lydia was tired of being weak and ignored. It was time to stand up and fight.

And so she came up with a new plan.

Braun had settled into his tiny room. The flimsy door shut, he was sprawled on a bed three inches shorter than his frame. One arm lay draped over his forehead, a cigarette between thumb and forefinger, while the other hand held Heinrich's papers. He studied them now with ravenous intensity. Braun had tried to sleep, but even with the gentle rocking of the train it was no use. Every time he closed his eyes he saw the incredible light, felt the wind rush over him like a breath from hell.

And if that wasn't enough, he had found more evidence. The steward had delivered a newspaper to his cabin, a local rag called the *Albuquerque Journal.* Braun found the article on page eleven, buried beneath a drab piece about the state budgetary process. *"Early this morning, an ammunition magazine exploded near Alamogordo. There were no reports of injuries..."*

Braun was not a newspaper man, but he knew there were deadlines. The blast had taken place at 5:30 this morning, yet there had apparently been a delay. Heinrich's theatrics suggested that 4:00 was the original target. It all made sense — the story had been planted by the War Department. There would have to be some explanation put forward, some account for the few night watchmen and freight train engineers who would undoubtedly witness the event. The article in the paper was further proof about the scope of this Manhattan Project. And proof that the whole thing had not been a dream.

Braun rose from his bunk and stretched. He flicked his cigarette out the window that was cracked open and ran a hand over the stubble on his chin. His stomach reminded him that he was neglecting it once again. It was time for a good meal and a decent cigar. He tucked Heinrich's file under the pillow, and gathered up his fresh clothes and shaving gear. *A gentleman doesn't go to lunch unclean,* he mused. Stepping from his compartment, he locked the door and headed for the washroom.

Thatcher waited thirty minutes before putting through a call to Newport. Sargent Cole confirmed that the train and time were correct. Baffled, Thatcher went to the ticket window. A young girl stood behind the counter, chewing gum and filing her nails.

"Perhaps you could help me," he said. "I'm looking for a young woman who came in on the last train. She's about your height and has dark hair, rather long."

The girl studied Thatcher for a moment before shrugging. "No, sorry mister." She went back to her nails.

Thatcher turned away with a sigh of frustration. Where had Lydia gone? Had she even arrived? He decided to walk down the street and look over the restaurants.

Back at the ticket counter, the young girl watched him from the corner of her eye. She was having a grand time thinking of all the scandalous possibilities. Most likely, Dreamboat had been the boyfriend, and the gimpy Brit soldier was the husband. She blew a bubble and it popped. Any way she figured it, she'd done the girl a big favor. "You owe me one, sister," she giggled under her breath.

CHAPTER 33

Lydia found the man she wanted in the dining car. Not knowing if Alex might be there as well, she leaned in and beckoned him over with a wave. He saw her, smiled, and came as requested.

"Hello, ma'am. I thought you got off in Albuquerque."

Lydia smiled conspiratorially. She dragged the old black man out of sight and into the next car. "Clifford, I'm so glad to see you!"

He'd been her steward all the way from Chicago. In spite of her mother's constant guidance that servants should "be held to their place," Lydia regularly befriended them, learning about their families and lives. Clifford lived in Chicago, had a wife and six children, and had been with the Santa Fe Line for nineteen years, after twenty with Union Pacific. He was also a very good steward.

"Where are you riding?" he asked. "I didn't see you up front."

"I have a seat in the day coach."

"The day coach? Young lady, what on earth —"

Lydia put a hand to his shoulder and giggled like a schoolgirl. "I need your help, Clifford."

"Help with what, miss?"

"You see, the reason I came out here is because I'm getting married."

"Married?" He smiled. "You never told me that. Well, congratulations!"

"Thank you. The big day is next Sunday in San Francisco."

"You mean you're headin' all the way out to San Francisco in coach?"

"No, no! That's the thing —" Lydia paused for effect and tried to look a bit shameful. "You see, my fiancé boarded the train in Albuquerque. He's up front. And he doesn't know I'm here. It's a surprise!"

The steward of nearly forty years understood in an instant. He grinned as old men did when appreciating the good folly of youth. "I see. Who is the lucky fellow?"

Lydia nearly blurted the name before realizing that Alex might have used an alias. "He's tall and blond." To be sure, she added, "With a scar here, on his temple."

"Ah! Mr. Holloway. Yeah, he's in my section."

"Oh, that's wonderful! Clifford, will you do this for me — watch him, and when he leaves his room, come get me and let me in. It'll knock his socks off to open the door and find me there."

The old fellow chuckled, "I seen a lot of things in my time — but all right, miss. You wait right here."

Clifford came back right away. "He's out of his room now."

"He's not in the dining car, is he? I want it to be a surprise."

"No, ma'am. I checked on my way back. He must be up front in the lounge."

"All right."

He led her through the dining car. Lydia was forced to nod when she recognized a woman, a boorish old dragon who'd gotten on in Kansas City. Once in the first-class car, Clifford stopped and knocked on a door. She must have looked frightened, because Clifford said, "Don't worry. I'm just making sure." There was no response, and Clifford used his pass key to open the door. Lydia slipped inside, and as he slid it closed the old man gave her a knowing wink.

Lydia turned the lock and sighed heavily. *There*, she thought. *Now what?* Alex could come back at any moment. She was scared, but also exhilarated. She'd put herself in the devil's own lair —

now she had to make good use of it. *Where is Alex heading?* Lydia wondered. *What is he up to?*

She went straight to two drawers that were built into the teak room divider and found a pair of socks, an undershirt, and a pack of cigarettes. In the narrow closet was a jacket. Nothing more. Lydia scanned desperately around the room. His ticket was on a small table. San Francisco, one way. Just as the agent had told her. *There has to be something else!* A newspaper on the bed caught her eye. And then she saw something edging out from under the pillow.

Lydia pulled out a stack of papers. On top was a handwritten letter. She leafed through the rest and saw papers covered with equations and diagrams. It all looked terribly scientific. She had taken the basic sciences in school, so Lydia recognized a few chemical symbols, but the balance, a mountain of Greek letters and formulas, were undecipherable.

She went back to the letter on top and began to read. *Rainer . . .* a German name, she thought . . . *Our plan is progressing well. In this bag are the documents you asked for. They are enough to convince anyone with a background in the field that my information about the Manhattan Project is invaluable. I have also detailed everything I know with regard to my travel plans. We must meet on the island of Guam. The ship we discussed will make port at 9:00 a.m. on July 27th. I will come ashore with everything at the first opportunity. From there we must rendezvous with the others—*

Lydia heard footsteps approaching. They stopped outside the door. She looked around the room in a panic. The only place to hide was in the closet, but it looked incredibly narrow. A key jingled in the lock. There wasn't time to do anything. Lydia froze in panic.

"I beg your pardon." Braun pulled his key out of the lock and put his back to the door, allowing an attractive woman and her toddler to pass in the narrow corridor.

The woman smiled, perhaps more than she should have, and her reply was packaged in the Deep South, "Why, thank you, sir."

She continued away, holding the hand of her son. Or perhaps a nanny with her ward, Braun mused. He paused for a moment to enjoy the view before putting his key back in the lock. Once in his room, he closed the door behind him and stuffed his shaving gear and dirty clothes into a drawer. Braun hoped the food here was decent. He was due a good meal. He turned to go back out, but then remembered that a jacket was required in the dining car. His hand had just reached the closet handle when someone knocked on the door. Instinctively, he came alert.

"Who is it?"

"Steward, Mr. Holloway."

He opened the door to see the familiar black man holding a bottle of Champagne and two glasses, a towel draped over one arm. "What is it?" Braun said.

The steward held out the bottle, but looked perplexed. He seemed to be searching the cabin over Braun's shoulder. "Um . . . compliments of the Santa Fe Line, sir."

Braun took the bottle and glasses tentatively. "Thank you."

The steward scurried away.

Braun closed the door. *Champagne? Two glasses?* "Something is not right," he hissed rhetorically. He felt a familiar rush, the glandular surge that kicked in when disaster was imminent. His heightened senses registered the next warning. A smell — perfume. The brand Lydia favored. He remembered the woman who had just walked by with the child — had she been wearing it? Or am I being paranoid? He saw the answer to that question on his bed. Heinrich's papers were lying in a loose pile. *He had put them under the pillow! Someone had been in his room!* Braun burst out to the corridor and spotted the steward.

"You!"

CHAPTER 34

Thatcher paced aimlessly around the station, still looking for Lydia. Another train was due to arrive soon and the place had gotten busier. He'd been waiting hours, far longer than it would have taken for Lydia to eat and come back. Something had gone wrong.

The porter he'd first spoken to was approaching with a trunk on a dolly. Thatcher was wondering what else he could ask the young man when he noticed the trunk's monogram — *LBC*.

He stopped the porter. "Excuse me! Whose trunk is that?"

"A young lady's."

"Medium height, dark hair, well-dressed?"

"Yes, sir. From back East, I'd say. It was strange. She asked me to take her trunk to the curb, but then never came for it. I have to take it to the unclaimed baggage room. Are you with her?"

"Yes, yes — so you didn't see her after she pointed out her luggage?"

"Actually, I did. I saw her at the ticket window. I figured she was buying a return ticket — people do that — but then I never saw her again."

Thatcher gave the man a dollar. "Right. Look after that bag."

He went to the ticket window. An older man was now in charge. "Excuse me," Thatcher said, "there was a girl working here earlier. Do you know where she is?" Once again, Thatcher was glad to be wearing his uniform.

The man was nearly bald with a small, compressed face. He looked Thatcher over and a starched, manager's frown fell across his features. "What's she done now?"

"It's nothing serious. I only need to speak with her."

The agent's eyes went outside and Thatcher followed them. He saw the girl across the street, walking away with a purse under one arm. She was done for the day. "Thank you!"

He caught up before she reached the first side street. "Excuse me! Miss!"

She turned.

Thatcher was sure the man back at the ticket window was watching. He stopped a few steps away, eyeing the girl like a father who'd just caught his daughter sneaking back in a window at three in the morning. It worked. Her shoulders drooped in defeat.

"This is *very* important," Thatcher insisted.

Her jaw fell still, as if the energy she put into her gum had to be transferred to arrange her thoughts. "Okay, yeah. I did see that woman you were asking about. She was in a big hurry to buy a ticket on the train that was about to leave."

"A ticket? Going where?"

"To San Francisco."

"San Francisco?" He muttered rhetorically, "Why on earth would she be going there?"

The young girl must have heard. "To be with her boyfriend."

"Her *what*?"

The girl rolled her eyes. "Tall, blond, dreamy. Look mister, I hate to be the one to break it to you —"

"A scar! Did he have a scar, here?" Thatcher touched his temple.

"So you know about him. I don't like getting in the middle of—"

She didn't get the chance to finish her words. The girl watched as the little Brit dashed across the street as fast as his gimpy leg would take him.

"Someone's been in my room!"

Lydia heard Alex's voice boom from the passageway. She squirmed out of the closet, finally able to breathe. *He'd been so close — his hand on the closet door, only inches away!*

Lydia knew she had to move. She curled her head into the corridor and saw Alex up front — he had poor Clifford pinned up against the wall and was shouting accusations. She hoped it was enough of a distraction. With only a few steps she could disappear through the door that led to the next car.

Lydia bolted, thankful for the carpet that muffled her sturdy low heels. Just as she reached the door, a little boy burst through squealing with glee. A moment later his mother came running in chase. Lydia looked over her shoulder. Her eyes met Alex's. For an instant, there was fury in his face as he let go of Clifford. But then there was control.

He put a hand to the steward's collar and straightened it, then said something in a quiet voice. Lydia couldn't hear, but she put herself in his place. She imagined his upper school accent — *Look, old boy, I'm terribly sorry about all this. I'll go have a word with the young woman and straighten things out. Please lock my room for me, and see to it that no one else gets in.* He began walking toward her.

Lydia burst through the door in a panic. Heads swiveled to gawk as she ran through the Pullmans. She looked back at the end of each car, but didn't see Alex. Lydia knew he would come. She kept moving, wanting to get as far away as possible, desperate for time to think. She slowed when she reached the day coach. There, one tiny set of eyes went straight to her — the terrible wretch who'd been staring at her. Lydia looked for Tommy. He was gone.

She pressed on, her eyes straight ahead, but feeling the stranger's awful stare. She wondered again if he was working with Alex. He might be a German spy. He might be anything. She passed him and kept going, frantic to get away from them both. At the end of the car, a door led outside to the back platform. She looked through the window and saw Tommy having a smoke at the back railing. Thank God, she thought. Lydia rushed outside.

Tommy turned and smiled. "Well, hello." His voice was loud enough to overcome the clacking din of the train. Then his smile evaporated. "What's wrong? You look like you've seen a ghost."

She didn't know what to say.

"Is that guy bothering you again? I had a little chat with him. He a slimy type, some kind of traveling salesman. But I set him straight."

"Oh, thank you, Tommy. Did he . . . did he have an accent of any sort?"

"Accent?"

"Yes, you know, like a foreign accent?"

"Naw. He was straight Midwest. You want me to go lean on him some more?"

"No, no. I —"

The door burst open and Alex appeared. Lydia backed away to the iron railing on one side. He stood still for a moment, clearly gauging the situation. More than ever Lydia wanted to get away, but there was nowhere to go. The train was traveling at full speed, and when she looked over the railing it was a blur of rocks, gravel, and iron. She would never survive a jump.

It only took Alex a moment. He relaxed. He nodded to Tommy as if they were at a dinner party. Alex pulled out a cigarette case and effortlessly held it toward Lydia. As he did, there was something in his eye, a knowing look, a slight gesture toward Tommy. He was telling her something. She shook her head to the offering and suddenly understood. He was going to kill her, of course. That was a given. The question was whether it would be necessary to kill the soldier as well. He was allowing Lydia a chance to spare the boy.

Strangely, these thoughts made her realize something. She knew Alex, and was beginning to think like him. What if she screamed? Alex had already made the calculations. He had placed himself between her and Tommy. He would strike her down and throw her off the train. Tommy, being a soldier, wasn't trained to raise an alarm. He would naturally attack Alex. And he was no match. Alex was in complete control.

She leaned back against the railing and searched desperately for a way out. Looking ahead, she caught a glimpse of where the train was headed. She saw something that made her mind spin. *If I can think like Alex, weigh every angle — it might work.*

"Tommy," she blurted, "this is my husband, Alex."

Alex raised an eyebrow. Tommy looked rather crestfallen, but put out a hand. Alex shook it.

"Tommy Moore. I'm headed out to the Pacific."

Alex smiled. The amiable Alex, hands deep in the pockets of his khaki pants. Moments ago he'd been rousting a porter — now he was at his gregarious best. He said, "No more Nazis to worry about, eh?"

Lydia said, "Alex and I are on our honeymoon, aren't we darling?"

Alex nodded, the luckiest man alive.

"Congratulations," Tommy said, flicking his cigarette butt off the back of the train. He edged toward the door.

Lydia took another glance ahead. She needed another minute.

"Alex was in the war in Europe, weren't you darling? What was your unit?"

Alex hesitated. He knew she was up to something. "The Forty-eighth Transportation Regiment. Not quite the Eighty-second Airborne, but we played our part. Now, dear, I'd like to have a private word with you."

Lydia felt it happening. The front of the train had hit the steep hill. Lydia knew about trains. The speed at which they were traveling would be cut in half during the climb. *Just a little longer.*

Tommy had had enough. "It was good to meet you both." He disappeared into the coach.

Alex looked through the window. *He's making sure the coast is clear.* Their own car was still level, not yet on the incline. The clanging of the wheels over the rail changed cadence, slowing like a clock that needed winding, nearing the end of its spring. Alex hadn't noticed it yet. She still needed more time.

"I had to find you," she blurted. "I had to see you again."

Alex stood at ease, a few steps away. He was completely confident—a cat happy to toy with a cornered mouse. "You've always been hopeless, Lydia. How did you find me?"

"I remembered when you were looking at the map in the library. Your finger was on Santa Fe. And that Major Thatcher said you might come here. I had to try and warn you."

"Warn me?"

"They're looking for you everywhere."

Behind the steel eyes she saw his thoughts turning.

"Why, Lydia? Why are you here?"

She allowed her head a tilt. "Isn't it obvious? I love you, Alex."

There! She saw it. A shift in his gaze. His thoughts had lost focus. "The last time I saw you, I'd just sent you tumbling down a staircase," he argued.

"I know. You panicked, like I did when I ran from your room just now." She kept her gaze locked to Alex, not allowing him to concentrate on the surroundings. "And what you did to Edward, as awful as it was—I know you did it so we could be together."

"You can't believe—" his eyes narrowed. "If you came here to warn me, then why were digging through my papers? Why were you in my room?"

Lydia's mind raced. *Just a few more seconds.* "Didn't you see the champagne? The two glasses? When I sat on the bed, the papers were there. I'm sorry if I messed them up."

Silence. A distracted gaze. The platform tilted slightly. They had reached the rise. Lydia moved quickly. She vaulted over the railing and got a footing outside. Leaning back, her hands clung to the platform, stretching for every possible second. Below, the rail bed was a blur. She heard the wheels churning and grinding just below her feet. All of it was dangerous, but less so than the man on the platform.

Her action had frozen Alex. He hadn't expected it. They stared at one another for an instant before Alex understood. His blue eyes came sharp, their raw intensity issuing the first strike. The same eyes Edward would have seen.

Alex lunged, his speed catching her by surprise. One hand

snagged her shoulder, snapping shut like a bear trap. She was hanging free, her feet still firm, pushing away, but Alex tearing and ripping from across the iron railing. A foot slipped loose and she saw the huge metal wheel spinning below. Lydia twisted wildly, not knowing where she would fall. Not caring. *Just get away!*

Lydia's other foot slipped, and her legs slammed against the frame of the car, inches from the wheels. Alex pulled and clawed from the other side, his fingers digging into her flesh. He refused to give up. Amid the clattering mechanical noise she heard the sound of fabric tearing. And then Lydia fell.

She crashed to the ground, tumbling and rolling. Limbs thrashed and flailed, scraping across gravel and down the incline of the rail bed. When it finally stopped, Lydia lay motionless, crumpled in a heap.

She felt pain in every sinew of her body. She tasted blood in her mouth. All of it proved the unlikely truth — that she was still alive. Lydia forced her eyes open. Amid the dust, she saw the train a hundred feet away, climbing the hill. And she saw Alex, leaning on the railing, watching her intently.

Lydia wished she was closer, to see the look on his face. As the top of the train crested the hill, she spit out a mouthful of blood and moved. First an arm underneath, then a shift of a leg. The pain was awful, but using every reserve Lydia did it. In sheer defiance, she stood and stared at Alexander Braun.

CHAPTER 35

The conductor gave his notice: "Winslow, Arizona, ten minutes!"

Braun would be ready. He had already apologized to the steward and, on hearing his side of the story, devised an explanation. He and his fiancée had just suffered their first row, and dear Lydia was presently brooding back in the day coach. She would come around soon.

There had been no alarms raised. Not yet. But Braun had to get off the train — he was running through a minefield. Tommy, the steward — and Lydia. Her perfume still lingered as he stuffed his belongings into his suitcase. The vision came again. Lydia, bloody and battered, standing by the track. *Damn, why can't I shake it?*

It had been a stunning performance. *I had to try and warn you . . . Isn't it obvious? I love you, Alex.* He had listened like a fool as she'd waited for the train to slow, waited for her chance. She had known he wouldn't follow — he had to stay with the train and the papers. A perfectly cunning deduction. Lydia. *Witless, feeble Lydia!* Braun slammed the suitcase shut, furious. But not because she'd gotten the better of him. He knew it was far more serious.

The train drew to a stop in a cloud of steam. Braun saw a station outside. The sign read: WINSLOW ARIZONA ELEVATION: 4,940.

He got off the train and instantly went to work, driving away what had happened. He had to work fast. There were no other trains on the siding — a westbound freight would have been ideal. Outside, he saw a truck carrying rock. He could jump into the bed, but it might be headed anywhere. Echoes from Frau Schumann. *Crowded places are best.* He needed a population center, a place to get lost.

A bus was scheduled to leave in twenty minutes, bound eventually for Los Angeles. He found a timetable and mentally recorded every stop it would make on the way. Braun walked quickly across the street. In a gift shop he found a map of Arizona. Braun studied it against the route he had just memorized. He could not stay on the bus long — the authorities would surely track it down. But he had to leave now, and it seemed the only way.

Braun went back to the station and purchased a ticket all the way through to Los Angeles. He boarded the bus, which was nearly empty, and kept the suitcase close by. He vowed never to let the papers out of his sight again.

When the bus left the station, he closed his eyes. Braun tried to deconstruct everything, tried to make his actuary's appraisal of the events on the train. But the disturbing vision intruded. He saw her hanging outside the railing. He saw her fall to the rocks below. Braun had stood with a torn sleeve in one hand before rushing to the back. He watched Lydia tumble and roll like a rag doll, her body battering down the embankment. His hands had clutched the iron railing with a force that might have bent it. When Lydia finally stopped her twisting, turning plunge, she remained still. Perfectly still.

And then Braun had done the most unimaginable thing. The thing that had absolutely puzzled him ever since. To a God he had never believed in, he'd prayed that Lydia would survive. And when she stood — wobbling, bleeding, but alive — he had felt the most indescribable joy.

A flurry of telephone calls ran between Michael Thatcher, Sargent Cole, and Tomas Jones. The local authorities caught up with the Western Express just outside Flagstaff, Arizona. It was a spot where Route 66 paralleled the rail line. Four police cruisers, the town's full complement, along with five officers frantically waving their arms, were enough to convince the engineer to apply his brakes.

The authorities searched the train for nearly an hour, giving particular interest to one first-class cabin. Interviews with the passengers and rail employees confirmed that a tall, blond man had in fact been on the train, but no one had seen him since Winslow. The officials also noted the absence of a young woman, identified as Lydia Murray, who was supposed to have been on board. Radio calls were made, and the information relayed by wire. The focus of the investigation quickly recentered thirty miles east, back in Winslow.

Seeing their job as done, the Flagstaff police pulled back and stood to watch as the train gathered steam once again. None took notice as a nearly empty Greyhound bus eased behind them on Route 66 and coasted into town.

A trucker carrying a load of hay found Lydia at dusk, limping alongside the road. She told the man her story, which was backed up by her miserable condition, and the driver made best time to Winslow. There, Lydia retold everything to the sheriff, who'd been looking for her. They all tried to guess where Alexander Braun had gone.

At seven that evening, Thatcher arrived at the station. He walked straight over, put his hands on her shoulders, and studied her with clear concern. Lydia understood — she had already been to the mirror. There were scrapes across one side of her face, cuts and bruises scattered all over her body. Her right elbow was severely swollen, but that was at least hidden by the shirt she had on, lent to her by one of the lawmen.

"Good Lord, you've been in another scrap. What happened?"

"I found him, Michael. I found Alex."

He took her by the elbow — the one that didn't hurt — and guided her to a quiet corner. The station was tiny, a wood and plaster square that might have been built a hundred years ago.

There were two officers on duty, both filling out paperwork to explain the day's lively events. Lydia recounted her story, Thatcher taking in every word.

"Damn! I'm sorry, Lydia. I must have arrived at the station in Albuquerque just a few minutes too late."

"I definitely could have used your help. When I saw Alex I didn't know what to do. I'm afraid I acted without thinking. It was terribly impulsive, wasn't it?"

"It was brave."

Lydia thought the word sounded strange. Had it been? Was that what bravery was — impulsiveness in the name of good cause?

"At least you found him," Thatcher continued. "That's more than I've managed in the last week. Tell me, have you talked to your father? He's been worried about you."

"Yes, I already called him. He insisted that I come straight home."

"I see. That's probably for the best."

Best for who? Lydia thought. She had nearly been killed, but she'd finally done something useful. If Alex had managed to leave Albuquerque unseen, he might have been lost forever. Lydia had found him, sent him scrambling.

"I have to tell you about the papers," she said, "the ones I found under his pillow."

"Papers?"

"Yes. I told you I went into his room. There was a stack of papers under his pillow. They were scientific — equations and formulas. On top was a letter addressed to someone called Rainer. That's a German name, isn't it?"

Thatcher nodded, "Usually."

"The letter said the papers were important. It was all about something called the Manhattan Project. Do you know what that is?"

Thatcher's gaze drifted.

"What's wrong?"

"Something I've suspected for a while — but this proves it.

The Manhattan Project is a tremendous undertaking by your government. It's a new weapon, very secret. All along we've been chasing Braun because we considered him a threat to this project. But think about it — sabotage is no use. Germany has lost. And now we know he's met with a German spy in New Mexico."

"That's where the letter and papers came from?"

"Almost certainly. Was this letter signed? Did you see a name?"

Lydia tried to remember, but nothing came. "No, I never got that far."

"So Braun and this agent have somehow stolen information about the project."

"But there's no one to give it to," Lydia said.

"Isn't there?"

"You just said it yourself — Germany is finished."

"Yes," Thatcher rubbed his forehead, "but it could have terrific value. What else can you remember?"

Lydia squeezed her eyes shut.

"Something about a ship making port for a meeting. And that I'm sure about — nine a.m. on July twenty-seventh."

He swiveled his head, and then pointed to a day calendar hanging crookedly on the station wall. "That's next Friday. What else? Where? What was the name of the ship?"

She tried to recall.

"We know when, but without knowing where —"

"Guam!" Lydia spat out.

"Guam? The island? That's in the middle of the Pacific Ocean."

"Is it? So what can we do?"

She watched Thatcher's taught features strain as he considered the options.

"Excuse me, miss," someone said.

Lydia turned. It was one of the deputies. "Yes?"

"We're down to our last car, so I've got to run Ed over to the train depot — he needs to ask a few questions. Normally, I'd lock up, but if you two want to stay that's okay by me."

Lydia looked at Thatcher, who said, "We don't have anywhere to go at the moment, so if you don't mind we'll stay."

"No problem," he said, putting on his gun belt. "I'll be back in twenty minutes." The two men left.

Before she and Thatcher could resume their conversation, the telephone rang. They looked at one another. Lydia shrugged and picked up the handset.

"Winslow Sheriff's Department," she said.

"Hello, I need to speak to whoever's in charge."

Lydia thought the voice sounded vaguely familiar. Then it came.

"This is Tomas Jones, FBI. It's quite urgent."

"Um . . . one minute, sir."

She held the phone to her chest, and her eyes went wide. "It's him!" she whispered harshly.

"Who?" Thatcher mouthed.

"Jones! He wants to talk to the sheriff."

Thatcher frowned, then said quietly, "Tell him the sheriff just left, but you'll take a message." He put an ear next to hers so they could both hear.

"I'm afraid he just left, sir. May I take a message?"

"Where is he?"

"Um —"

Thatcher fumbled across the desk for a pencil and scribbled — *Looking for German spy.*

Lydia caught up. "He's out looking for a German spy."

"Right. Any luck yet?"

Thatcher shook his head, then wrote — *And you?*

Lydia nodded. "No, sir. Does the FBI have any information about the suspect I should pass along to the sheriff?"

"No. We're looking, but nothing yet. I have a pair of men headed your way from Phoenix — they should arrive soon. Have the sheriff give them whatever they need so we can find this guy once and for all."

"Of course, sir."

"There's a young woman, Lydia Murray. I understand you have her at the station?"

Lydia nearly giggled. "Yes, she's right here." She immediately regretted the answer, realizing that Jones might ask to speak to her. Lydia was contemplating a change of voice when Jones let her off the hook.

"Good. Keep track of her. Her father is a bigwig back East — he's coming out to collect her."

"Okay."

"Oh, and one more thing. There's an Englishman, a Major Michael Thatcher — has he turned up there?"

"Not that I know of, Mr. Jones."

"Well if he does, arrest him. Immigration charges — whatever the sheriff can come up with. We want him."

"Is he a spy too?" Lydia prodded mischievously.

"No, just a danged pain in the ass."

Before hanging up, Jones gave a number where he could be reached.

"All right, Mr. Jones, I'll have the sheriff get in touch if we find anything. Good-bye."

Lydia put the phone to the cradle and looked at Thatcher. She saw a slight curl at the corners of his mouth. They burst out laughing at the same time. Lydia bent at the waist, the laughter aggravating her pain, but there was nothing she could do. After all that had happened it felt incredibly good.

She said, "I can't believe I just did that."

He wore a satisfied smile. "You should do it more often."

"Lie to the FBI?"

"No, laugh."

She sighed. "I used to do it a lot. But lately —" Lydia paused, not able to finish the thought. She began to ponder what would happen next. "My father is on the way, Michael. He'll tell me I've had my little adventure, and now it's time to go home."

He looked at her pensively. Lydia knew what he was thinking.

"Of course, I have my passport," she said. "I never travel without it."

"Nor do I," he replied. "What we really need is transportation. I think it's time I put through a call to my boss in England."

Thirty minutes later, the sheriff arrived to find two FBI men outside his station. They all went inside and found a note tacked to the wall by his desk.

Please forward to Tomas Jones, FBI.
Braun headed to meet with unknown ship
making port in Guam on July 27, 9:00 a.m.
See you there.
                    Michael Thatcher, Pain in the Ass

CHAPTER 36

The Russian Consulate in San Francisco was a nondescript affair, its modest Victorian façade blending nicely among a row of similar buildings. Surrounded by a fence, the narrow entrance was just wide enough for a pathway that could be flanked by a pair of guards.

The two on duty had every reason to be happy young men — happy to have spent the war battling the menace of capitalism in northern California, as opposed to the Wehrmacht on the European front. Here, the food was plentiful, the weather agreeable, and the guards had little to do beyond scheming with regard to how they could extend their assignments.

That being the case, as the two stood with rifles hung loosely over their shoulders, one was chatting up the ambassador's daughter. She was a plump cow who might have been doomed to spinsterdom if not for her father's lofty position. The other soldier had his nose buried in a Russian-to-English dictionary. He gave particular attention to certain vital words — girl, movie, beer, bed — along with a few verbs to encourage the sequence. Neither man saw the brick coming.

It slid across the sidewalk at considerable speed, hit a rut, and tumbled the last few yards, coming to rest directly at the feet of the language student. He was surprised enough to lower his book, but not so much as to grip his Kalashnikov which was, in fact, not even loaded. He scanned the busy sidewalk just outside the gate. People were scurrying about, and two cars had just passed — a sedan in one direction and a taxi in the other. He first thought that it was an insult of sorts, a pathetic little political statement. He hadn't seen much of it in his two years here, but Russia and America were becoming less allied and more estranged with each passing day. He looked to his partner, who hadn't even noticed.

"Andrei!"

The other man broke away from his shmoozing.

"What?"

"Look! Someone just threw this at us!" He pointed to the brick.

"What do you mean?"

The student picked it up. Strangely, an envelope was wrapped around the brick, secured with rubber bands. It was addressed in English: The Consul General. These words he had been required to learn some time ago.

His partner came over and looked at the brick, then out to the street. The ambassador's daughter got involved next. With one look, she snatched it away.

"Give me that, you idiots! It might be important."

She disappeared into the embassy, leaving the two guards staring at each other in her wake. They said it in English, and in unison.

"*Bitch.*"

Pavel Kovalenko sat at his desk feeling troubled. It was his Russian nature to be a pessimist, but the more he pondered his future, the more depressed he became. Officially, he was the Russian Consulate's chargé d'affaires, a diplomatically useful title that masked his true position — Kovalenko was the head local officer of The People's Commissariat of Internal Affairs, better known in the west as the NKVD. It was Russia's internal security service, tasked to keep a watchful eye over every military unit and diplomatic outpost in the world. Or as Stalin was fond of saying, "Even the purest of revolutions require counsel."

Kovalenko was a colonel, a recent promotion that his wife had begged him to decline. As if there had been a choice. He had long worked under the illusion that the higher up one rose in an organization, the more secure life would be. Perhaps in America, he thought, but not in the People's Commissariat. Here, each promotion brought greater responsibility, but also greater uncertainty. Screwups at this level met a very unkind end, and war had only magnified the stress. Still, Kovalenko reckoned, things could be worse. There were hundreds of NKVD colonels right now enduring far less desirable circumstances — harassing the Red Army, busting heads in Gulags.

Pushing the work on his desk away, he looked out the window. It framed a wonderful view of the Presidio. Kovalenko liked America. He often imagined that he might have gone far in this country. Here, he would have been a businessman, the Ford Motor Company, perhaps. As it was, Kovalenko remained, in best terms, a bureaucrat. He sighed, and decided he needed something. What would a capitalist magnate do?

"Irina! Coffee!" he bellowed through the door to his secretary.

She acknowledged the request.

"And no cream," he added, looking down at his waistline. It seemed like he was finding a new notch on his belt each week. Kovalenko was a broad man, strapping in his younger days — but the straps had begun to loosen at a disturbing pace. Nearing fifty, the years had turned against him, his hair coming full gray, framing a wide Slavic face that had recently acquired jowls. It was all related to the stress of the job, he decided.

These were his weary thoughts when Katya, the ambassador's daughter, burst in. The girl was a pain in the ass, but smart enough to know the true order of things — it was not her father, but Kovalenko who ran this little outpost. She slammed a brick onto his desk theatrically.

Kovalenko saw the attached envelope, addressed to the counsel general. "Where did this come from?" he demanded.

"Someone just threw it at our guards." Katya then smiled wryly. "Unfortunately, they missed."

Kovalenko picked it up, slid off two rubber bands, and weighed the envelope in his hand. It seemed rather heavy. He started to open it, but then saw Katya looking on eagerly. He nodded sharply to the door, shooing her away. With a pout, she waddled off and disappeared.

Kovalenko opened the envelope. Inside were ten pages, all in English, the same meticulous, handwritten script. Kovalenko's English was reasonably good, but much of what he saw was scientific jargon, symbols and equations. On the last page was a cryptic message. *Embarcadero, South end. One person only. 21 July, 3:00 p.m.*

Two days from now, Kovalenko thought. Someone was giving him time. Time to send this information, whatever it was, to a higher level. He read through it all once more, but the science escaped him. Perhaps a professor from one of the universities, he reckoned, trying to sell his research. Or give it away — there were any number of communists in the local academic community. At any rate, it might be important. There was only one thing to do.

He wrote a short, concise statement regarding how the papers had arrived at the consulate. Kovalenko then put it all into a folder. He trundled downstairs to the basement communications room. The officer on duty, a new woman, was sound asleep. She had probably been here all night. It struck him that she was not unattractive — his wife had been in Moscow for the last six months. Never one to miss an opportunity, he gently rubbed her back. "Wake up, dear."

She did. "Um . . . sir, I'm sorry. I was —"

"It's all right. Take these papers. There are formulas and diagrams, but encode as much as you can, then send it to headquarters."

Straightening up, she looked over it. "There are ten or twelve pages here. It will take —"

"Whatever it takes, please do it!" he ordered, not allowing his libido to sidetrack what had to be done. "And secure it in the safe when you are finished."

He left the room feeling lighter. It occurred to him that the entire matter might be a test. Headquarters relished that kind of thing. If so, everything had been done squarely by the book. Pavel Kovalenko had nothing to worry about.

A soft tropical breeze blew across Karl Heinrich's nearly bald head as he rode in the Navy skiff across Pearl Harbor. Things were already getting better, he thought. He'd only been in Hawaii one day, yet for the first time in a year his skin was not cracked from dryness.

In the distance, moored just off Ford Island, was the USS *Indianapolis*. Heinrich had seen her pull into port this morning, a brute among brutes. But now, as he closed in, she looked even bigger, her gray hull looming like a sleek mountain against the backdrop of the country's biggest debacle.

To Americans, including the scientists at Los Alamos, it was still the war cry: *"Remember Pearl Harbor!"* Heinrich had expected to see Armageddon, a junkyard of scuttled relics. *Arizona* and *Utah* remained, but there were few other telltales of that day nearly four years ago. Now, the place buzzed with activity — ships, aircraft, and soldiers everywhere. Pearl was back in business, a through point for the tools of America's war machine. And Heinrich knew there was no bigger tool in the box than the sledgehammer that lay in two containers on the ship in front of him — 20,000 kilotons. That was the new estimate for Little Boy.

Heinrich had stayed in New Mexico for two days after the Trinity test. Information was analyzed, calculations made. The next atomic blast would be the one that counted, the one the world would see, and the results of Trinity had to be incorporated to maximize every effect. He carried with him the final guidance for the team that would assemble the bomb on Tinian. The precise altitude for fusing — 580 meters. Options for delivery geometry, with respect to terrain and time of day. Fine tuning,

Heinrich thought of it, as one would a radio station that suffered heavy static — only with far more barbaric results. These new figures were in the suitcase chained to his wrist. The same suitcase that held a massive compilation of secrets regarding the entire program.

The vision of the Trinity test was still fixed in his mind. Heinrich had watched the incredible success from one of the observation bunkers. After his initial shock, a strange corollary had come to mind. He remembered, perhaps a year ago, seeing a newsreel about Germany's V-1 rocket. The film had showed the rocket blasting skyward, then broke away to show Hitler as he reveled in the spectacle. The Führer had clasped his hands together in joy, delighted at the new strength his scientists had given him. *If only he could have witnessed*, Heinrich imagined, *the power that I will give the Fatherland.*

The skiff pulled alongside *Indianapolis*, coming to rest at a boarding platform. Dull gray armor seemed to rise straight to the sky. Yet while the ship had appeared sleek and modern from a distance, up close *Indianapolis* showed her scars. Fittings above the waterline spewed brown water, staining the gray steel. Rust was evident along joints and creases, and the hull itself carried any number of dents and lesions. She had been to the battles.

Heinrich spotted a familiar face from Los Alamos on the boarding platform. Major Lynn, U.S. Army, had been placed in charge of security for the voyage.

"Hello, Dr. Heinrich," he called.

Heinrich waved. "Hello, Major."

Lynn took Heinrich's second bag, containing his personal effects, as the scientist clambered awkwardly over a gangplank, the heavier case clutched to his chest.

"Welcome aboard. How was your trip?"

"Oh, fine," Heinrich said. "And yours? The crossing has been uneventful?"

"A little weather, but nothing severe." Lynn guided him to a passageway. "Let's get you bivouacked."

Lynn led through a maze of passageways under the ship's

stern quarter. Heinrich had never been on such a large vessel, and he marveled at the complexity of it all. Over the narrow corridor, dim lights were encased in protective frames of steel wire, providing light in muted economy. Ventilation ducts and bundles of wires snaked across the ceiling. Every so often he was forced to step up and through an oval steel doorway. He guessed that these were the watertight doors he had always heard about, used to separate the compartments if sections of the ship began to flood. The thought was discomforting, and for the first time Heinrich felt a pang of fear not related to his being a spy — he was about to enter a war zone.

"Are our quarters higher up?" he asked.

Lynn spoke over his shoulder, "Yep. We're up in captain's country. That's what they call it around here. But first I want to show you something."

Lynn's feet clomped across the hard steel floor as he navigated stark, utilitarian passageways. He paused at an intersection, looked left and right, and then scratched his head.

"What is it?" Heinrich asked.

"Damn Navy," he said in a low voice. "They don't put up signs to tell you which way is which. I've never been on this deck before."

An enlisted man came by. "Can I help you, sir?"

Lynn said, "No, no thanks." After the navy man was gone he turned to Heinrich and said, "I'll figure it out."

Heinrich made a note of this. The ship was huge, complex. The moment might come when he would need to know his way around. He'd have to find some kind of diagram. Or, if necessary, he would explore and make his own — the physicist had solved far more complex problems in his time.

Lynn climbed a staircase and eased through another watertight door. Heinrich followed awkwardly, the heavy case clattering from side to side as he went up. At the top he found Lynn in a wider passageway.

"*Indy* is the flagship of the Fifth Fleet," the American explained. "This is the Flag Staff Quarters, although they're not in residence. We're on our own for this cruise." He led to a door labeled: FLAG LIEUTENANT. Two large men in uniform — Heinrich thought they might be Marines — were standing watch. They came to attention as Major Lynn approached.

"At ease, boys. This is Dr. Heinrich. He's one of the scientists who helped build this thing. I'd like to let him in for a minute."

One of the guards became spokesman, "All right, sir. But you'll have to escort him. Those are our orders. Nobody goes in without you."

"Sure." Lynn led the way through the door.

Heinrich followed. He smiled and nodded at the guards, but said nothing as he passed. He had learned long ago to keep quiet in the presence of such men. His accent was severe, and while his peers at Los Alamos accepted his nationality freely, not all Americans were so accepting.

The room inside was small, but looked larger because everything had been stripped out. It was simply a rectangular space, a few fasteners hanging from the walls to suggest where a bunk or desk might have been mounted. There was, in fact, only one thing in the entire room — a lead bucket, roughly two feet high, and slightly less in circumference. It was strapped securely to anchor points in the floor. Lynn parked at the door.

Heinrich went closer to the bucket. He knew what was inside. It was the stack — nine uranium rings, each 6.25 inches in diameter, with a 4-inch hole in the center, all held in a 7-inch high canister.

The heavy lid was free, no locks to secure it in place. He looked over his shoulder at Major Lynn. "May I?"

"You helped make it. But are you sure it's okay — I mean with the radiation and all?"

"Uranium 235 has a long half-life, Major, which means the rate of decay is extremely slow. Brief exposures are quite acceptable."

The officer shrugged, clearly not understanding, but accepting the word of a scientist. Heinrich put his suitcase on the floor and lifted the thick lid slowly, as if expecting a demon to jump out. Inside he saw it — so simple and small, a stack of well-machined metal rings. Nothing to suggest the fireball of hell he had seen at the Trinity test. The ridiculous notion came to his head that he should take it, stuff it in his suitcase. For ten seconds he could feel like the most powerful man in the world. Heinrich replaced the bucket's lead top. *No*, he thought with satisfaction, *I am already that.*

Lynn led Heinrich to his quarters.

When they arrived, Heinrich thanked him. "It was kind of you to allow that."

"No problem, but it was a one-time deal. Your two colleagues have been all over it, but I thought you should at least get one look, Dr. Heinrich. I know how hard you worked."

"You don't know the half of it."

"The other crate, the big one, is up in a hangar on deck. Of course, that one's not much to look at — just a bunch of hardware and wires."

"Indeed."

"Oh, your buddies wanted me to pass along that they'd meet you in the officer's mess at five."

Price and Hudson, both engineers, had escorted the components all the way from Los Alamos. "I will be there," Heinrich said.

"We've had a safe installed in your room. You can keep your papers there. Set the combination to whatever you like — the instructions are on top."

Heinrich saw the industrial gray steel box bolted to the floor in a corner. "Yes, that is good." *Very good.*

Twenty minutes later Karl Heinrich was settled. He stretched out on his bunk and stared accusingly at the vent in the ceiling. Little, if any, air was circulating. The room was hot and uncomfortable, and he felt his clothes already sticking to his skin. Heinrich sighed. It was a small thing. He had to appreciate the rest — everything was going according to plan. Perfectly.

He began to drift off, feeling the toll of his travels. Heinrich dreamed about of the coolness of Bavaria, the crispness of summer in the mountains. *Like winter in Argentina . . .*

*   *   *

The message to the Russian Consulate came that morning:

KEEP MEETING AT EMBARCADERO. NOTHING CAN
TAKE HIGHER PRIORITY. YOU ARE AUTHORIZED TO
OFFER ANYTHING TO RECRUIT THIS CONTACT.
COMRADE KOVALENKO, YOU WILL BE HELD PER-
SONALLY RESPONSIBLE FOR SUCCESS OR FAILURE.

Pavel Kovalenko read it only once. He then headed straight
to his liquor cabinet.

CHAPTER 37

Braun watched the Russian pace nervously across the heavy wooden dock at the head of Pier 1. The Embarcadero was busy. Travelers and office workers scurried in and out of the adjacent Ferry Building. Others strolled more casually, tourists and sight-seers enjoying the cool, sun drenched afternoon.

It was 3:15, well past the instructed rendezvous time. He saw the man take a flask from his jacket and, none too discretely, take a hard swallow. Braun knew what he was thinking — *I don't even know who I'm looking for.*

He had been watching the consulate for two days. A small operation, it didn't take long to deduce by the reactions of the guards who was in charge. He had found out the name, Koval-enko, and Braun supposed he was NKVD, though it really wasn't important. He was a marshmallow of a man, at least fifty years old, probably fifty-five. And not very fit — Braun had watched him become winded climbing the hill to the consulate. He had the aspect of a civil servant, not a soldier — Braun suspected he could have found either, and he registered this as a positive.

Today, Kovalenko was not alone. He had brought help, two men who looked in far better shape. At 3:20, Braun decided it was time. He approached from behind, masked by a threesome of chattering women.

Braun spoke in Russian, "Hello, Kovalenko."

Kovalenko turned, tension deep in his soft veneer.

"Hello," he replied.

Up close the man looked even older than Braun had supposed. His cheeks were florid, the eyes bloodshot. He looked like he hadn't slept well. Braun held out an arm, suggesting a stroll. Kovalenko fell in at his side, and Braun set a casual pace. He switched to English, "My Russian is passable, but I think we should use English. Others will pass near. Also, it is important that we have no misunderstandings."

"Of course," Kovalenko replied, his voice surprisingly thin and reedy for such a big man.

"Tell your men to leave."

Kovalenko stuttered, "What do you mean?"

"The one by the Ferry Building, and the other at the end of Market Street. Give them a nod, whatever it takes. Make them go away."

The Russian hesitated.

"Do it now or I will leave!" Braun insisted.

Kovalenko turned and stared obviously at each of his men, shooing them away with a wave of his arm. They looked mystified, so he amplified the effort. The two joined up and, like a pair of hunting dogs with their tails between their legs, disappeared to a side street.

"Now, come with me," Braun said. He took Kovalenko by the elbow and guided him to a waiting taxi.

"Where are we going?" Kovalenko asked, concern clear in his voice.

Braun pushed slightly to get him into the cab. The driver started off—he already had his instructions. Braun looked at the Russian and smiled. "You are going to buy me dinner."

Ten minutes later they walked into Roman's, a classically overpriced Italian restaurant.

Braun addressed the maître d', "You have a table reserved for Kovalenko."

The man nodded and guided them through a nearly empty

dining room. They were seated three tables away from the nearest company. Once free of the maître d', Braun said, "There will not be a crowd for at least two hours. I selected the time of day and the restaurant so that we might speak freely."

Kovalenko was more comfortable now. He said, "How do you know my name?"

"I've been following you for some time. I know your name, where you live, and I know about that little blond tart you see regularly." Braun had, in fact, only seen her once, but it was a reasonable deduction.

Kovalenko kept an even keel. "And you are?"

"Alex will do."

"American?"

"My nationality is a complex thing. And not relevant."

"But you are here to tell me what is?"

"Have you reviewed the documents I sent?"

"Sent?" The Russian grinned. "You make it sound like a postal delivery."

"The purpose was served."

"I passed them on to higher authorities."

"And?"

"And we are interested in what you present. I've been told that if you have as much information as you claim, we can pay handsomely for it."

The waiter approached with menus. Braun said, "I will put this to a test." He addressed the waiter, "Barolo, 1939." The waiter nodded and disappeared.

"Nineteen dollars," Braun said.

Kovalenko frowned. "I am trying to remember how much I have in my wallet." He gave a Slavic shrug. "Perhaps we should enjoy a good meal first. We can talk business afterward."

"Why not?"

Braun ordered veal, Kovalenko, the duck. The two made small talk, casual banter about the future of Russia and Europe, and how the Americans would pursue the end of the Pacific war. The meal was superb, though Braun did not enjoy it as much as he might have. Kovalenko was soft, a bureaucrat, but such men could be thick with guile — he would have to keep his guard. Afterward, Braun took a brandy. Kovalenko kept a cigarette and a Scotch in constant play. It was the Russian who eventually drifted to the point.

"The information you are offering — it is scientific in nature. I suspect you are not a scientist. Therefore, shall I assume you've stolen it?"

Braun paused, deciding how much to give. "There is another man. He is deeply involved in this American project. A spy."

"For whom?"

"Germany."

"*Germany?*"

"And you should know that he still believes his work will go to the Nazis."

Kovalenko scoffed. "Does he not read the papers? Does he not have eyes and ears?"

"I've convinced him that the German Reich is still functioning — only displaced."

Kovalenko chuckled and lifted a tumbler to his lips.

Braun warned, "He is not a stupid man, I assure you — only blinded by the same hatred that took so many Germans down Hitler's foolish road."

"What is his name?"

"That I will keep to myself."

"And your friend, this Nazi, he holds the information now?"

Braun explained how Heinrich kept a suitcase jammed with thousands of documents.

"He works with you — why? Does he think you are a Nazi as well?"

"Something like that. We are to meet next week. He is traveling on a ship, the USS *Indianapolis*."

"And you wish us to take over this ship?" Kovalenko guessed.

Braun's eyes glazed over. He was disappointed in the Russian. "No. It's a heavy cruiser, you — " he held back the last word.

Nothing would be gained by antagonizing. "I am to rendezvous with him on the island of Guam. And since I am the only one he will trust, I must meet him alone. Our bargain will be this — I keep the meeting, dispose of him, and deliver the documents to you."

Kovalenko paled slightly. "And he trusts you enough to —"

"I agree!" Braun interrupted loudly as the waiter approached. He kept blathering in the overt voice of a man who'd tipped one more drink than he was accustomed to, "The Russians alone would never have been a match for Hitler's Wehrmacht!"

The waiter left the check discreetly in the middle of the table, then shuffled away. Braun pushed it toward Kovalenko.

The Russian reached for his wallet. "And I suppose you have a price in mind for your work?"

"One million U.S. dollars — half tomorrow."

The Russian laughed freely for the first time, still chuckling as he pulled cash from his wallet. "You Americans do have an excellent . . . how do they say it . . . sense of humor!"

The two engaged eyes and Kovalenko's smile evaporated. He said, "Surely you cannot be serious! My superiors —"

"Your superiors," Braun cut in, "will agree without reservation. My information can save them a thousand times as much. The fee is absolutely nonnegotiable. I have no affinity for mother Russia. Other countries would easily recognize the value of what I offer." Braun hadn't really considered it, but he suspected there was enough truth in the threat to make it stick. He dictated his final instructions.

"I will deal only with you. Meet me tomorrow, same place, same time, and bring half the fee. If I spot anyone else this time, you will never see me again. Wait ten minutes before you leave." Braun got up and walked away.

Kovalenko sat still. He watched the man he knew as Alex move smoothly to the door. A million dollars, he thought miserably. How could he put forward such an offer to headquarters? They would be livid. Kovalenko wondered how high this fiasco had already gone in the NKVD. Had the chief of the American zone seen it yet? Moscow was clearly interested in Alex's information. The cable had authorized Kovalenko to offer anything — but they could never have imagined such madness. He wished the stupid brick had never come to him. He wished he was one of the colonels breaking heads in a dark corner of Lubyanka's basement. If he wasn't careful, Kovalenko knew he could soon be on the other end of it.

And it wasn't only his superiors who worried him. He wanted nothing to do with Alex, or whatever his name really was. Kovalenko was a good judge of men. He had risen far in a cut-throat organization, and it was largely thanks to his ability to assess people. Thieves and liars, police and thinkers — Kovalenko thrived on the accuracy of his instincts. From the initial letter, he thought this contact might be a harmless college professor wanting to support the Communist cause. But at the Embarcadero, Kovalenko had quickly decided otherwise. It was the way Alex moved, the way he eyed Dmitri and Sergei.

Alex was a killer. Of this, Kovalenko was sure.

CHAPTER 38

"What kind of airplane is it?" Lydia asked as she and Thatcher walked across the cement parking apron.

The big silver transport ahead of them was one of dozens in a row that looked exactly the same. The only thing to distinguish this particular craft was the markings on the tail — it was the only one without the star emblem of the U.S. Army Air Force.

Thatcher said, "It's a C-47. The Americans have been building them by the thousands."

"And this one's Australian?"

"Yes."

A young man in greasy coveralls — the loadmaster, Thatcher had explained — greeted them at the back stairs."

"G'day. So you're the two that need a lift?"

"Yes," Thatcher replied. "We'll try to stay out of your way."

"Not to worry," the airman said, "make yourselves comfortable."

Thatcher climbed up first. Lydia followed, and as she did, she felt the Australian's eyes on her — ogling like the boys had in high school. She supposed that's where he'd been not long ago.

Inside there was barely room to move. Wooden crates were piled high, matching the contour of the ceiling. They were all stenciled with labels — welding torches, powdered milk, lightbulbs, and whiskey. The larger crates were tied down, secured to the floor and walls, while the smaller boxes sat wedged in gaps. Altogether, Lydia imagined it must weigh tons.

She followed Thatcher forward, having to turn sideways to squeeze through gaps in the mountain of cargo. Just behind the flight deck, a pair of webbed bench seats were situated on each side. He dropped his suitcase to the metal floor. "I should go introduce myself to the pilots."

They had tried to find a commercial flight to Guam, but there were none. The only option was military transport, and Thatcher had somehow gotten approval to drag her along. He had a way of doing that, she'd noticed, a knack for getting what he wanted. Lydia took a seat on the rickety bench. It was ridiculously uncomfortable. *If father could see me now.*

Thatcher came back and took a seat beside her, settling in with ease.

"You're used to this kind of thing, aren't you?"

"Well, yes. I suppose so. Have you flown before?"

"Twice. But it was a better air line than this. I didn't much like that purser."

He laughed. "I'm afraid it will take at least three of these flights to get us to Guam. Can you manage it?"

"I might come to like it, actually. So your boss, Colonel Ainsley, arranged it?"

"Reluctantly. His first inclination was to bring me back to England. But when I told him about all that's happened, Roger had no choice. He insisted I go to Guam. As far as getting the flight, we knew the Americans wouldn't help and the RAF had nothing passing through. The Aussie's were our best bet. He called in an old favor."

"A side advantage of Colonial rule?"

"Well — Australia. I think Roger liked that. It's where we've always sent our undesirables. Although with any luck we won't have to go that far. I think there's a good chance we can find a shortcut along the way."

"Did you tell the colonel I was going with you?"

"No. Did you tell your father?"

"Of course not. He thinks I'm on a flight headed back East right now."

The engines whined and spat as they spun to life.

"It's very loud," Lydia shouted, her hands over her ears.

"Wait until we take off!"

Indeed, engine noise seemed to shake the entire plane as it careened down the runway. The boxes and crates teetered precariously, straining against tie-down straps. Without them, Lydia was sure they'd have been crushed. The young loadmaster was slouched on the opposite bench, grinning, but looking very tired, his head nodding to one side.

The noise lessened once they were in the air. Thatcher unstrapped their seat belts and pulled Lydia to a window. Below, she could see Los Angeles, an impossible maze of concrete and metal. Soon, the city drifted away and there was nothing beneath but the deep blue Pacific.

"We'll be seeing a lot of that," Thatcher remarked.

"And so will Alex," Lydia found herself saying.

"Yes. He might be looking at the very same view right now."

"Do you really think he has a chance, Michael? We know where and when to look for him. The FBI are involved, aren't they?"

"According to your father, Jones has been given everything. He'll have to pursue it now. Of course, he's always seen Alex as a direct threat — you know, a saboteur. But you proved it on the train, Lydia — he's carrying information on the Manhattan Project."

Lydia felt a chill. Edward, she thought. The flight instructor, Mitchell. And the poor old Indian who'd gone to help after Alex's plane had crashed. She wondered how many others there had been. "Do you think we can stop him?"

There was no answer, but she felt a comforting hand on her tense shoulders. It was just what her father would have done. She looked appreciatively at Thatcher, who was pretending to look out the window.

"Michael," she said, "what was your wife's name?"

He turned toward her, clearly surprised by the question. "Madeline."

"Madeline," she repeated. "What a lovely name." Lydia turned back to the window and smiled.

Kovalenko strode past his secretary, heading toward his office.

Irina jumped up. "Sir, wait!"

Kovalenko paused. Then he heard voices behind his door.

"In your office —" she began.

"No one is allowed there in my absence!" He burst inside. "What's the meaning of —" Kovalenko went pale. Standing behind his desk was a man he recognized instantly. Bald, short, puffy lips — and a viper's eyes behind pince-nez glasses. Lavrenti Beria. Head of the People's Commissariat of Internal Affairs, or NKVD. After Joseph Stalin, the second most powerful man in Russia.

"C . . . Comrade Beria. What a surprise."

Beria's eyes drifted toward him, and Kovalenko suddenly felt cold, as if a Siberian wind had swept into the room. There were two other men — nondescript bodyguards or aides. Neither said a word.

Beria smiled, or tried to. "Comrade Kovalenko. I don't believe we have met."

Actually Kovalenko had seen Beria once before, at a speech he had given to a group of Foreign Service NKVD officers. Kovalenko remembered him as being quite lively and vibrant. Clearly, the war had taken a toll. Beria had gained weight, and his skin held a gray, deathly pallor.

"It is an honor," Kovalenko prattled, "I did not know you were in America."

"Nor do the Americans," Beria said, his smile broadening. "I came here directly from Germany, the Potsdam Conference."

Kovalenko had read about it in the papers. Stalin, Churchill, and Truman doling out the world like poker players splitting a pot. "You have come a long way, then."

"I have a good reason." Beria pushed a chair noisily across the hardwood floor. "Please, Kovalenko, make yourself comfortable."

Kovalenko sat.

Beria stuck his head out the door toward Irina and asked very politely for tea. He became more animated, his tone unnervingly pleasant. "It has come to my attention that your consulate was approached by a man who has offered to sell a collection of scientific papers."

"Yes, I met with him only an hour ago."

"Good, good. You kept the meeting."

"Of course."

"And you were wise to send this matter immediately to higher authorities."

Kovalenko did not feel wise. If he had known the papers were going to bring Lavrenti Beria to his office, he would have run to the Golden Gate Bridge and thrown them straight into the ocean.

Beria leaned against Kovalenko's desk, his backside up against the nameplate. "Do you know what this involves?"

"Not really. We did not talk about the subject matter. I was only following my instructions to facilitate the exchange." In a moment Kovalenko would later look back on with pride, he undertook a detailed, lucid account of his meeting with Alex. When he finished, Beria exchanged a look with one of his silent underlings.

Beria said, "This man told you that he has *thousands* of pages of information?"

"Yes. He said it covered every aspect of an American project of some sort."

A knock came at the door. Irina brought in the tea. She was as white as fresh snow. Beria poured two cups and handed one to Kovalenko, who could only think — *Vodka, that's what I need.*

"Kovalenko, allow me to explain." Beria's voice assumed a lyrical tone, as if reading a bedtime story to a child. "In the days immediately after the fall of Berlin, our Red Army brothers captured a German in Austria. He was taken into custody and questioned, but it took many weeks to discover his true identity. Does the name Hans Gruber mean anything to you?"

"He was in the SD, was he not?"

"Yes! Very good. He was a colonel, a senior man in the Operations Directorate. Once we realized this, he was brought to Moscow, to Lubyanka. Unfortunately, our hand of persuasion was — a bit too heavy. He expired." Beria said this as if talking about a loaf of bread that had turn moldy. "This was two weeks ago. In his last hours, however, Gruber did provide some intriguing information. It seems that the Germans were able to insert a spy into a very secret American weapons project."

"The friend that Alex told me about?" Kovalenko managed.

Beria looked pleased. "Perhaps, perhaps not." He put down his tea and walked slowly toward the window. "But there is a way for me to find out. So tomorrow, I will keep the meeting with Alex."

"You? But with all respect, Alex was very specific that only I should come."

Kovalenko saw Beria's head cock slightly to one side. *Dear God*, he thought, *what am I saying?* "Of course —"

Beria cut him off with a raised hand. "You should know something else, Kovalenko." His voice was sharper now, brittle. "When I was in Potsdam, with Stalin, word came that the Americans have tested this new weapon with great success." Beria turned toward him, his face now altogether different. The eyes were cold and void, and the veins at his temple spidered darkly. Yet somehow Kovalenko had the impression Beria was not addressing him, but rather talking to himself, airing his frustration. "When Stalin heard of this, he went mad. I tell you, Kovalenko, I have stood by him through a revolution and a war — a war that has cost over twenty million of our countrymen their lives — and never, *never* have I seen him so angry. There was indeed a moment when I feared for my own life."

Beria's underlings had receded to the corners, perhaps having sensed the impending storm. Kovalenko held motionless, his hands gripping the arms of the chair like a man about to fall off a cliff. He knew that Beria himself, as head of the NKVD, was responsible for taking at least ten million lives during the revolution. The consequence of one more — Kovalenko's, perhaps — could not be more trivial.

"You see, Kovalenko," Beria continued, "we are at a very critical juncture in the path of our world. The war is nearly done, and the winners are dividing the spoils." He then spoke as if quoting holy verse, "Whoever has this new weapon, this power, will dictate to the rest."

The head of the NKVD then calmed, his eruption over. He looked directly at Kovalenko, and said, "So here is what we will do —"

CHAPTER 39

The Embarcadero was less busy. A cool rain and vigorous wind had driven away the casual traffic, leaving the docks and sidewalks to carry only the business of the day. Seagulls sat hunched on pilings, their beaks tucked into their chests. Braun did much the same as he stood in a heavy overcoat and watched Kovalenko from a distance. He did not like what he saw.

The Russian had been right on time, loitering at the same spot they'd met yesterday. But twenty yards away two new men, replacements for Sergei and Dmitri, were blatantly obvious. Even worse, another man had joined them, a short, stubby man in an overcoat who, in spite of his build, seemed strangely agile. The only verse of good news was that this new man carried a briefcase.

Standing near a canvas awning that fronted a busy hotel, Braun considered his options. He could wait, but the extras would not go away. The Russians were presenting not a choice, but an ultimatum — show up if you want, but we are in charge. Braun decided he had to go forward. But he would meet intimidation with intimidation.

He walked briskly across the street and made a beeline to Kovalenko. The Russian saw him coming and forced a nervous smile. Braun spit out the first words.

"Did you not understand?" he said combatively. "You were to come alone!"

Kovalenko held up his palms, and spoke in a plaintive whisper. "I had no choice." He nodded to a bench where the new man was now seated. The bodyguards had backed off — out of earshot from the bench, but close enough to help if needed. Kovalenko hissed, "Do you have any idea who that is?"

Braun took a good look at the man on the bench. There was something vaguely familiar, but no name came to mind. "No. Should I?"

"It is Lavrenti Beria, head of the NKVD."

Braun reset his eyes on the man. He had seen a few pictures of Beria, usually standing at the shoulder of Stalin himself. *Jesus,* he thought, *it is him.* "Why is he here?" Braun demanded.

"He wants to talk to you, of course." Kovalenko turned and simply walked away.

Lavrenti Beria smiled and moved to one side of the bench, making plenty of room. Braun looked across the Embarcadero. Even in the drizzle, there were people milling about. They would not try to snatch him away — not here. Braun walked directly to the bench.

Beria spoke in heavily accented English as Braun approached, his voice light, almost glib, "Alex, my name is —"

"I know who you are," Braun said, even more casually. He might have been meeting a new relative at a wedding — not the man who, by all reliable accounts, was one of the most notorious mass murderers the world had known, right up with Hitler and Himmler themselves. Braun felt himself being weighed, and he continued, "The question is, old man, why are you sitting on a park bench in the rain — in America?"

Beria rose to the challenge and bantered back, "Comrade Kovalenko is efficient, but I thought that my being here would impress upon you the importance of our work."

"Our work? The importance of our work will be most clear if you are carrying a half million U.S. dollars in that briefcase."

Beria gave the case at his feet a pat. "Three hundred thousand — not an easy thing on short notice, but I believe it shows our sincere interest. The rest will come, you have my word. But, of course, there are requirements. Please —" he gestured to the bench.

Braun sat slowly. The number had distracted him. It was only a fraction of what he'd asked for, yet the thought of being so close to such a massive sum made his head swirl. He tried to keep his wits. "Requirements?"

Beria waxed, "There is a saying where I come from — 'One does not always swim in waters of one's own choosing.'"

"Are all Russians poets?"

Beria's dead, gray lips curled up at the corners. "Perhaps it is so."

"What are you getting at?"

"This friend of yours, the German. I think I know who he is." Beria looked at Braun intently.

"Good," Braun shot back, "then you know the value of what he holds."

"Perhaps. But your own plan to take his information, dispose of him, and exchange it for cash — this is not wholly acceptable."

Braun considered it. "You want the German as well."

Beria nodded.

"He won't help you, if that's what you're thinking. He's a Nazi, straight off the SS assembly line."

"I appreciate your opinion, Alex, but our methods of persuasion can be most productive."

"I can imagine," Braun said.

"No," the head of the NKVD replied, "you cannot." Beria paused. "And there is more yet. Once the German is in our hands, it would be very helpful if his disappearance was not noticed."

"That would be a trick. I suppose you have something in mind?"

Beria explained his idea.

When he was done, Braun looked at the Russian more closely. There was a lively glimmer behind the pince-nez glasses, a smirk in the swollen lips. Braun had always considered himself ruthless, albeit in the name of his own good cause. But the man seated next to him was on another level. "You want it to appear that this man remains on the USS *Indianapolis* after she sails — and then you intend to sink her?"

"If done correctly, the ship will be only another casualty of this long, terrible war."

"Will I have a hand in it?"

"Yes, Alex. We will pay what you ask, but you must do more. You must carry a package on board this ship and leave it, then take your friend and escape in a way that will not be noticed."

"Package? You can't mean a bomb."

"No, this would not be practical. You must carry a radio transmitter."

Braun began to see the outline, but had not yet come full circle. "How could this work? A transmitter to broadcast the ship's position and then — a torpedo?"

"Yes, Alex, good. A submarine."

"But a Russian sub could never risk attacking —" Braun paused.

Beria nodded, urging him on. "Figure it out Alex. You have a knack for this."

Of the countries that kept submarines in the South Pacific, only one would be interested in sinking an American heavy cruiser. "A Japanese sub?"

The Russian stabbed a chubby index finger into the air to register the hit.

Braun decided Beria was enjoying his little charade far too much. He said, "How can *you* get a Jap sub to sink an American ship?"

"We do, as it turns out, have access to a small fishing trawler in this area — a boat that does little fishing. With a beacon to guide, it could intercept such a large American ship. Remember, Alex, the United States and Japan are at war, but my country is not yet formally engaged with Japan. There are still quiet relations between our countries. We let slip where *Indianapolis* might be — perhaps a few radio calls at the right time."

"Why would the Japanese trust you?"

"The Imperial Navy has had few successes lately. I think they might trust us enough to investigate such an opportunity. In any event, this part of the operation would be left to us. I explain it only so that you understand the relevance of what we are asking you to do."

For a moment Braun considered how many men would be aboard a ship like *Indianapolis*. Eight hundred? A thousand? He was sure Beria had no idea. Braun's thoughts moved ahead to distill more practical matters. "I'll have to get aboard *Indianapolis* before my contact gets off."

"Do you have any ideas?"

What came to Braun's mind was simple enough. And simplicity was always good. He told Beria what he would need.

"Yes," he replied, "I can get you these things."

"And I'll have to go there right away, to lay the foundation."

"I can give you the aircraft I came in on." Beria then nodded over his shoulder, "My two men will go along to help."

Braun hesitated. He looked squarely at the Russian's reptilian features. Here was a man who had just whimsically plotted the death of a thousand men.

"No," Braun said. "Your men do not come. I want the aircraft, one pilot, and—and Kovalenko."

"*Kovalenko?*" Beria burst out. "We are going to pay you an incredible sum for your work. Kovalenko is not acceptable."

"All the money on earth is no good to me when I am dead. One pilot and Kovalenko."

"Absolutely not! I will—" Beria stopped in mid-sentence.

Braun knew why. It must now be in his face, in his eyes. The familiar sharpness had come to his mind, the acute concentration. He knew precisely where the two bodyguards were. He knew where Beria's hands were. Where his neck was. In the next ten seconds, Lavrenti Beria would realize who was in control, or he would die. His bodyguards would not save him, nor would his own abilities. The Russian's eyes snapped back and forth between his help and his adversary. Yes, Braun thought — Beria knew his thoughts exactly.

"All right," Beria allowed, his tone suddenly very different. "I consent to this."

The rising, uncontrolled wave in Braun's mind began to slowly recede. He added, "And I don't want to see anyone else in Guam. When I deliver the German, you will have to trust Kovalenko and the pilot to handle him."

"Agreed," Beria said. "But there is one more thing, Alex."

Braun narrowed his eyes.

"I told you that I think I know who your German scientist is. If it is the right man, his information could indeed be worth all this trouble."

"It is worth much more. I have seen the results with my own eyes."

"Still, if you can answer one question, Alex, it will convince me beyond a doubt. What was his code name?"

Braun wondered briefly how Beria could know this. But then he remembered — the man *was* a spy master.

"Die Wespe," Braun said. "The Wasp."

Lavrenti Beria smiled.

CHAPTER 40

The USS *Indianapolis* carved into the crystalline blue waters of Apra, Guam, on the morning of July 27th, 1945. The deep-water harbor was a largely natural formation. Cradled by the Orote Peninsula to the south, and Cabras Island to the north, modest hills of bleached white coral stood protectively around the glistening waters. The few enhancements to the natural breakwater were thanks to the U.S. Navy Seabees, who had been in possession of the island for nearly a year since the occupying Japanese forces had been evicted. The Seabees, starting from scratch as always, had turned a strip of barren coral rock into one of the world's busiest sea ports.

From the highest ground available, a short coral bluff, Lydia watched the huge ship lumber into the center of the harbor, gradually fall still, and then drop her massive anchor. It reminded her of a big dog marking its territory. There were several other ships in the harbor, a mix of sizes and purposes, but none were on the scale of *Indianapolis*. Lydia looked over her shoulder, wondering where Thatcher was. He had gone to use the telephone in the Naval Operations building. Tomas Jones had sent word that he'd be arriving with a team of FBI men to watch the harbor this morning. Oddly, she and Thatcher had seen no signs of them yet.

Thatcher came back hurriedly.

"Any luck?" she asked.

"No. They left the States three days ago, but nobody seems to know where Jones and his team are."

Lydia looked across the harbor. A small gray boat churned out toward *Indianapolis*, trailing a thin line of black smoke over the sunlit water. "But people will be coming ashore any minute. What can we do?"

"There's not much choice. We'll go down ourselves and see who comes off."

"But we don't even know who we're looking for," Lydia argued.

"No. Not unless we can spot Alex Braun."

Watching the small utility boat plow across Apra Harbor, neither knew that they were, at that very moment, looking directly at him.

He was seated on the aft bench of the small Navy tender. The craft plodded steadily through aquamarine water, its diesel engine growling at a constant pitch. As they closed in, Braun regarded the ship that lay before him.

She was ugly to begin with, a leviathan whose angular lines and blunt moldings were a pure crime of function over form. If this was not enough, she bristled with guns and antennae, the tools of destruction that were the very essence of her existence. Braun had seen beautiful ships. During the summer before his mother had died, they'd sailed to Europe on the S.S. *Normandie*. Even now, he remembered vividly that vessel's elegant flow and workmanship. Smooth, feminine curves. Cultured materials fitted by the hands of skilled craftsmen. Even Edward's little boat, *Mystic*, had held a certain grace. But the thing before him now was an abhorrence.

It made his task, to some degree, less unpalatable. When the war was over, *Indianapolis* would fall obsolete. Driving her home now to Davey Jones' Locker would simply save the world another rusting, mothballed eyesore. The fact that over a thousand men would be put in harm's way registered only as a footnote to Braun — here in the Pacific, the war still ran, and in the calculus of armed conflict such a disaster could not be differentiated from the bombings of Dresden or Tokyo. Braun had killed before, and while it had always involved one victim at a time, the mass of agony he was about to unfurl seemed no worse by way of its scale.

He pulled the sea bag at his feet closer. It had been given to him by Kovalenko, and contained everything one would expect a basic seaman to carry. Spare uniforms, a few personal effects, and—a touch Braun rather liked—a Bible. The bag also carried one thing no basic seaman would keep—a simple, yet powerful radio transmitter. It would activate intermittently over the next two days to act as a beacon.

Kovalenko had assured him that his bag would not be searched. Back at the pier, a sentry had gone over his orders and War Department ID card. Beria's people had done a fine job—the photograph, fingerprints, and physical description were all quite legitimate, and the ID even showed a slight stain from spilled beer. The guard had thumbed Braun past without a second look at his ubiquitous sailor's sea bag.

The tender pulled up alongside the big ship's boarding area, and Braun spotted a half dozen uniformed officers milling about in wait. He was not surprised. Though Braun had served in the army, he suspected officers were a predictable lot, regardless of service or country. The captain and his staff would probably be the first to go ashore. They'd mingle with their peers at headquarters, make a few token decisions about when and how *Indianapolis* would depart. Then the group would recess for an extended lunch at the Officer's Club. There, they'd gossip about promotions, assignments, nurses, and — if the mood struck — the war.

Lines were tossed, and the tender, rocking on small seas, was secured to the unmoving island that was *Indianapolis*. Braun scanned behind the gaggle of officers. He finally saw what he was looking for—Karl Heinrich with a suitcase chained to his wrist. The scientist did not see him, but then he wouldn't be looking for Braun here, and certainly not in a U.S. Navy uniform.

Braun stepped onto Indianapolis, following two other seamen. He tried to make eye contact with Heinrich, but the little German was talking to a Marine who was stationed at the gangway. The man was big and had the look of a fighter. Not that it mattered for the moment. Right now the only thing was to get Heinrich's attention. Braun had to keep him on the ship.

"Orders!"

The gruff command surprised Braun. He turned to see a weathered petty officer, his shoulder heavy with stripes. The man's hand was extended impatiently. Braun, uniformed as the lowest of the low, would get no respect. The Russians had wanted to make him a junior officer. Braun had argued that, while it might allow some small degree of authority once aboard, the commission would also bring duties and responsibilities. Instead, he had been suited as a basic seaman, his orders for kitchen duty. The expectations were slim — salute any officer, respect enlisted superiors, and know port from starboard. It was a part Braun could play convincingly.

He fished his orders and ID from a pocket. As the man looked them over, the group of officers began boarding the launch. At that moment, Heinrich looked up. The German did a double take. He went rigid, his eyes becoming huge circles.

Braun blinked slowly, deliberately, to indicate calmness. He then gave an almost imperceptible nod away from the launch.

"Any contraband in there?" the petty officer demanded as he handed back Braun's orders.

"Just a few bottles of whiskey, chief." Braun smiled.

The gruff man eased up and chuckled. "Yeah, well you just save one for me, sailor. And tell the cook to stop using that goddamn horse meat in the stew."

Braun slipped his papers back into his pocket and smiled again. "You bet." He walked toward the main passageway and saw Heinrich speaking to the Marine again. Rounding a corner, Braun was out of the crowd's sight. Heinrich appeared a moment later.

"What are you doing here?" he whispered. "I thought we were to meet on shore!"

"Steady, Karl. We have thought things through very carefully. You must trust our planning." Braun watched the effect of these words.

"We? You have had contact with those in —" Heinrich looked over his shoulder, afraid to say it out loud.

"Yes, yes Karl. Our plans are progressing well. But we cannot talk about it now. You must tell me some things."

The scientist nodded eagerly.

"When does the ship sail?"

"Sometime tomorrow morning, they say."

"Good. Will there be other tenders, other chances for you to go ashore?"

Heinrich shrugged. "I wanted to get off right away. They told me this was the first opportunity. I know there is no shore leave for the sailors, but I heard a few officers talking about going ashore later."

"All right, Karl, listen closely. Come back tonight, at 4:00 a.m., to this very spot."

Heinrich nodded.

"And you must come alone."

"That will be easy. The rest of the scientists from Los Alamos left the ship back in Tinian. Now, I am the only civilian — and of course the only German. No one here has a word for me."

"They do not guard you?"

"Not anymore. All the important documents went with the cargo to Tinian." He grinned conspiratorially and raised his suitcase slightly. "All that is left is my dirty laundry."

Braun looked at the suitcase and his thoughts stumbled. "Yes — make sure you bring everything tonight."

"We will leave then?"

Braun nodded. He pulled a paper from his pocket, something on Navy letterhead he'd scavenged from a trash can on the pier. He handed it to Heinrich. "Go wave this at the guard. Tell him your instructions have changed and you won't be getting off until the next port. And tell anyone else who will listen."

Heinrich was clearly curious at this strange request, but he agreed, "All right."

"Go, Karl. Go now. I will see you tonight."

The scientist disappeared around the corner. Braun could not stay to watch over him. He turned and began to move, search, and record. Passageways, staterooms, storage compartments, and gear. Braun could not learn the entire ship, but he would know certain sections intimately. He had sixteen hours.

The act of highest risk would come first — he had to hide and activate the transmitter. The Russians wanted it high, yet in a place where it would not be discovered. Then he would gather what he and Heinrich needed to extricate themselves. Finally, Braun would hide — a ship this size must have any number of seldom used closets and alcoves. He did not intend to search out the kitchen, suspecting it would be days before someone realized that the green sailor who'd boarded in Guam had never reported to his duty station.

As Braun scoured the ship, his mind faltered briefly as he thought of the suitcase. It was the first time he'd seen it, and he felt like a pirate getting his first look at a treasure chest. It had been only inches from his grasp. Braun cursed the Russians for demanding Heinrich himself, and for making him stage the scientist's disappearance. So many complications.

All had gone well so far, but Braun had felt the same confidence on other occasions. Flying a little airplane through clouds over New Mexico, only to be thrown into a mountain. Standing in a cool rain on the Embarcadero, only to collide with the head of the NKVD. And lounging on a train in Arizona, only to encounter Lydia. Hopeless, cunning Lydia. Her image came to mind, and Braun wondered where on earth she was at this moment.

Tomas Jones was surrounded by a thousand miles of ocean in every direction. He was stuck on a tiny mound of coral in the Marshall Islands, along with his contingent of eight FBI men.

They all sat sweating in a thatched hut, even though it was early evening, and watched as a pair of mechanics jacked up their C-47 transport, the big left tire rising off the ground.

A similar craft had brought them in yesterday, only to be sent back stateside on a mission deemed more important. No amount of complaining by Jones had been able to cut through the red tape, and they'd watched their perfectly good airplane disappear into the eastern sky.

The Army had been merciful enough to provide an alternative, a spare aircraft that unfortunately had a partially collapsed landing gear. They promised it would only take a few hours to repair — once the parts arrived. And arrive they had, only twenty minutes earlier. The mechanics were moving now, but clearly at a pace that reflected the heat.

Jones was in a lousy mood. He trudged over to a large tent and saw the officer in charge, a captain, just hanging up a telephone. "Captain, do you understand how important it is that we get to Guam ASAP?"

"Look, Jones, I'm trying. That was HQ on the phone and they wondered the same thing. What's all the fuss? And what the heck is the FBI doing in the South Pacific?"

Jones heaved a sigh. He needed to unload to somebody. "Ahh! We're chasing a damned Nazi spy."

"A Nazi?"

"Can you believe it? This all came to a head in the last few days. The Army has some super-secret project, and who do they take right into the middle of it? A German scientist, for cryin' out loud."

"Jeez."

"They raided his room and found a camera, some code books — lots of suspicious stuff."

"So you're chasing him down?"

"Yeah. We got a lead from," Jones hesitated painfully, "a British officer. He thinks this spy is gonna turn up on Guam."

The captain looked out through the door of the tent. "My guys have the old strut arm off already. When do you have to be there?"

"9:00 a.m. on the 27th. The pilot says the flight will only take about six hours, so if we can get out of here before midnight we'll still make it."

The captain looked at the wall calendar. "I've got some bad news for you, Jones."

"What?"

"It happens all the time — we Americans aren't exactly a worldly lot. You see, there's this thing called the International Date Line."

"The what?"

"The International Date Line. You crossed it yesterday. Here in the Marshalls — or I guess more importantly for you, in Guam — it's already the 27th."

An apoplectic Tomas Jones rushed to look outside. "Can't I catch a break!" he shouted.

At that very moment, the two mechanics dove out from under the C-47 as it wobbled, then fell off the jack. The airplane crunched down on a wingtip and sat precariously balanced for a few seconds. Then, with an audible crack, the wing snapped in half at the midpoint, and the entire machine collapsed into a lopsided heap.

Jones threw a roundhouse punch at the tent, his hand striking the hidden metal frame. *"Shit!"*

CHAPTER 41

At four o'clock in the morning *Indianapolis* was like a tomb, the air still and strangely cool. Karl Heinrich heard snoring as he made his way past compartments where crewmen were racked, and the ship's plumbing and ventilators murmured occasionally. Otherwise the place was silent. He imagined how much different it must be when the big ship was engaged in combat — shouting, explosions, the huge guns above spewing their massive shells. Heinrich was happy to have fought the war on his own terms.

He passed only one crewman, a sleepy junior officer who had not bothered to challenge Heinrich's cause for walking around at this hour with a suitcase tucked under his arm. It was a good thing, because Heinrich only been able to prepare one weak response — that he was lost.

Approaching the gangway, he kept to the shadows. He saw a sentry on duty, another Marine, this one smaller and less imposing than the man who'd been on duty earlier. This guard looked drowsy, slumped on a metal chair with his feet propped on a rail. Heinrich heard the slightest sound and he turned. Rainer beckoned him toward a passageway. He scurried to follow.

Rainer said nothing, but walked at a quick pace. After five minutes of turning and twisting, he led through a heavy, watertight door. Heinrich was greeted by darkness and a light breeze that was not strong enough to overcome the most unmistakable scent — rotting garbage. They were on a platform at the fantail of the ship, perhaps two levels above the waterline. Heinrich knew the kitchen was near, and he calculated that this was where the ship's garbage was dumped overboard. Rainer began digging through a large wooden box mounted on the deck.

"What are —"

Rainer cut off Heinrich's words by putting a vertical hand to his lips. "Quiet, Karl," he whispered. "There is a man on watch three decks above." He pointed straight up.

Heinrich looked up cautiously and matched Rainer's whisper, "What are we doing here?"

"We are leaving."

"How?"

Rainer produced a wool blanket and a bulky package from the stowage box. The package was stenciled militarily: EMER-GENCY LIFE RAFT: TWO PERSON.

"Can you swim, Karl?"

"Swim? No, and besides —" Heinrich looked down into the water, "there are sharks out there. They follow the ship for the garbage."

Rainer pulled a lanyard on the raft, and with a soft hiss it inflated to full size. "They don't dump anything in port, Karl." Rainer looked up at the sky. "The moon comes and goes. We must wait until it falls behind a cloud."

Rainer grabbed a rope that was already attached to the railing. It was thick, with large knots tied at intervals. He secured the free end to the raft, then fed it over the side.

"How far away is the shore?" Heinrich asked.

"Two hundred meters. No more." Rainer handed him a life preserver. "You'll need this."

Heinrich started to put it over his head.

"No, Karl! If you fall it would break your neck when you hit. Carry it on your arm for now."

Flustered, Heinrich did as he was told.

"Give me the suitcase."

Heinrich hesitated. His prize had never been in another's hands.

"I am stronger," Rainer insisted. "Give it to me."

Heinrich did, and watched as his countryman wrapped it in two layers of thick oilskin, then secured his work with twine.

"Now, over!"

Heinrich looked into the blackness below.

"Go!"

He straddled over the safety rail and clambered awkwardly down the rope. At the bottom he clutched the life preserver tightly and dropped into the water. He could, in fact, swim, although it had been years. He looked up and saw the suitcase just over his head. Rainer slipped into the water next to him and yanked on a second line that was now in his hand. The rope with the knots fell into the water with a splash. There would be nothing left, Heinrich thought, no sign of their escape. He has thought of everything.

Rainer flipped the suitcase, still dry, into the raft. He then put the dark, wet blanket over it all. The yellow raft became a murky, indiscriminant blob on the water. He helped Heinrich pull on his life preserver. Just then, Rainer looked up. A heavy cloud floated overhead to obscure the moon.

Rainer spoke quietly in German, "You see, Karl? Luck is on our side."

Those words, spoken so purely in his native tongue, made Heinrich forget any misgivings. "Rainer," he said, "I cannot believe we lost the war having men like you on our side."

Rainer grinned. He pulled the blanket over their heads, and they pushed off toward shore.

Thatcher watched Lydia sleep. She was slumped in a wicker chair, her head cocked coyly at an angle and resting on a wadded beach blanket they'd found. Lydia had almost lasted the entire night, finally drifting off an hour ago. But Thatcher noted it was a fitful sleep as she shifted constantly. Whatever dreams were circulating, he hoped they were better than his own.

They had moved closer to the naval facility, finding a perch on the deck of a bar that was the closest vantage point for watching the tender dock. The place had closed shortly after midnight. It was a sailor's bar, scuffed floors and cheap wood stools, everything drenched in the bitter smell of spilled beer. Clearly, the big ship at anchor in the harbor had not granted general shore liberty—otherwise, the place would probably still be open.

They'd been watching for the better part of a day. In that time, the tender had made three trips to and from *Indianapolis*. Thatcher and Lydia had observed carefully—a total of sixteen men had gotten off the tender. Every single one was in the uniform of a naval officer. This alone was no guarantee that one might not have been Die Wespe, but they had all stayed together in groups. The first load had been the captain and his staff. Then two small parties of midlevel officers. Thatcher had looked for anything amiss—a haircut out of regulation, a uniform worn improperly, a loner edging away from the pack. There was no way a German spy, a scientist from Los Alamos, could comfortably blend into such a crowd.

An airplane flew overhead, its radial engines jarring the early morning silence. Lydia stirred.

"Oh, Michael, I'm sorry. I fell asleep."

"It's all right. You didn't miss anything. The tender hasn't left the dock."

"And there's still no sign of Jones or his men?"

"No. It seems we're on our own."

"Michael, look!" She pointed out toward *Indianapolis*.

Thatcher didn't see anything new. "What?"

"The smoke."

A moderate stream of black swirled up from the main stack. "What about it?"

"I've been on ships before, Michael. She's lighting her boilers. I think she's about to sail."

The swelling cloud did look heavier, Thatcher realized. He probably hadn't noticed because it had built gradually. "You're right. She's leaving soon."

"But we haven't seen anything of Alex or this spy he was supposed to meet. Do you think their plans changed? Maybe they already met in a different port."

Thatcher's instincts told him otherwise. "No. *Indianapolis* arrived here right on schedule. We've just missed something."

They both watched the big ship's anchor rise up from the water.

"We can only assume they're here on Guam," Lydia reasoned. "And if that's the case, where would they go next?"

Thatcher's eyes came alight. "Yes." His thoughts returned to the dilemma he'd been wrestling for weeks. The one question that had bedeviled him. What was the point of it all? These two men had valuable information on the Manhattan Project, but what good was it with Germany defeated? An odd vision came to Thatcher's mind — the bulletin board at Handley Down. *Situations wanted. Instant wealth.* And then he understood.

"Lydia! Assume Alex and this spy, Wespe, have valuable secrets about some new weapon. It's no use to Germany anymore, so what would do they do?"

"Well . . . they could sell, it I suppose."

"Exactly! And do you remember — two days ago, when we arrived at the airport? There was one airplane that really stood out."

"I saw lots of airplanes. The place was thick with them."

"Yes, but one was out of place."

"What are you getting at, Michael?"

"There was an Ilyushin."

"I'm sorry, but that doesn't mean anything to me."

"It's a medium transport aircraft. More to the point, it had a big red star on the tail."

"A Russian —" Lydia clearly saw it as well. "Michael, that's it!"

CHAPTER 42

The airfield was located on the island's very northern tip. With classic lack of imagination, the Army had designated the place North Field — though one mischievous staff officer had pushed for West Field, arguing that it would completely throw off the Japanese in the event of an attack. Six mile-and-a-half long airstrips —credit again to the Seabees — lay up against the sea, carpet-like runners of rock and steel that launched wave after wave of long range B-29's against the Japanese mainland.

Braun and Heinrich arrived in the back seat of a U.S. Army military sedan that Kovalenko, in the driver's seat, had somehow managed to commandeer. Braun thought it a stylish touch that the Russians were stealing America's greatest secret with the help of their motor pool.

The journey had taken thirty minutes. Kovalenko had been ready with dry clothing after plucking them out of Apra Harbor at the rendezvous point. Heinrich was still pulling on his dry boots.

"These boots, they do not fit!" he fussed.

"Just do your best, Karl. We'll find something better after we get on the airplane."

At a checkpoint, Kovalenko flashed the drowsy guard some kind of authorizing paper. Whatever it was, it had clout, and they were waved right through. The scrutiny might have been tougher had they been going to the "business end" of the airfield, where seemingly endless rows of B-29s were being loaded and readied for their next missions. Fortunately, they were going to the Transient Ramp. It was a tiny corner of North Field where a handful of transports sat idle, their fin flashes a mix of services and nationalities.

Braun caught Kovalenko's eye in the rear view mirror, and he wondered what the Russian was thinking. The man had not said a word since picking them up, but this was by design. Heinrich was not yet suspicious — but he certainly would be if he heard Kovalenko's severe Russian accent. Braun had not yet seen the most important thing — his money. Until he took possession of seven hundred thousand dollars, he would keep Karl Heinrich and his heavy suitcase very close indeed.

Heinrich finally wedged his boot on. Braun looked him over. A mechanic's khaki overalls strained at the seams. Scuffed boots, and a cap with a brim. Nothing to indicate rank or insignia. Just an anonymous wrench turner. Braun was dressed in a similar fashion, wearing workman's pants and a ubiquitous cotton shirt. All they had to do was get Heinrich and his collection of secrets calmly across a hundred feet of hardpan coral to the aircraft, a heavily modified Ilyushin transport. The pilot would have the engines running, ready to dash. For his part, Kovalenko was dressed as the co-pilot. It was rather unconvincing — his age and lack of fitness did not conjure up the image of a military aviator — but then, it *was* a Russian plane. The American soldiers might snicker and point, but there was nothing to raise an alarm.

Kovalenko drew the sedan to a stop just short of the aircraft ramp. The Russian gave Braun an almost imperceptible nod, then got out of the car and hurried toward the waiting Ilyushin. One of the aircraft's engines was already idling, and the second spit smoke as it started to turn. Braun watched from the car as Kovalenko climbed up a short set of stairs and disappeared into the airplane.

Thatcher and Lydia arrived on the hourly military bus that shuttled worker bees between the island's two main hives — the Navy base at Apra, and the Army Air Force's North Field. Lydia craned her neck to find what they were looking for — a mid-sized airplane with a red star on the tail.

"I don't see it," she said.

Thatcher concurred, "It's hard to see anything with all this hardware."

North Field was presently one of the busiest airports in the world, according to the pilot who'd brought them in. When Lydia looked out, she saw hundreds of huge bombers. For the moment, they sat still, surrounded by a flurry of carts, trucks, and men. But soon the fleet would be ready for the next big wave.

The bus stopped to let everyone off near a large tent that was labeled: MESS HALL. Thatcher took her hand and led the way, weaving amid a city of tents and prefabricated buildings. As they cleared a stinking line of latrines, Thatcher stopped cold.

"There!" he said.

Lydia saw it a few hundred feet away — the Russian transport, one engine already running. And walking across the ramp were two men dressed in workman's clothes. One she recognized instantly. "It's Alex!"

Thatcher nodded. "And the other man must be Wespe. Look at the case he's carrying. I'll bet I know what's inside."

"What can we do?"

Thatcher's eyes searched all around.

"There were Military Police back at the gate," Lydia suggested. "We have to go get them."

"They'll never get here in time. That airplane's ready to taxi." Thatcher scanned the area. "You go for the MP's."

"What about you, Michael?"

He gripped her shoulder and pointed. "There! That's what I need! "

Lydia saw a small utility tug. It was parked untended, and attached to the back was a trailer loaded with bombs.

"I don't understand!" Heinrich demanded as he was being hustled across the ramp. "This is a Russian airplane!"

Braun was prepared. "What did you expect, Karl? The Luftwaffe?" He smiled knowingly and spoke over the roar of two
radial engines, "I told you — our new leaders are clever. It is a
Russian aircraft, yes. We captured it years ago, and now it has
turned quite useful." Braun let this sink in. "Can you imagine a
better deception, Karl?"

Heinrich eased. "Yes . . . I see. It *is* a good idea. The pilots,
they are German?"

"Of course. They speak a bit of Russian, just to be convincing. But both are SS men."

"All right, Rainer."

Kovalenko appeared in the aircraft's entry door and
beckoned them with a wave. Braun didn't like how things were
flowing. He grabbed Heinrich's elbow and stopped him twenty
paces away.

"Stay here, Karl," Braun instructed. He pointed to the suitcase. "And hold on to that grip."

Braun walked quickly across to the airplane, leaving Heinrich
and his priceless trove of information safely in the open. With the
engines running, he nearly had to shout at Kovalenko. "Where is
my money?"

"Here." Kovalenko slid a large briefcase into view.

"Give it to me now," Braun demanded.

Kovalenko shook his head. "First bring the scientist and his
papers."

The two glared at one another. The sequence of the exchange
had not been discussed — not this far. Braun was now improvis-
ing. Kovalenko pulled the briefcase back slightly from the door
and opened it. Stacks of fifty dollar bills bulged inside. He then
snapped it shut. "Bring Wespe. Once he is aboard, you can have it."

"How will you keep him aboard after I leave?"

Kovalenko twisted just enough to show a gun tucked ama-
teurishly into the back of his waistband. Braun recognized it as a
Tokarev Tula. He hesitated. Would the Russian use the gun against
him? No, he decided. Otherwise he would not have shown it. In
any event, Braun was confident he could find a way past

Kovalenko. And off of this infernal island. He turned and jogged toward Heinrich.

"All right, Karl," Braun announced, "it's time to go!"

Heinrich cradled the case as if holding a newborn child. He began to follow across the crushed coral. But when Braun reached the airplane and looked back, Heinrich had stopped again.

"Come on!" Braun shouted.

Suddenly, Kovalenko rushed down the stairs and toward Heinrich.

Braun took the chance. He reached into the airplane and pulled the briefcase closer. When he unlatched the locks, an array of fifty dollar bills stared up at him. He felt an instant of elation — but it was short-lived. He raked a stack of bills with his thumb, then a second. Only the money on top was real, the rest carefully cut stacks of paper. Furious, he turned.

Kovalenko was at Heinrich's elbow, ushering him to the airplane. Braun heard Heinrich ask, "Where is our first stop?" The words were in German.

Kovalenko reacted badly. He froze, a bewildered expression on his face.

The little German scientist suddenly understood. With a speed that surprised Braun, Heinrich swung his suitcase into Kovalenko's ribcage. The Russian doubled over, and Heinrich pried the gun from his belt. Kovalenko recovered enough to snatch at the weapon, but Heinrich was smart — using both hands, he kept the gun close to his chest, operating from a position of strength. A single shot rang out, and Kovalenko crumpled to the ground.

Braun was already moving. He pulled the worthless briefcase to his chest, using it as a shield, and rushed Heinrich. The German got off one shot, but it was absorbed by the thick wads of paper in the briefcase. Braun battered into Heinrich, locking onto his gun hand as they both went sprawling.

From there, it was no match. Braun was far stronger, far more experienced. In seconds his hands were wrapped securely around the Tokarev. Braun twisted the short barrel toward the

German and jammed it into his bulging gut. He looked at Heinrich, saw his face flush with fear, saw the eyes bulging. Braun's own gaze was steady, composed — both men knew who would win.

Braun found the trigger. On the first shot the Nazi looked stunned. On the second he let out a churning wheeze. With the third, angled higher, into the heart, the body of Die Wespe fell completely limp across the hard crushed coral. Braun pried the gun away and looked at Kovalenko. The Russian was lying perfectly still in a spreading pool of red. The MP's had not reacted yet — Braun knew he had only a minute, perhaps two, and his brain did the calculations. He reached a solution in two parts — the suitcase containing Heinrich's documents, and the aircraft waiting a few steps away.

Braun snatched the case and bounded up the steps into the Ilyushin. The next problem was seconds away. He knew the pilot was an aviator — the man had brought them here from San Francisco — but was he also NKVD? Was he armed? Braun rushed the flight deck, gun leveled, and the answer was instantly clear. The man sat half turned in his seat, strangely calm. Resigned. He knew what Braun would ask of him.

"Where we are going?" the pilot asked in broken English.

"I don't care!" Braun yelled, pointing the gun at the man's head. "Anywhere! Just go!"

The pilot released his parking brake and gave power to the big radial engines. The Ilyushin began to move, lumbering toward the runway. They'd gone less than fifty feet when the pilot slammed on his brakes, nearly throwing Braun to the deck.

The pilot spewed a stream of obscenities in his native language.

"What is it?" Braun shouted.

The pilot gestured with both hands for him to look down, over the glare shield. Braun scrambled up to the empty copilot's seat and looked low under the nose. Some suicidal idiot had just cut them off with a loaded bomb cart.

CHAPTER 43

Lydia's mission had been to bring the MP's as quickly as possible. She'd only made a hundred feet across the parking apron when she heard their whistles and saw them coming at a dead run. The alarm had been raised, but they were still two hundred yards away.

She turned back and spotted Thatcher as she ran. He was driving the tug wildly, careening across the ramp with a load of bombs still in tow. He brought it all skidding to a stop smack in front of the airplane. Thatcher jumped off as a collision seemed imminent, but the pilot slammed on his brakes and the big airplane's nose rocked down as it ground to a halt. Thatcher did a half circle around the right side of the airplane, just clearing the propeller that still spun in a blur. Lydia couldn't imagine what he was up to as he crouched down behind the big right wheel.

She was close now, and Lydia ducked into the shadow of another airplane. An instant later, Alex came bounding off the Russian craft. He had his gun poised, sweeping left and right in a crouch as he ran to the tug. He climbed on, started it, and drove the thing clear.

With Alex distracted, Thatcher moved on the opposite side of the airplane, scurrying toward the back. He stopped just in front of the tail and began prying against the side of the cabin. Lydia realized there was a door. It was farther back and larger than the entry door on the other side — probably used for loading cargo. Thatcher expertly released the latches and had it open in a matter of seconds. He boosted himself up and disappeared, the door swinging shut behind him.

Against the churning vibration of the airplane's engines, Lydia heard a whistle. The MP's were closing in, but they'd never make it in time. Alex was already scrambling back inside, and the big airplane began to move. She had to do *something*. She'd just seen Alex kill a man. Now Thatcher was with him, alone. And Alex still had the gun. He had every advantage.

Lydia eyed the cargo door. It was still hanging loose on its hinges, the latches undone. There was no time to think. She scampered from her hiding spot and ran like she'd never run before.

Braun pointed the pistol at the pilot and screamed, *"Go!"*

There was no hesitation — the airplane began to move. He looked out the entryway and saw MP's running, handguns drawn. Braun reached for the handle to draw the door closed, but it was locked in place. He was trying to find the release mechanism, his body squarely in the opening, when the blow came. Something smashed into his left arm. The Tokarev went flying out onto the ramp. Braun went for balance, spreading his feet and arms to the corners of the door frame. A flash came from behind and he ducked as hard steel glanced off his head. Braun was stunned. He tried to hold on as he strained for consciousness.

At that moment, the big airplane turned and accelerated under full power. He senses that his adversary was thrown off by the movement, and it gave Braun time to recover. He turned, his stance was wide, his hands up to deflect the next blow. But nothing came. The blurry shape in front of him was struggling to right itself.

Slowly, Braun's vision cleared. He heard the other man curse. Lifting a sleeve to wipe the blood from his face, Braun could not believe what he saw. The gimpy little Englishman. The same man who had started all his troubles back at Harrold House.

"You!" he hissed.

The Englishman stood. He was hanging onto the aft bulkhead, and they stared at one another as the aircraft sped down the runway. A window suddenly exploded, and Braun threw himself to the deck as bullets plinked into metal and glass. He saw the shooters flash by outside — two MPs emptying their handguns into the huge Ilyushin. An instant later, the hail ended.

The big airplane levitated slowly, lumbering into the calm morning air. Braun got back to his feet. The Englishman was brandishing a wrench. If he was hopelessly outmatched, his eyes didn't show it. They held nothing but fight. The man lunged at Braun with agility that belied his infirmity. The wrench whizzed by Braun's ear, and whacked painfully into his shoulder. But then Braun used his size. He kept the Englishman close and clamped down on the arm that held the wrench. A head butt caught Braun flush in the face, crunching against his nose. The pain was excruciating, but anger and adrenaline overcame it. He twisted toward the Englishman's bad leg and sent him spinning. His skull smacked hard against the metal sidewall, and he crumpled to the deck.

Grimacing, Braun spit out a mouthful of blood. He looked up front and set eyes on the pilot, who was watching the events in back. Braun had no idea who the man had been rooting for, but everything was clear now. "Keep it headed west!" Braun demanded. The pilot turned back to his controls.

Cautiously, Braun moved closer and inspected his adversary. Thatcher, he remembered. Major Michael Thatcher. The man was dazed, but not dead. Not yet. Braun looked at the still open door. Wind whistled past the opening, a rush of noise that Braun remembered from his parachute training. He contemplated tossing Thatcher out, as he'd done with old Mitchell. But then he had second thoughts. Thatcher might have valuable information.

Braun looked across the deck. Heinrich's suitcase, at least, was still there. Its tremendous value remained in his grasp. But he had to get away, and to do that Braun needed to know exactly who was after him, how much they knew. He might very well throw the little Englishman out the door — just not yet.

* * *

Lydia watched intently from behind the steel bulkhead that separated the main cabin from the aft cargo compartment. A heavy sheet of canvas was strung across the small opening that connected the two sections. It was loose on one edge, and Lydia supposed that was how Thatcher had gotten forward to confront Alex.

She only wished she could have helped. On crawling through the cargo door she'd found a mountain of luggage, supplies, and equipment to overcome. The violent maneuvering of the airplane on the ground had sent her reeling twice, and she'd gotten to the bulkhead just in time to see her partner thrown against the wall. Her heart skipped as he lay motionless, but then she saw Alex drag him forward and bind his hands and legs. Thatcher was still alive.

Lydia watched Alex as he moved up front and took the co-pilot's seat. He was addressing the pilot — not conversationally, but with intimidation. Alex was giving instructions. The pilot, a Russian she imagined, was not necessarily on Alex's side. Given the carnage that had already taken place, he was probably just out to save his own skin.

Lydia had heard Alex's first demand — *Keep it headed west!* As the airplane droned onward, she knew time was not on her side. Lydia turned and quietly rummaged through the luggage and equipment, looking for something to help her against Alex. The labels were in Cyrillic, but most was obvious enough — spare tires, tools, cans of grease and oil. Nothing that would give her a chance. She went back to her vantage point and her heart soared. Thatcher was stirring against his restraints.

The wind rushed across the still open entry door nearby. Lydia imagined pushing Alex out — was she cold enough to do it if the chance came? Had she become like him? Lydia did not have the answer to either question. She desperately scanned the forward part of the airplane. If nothing else, the noise from the open door would mask any sounds.

Think, dammit! Think like Alex! And then Lydia's eyes locked onto something — it was just to her right, against the bulkhead. The weapon she needed.

Braun saw nothing but blue water in every direction. He had no desire to battle the ocean again. Keeping an eye on the pilot, he was encouraged that he knew enough about flying to keep the man honest. They had sufficient fuel to make the Philippines. There, Braun would force a landing at an obscure field, a road if necessary. And then he would take Heinrich's treasure and disappear.

Looking back, he saw Thatcher stir. The Englishman's eyes opened, and he groaned. Then his hands began to twist, testing the bindings. Braun had done his best with what was available, but the man might eventually worm his way free — he was nothing if not persistent. Braun walked back and bent down to face Thatcher.

"So, Major, you are back with us?"

The reply was defiant. "I hope I look better than you."

Braun grinned and touched the goose egg that had erupted just above his scar. His face would also be smeared in blood. "Yes, my friend, you put up a good fight. But you have lost."

"I'm behind at the moment." Thatcher was able to lock eyes with the pilot.

"No, Major, our Russian friend will not help you. He knows what is best for him." Braun's tone grew lighter, "You know, I have wondered for some time — how did you track me to Newport?"

Thatcher hesitated before explaining. "Back in England I interrogated a young corporal, Hans Gruber's secretary."

Braun strained to remember. "Yes . . . yes. I do remember him. He gave you my name?"

"That and a few other things. He was destroying some of Gruber's files, but he looked them over first."

Braun nodded vigorously. "Yes. That makes sense."

"So now you tell me," Thatcher said, "what are you going to do?"

Braun gestured to the suitcase in back. "I still hold the secrets of the world's greatest weapon. I have seen this thing, Major. I was a witness to the test. Someone will pay a great deal of money for the information."

"Money? Is that what Newport was about? You never really cared about Lydia, did you?"

Braun grasped at the question, but it was like trying to catch a thrown dagger. "No," he blurted, "of course not. Though we might have ended up together had it not been for your interruption." This idea surged in Braun's mind — the man before him had ruined everything. "I am growing weary, Major," he spat. Braun grabbed Thatcher roughly by the collar. "Who else is after me at this moment? And what do they know? If you do not answer these questions right now —" Braun stopped in mid-sentence and tensed. Something was wrong. He saw it in Thatcher's eyes. He followed the Englishman's gaze and looked over his own shoulder. There, standing by the open door, was Lydia. In her hand was Karl Heinrich's suitcase.

"Stay where you are, Alex!" Lydia shouted to be heard over the noise, but also to take command. Even she was surprised by the confidence that radiated in her voice.

Alex said nothing. He stood tall and simply stared. Lydia tried to read the expression on his face. He had to be surprised, but there was something else. Something she didn't recognize. "If you come any closer, Alex, I'll throw it out the door!" To emphasize the point, she undid the latches on the heavy case. It cracked open slightly, and the edges of a few papers eked out to flutter sharply in the turbulent air. "Untie Michael," she demanded.

Alex finally spoke. "Lydia. What in God's name are you doing here?" He began to move closer.

"Stay where you are!" she shouted.

He seemed not to hear. His eyes were locked to hers, not even seeming to register the suitcase she had thought would command his attention. *What is he thinking?* She cracked the case further, and a handful of pages fluttered out and were swept away in the windstream. Alex stopped a few feet away.

"I'll do it, Alex! You know I will!"

He lunged and grabbed for her arm. Lydia was ready. She swung the case outside and it snapped open. Stacks of paper flew out, a flurry of white swirling behind into the empty sky. Alex was on her. In the struggle Lydia lost her grip on the handle, and the suitcase was gone. They fell to the floor in a tangle, Lydia slipping toward the door.

"No!" he screamed.

Just like on the train, Lydia thought she would fall. But this time Alex had her. He pulled her back inside. With a fierce grip on her shoulders, he brought her away from the door. Alex's grip loosened, but he kept holding on, locking her at arm's length. Lydia braced for a strike, the back of a hand across her face. She expected anger, but what she saw instead was carved into his every feature. Confusion. The mercurial, indomitable Alexander Braun seemed utterly bewildered.

"Do you know what you just cost me?" he said.

Lydia was defiant. "And how can *you* say that to me?"

They stared at one another for a long moment. Then an engine sputtered.

The pilot spewed a stream of harsh Russian that could only be expletives. The starboard engine coughed again, then shuddered to a stop with a sickening vibration. The Ilyushin lurched to one side as the pilot slapped at levers up front. The port engine went to full power.

"Fuel!" the pilot yelled.

They all looked out at the affected engine. Liquid was streaming out from a pair of jagged holes in the metal cowling.

Thatcher said, "The MP's were shooting at us — they must have nicked a fuel line! Can you do anything?" he shouted to the pilot.

The Russian shook his head violently. "We fly on one engine, but not far!" He pointed behind as the aircraft began a turn. "We must to go back — Guam! This is only way!"

The port engine screamed at full power. Alex broke away

from Lydia. He went up front and looked at the gauges, trying to make sense of it.

"We can't go back! Head somewhere else!" he ordered the pilot.

The man ignored him. "I am pilot. There is no choice. Forty minutes, and we are back in Guam. Either that, or —" he pointed down to the indigo blue Pacific.

CHAPTER 44

The stricken Ilyushin was level at three thousand feet. It was the best she could manage on one engine, but they'd made it halfway.

Lydia watched Alex, who was in the copilot's seat. He was arguing with the pilot in a mix of English and Russian, trying to find an alternative to going back to North Field. Thatcher sat next to her, still in restraints. Alex had not bothered to bind her hands, and Lydia wondered why. Did he not consider her enough of a threat? Given a chance, she'd be happy to prove that notion wrong. In any event, the airplane was headed back to Guam now. They might all get out of this yet.

She was studying Thatcher's bindings, wondering how quickly she could undo them, when Alex and the pilot had a particularly heated exchange. The Russian tapped an instrument on his panel. Alex went to the port side window and looked at the good engine.

"What now?" Thatcher asked.

"The port engine," Alex replied.

Lydia looked out and saw a thin black streak along the side of the metal casing.

"It's operating at such a high power setting, we're losing oil. The engine's going to seize." Alex turned to the pilot. "How long?"

"Five minutes!" came the reply. "Maybe ten!"

"How far to shore?" Lydia asked.

Thatcher replied, "More than that."

"So that's it," she said. Lydia looked down at the ocean. "There's still a chance," she said hopefully. "If we can survive the impact."

Thatcher addressed the pilot, "Where's the service port?"

The Russian gave him a look like he was crazy.

"Where?" Thatcher demanded.

The Russian pointed to a small door at the midpoint of the engine.

"It might work," Thatcher said. He explained his idea.

Lydia agreed with the pilot — he was mad. "You can't be serious, Michael."

"There's a strut right there to hang on to. We break the window, and pull back power to lessen the wash from the propeller. Someone crawls out and adds oil — we have a case of it in back. It's simple, really."

The pilot certified the idea as insane, but had no objections if someone wanted to try.

"Who's going to do it?" Lydia wondered.

Thatcher looked at Alex. "You're the strongest."

Alex seemed to think it over. He looked outside, down at the water. He eyed Lydia.

"No, Major. I'm afraid if I went out there, I might find my way back inside blocked." He pointed defiantly at Thatcher. "You do it."

Thatcher met his gaze, and raised his bound hands. "All right. Get these off."

They punctured two cans and poured the oil into an empty vodka bottle — the pilot had watched forlornly as they'd poured his personal stash out the door. Thatcher figured the bottle's long neck would give him a better chance. He took off his jacket as Braun broke out the window with a monkey wrench. Thatcher stood at the opening and mapped out his steps. He had a screwdriver in a pocket. The bottle of oil would stay in his left hand.

Braun returned from talking to the pilot. "He says you'll have about two minutes before he has to add power. When it's coming, I'll pull your leg twice to give you twenty seconds notice. He doesn't think you'll be able to hold on once the prop wash hits at full power."

"Michael," Lydia said, "if you show me what to do, I can try." She looked him in the eye and said, "I've got two good legs."

"No!" Braun said. "Absolutely not!"

Thatcher agreed. "No, Lydia. I can manage."

With that, Thatcher looked up to the pilot and nodded. The engine went to idle, its rumble almost gone, and the nose of the airplane fell slightly. They were now gliding down.

Thatcher wedged through the window and placed his good leg on the thick wing strut. The big Ilyushin was flying at her minimum speed — sixty knots was the least she'd do without falling out of the sky — but even then, the wind was nearly hurricane force. Thatcher leaned into the stream, finding his balance, and stretched out toward the access panel. He pulled the screwdriver from his pocket, and when he got the door opened it flipped back in the windstream. He tossed the screwdriver away, and found himself watching as it twirled into the ocean below.

The filler cap came off by hand. Thatcher switched the bottle between his hands, but as it came across his face, oil splattered into his eyes. Blinded, he wiped his face across a shirtsleeve that was rippling in the wind. His vision was blurred by the viscous brown goo, but he got the long bottle neck in place and began to pour.

His right leg was tiring, the muscles straining at odd angles as it wrapped around the strut. He looked down and saw the Pacific. It seemed incredibly clear. Incredibly close. Thatcher felt two tugs on his leg. Twenty seconds. The bottle was only half empty. He kept at it, the brown liquid spilling and spraying, but most of it going to the engine. When the bottle was finally empty, Thatcher tossed it away. He fumbled with the filler cap. If he couldn't get it back on, it would all be for nothing — the oil would only have another avenue of escape from the engine. Thatcher wondered how many more seconds he had.

He got the cap in place, but when he looked down Thatcher thought it was too late. They were no more than twenty feet in the air. He braced, and then it hit — the engine roared to life. Wash from the propeller struck like a massive wave, pulling every part of his body back, tearing him away from his handhold. Thatcher felt his oily fingers slipping. He tried to wrap around the strut, hooking one elbow and his good leg. It was no good. The rush of air was too strong, his grip too slick from the oil. His hand gave way.

Thatcher braced for the fall, but then his belt caught on something. His upper body flailed back in the windstream, but he still didn't fall. His eyes were closed against the maelstrom of wind, and he reached back to grab whatever was holding him in place. He felt a hand.

All at once, the engine fell back to idle power. Thatcher squinted to see Braun halfway out the window. He pulled Thatcher toward the fuselage, and seconds later they were both back inside. The pilot instantly reapplied full power, and the Ilyushin began another sluggish climb.

Thatcher hunched over breathlessly, his hands on his knees, Lydia at his side. He scanned the pilot's instrument panel, trying to find the port engine oil quantity gauge. He then looked up at Braun. The man was completely disheveled — bloody face, clothes torn, hair askew. Thatcher nodded to the spy. "Thanks for that."

Braun paused to eye Thatcher for a moment. He then shrugged it off. "We may need you again, Major. It is possible we'll require one more service to make land."

Thatcher gave no reply.

CHAPTER 45

"Are you all right?" Lydia asked.

"Couldn't be better," Thatcher said.

Lydia found a first-aid kit and tended to him. As she did, she eyed Alex. He was in the copilot's seat studying charts, talking to the pilot in Russian. She spoke in a low voice, "Michael, he's not going to let the pilot take us back to North Field. The place is already swarming with MP's."

"I know," he said. "He's probably trying to convince the man to land elsewhere."

The pilot shouted excitedly in Russian, and pointed out the front windscreen.

Alex turned toward the back. "Land-ho," he announced.

"Where are we going?" Lydia demanded.

"That is for me —" Alex stopped in mid-sentence. He shot a look at the pilot.

Then Lydia heard it — a vibration, steady but growing.

Everyone looked to the port engine. It had been running at full power for a very long time. The pilot pulled back on the throttle, but the vibration only increased. Soon the entire craft began to shake. Lydia could barely see, her vision rattled to a blur. Then the engine exploded.

Parts sprayed into the fuselage, ripping through glass and

metal. Lydia ducked to cover Thatcher. When she looked up, the left wing was on fire, the engine a tangled mass of metal. Then she saw the pilot. The Russian was slumped to the side across the control panel, his head covered in blood.

Alex dragged him out of the left seat and took his place. He struggled fiercely against the control column.

"Can you fly it?" Lydia shouted.

"It's a glider now! All I can do is try to crash it well!" Alex looked over his shoulder. "Get up here, Lydia."

She scrambled forward. The ocean grew larger in the windscreen.

"Strap into that seat," Alex ordered. "We're going to hit hard."

There were no other seats, and Lydia said, "What about Michael?"

Alex looked back. "Go stand by the door, Thatcher! I'll get her as slow as I can, and right before she hits, jump!"

"Jump? He can't do that!" Lydia argued.

"No," Thatcher said, "he's right." He pried himself up and moved to the door.

Lydia put on her seatbelt.

Alex fought with the controls. "It's really heavy," he said, "mushy. I don't know if I can control it."

He looked her over. "Shoulder straps!"

Lydia wasn't sure what he meant. Alex reached across with one hand and pulled two straps from behind her seat. He secured it all and pulled everything tight. The two locked eyes for just a moment, then Lydia looked out the side window. It seemed like they were skimming across the waves.

"Get ready, Thatcher!" Alex shouted. "Now!"

Lydia saw Thatcher disappear out the door. When she turned back around, the right wing clipped a wave, and a curtain of white enveloped everything. The airplane cartwheeled a half turn before the windscreen imploded in a wall of water. Everything disappeared.

* * *

Braun was stunned. He felt a cool wetness enveloping his body —
strangley calm and serene. Then he realized he was face down in
the water.

Braun snapped his head up and shook it violently, taking the
water from his eyes and the fog from his brain. When he tried to
move, everything seemed surprisingly intact. He began to remember. Looking around, he saw the Ilyushin, or what was left of it.
Only the tail and the spine of the fuselage were still visible, wal-
lowing atop the ocean swells a hundred yards away. He had somehow been thrown clear. Yet again, Braun had survived.

The thought nearly brought a smile until he remembered —
Lydia. Had she been thrown clear as well? Braun quickly scanned
the ocean around him. He saw a wing and a few bits of debris.
But no Lydia. The Ilyushin already appeared to be lower in the
water — she was sinking fast.

"Lydia!" he shouted, hoping for some weak response. He
heard nothing. Braun began to swim. He tore through the waves
as the big airplane's fuselage began to disappear. When he reached
it, the cockpit was already under, but Braun found a gaping hole
midway back along the fuselage. He pulled himself though, flowing easily inside with the torrent of water. Getting back out might
not be as simple, he realized.

The water inside the barrel of the airplane was up to his
shoulders. He scrambled forward, a mix of running and swimming, until he heard a sound that gave him an incredible lift — a
soft, unintelligible moan.

"Lydia!" Braun found her semiconscious, still strapped into
her seat. She was battered and incoherent, but alive. Water rushed
in from the other side of the cockpit. There, the sidewall, windows, and captain's seat were simply gone.

"Come on! We've got to get you out!"

The water was nearly up to Lydia's neck. She moaned again
as Braun worked his hands blindly in the water to release her
straps. He found the latch and pulled, but just at that moment
the airplane lurched. There was a terrible noise, a groan, as if the

big ship was expelling its last painful breath, and then the fuse-lage buckled behind them. The aft section seemed to fall, and everything rotated. What was left of the cockpit now pointed straight up. For a moment, Braun saw blue sky through the window, but then it disappeared in a swirl of foam and slapping waves. They were headed down.

"Come on, Lydia!" With the cockpit elevated, the remaining air now surrounded them. Braun saw that Lydia's right arm was badly broken. The water rose even more quickly now, and as he tried to lift her from the seat, he looked up through what had been the front window. Braun saw the ocean's surface clearly — it was definitely receding. They were already ten or twenty feet down, sinking like a stone.

It was a death trap that would only stop falling when it hit the bottom. Braun knew he could make it to the surface if he went now. But not with Lydia in tow. And he knew she'd never make it alone. Lydia, the ocean, his own well being — it all triangulated in his mind. Then he remembered the life vests.

Still cradling Lydia, Braun reached behind her seat and groped in the stowage pocket with his hand. He found what he wanted — the emergency life vest. He worked it around her neck and secured the strap, then positioned Lydia carefully near the breach in the sidewall, where the remaining air was fighting a tumultuous, losing battle with the sea.

"Lydia!" he screamed, shaking her shoulders.

Her eyes opened, but the gaze was lazy, unfocused.

"Listen to me, dammit!"

There was a glimmer of comprehension as her soft green eyes locked to his. The water was back up to chest level. "Take a deep breath! I'm going to send you up!"

Lydia looked around briefly, registering their predicament, seeing the vest strapped around her. Braun might have expected panic, or at least fear. Instead he saw only one thing etched into her face — determination. She nodded. "All right."

Braun made sure she was clear of any obstructions, and

Lydia drew in a full breath. He reached for the inflation lanyard on her vest and they locked eyes once more. Braun felt like he was taking a snapshot of her face. The battered cheek, wet hair plastered across her forehead. *All so incredibly* — Braun cursed himself for the hesitation. He pulled the lanyard and guided her clear. In a rush of air and water, Lydia was gone.

He watched her rise in a maelstrom of bubbles as the water level reached his own chin. He had considered going up with her, but his added weight would have slowed the ascent. With only a small pocket of air remaining, Braun took his last breath. As he did, he was suddenly beset by a sickening realization. There had been a second vest — but it was gone, lost with the pilot's seat. How had he not realized it? What had he been thinking?

He scrambled out, trying to clear the wreckage. His shirt caught on something, and Braun tried to wrestle free. As the airplane pulled him farther into the abyss, he looked up, his vision blurred by the stinging salt water. The surface was less distinguishable now, simply a lighter shade against the darkness surrounding him. How deep could he be? Fifty feet? A hundred? There was an urge to close his eyes, to take his minute of calm. But in a minute his body would be crushed by the depth.

Braun finally ripped free, his lungs demanding air after the exertion. He again looked up to find the surface. He saw the sun, a faded orb, obscure and distant. It reminded him of the sky on a snowy Russian morning. Then Braun's eyes captured something else — a tiny dot dancing near the surface, a lone figure awash in muted sunlight. *Lydia.*

The vision above him faltered. And soon it faded to nothing.

Lydia burst to the surface gasping for air. The brightness was incredible. She slapped frantically against the waves, as if trying to keep afloat. Her right arm blazed in pain, every movement a torture as she gasped for breath. She then heard a distant voice.

Lydia . . . Lydia.

A shudder coursed briefly through her nervous system. But

then she saw the source — it was Thatcher, clinging to a piece of wreckage thirty yards away. Lydia gave him an awkward wave with her good arm.

"Are you all right?" he shouted across the divide.

The question was a simple one, yet a thousand thoughts spun in her mind. She tried to wave again, then saw Thatcher pointing toward the sky. Lydia looked up and saw an airplane overhead flying low, lazy circles.

A strange tranquility set in. The ocean seemed to still, and Lydia lay back, allowing the vest to keep her afloat. The pain in her arm lessened as she relaxed. With each new breath, Lydia gained clarity. Bits and pieces flowed to her marginally coherent head — the violent torrents of water, Alex pulling her free. And the look on his face right before he had inflated her vest — the same odd expression she'd seen after throwing his precious papers into the sky. Only now did she recognize it for what it was.

Lydia looked all around, drawing her gaze carefully across the sea. Alex was not here. He was gone.

Two hundred miles to the west, a small Russian fishing boat received the first faint signal. Her captain adjusted course accordingly. The man who was truly in charge, an NKVD colonel, made a series of plots on his chart. He then issued the first of what would eventually be four messages. *Contact established.*

The Japanese submarine I-58 acknowledged.

CHAPTER 46

Thatcher woke to the gentle din of rain tapping at his window. The impulse to move was not a strong one, and so he lay in bed with his eyes closed and listened. Aside from the rain, there was nothing. Nothing at all. He had never been one to appreciated things like silence, yet today, somehow, it seemed a like a treasure.

It had taken over a week to get back to England, and it all seemed a blur. After a few days in a clinic on Guam, Thatcher had delivered Lydia to her grateful family in Newport. He'd spent a day there, mostly giving her parents a glowing account of their daughter's exploits. That evening, he and Lydia had spent a few hours alone in the kitchen — at the same table where they'd first gotten to know each other late one night over a month ago. The next two days were lost to travel. And finally Thatcher was home.

When he tried to rise, his limbs felt heavy, as if the bones had been replaced with leaden rods. He sat up slowly and, like each morning for the past week, found today's pains to be slightly more bearable than yesterday's. Dim morning light filtered in through the windows, and he looked at the unset alarm clock by his bed. Ten thirty. He had slept for sixteen hours — and was already four hours late for work. Today would be Thatcher's first day back at Handley Down since he'd left over a month ago.

He pried himself out of bed and cracked open the windows,

hoping to stir the stale air that had gathered in his absence. His next stop was the mirror — a grievous mistake. One side of his head displayed a gash with ten stitches, and his jaw was still swollen on the opposite side. On top of this, he hadn't shaved in three days, and his hair was completely askew. Thatcher sighed. He went through the motions as best he could — washing, dressing, breakfast, and tea.

Before heading outside, he paused at the nightstand. As always, the picture of Madeline was there. Thatcher studied it for some time before picking up the unopened envelope that leaned against it. Lydia had given it to him in parting, with instructions that it should not be opened until Thatcher had arrived back in England. Yesterday he'd been tired. But also fearful. He'd been thinking a great deal about Lydia Murray, and what the letter might or might not say.

Thatcher sat on the bed, took a deep breath -— and slid the letter into the pocket of his jacket.

He rode through the gate at Handley Down thirty minutes later. The guard shack was vacant. He parked his bicycle and went straight to Roger Ainsley's office.

When Thatcher limped in, Ainsley looked up from his desk in astonishment. "Good Lord, Michael!" He rushed over to help, but Thatcher shooed him off.

"I'm fine, Roger. Really." Thatcher eased into a chair. "Much improved, actually, from when they fished me out of the Pacific."

"All the same, you should have told me." Ainsley crossed his arms defiantly. "I simply won't have you here in this state, Michael. You must take time off to convalesce. I won't hear any argument."

For once, Thatcher gave none.

"Can I send for tea?"

"No, thank you."

Ainsley edged back behind his desk. "Have you seen the newspapers?"

Thatcher shook his head, and Ainsley spun the *Times* across the hardwood writing surface. The headline displayed prominently: ATOMIC BOMB DEVASTATES HIROSHIMA

Thatcher skimmed through the article. "Dear God — 100,000 dead?" He pinched the bridge of his thin nose. "So this is what it was all about — what Braun was trying to sell to Russia."

"Yes. And he would have done it if it hadn't been for you."

Thatcher tilted his head back and stared at the ceiling. "Actually . . . there was another person who had an even bigger part in stopping him."

Ainsley raised an eyebrow, but didn't ask the obvious question. Instead, he said, "There's something else. Page 9, bottom left."

Thatcher leafed through and found the second article: U.S. SAILORS SPEND FOUR DAYS ADRIFT. Again he read, and again he felt his stomach churn. "*Indianapolis.* Do you think Braun had something to do with it? Or the Russians?"

"I think it's a hell of a coincidence," Ainsley replied.

"Eight hundred men — it ought to be investigated."

"It ought to be. But it's been a long war, Michael. I have a feeling we'll probably never know if there was any connection."

Thatcher nodded, then paused to consider it. "Perhaps it's best that way."

The telephone rang, and Ainsley answered, falling victim to his daily chores.

Thatcher briefly considered venturing across the hall to his own office, to inspect the mountain of papers that must certainly have accumulated in his absence. Instead, he pulled Lydia's letter from his pocket. After some hesitation, he forged it open and read.

Michael,

> *We've been through a great deal together. I asked you to not open this letter until your arrival in England because I know it will take time for us to collect our lives.*

You are, I think, the bravest man I've known. I realize there is an ocean between us now, but I dearly hope that someday we might see each other again. I say this not with the prospect of looking back to reminisce over the terrible events we left behind. Instead, I think you and I, more than most, can appreciate the possibilities of what is yet to come.

With deepest affection,

Lydia

Thatcher read the letter three times. He then folded it carefully and sat very still, playing her voice in his mind. And what *would* come? The future tense had been foreign to his thoughts for so long.

Ainsley hung up his telephone. "Apparently we'll be getting another tomorrow — a colonel from the 7th Army Headquarters who —" Ainsley stopped in mid-sentence and stared at Thatcher. "Are you hearing any of this?"

When the question broke Thatcher's thoughts, he could think of only one thing to say. "I think you're right, Roger. I'm going to take some time off."

Ainsley walked around his desk and put a hand on Thatcher's shoulder. "Take as much as you need, Michael. God knows, you've earned it."

Thatcher left Ainsley's office and passed his own without a glance. There would be others to find, he knew. It might take years, even decades to track them all down. In time, he would do his share. But not today. And not tomorrow. As he walked down the hall his pace quickened. He could almost hear Madeline's strong, clear voice urging him elsewhere — *It's time to live now, Michael. Live!*

Outside, Thatcher struggled onto his bicycle and began to pedal surely through the warm August rain.

AUTHOR'S NOTE

The sinking of the USS *Indianapolis* has long been shrouded in mystery, but the same can be said for any number of events that occurred during World War II. The true circumstances of such tragedies are, of course, generally more ordinary than writers of fiction would imagine. What is not at question are the sacrifices made then, and continuing to this day, by the generation who fought those battles both at home and on the fronts.

To them, my utmost thanks and respect.

Sarasota, Florida
February 2008